ISBN-13: 978-1717460509

ISBN-10: 171746050X

Text Copyright © 2018 Angela Warwick

All Rights Reserved. No part of this publication may be reproduced, stored in a retrieval system or transmitted in any form, or by any means, without the prior written permission of the author, nor be otherwise circulated in any form of binding or cover other than that in which it is published and without a similar condition being imposed on the purchaser.

Cover Art © 2018 Nick Warwick

All Rights Reserved

BEHIND THE MASK

The Story of Jane Seymour

Angela Warwick

Also by Angela Warwick

Moth To The Flame – The Story of Anne Boleyn

Vyvyan's Vicarage

Return To Vyvyan's Vicarage

Chapter One

The attic windows were small and high, reflecting the afternoon sunlight across the faded oak floor. As the door to the small room opened slowly, the slight stirring of the air sent dust motes swirling upwards momentarily before they rained gently down, caught in the sunbeams piercing the tiny diamond leaded window panes. The little girl skipped daintily over the boards and plumped herself down comfortably in the far corner of the low-ceilinged room, carefully spreading her skirts around her. Once satisfied with the arrangement, she pulled a small wooden doll from her sleeve and gazed intently into the painted eyes before propping it against the wall where it lurched drunkenly to one side.

Modesty forgotten, the child slid down to lie on her stomach, hands cupping her chin, legs bent up the knees to allow her feet to waggle in the air. Suddenly her attention was caught by a movement on the floor close by; a fat black beetle pushed its way from a crack in the roughly plastered wall and began a stately plod across the floor towards the half open door. Quick as a flash her podgy hand shot out to capture the insect, giggling as the tiny feet ticked her palm. Dropping the beetle on the floor in front of her she observed the creature turn in a small circle before continuing on its interrupted path. Carefully she picked it up with finger and thumb and held it close to her face watching its little legs paddling aimlessly and its antennae waving.

Shuffling into a sitting position, she increased the pressure of her hold and the beetle, perhaps sensing danger, became motionless. The child's amused expression suddenly hardened as she deliberately began pulling the legs from the insect's body, one by one.

"Mistress Jane! Mistress Jane!"

The child paused in her careless torture and looked towards the attic door, hearing her nurse's voice rising from the floor below.

"Mistress Jane!" As the nurse's heavy footsteps drew closer, Jane jumped to her feet, dropped the insect to the floor and stamped on it. Stooping to pick up her doll, she smoothed her skirts, assumed her most innocent and carefree expression, then skipped leisurely towards the door, blond curls dancing.

Her nurse pushed the door wide and stood with her hands on her ample hips, glaring down at her charge. "Whatever are you about up here all alone Mistress Jane?"

Jane gazed innocently into her nurse's exasperated face then shrugged her shoulders and smiled impishly. "Just playing."

Knowing the child of old, the nurse surveyed the small attic room with narrowed eyes, then caught hold of Jane's hand and pulled her towards the squashed beetle, almost unrecognisable amongst the glistening tangle of its remains. Grimacing at the mess, the nurse bent towards Jane, put her hands on her shoulders and gave her a none too gentle shake. "No doubt you tortured the poor creature before you killed it. Why do you keep doing such things?"

Jane opened her baby blue eyes as wide as she could and stuck out her lower lip. "It was an accident. I didn't mean to do it."

The nurse straightened and shook her head slowly. If this child was in any way contrite, then she, Kat Symons, was the Queen of England. She tried again. "What had the poor thing ever done to you? How would you feel if you were a tiny insect and some great big cruel girl hurt you?"

Jane's expression was unreadable and not for the first time, Kat feared for the child's future. She sighed and caught hold of Jane's arm. "Come away downstairs now. I shall have to tell your mother and father that you are a nasty, thoughtless child with no care for any of God's creatures."

Jane shrugged again and allowed herself to be steered towards the narrow staircase. Standing aside, Kat motioned for Jane to descend the stairs ahead of her, mindful of the last time. The time when Jane had followed her down and planted two determined hands in the small of her back and shoved her down the entire flight. How she had stood tearfully in front of her parents and maintained that Kat had tripped over her apron and accidentally fallen. Kat was under no illusions about Mistress Jane Seymour;

small child that she was, she believed her to be cruel, spiteful, cunning, manipulative and without conscience.

Jane allowed herself to be herded down through the house and along the narrow flagstoned passageway to the kitchen. There, she took her customary stool at the end of the broad table, bleached by constant scrubbing and regarded Kat stonily from beneath her creased brow. The cook, her eyes darting from Jane's sulky face to Kat's infuriated one, said nothing as she slid the small trencher of food towards the child. Jane directed a venomous glance towards cook's retreating back and began pushing at the chunks of bread and cheese disinterestedly with a leisurely forefinger. After a quick glance over her shoulder at the girl, cook drew Kat away from the table and towards the fire. "What is the matter? What has gone on?"

Kat turned her body towards the fire grate so that her face was hidden from Jane. "Up to her usual tricks" she confided. "She couldn't find a small bird or animal to mistreat so she took her temper out on a bug she found in the attic."

Cook's homely face assumed a worried frown as she shook her head slowly. "I don't know what ails her and that's a fact. She has the face of an angel and a heart as black as soot. But after that awful business in the barn yard last week ..."

Kat nodded gravely, thinking back to the clutch of newly hatched goslings, found drowned in the muddy ditch behind the cow byre. "I keep hoping and praying that it wasn't her, but she had been watching the cows being milked, and her gown and hands were covered in mud."

"Still might have been an accident" cook soothed. "Young creatures will wander; similar things have happened countless times in the past."

Kat could feel Jane's eyes boring into the back of her head but refused to look round. "They were hatchlings" she whispered urgently. "They were barely mobile and it was the first time the goose had left the nest."

Cook risked a glance back at Jane and noted the hostile stare directed at the two of them. "Happen she'll grow out of it. She's left too much to herself that one; she has no playmates her own age and her siblings don't so much as spare her a kindly word."

"She is too much on her own" Kat agreed, "but I don't have the time to watch her every hour of the day and between you and me, I do not care overmuch for her company."

"Will you mention anything to her mother or father?"

Kat considered, then shook her head. "I can't see it would make much difference. Sir John is always too busy and directs anything domestic towards his lady. I've tried talking to her, but she just waves it all away and calls it childish misdeeds."

They both jumped in alarm as the trencher hit the wall beside them with some force, scattering the food as it clattered to the floor. Turning, they found Jane standing close behind them. "I am not hungry" she told them, "and your bread..." she turned towards cook, "tastes like cow dung." Smiling sweetly, she took in their horrified expressions, then swung on her heel and skipped lightly out of the door.

Chapter Two

Lady Margery Seymour stood in her solar, looking out through the great oriel window on to the deer park below. In general, she was a contented woman. Her husband was hard working and dependable, she had a large and thriving family and her estate was sizeable and profitable. As a young woman she had served her aunt the Countess of Surrey at court, so she had led a full and interesting life. Her father may have initially hoped that she would make a grander marriage as through him she had the blood of King Edward III running through her veins, but John Seymour had already been a member of the family due to his wardship being granted to her father when his own died. So much property and lands had come with the young John in his minority, that her father decided to keep it all in the family by marrying the two of them. And up to now, on the surface anyway, it had all been a resounding success. She mused further and so deep in thought was she that she had no idea someone was standing in the doorway, not until Kat gave a discreet cough.

"Kat?" Lady Margery turned slightly, looking over her shoulder.

"I'm sorry to bother you my lady, but might I have a word with you about Mistress Jane?"

Margery sighed heavily. "What has she done now?"

"It's not so much what she has done my lady, although I call torturing any of God's creatures a wicked thing, it is more that the child is so solitary and has too much empty time on her hands. Now I know it is not my place to dictate your plans for Mistress Jane, but might she not benefit from being placed in a neighbouring household? One with other girls her own age so that she may learn to use her time as befitting a girl of her station?"

Margery sighed again and turned to face Kat, who stood awkwardly just inside the door, twisting her apron with anxious fingers. "You are right Kat…"

Kat's expression brightened hopefully, just for the briefest second, until Margery continued. "It is not your place to dictate to me how my family should be brought up. I have undertaken to teach all of my daughters anything they need to know about the world in which they will live. Your duties are to supervise them when they are out of the nursery and not occupied with their lessons. Are you having a problem fulfilling this duty? Because if so I will seek to employ somebody who can."

As always when under Lady Margery's imperious gaze, Kat became flustered. "Yes, my lady… I mean no, my lady… ". Kat paused and took a deep breath. "I can supervise the children as you wish, of course I can, but …"

"Then I suggest you get back to your duties." Lady Margery ended the conversation abruptly, turning back to the window.

Kat curtsied to Lady Margery's back and hastily left the chamber, hurrying back to the comparative safety of the kitchen.

Cook came to meet her. "How did it go? Did she listen to you?"

Kat shook her head sadly. "No, as usual she turned the conversation to make it seem that Mistress Jane plays up because I don't manage her properly, rather than considering that the problem might lie with the child herself."

Cook turned back to the hearth, basted the large beef joint and poked the dozing turnspit with her toe. "It looks like we'll just have to carry on as we are then. It's not like it will be for ever; she'll grow up soon enough. It's just a question of watching her and trying to stay one step ahead."

"Easier said than done" Kat muttered.

After leaving the kitchen, Jane had wandered off towards the nursery, but when she saw Kat heading for her mother's solar, had followed her and listened to the exchange. Hearing her mother admonish the nurse and threaten to replace her had gladdened Jane's heart; she hated Kat always chasing after her and spoiling her fun. Still, that said, perhaps she was better off with someone she already had the better of;

who knew what steps a new nursemaid might take to pull her in to line. Smiling to herself she skipped on through the long gallery, up the stone steps and towards the suite of rooms used for the children. Following the sound of wailing, she pushed open one of the heavy oak doors and peeped in.

Her new baby brother Anthony lay stark naked on a sheepskin rug on the floor, screaming at the top of his voice and waving his limbs angrily. Meanwhile the nursemaid ran around like the busy bee she was, selecting napkins and swaddling robes. Seeing there might be some fun to be had, Jane pushed the door wider and went inside, plumping herself down on the rug beside the baby and poking him in the ribs to try and get his attention.

"Stop that Mistress Jane!" The nursemaid had seen that she seemed more set on hindrance than help. "Play with him by all means…here..." She handed Jane a small silver rattle. "Attract his attention with this rather than risk hurting his fragile bones." Jane shook the rattle in his face disinterestedly but the baby, after the merest glance and gurgle, resumed his yelling, causing Jane to drop the rattle on his head and skip off to see what her other siblings were up to.

The nursemaid tutted, scooped the baby up and began dressing him, at the same time pushing the door Jane had left open shut with her foot, to preserve the warmth in the room.

Jane was disappointed to find that none of her older brothers were there. Edward the eldest was already eighteen and started on his career, but she had expected that Henry or Thomas might be present. She walked around their chamber, picking up their possessions and then dropping them back down again before turning her attention to the younger children.

Elizabeth was two years younger, a plump pretty child who wanted to do little else but play with her dolls and help nurse with the younger children. Jane had little time for her. Seven-year-old Dorothy was almost as bad; she idolised Elizabeth and avoided Jane because Jane was the one who would pinch her slyly and make her cry.

That left four-year-old John and two-year-old Margery, both too young to be of any interest. Jane looked around at them all, chewing her thumbnail thoughtfully. Should she stay here and cause a little mayhem or explore further? Before she could decide, the door opened and her mother entered. The nurses, surprised, curtsied, whilst the younger children raced to greet her.

Although Margery could not be described as an overly affectionate mother, she loved her children and always made it her business to spend time in the nursery every day. She never specified an arrival time because she felt that it would ensure that standards were always kept high if they never knew when to expect her.

Jane was the only child who hung back on this occasion, and after Margery had hugged and spoken with the other children and cooed over the baby, she came to sit beside her. "And what have you been doing today Jane? Have you kept yourself properly occupied?"

Jane switched on her most innocent expression, smiled sweetly and nodded enthusiastically. Margery nodded. "I am glad about that. Now, where is Kat?"

"I don't know, I have hardly seen her today. She's spent most of her time talking to cook in the kitchen." As Margery's expression hardened, Jane smiled inwardly. It had been a good day.

Chapter Three

As cook had prophesied, Jane did soon grow up, although her early promise of beauty was not fulfilled. Kat, prematurely aged by running around after the Seymour children, thought that Jane's looks as she passed through her teenaged years, were the looks she had brought upon herself by her behaviour and interactions with others. Her rosy childhood complexion had paled until it was the colour of chalk, her beautiful blue eyes, although still blue, seemed too big for her brow and fairly bulged out of their sockets, whilst her mouth, once rosebud plump, seemed to have grown smaller, with remarkably thin lips which she generally held pursed in disapproval or malice. Only her hair remained the same colour, corn yellow, but since she generally kept it covered, it did nothing to offset her rather severe appearance. Her nature had not improved, although she had learned to project what she wished others to see. On the surface she was quiet, obedient, demure and almost overly prim and proper. Underneath she was nosy, spiteful and prone to listening at doors. She was less inclined to be cruel as she matured, but privately Kat felt that was more down to lack of opportunity than anything else. With servants and those she considered beneath her, she was insufferably haughty and frequently rude and belittling. She had become an accomplished liar and had both adopted and perfected her mother's habit of turning any negative conversation into an attack upon the other party.

Margery watched her with troubled eyes, wishing she had paid more attention to Kat's concerns in Jane's early years. She could see for herself how Jane's early disposition still impacted upon her barely adult self. Although her needlework was of high standard, her reading and writing more than adequate and her domestic abilities second to none, she could not help but wonder what would become of her daughter as she grew older.

At almost twenty years old, Jane seemed already destined for spinsterhood as not one offer of marriage had come her way. For herself, Jane was not too worried as she knew there would always be widowers who needed a wife who would be both nurse and housekeeper. Unlike many young girls, she did not dream of a handsome knight who would fall in love with her and carry her away to live happily ever after. All she really wanted was to be able to do exactly what she liked in her own household, which would be run according to her own strict instructions.

Jane was passing time in the long gallery one day, moving idly from window to window when she was distracted by a squeal of delight from the broad chamber across the passageway. She was just moving towards the door to see the cause of the commotion when her sister Elizabeth came dancing in, spinning around in circles, her skirts flying immodestly high.

At seventeen, Elizabeth was the undisputed beauty of the family, little changed from the enchanting child she had once been. Jane tolerated her but could not hide her jealousy at the suitors the girl had already attracted. Despite Jane being the eldest daughter, as soon as anyone set eyes on Elizabeth they were captivated and Jane forgotten once more.

Jane waited until Elizabeth had calmed a little before asking the obvious questions "Why all the excitement? What is afoot?"

Elizabeth ran over to her, grabbing her arms excitedly. "I am to be married!" she exclaimed. "Sir Anthony Ughtred has asked for my hand!"

Jane was unimpressed. She knew of Sir Anthony, admittedly a distinguished soldier with a long and illustrious career, but also a widower who was already approaching fifty years of age. "You have met this man?"

Elizabeth looked vague "No, not exactly, but I have seen his portrait and I know he is much favoured by the King."

"He's old enough to be your father!"

Elizabeth flushed angrily. "Why should that matter? He is a kind man and he will give me a good life."

Jane sniffed. "Is that the summit of your ambition? It certainly would not do for me."

Elizabeth laughed pityingly. "Considering no-one has made an offer to you, you seem overly choosy. Where are your suitors sister?" Elizabeth walked to the window and looked down in to the courtyard, shading her eyes the better to see beyond into the park. "Oh, wait. Is that a long line of hopeful amours on the horizon? No. All that awaits out there is a flock of sheep."

Jane regarded her steadily, not troubling to hide her dislike. "Mock all you like. Just you wait and see." She projected a confidence she did not feel.

"Sir Anthony would not be good enough for you, no doubt!"

"Certainly not. I have standards."

"So you have set your sights where exactly, a duke, a prince, a king?"

Jane smiled frostily. "Any or all would be quite acceptable. When will your marriage take place, soon?" Privately Jane felt that the sooner Elizabeth was out of the way, the more chance someone's eye might alight on her.

"There is to be a lengthy betrothal" Elizabeth replied. "He is detained overseas and seeks a more settled post before marriage."

After a brisk gallop in the red deer park, Jane felt a little happier. Elizabeth would soon be gone and now she was betrothed she would attract no more offers for her hand. Throwing her horse's reins to the groom, she bunched up her long riding skirts, draped them over her arm and made her way into the house. Lady Margery was ascending the staircase as she passed through the hall. "Ah, Jane" she called, "I have been looking for you."

Jane stopped and looked up at her mother. "Oh? I was riding in the deer park. It needs restocking I think."

"I am sure Palmer has it all in hand." Margery dismissed Jane's comments, she had news to impart. "I take it you have heard of Elizabeth's good fortune?"

"Good fortune? Ha!" Jane's laugh was sarcastic. "If you can call marriage to a man old enough to be her father 'good news', then yes, I've heard."

"You should be pleased for your sister!" Margery admonished. "It is a good match and she will be well taken care of."

Jane looked unconvinced and was just about to continue on her way when her mother hurried towards her and placed a restraining hand on her arm. "There are also tidings for you" she began. "Sir Francis Bryan is here, he has news from court."

"And that concerns me how?" Jane didn't much care for Francis Bryan's reputation or cavalier attitude.

"The Queen is in want of a maid of honour. He has put your name forward and she has provisionally accepted you."

Jane took a moment to absorb that information, then bestowed a rare smile upon her mother. "I would be most honoured to serve Queen Catherine, she is a great lady. If you can give me a few moments mother, I will change and come to greet Sir Francis."

Jane bounded up the back stairs in high good humour. At last she had been gifted a way out of this cloying and very public household. Away from the prying eyes of her parents and with a chance to make a name for herself in the most glittering court in the world. Her siblings were growing up and would soon be clamouring to find their own places; what better time to strike out.

She may also see more of her favourite brother Edward who was pursuing his military career under court patronage. His new wife had been sent to Wolf Hall because of lack of marital lodgings and had just announced her pregnancy, so Jane was more than happy to leave behind all the sickness and nastiness which accompanied that condition. Her only regret was that she might never find out exactly why her frequently weeping and wailing sister-in-law was so often closeted with Sir John. Privately Jane felt that something was not quite right and was quite positive that her mother shared the same view.

Once in her chamber, Jane changed quickly out of her riding habit and into a modest, plum coloured gown with a black embroidered kirtle. Carefully she smoothed her hair under her gable hood, then frowned at her reflection in her tiny looking glass. Like many pale skinned women, violent exercise and keen winds did very little for her looks. Rather than a healthy glow, her white skin was dotted with livid dark red patches which almost matched the redness of her eyes which still watered from the homeward gallop. A quick dab at her face with a moistened kerchief made little difference, so she abandoned any attempt to resurrect the smooth pale complexion which was her one very small claim to beauty and decided to try to impress with her demeanour instead.

Halfway down the long gallery, Jane slowed her brisk pace to a sedate glide, and arrived at the half-closed door of the broad chamber without attracting the attention of those within. As was her habit, she listened for a moment before making herself known, blocking out Kat's voice in her head which told her that those who listen at doors rarely hear any good of themselves. Jane was convinced that if Sir Francis had come to take her up to court, then surely this was the one time when she would hear something flattering. But alas, all she could discern beyond the solid oak door was a low hubbub of conversation, so head held high, she pushed the door wide and entered.

All looked towards her as she swept grandly in. Her mother and father were there, along with Sir Francis who had arrived with two companions, all attended by a handful of servants who were occupied bringing food, pouring wine and building up the fire in the great hearth.

Her mother came forward to greet her, her expression disappointed. "You could have made yourself a little more respectable" she hissed. Then all smiles, she turned back to the company and led Jane forward to Sir Francis. "My daughter apologises for keeping you waiting gentlemen" she began, "but she has been riding, hence her dishevelled appearance."

Jane crossly shook her arm free of her mother's grasp. "I can speak for myself mother, I am not a child to have you make my excuses for me." Ignoring her father's warning glance, she approached Sir Francis and bobbed a respectful curtsey. Nothing too low or deep, because he was only a knight. She was reserving her deepest obeisance for when she was finally in the presence of royalty. "Sir Francis, I am delighted to meet you again."

Sir Francis Bryan, accustomed as he was to the court beauties, blinked a little at the apparition before him. She was as he expected, a bit of a country bumpkin, albeit a well-bred country bumpkin, with her reddened skin and pale watery eyes.

"Mistress Seymour." The courtier in him came to the fore as he extended his hand to her. "You have grown into quite the young lady since I last saw you."

"I doubt that very much Sir Francis" Jane replied tartly. "It cannot be more than six months since you were last here and I hardly think I can have changed overmuch." Feeling her mother's eyes boring into the back of the head, Jane relaxed her stiffness a little, flashing him a quick if insincere smile and inclining her head in a manner she hoped would be considered gracious.

Sir Francis chuckled inwardly. Country bumpkin or not, she was amply equipped to stand up to the eternal squabbles and backbiting at court. "Mistress Seymour, as you have likely been told, the Queen requires a new maid of honour in place of one recently promoted upon her marriage. Since Lady Margery had recently informed me that you were still at home, I thought you would be admirably suited. Queen Catherine was gracious enough to grant my request and wishes to meet you before you are sworn in. Will this arrangement be acceptable to you?"

Jane pretended to consider, then graciously inclined her head once more. "It would be most acceptable Sir

Francis, thank you. May I ask, what was it which swayed Her Grace in my favour?"

"I stressed your piety, your gentleness, your patience and your excellent needlework. Her Grace was well pleased."

Out of the corner of her eye, Jane saw her mother and father exchange glances then turn as one to busy themselves with offering more refreshment to Sir Francis's companions.

Jane chewed the inside of her cheek as she considered his words. Piety, maybe. That was a cloak which could be donned or discarded at will. Gentleness? Not something she was generally accused of. Neither was patience, although it would be easy to assume if harder to maintain. Needlework, yes. She was good with her needle. Aware that he was waiting for her response, she smiled haughtily. "I believe that I can be all the Queen expects of me."

Sir Francis raised his goblet to her and took a celebratory swig. "Then all is arranged. Can you be ready to leave on the morrow?"

"Most certainly."

Lady Margery stepped in her expression one of concern. "Sir Francis, she has not the attire for court."

"Do not concern yourself my lady. Livery is already arranged and Mistress Jane will have access to materials held in the Great Wardrobe should grander attire be required for celebrations and feast days".

Chapter Four

The court was newly arrived at Greenwich from Whitehall, so was even more a hive of activity than usual. Due to the general tumult and the lack of stabling, Francis left their horses in livery at a hostelry of his acquaintance and ushered Jane into a barge at Westminster steps whilst her baggage continued by road. It was her first time in London and she had plenty of opportunity to look about her and gather her thoughts whilst being rowed along the eight mile stretch of river. The boatman, possibly new to his occupation, missed the smaller landing stage east of the main steps, and put Francis and Jane down on the wide water steps underneath the windows of the King's presence chamber.

"Let us hope the King is elsewhere" Sir Francis nodded up to the large glazed windows on the first floor. "This area is reserved for the landing of royalty and nobility, not a humble knight escorting a new maid of honour!"

Jane gazed boldly upwards, prepared to stand her ground and stare down anyone who would presume that she was not worthy to tread in the footsteps of those who considered themselves her betters.

"Quickly Mistress Seymour." Sir Francis had paid the boatman, stepped gracefully ashore and was offering his hand for her safe disembarkation. "If we hurry this way," he indicated to the left, "we can turn down between the chapel and the lodging house and be admitted through the entrance off the middle court."

Jane looked at him blankly, she had no idea what he was talking about, but followed his lead. Greenwich Palace was a huge sprawling building, and Jane soon found out that it was far quicker to be told the proposed route than it was to walk it. However, they made the journey without incident and were admitted into the palace promptly without challenge, Sir Francis being well known about the court.

"The Queen will be in the watching chamber at this hour" Sir Francis informed her. "This way." He led her quickly down a narrow passageway, then up a flight of stone stairs to the first floor. At the top of the stairs was a long, wide, sumptuously decorated landing, with high, grand double oak doors at each end with armed guards in attendance.

"The Queen is this way" he hurried her to the right.

Jane stopped. "And that way?"

"The King." Francis grimaced. "If I were you I'd keep well clear; he's been in a high old temper these past weeks." Jane looked at him curiously, but he was not about to confide exactly why the King was out of sorts. The fact that the King was infatuated and some said, wished to marry, a lady of the court was no secret; Jane would soon enough become acquainted with both the rumours and the lady herself.

As they approached the doors to the Queen's chamber, the guards stood down their weapons and pushed open the double doors. Inside was a small ante chamber, beyond which was another set of closed doors. Sir Francis stepped forward, knocked smartly on the wood panel, then opened the left-hand door and ushered Jane in ahead of him.

The room was full of women, quietly sewing linens or working on embroidery. Jane scanned the figures one by one and soon identified the Queen. Catherine sat to one side on a plain straight-backed chair slightly higher than the stools on which most of her women sat in a semicircle around her. She did not acknowledge their presence for some moments, giving Jane time to get a good look at her. Catherine looked tired and her face was lined with worry and what looked like the beginnings of ill health. She wore a plain heavily embroidered black velvet dress and an elaborate gold crucifix. Her greying hair was mostly obscured by the pearl encrusted black velvet English style gable hood she wore.

Jane noticed that some of the younger ladies were eying Sir Francis speculatively, as did the Queen. Without so much as a glance towards them she murmured warningly "Ladies." Then seconds later, after calmly finishing her row of stitches, she set aside her linen and rose to her feet. Immediately, all others in the room did the same.

"Sir Francis." Catherine held out her hand as he

executed a deep and respectful bow before kissing her fingers lightly. "This then is Mistress Seymour." As the Queen turned towards her, Jane dropped into a deep curtsey, too overcome to speak.

"Rise, child." Catherine stepped towards her and motioned her to her feet. "Sir Francis has been your most able champion; we have heard many good things of you."

"I thank Your Grace." Jane found her voice at last, but still did not dare to raise her eyes any further than the waist of the Queen's gown.

"Mistress Seymour. Jane." Catherine stepped forward and gently lifted Jane's chin until their eyes met. After a searing scrutiny, Catherine smiled gently. "I think you will do very well."

Stepping away from Jane, Catherine looked to one side and held out her hand. "Constance, the oath if you please." One of the younger maids stepped forward and bowed her head as she placed a small parchment into the Queen's outstretched hand. "Thank you, Constance."

After running her eyes briefly over the parchment, Catherine handed it to Jane. "Now Mistress Seymour, if you would just read this aloud and promise to abide by the rules and regulations of the household, you can consider yourself inducted. Constance can then show you where you will sleep and help you settle in."

"Your Grace." Jane curtsied again as she took the document from Catherine's hand then dutifully read the script aloud.

"Very good Jane." Catherine motioned Constance forward and indicated that Jane should return the parchment to her. "Before you go, may I present my daughter the Princess Mary, who is visiting with us from Ludlow for a few days."

A small slightly built girl moved gracefully forward from the shadows at the back of the room. She was quite the daintiest creature Jane had ever encountered, almost impossibly fragile, her features small, her eyes bright and interested.

"Lady Princess." Jane curtsied deeply, taking the slender hand which was extended to help her rise.

"We are pleased to make your acquaintance Mistress Seymour." Princess Mary had a surprisingly deep and gruff voice for one so delicate. Jane was not exactly sure what age she was but thought her around twelve or thirteen. "I rarely visit court these days, but when I do it gladdens my heart to see my lady mother is well served. She is fortunate in her women." Mary looked around the room as she spoke. "And I feel sure that in you she has made another sound choice." Mary smiled at Jane in a most friendly manner and Jane smiled back, momentarily forgetting that she was in front of not only a royal princess, but the heir to the throne. For a split second, they were just two girls not so very far apart in age who in another situation may have been good friends.

"Sir Francis." Catherine had suddenly noticed him still standing just inside the door. "Your task is complete, you have delivered Mistress Seymour safely into our care. You may withdraw. Constance? Take Jane along now and help her settle in."

Once outside, Sir Francis swept Jane a courtly bow and settled his feathered hat back on his brow. "I bid you farewell for now Mistress Seymour and wish you much success in your court career."

Chapter Five

Jane soon had the measure of Constance, like herself a country girl, but unlike Jane, very soft and trusting. Once Jane had learned all she needed to know about the way Catherine's household was run, she cut her association with Constance without compunction. This in no way distressed the gentle Constance who after a few weeks in Jane's company grew tired of her rudeness and haughty ways.

Constance had hoped that she and Jane could be friends since they were both less well born than many of the Queen's ladies, but Jane made it abundantly clear that she required no confidante with whom to giggle in corners, she was perfectly happy with her own company. This attitude also alienated her from the rest of the waiting women, who excluded her from their gossiping and merrymaking. Jane reverted to her favourite pastime of listening at doors and from behind curtains in order to keep up with the latest court tittle tattle.

The Queen made no comment on Jane's behaviour outside her royal duties but was well aware that she was not popular.

The main topic of conversation for all was the state of the royal marriage. As Sir Francis had predicted, it took her no time at all to learn that Mistress Anne Boleyn was behind the Queen's private heartache and although she had only seen her from afar, hated her for the distress she was causing her royal mistress. Jane believed that the King was totally blameless, he was but a man ensnared by the allure of forbidden fruit.

After a cool spring, come midsummer's day the city was in the grip of a sudden and intense heatwave. The river, never fragrant at the best of times, began emitting a fetid stench which made those who lived on its banks nauseous and restless. That some sort of sickness or plague would strike became a reality rather than a possibility and those who had lived through similar times became worried and alert to the slightest adverse symptom in themselves or others.

There was not long to wait and soon cases of the dreaded sweating sickness were being reported from across the city.

At court, all the talk was of the divorce hearing at Blackfriars when Catherine fell upon her knees before Henry and begged him to consider their long and happy marriage. The King continued to deny her, certain that she had been a true wife to his brother Prince Arthur and was therefore flouting God's law in determining to remain as his wife.

The Queen and her ladies spent long hours praying to God to show the King the error of his ways and Jane discovered a new respect for her dignified and stoical mistress and did all she could to comfort and cheer her.

By now, Anne Boleyn was set up in her own household not far from an area of the city badly affected by the sickness. It was only a matter of time before it was brought to her door, despite rigorous rules denying entry to anyone who had come directly from the city precincts. But the sickness followed no rules and had scant respect for whoever it infected, be they from the highest estate in the land or the lowest.

Even as Anne Boleyn prepared to move her household to Waltham in Essex, along with the King, news was brought to her that one of her maids had taken the sickness and would surely die.

Once this news reached the Queen's household there was much rejoicing. Anne Boleyn would not now follow them to Waltham and set up a rival court because she had been in direct contact with a carrier of the sickness. She would have to go wherever she felt she might be safe but she could not come near the King until enough time had passed to prove that she had not been infected.

Whereas Catherine's ladies were not slow in wishing all manner of plague down on the interloper's head, Catherine took great pains to pray for everyone stricken, and was even heard to pray for Anne Boleyn's deliverance from danger.

Whilst her long-serving women accepted that their mistress was adept at turning the other cheek, Jane could not understand her tolerance. Surely now was the time to call God's wrath down on Anne Boleyn's head and petition for him to remove her from the face of the earth. She became more and more agitated at Catherine's patience and forbearance until she could no longer hold her tongue.

"Your Grace, do you have no spleen against that other woman, she who seeks to oust you from your royal estate and take your place?"

Catherine had been leaning back in her chair with her eyes closed, listening to one of her musicians gently strumming his lute. At Jane's question, her eyes opened and her brows raised high in surprise. "Jane, one thing you could never be accused of is sugaring the pill. It seems that tact is a stranger to you."

Jane flushed, wondering if she had overstepped the mark. Catherine had been tolerant of some of her outbursts in the past, but she accepted that she was delving into the Queen's most personal feelings and could well provoke the royal rage. It was not often that Catherine lost her temper because her self-control was rarely breached, but when it did happen it could be terrifying.

"I can only apologise for my directness Your Grace, but it pains me to see the agony this woman causes you, yet your only reaction is gentle compassion."

Catherine sighed and looked down at her hands, about which were twisted the rosary beads given her by her mother when she left her native Spain to marry Prince Arthur. "Jane, you know your bible; our saviour teaches that tolerance and compassion in the face of our enemies is the only way to salvation. Anyway, I pity her."

Jane was mystified. "Your Grace?"

"Look into her eyes when you can and you will see that her burning ambition will be her undoing. Much as I may suffer in the months to come, I believe that she will come to a far worse fate."

When news reached the court that Anne Boleyn, newly returned to her childhood home at Hever in Kent, had taken the sickness, Jane truly came to believe that Catherine must be some kind of holy prophet. She had said the woman would suffer and she was most surely suffering now. Whilst Catherine murmured prayers for her recovery, Jane fervently prayed that she would die and roast in hell forever.

Jane's prayers were not answered, but Catherine's were. Anne Boleyn, strong as an ox, recovered her health in full, whilst her sister's husband William Carey succumbed with seemingly no resistance. Whereas it was not uncommon to recover from the sweating sickness, provided good and prompt medical attention was given, it was rare for there to be no long-term effects. Catherine's ladies whispered amongst themselves that it must be proof positive that Anne Boleyn was in league with the devil himself.

Within days of news reaching the court that Anne Boleyn had survived, a messenger arrived from Wolf Hall with a letter for Jane. The messenger was a long-standing servant of her father's and she read in his eyes as she took the letter from his hand that it was not good news. A soldier all his life, Sir John Seymour was nothing if not practical and brief when penning missives to members of his family. However, on this occasion he was uncharacteristically incoherent and emotional. It seemed that the sweating sickness had reached Wolf Hall, carrying off several house servants as well as Jane's two youngest siblings twelve-year-old Margery and ten-year-old Anthony. According to Sir John, both children had fought long and hard and the end when it came was very sudden and unexpected. It was very clear that their deaths had caused much sorrow at home, but the letter ended with a cryptic postscript advising her that she may shortly hear news which may surprise and shock her, particularly if it were to be conveyed by her brother Edward.

Jane frowned and thought back to the last time she had been at home, six months previously. Immediately she recalled the long and intense conversations she had witnessed and on occasion overheard between her father and Edward's wife. It would likely be something to do with that, particularly if Edward was on another of his rather frequent rampages.

The messenger, who still stood before her studying her face, thought that he may see some kind of emotion when she read of her siblings' deaths. But no expression other than interest had passed over her face, at least until she read the passage at the very bottom of the parchment, when her eyes narrowed calculatingly and her mouth hardened. Deep in thought, she carefully folded the parchment before meeting the gaze of the messenger. "Is there a reply Mistress Seymour?"

She shook her head. "No."

The messenger, who had been instructed by Sir John

to bring back some sort of response, tried again. "Nothing at all?"

Jane sighed impatiently and glared at him. "Are you missing some of your wits? I said no!"

"But Sir John said …."

"I do not care what Sir John said. Tell me, is my brother Edward here at court?"

"He is. I also have a letter for him."

"Then when you see him, ask him if he will meet me at his convenience to speak of matters at home."

"Assuredly. And there is not even a verbal message for your family?"

Jane tossed her head and sighed again. "Very well, give them my condolences on their loss if you must."

For the rest of that day, she remained alert, turning at every footfall in case it was Edward coming to see her. He kept her waiting until after evening vespers and when he did arrive, it was with a very short temper and an arrogance which had increased and developed as he matured. He did not waste time on niceties, but barked "What is it sister? I have better things to do than scuttle over here like some minion at your bidding."

"I am glad you could manage to spare me a few moments of your time" Jane replied sarcastically. "I take it you have read the news from home?"

"Aye." He softened a little and lowered his eyes. "I was sorry to hear about Margery and Anthony; no doubt our mother is greatly distressed."

"And our father also." Jane could not resist the sly comment, although she was taken aback at the angry reaction it provoked.

"He does not deserve our thoughts and sympathy, our mother does."

"Why? What has he done? He put a postscript in my letter to say that I may hear ill of him, particularly from you."

Edward's jaw was set so rigidly, he spoke almost from between clenched teeth. "He has seduced Catherine."

"Catherine your wife?"

"Yes of course Catherine my wife, who else?"

"Well!" Jane did not know quite what to say. "I thought there might be something afoot, with them being closeted together so often, but I never expected this of him."

Edward regarded her curiously and with rising anger before thrusting his face close to her own. "You knew about this and did not even think to tell me?"

Backing away, Jane held up her hands to ward him off. "I did not know anything for sure so why would I risk causing upset where there need not be any?"

Her brother laughed. "It is not something which you have hesitated over before is it? Dear sweet Jane, of course you would never say anything ill of anyone would you? Do not presume to act all innocent with me, what did you see? If you saw nothing then for sure with your penchant for listening at doors you would have heard something!"

As he approached her menacingly, Jane held up her hand imperiously, causing him to stop in surprise. "I saw nothing and heard nothing worth reporting. Do not presume to blame me for your wife's failings or those of our father. If you want someone to blame, maybe you should look to our mother. I am sure that she had her suspicions."

"Surely she would not condone something like this?"

Jane shrugged. "I do not know. She would not be the first wife to turn a blind eye to her husband's philandering."

Edward was by now striding up and down the small chamber in extreme agitation. "I cannot believe she would allow something like this to go on under her nose."

Jane smirked. "You know mother, she can close her eyes to anything in order to guarantee herself a quiet life." Then a sudden thought struck her. "Edward, what of the boys?" Catherine had given birth to two children in quick succession.

He shook his head ruefully. "I do not know, I cannot think straight. They are without a doubt their mother's children, but who is their father, her husband or her father in law?"

"Edward, you cannot think …"

"Well, who is to know? We look alike, father and I. Maybe the elder boy is mine, but I very much doubt the younger can be."

"What will you do?"

"The only thing I can do. Put her away from me and repudiate the marriage."

"But there will be scandal!"

"Ha! You think I care about that? The hell with what people think, I will have her known for the harlot she is. And him for the back-stabbing excuse for a father he is."

"You care not then that your sisters would be denied any high-status marriages?"

"Elizabeth is betrothed and I do not believe Sir Anthony would be overly perturbed by adverse news, he is well satisfied with her. Now Margery has gone, it is only you and Dorothy who may feel the effects. According to mother, you are set to remain a spinster. Dorothy is blossoming and may yet outshine our sister Elizabeth, so do not fear for her."

"Why does mother say I will never marry? I am young, I am sure to be noticed by someone; there are many here in want of a wife."

Edward looked at her pityingly. "Have you bothered your looking glass lately sister? Yes, there are many here seeking wives, but your looks do you no favours. Your very nature is plain to read from your face; you are sly, spiteful and proud. Hardly qualities most men seek in their wives."

"I thank you for the character assassination brother." Jane had sarcasm which far outshone Edward's. "I will have you know that I can be as modest, demure and obedient as any woman at court. You just wait and see."

Chapter Six

The King was stubbornly set on a speedy divorce from the Queen so that he could marry Anne Boleyn. Cardinal Wolsey, who had been working most assiduously on the King's great matter to achieve this for his royal master was deemed by Anne and her supporters to be not working hard or fast enough. The King allowed himself to be persuaded likewise and ordered Wolsey's arrest. When the news reached the pope, he decreed that the matter of the divorce could no longer be deliberated in England, the decision, if and when it came, would come from Rome.

Although the King stripped the Cardinal of his property and grand offices, he did allow him to remain as Archbishop of York provided he took himself to that diocese without delay and remained there out of sight of his furious monarch. Wolsey wasted no time in making ready and was soon heading a long procession of his household and what goods he was left with on the road to York.

This however did not satisfy Anne Boleyn, who was afraid that the King might relent and allow his old friend Wolsey back into his life. Allowing her hot temper full rein, she endlessly pushed home her point that Wolsey's actions in delaying the divorce and the fulfilment of his King's desires was nothing short of high treason. She knew the King would give in to her sooner or later but even she was surprised with the speed with which he did relent. Wolsey was at Cawood, seven miles short of York, and at dinner in the castle there, when the King's men arrived to arrest him and take him back to London to face trial.

The Earl of Northumberland, the same Henry Percy whom Anne had once loved and sought to marry, was accompanied by a large contingent of soldiers and a trusted member of the King's privy chamber, Master Walsh.

Wolsey was not altogether surprised by their arrival but refused to comply with the arrest until he had seen with his own eyes the copy of the order which gave them their authority. It was left to Master Walsh to explain that he could not have sight of it because it also contained many instructions to which the King did not want him privy. Although Wolsey still refused to submit to Henry Percy, he allowed Master Walsh to arrest him because since he was of the King's privy chamber, he presumably had direct authority from the King to do so.

Wolsey had been unwell for some weeks. Describing himself as heart-sick at the King's distrust of him, the journey southwards had to be taken in short stages to allow Wolsey to rest. By the time they reached Leicester, he was almost falling from his mule in sickness and exhaustion, so they took him to the nearby abbey so that the monks could attend to him. Despite their best efforts, Wolsey became worse and died a few days later.

Mistress Boleyn was much aggrieved by the King's obvious sorrow at his old friend's death whilst Queen Catherine prayed fervently for the salvation of his soul and bid her women do likewise. She had only tolerated him in life, but in death recognised that he had served the King faithfully until his last breath.

Two months later, Jane's sister Elizabeth married Sir Anthony Ughtred. Jane did not attend the ceremony because she felt that her sister had let the family down by accepting a place in Anne Boleyn's court. Sir Anthony was an open and loyal supporter of the Boleyn cause and soon after their marriage the King granted him the manors of Lepington and Kexby, both of which were formerly held by Wolsey until his disgrace and downfall.

Jane took no pleasure in having her sister wed and settled with fine estates, she was both jealous of her good fortune and angry that she chose to support the usurper rather than the true Queen.

Queen Catherine kept to her household routine and her devotions, fervently praying for the King to be delivered from the temptations of the woman who sought to bewitch him away from his lawful wife. As far as she was aware, the affair had not progressed.

Anne Boleyn still spurned the King's bed and although he spent much time with her and her friends, it was to Catherine he returned each and every night.

Therefore it was a great and unhappy surprise to her when one day in July he rode away from Windsor with Anne and several members of his household and did not return.

After several days with absolute silence from him and any close to him, messages arrived at Windsor for both Catherine and Mary. Mary was ordered to leave Windsor forthwith and take up residence at Richmond whereas Catherine was instructed to take her household and settle at a large, remote country house in Hertfordshire called The More.

Advising Mary not to disobey her father, she saw her safely off to Richmond before writing urgently to the King to protest at both the remoteness of the location and of the unsuitability of The More for her sizeable household.

For several months heated missives sped to and from the Queen at Windsor and the King at Greenwich, but eventually Catherine realised that she could hold out no longer and five months after the original order she packed up her goods and servants and travelled into exile.

The More was less of a shock to Jane than it was to many of the other ladies. Granted it was no palace and short on gaiety and modern amenities, but it was a building only thirty years old and in generally good repair. Until very recently it had been owned by Cardinal Wolsey and had only passed into the King's ownership a few months previously following Wolsey's disgrace. Wolsey had made certain alterations to the house to ensure that should it ever be granted a royal visit, adequate facilities were available for both King and Queen.

Accommodation was arranged around an inner court within a wide and deep moat. A recent alteration had seen a long gallery built out from the King's watching chamber which extended not just over the privy gardens but also a bridged a small lake which was an offshoot of the moat. Jane thought it a most agreeable place, only slightly larger than her own family home and far more luxuriously appointed. There was an orchard to one side and a sizeable park bounded by the river Colne.

The house required a certain amount of freshening and airing, but Jane and the other servants gladly did all that was required, and once a few months of neglect were chased away and all the fires lit in the main rooms, The More became a peaceful refuge from the political upheaval of the King's court.

Catherine, grateful for the tender ministrations and solicitous care of her ladies, still refused to call herself anything than the Queen of England, despite the King's order that she should no longer use that title and felt that her continued sojourn so far away from the King and his court was not becoming to her status. News from court was scant and she was forbidden any contact with her daughter.

Once she and her household had truly settled, Catherine found The More a pleasant residence, if a little cut off from London. Her contentment was not to last; barely twelve months later she was ordered to move again, this time to Ampthill Castle in Bedfordshire.

If she had felt The More to be remote, it was nothing compared to Ampthill which stood in parkland amid acres of unoccupied countryside. It had once been regarded as a palace when it was built more than one hundred and twenty years earlier for the bride of Sir John Cornwall. She was a sister of Henry IV and Sir John wanted her new home to befit her royal status.

However modern the facilities were considered to be in the 1400s, by the time Catherine arrived there in early 1533 with her still sizeable household, what awaited her was accommodation of barely habitable standard. When the King first acquired the estate in the early 1520s, he had been a frequent visitor for the hunting was good. As state matters slowly took precedence, Ampthill fell by the wayside because of both the distance from London and the poor roads which made any journey long and arduous.

As she approached the castle, Catherine, who had never been there before, saw it occupied rising ground and was comprised of four wings ranged around a central courtyard, with small towers at each corner. The gatehouse through which they passed was on the eastern side. Inside, there were large kitchens and a great hall, over which were built the state rooms and private quarters which Henry had used during his sojourns there.

Like The More, the place had not been occupied for some time and the curtains and hangings were damp and mildewed. Unlike The More, it did not improve with freshening, airing and heating. The all-pervading odour of mildew persisted and even Catherine's clothes and those of her ladies, no matter how carefully dried and stored, took on a similar aroma.

Catherine however refused to be brought down by her surroundings. "Cheer up ladies" she would say, when she saw their low spirits and sad faces. "We have a stout roof above us, warm fires and good food. That must suffice for us because it could be far worse."

However, it is doubtful she would have remained so relentlessly cheerful had she known what was going on at court in her absence.

Chapter Seven

Catherine and her household had been at Ampthill for around three months when a large deputation, including the Dukes of Norfolk and Suffolk arrived at the gatehouse and requested audience.

Catherine saw to it that she exercised what little power she still had by making them wait whilst she performed a long and complicated toilet. Only when she was satisfied that she was looking her best did she emerge from her bedchamber and make her way to that area she had come to call her presence chamber. Visitors were few, but those who came were shown into this large chamber which had been made as grand and comfortable as possible by her devoted servants.

Upon making her entrance she saw a great many men and nobles milling about. Suffolk was slumped in a chair looking despondent whilst Norfolk paced up and down in front of the windows like a man demented.

She cleared her throat and spoke "Gentlemen."

Norfolk immediately ceased his wanderings and strode across to her, executing a very perfunctory bow which made Catherine's brow crease in annoyance. This was not the way a Queen should be greeted by the highest noble in the land. Fixing him with a haughty stare, she extended her hand for him to kiss. He looked surprised, but took it anyway, barely touching the back of her hand with his lips. Without preamble, he launched straight into the news which struck Catherine like a dagger to the heart.

"Your marriage to our gracious lord King Henry will shortly be ruled invalid on the grounds that your first marriage to Prince Arthur was lawfully consummated."

"By whose authority?" Catherine demanded. "To my knowledge, the pope has not yet ruled on the matter."

"The pope has no authority in England" Norfolk sneered. "We are free of the jurisdiction of Rome, all decisions such as this now lie with the senior clerics of the Church of England."

"I do not recognise a Church of England. I will submit only to the pope's ruling on this matter."

"You will submit to the King's will or be liable to a charge of treason!" Norfolk shouted, causing

Catherine to take a step back in alarm. Jane however stepped forward and stood at her mistress's shoulder, hands extended slightly for fear that Catherine might faint. Norfolk continued his rant

"You left the King no option with your continued and willful stubbornness. He has been far more patient with you than you deserve; for many years he has been waiting on the pope's ruling in order to break free of his shackles. He now feels that the time is right to shrug off the influence of Rome and make his own rules for England."

"Then something has changed" Catherine looked at him curiously. "Tell me, why now?"

Norfolk pursed his lips and glanced sideways at Suffolk. "The King and Mistress Anne Boleyn were married at Whitehall two months ago. Yesterday in council the King announced that she is with child."

Catherine gasped and staggered a little. Anxiously Jane supported her weight and felt the Queen's knees give way in her distress. As other ladies came to prop up their stricken mistress, a chair was quickly brought into which Catherine sank gratefully. After a few moments, she spoke. "This then is the reason" she nodded wisely. "It is not the King at all, it is her. After all the years of making him wait for her favours, she became impatient and decided to play her hand. She knew that once with child, he would not delay matters a moment longer to ensure that it was born in wedlock."

Jane, standing behind Catherine's chair, nodded fervently in agreement, causing Norfolk to fix her with his steely stare. With open hostility, Jane stared back.

Catherine was tapping the arms of her chair with quick and agitated fingers. "What other news?" she asked fearfully. "It does not take such a large contingent of nobles to convey the news of a marriage, unlawful as it is, and a bastard child. The King has no doubt decided what is to become of me, so tell me now."

As Norfolk opened his mouth to do just that, Suffolk laid a warning hand on his arm causing him to stop in surprise. "There has probably been enough shock and upset for now and we should take our leave."

"Very well." Norfolk shook his arm free. "I would advise you Madam to consult with your chamberlain when you feel able. We have conveyed certain instructions to him with which he can acquaint you."

Catherine nodded distractedly and waved her hand in dismissal. One by one, the deputation left the chamber, some making respectful bows, others barely acknowledging her.

It was some moments before she spoke. Constance fetched her some wine whilst her other ladies hovered anxiously nearby. As she replaced the goblet on the silver tray, she asked Jane to fetch Lord Mountjoy, her chamberlain.

He arrived promptly. A small man in his middle fifties, he had served Catherine faithfully for over twenty years. He stood before her, biting his lip and wondering how on earth he could convey what needed to be said in gentle terms.

Catherine smiled, doing her best to set him at ease. "Just tell me William, I am as ready as I will ever be."

"Dearest Majesty, I am to inform you that you are no longer to be called Queen or expect any concessions with regard to your former title. With immediate effect you are to be known as the Dowager Princess of Wales, to reflect your status as widow of Arthur Prince of Wales. Furthermore, from one month after Easter the King will no longer pay your personal or household expenses as you are no longer entitled to a royal household and directs that you should retire to a small private house of your own. He will provide you with a small allowance as befits the widow of his brother."

Catherine had been leaning forward in her chair, watching his face and listening carefully to all that was said. As he finished, she leaned heavily back, shaking her head sadly. "William, kindly write to the King on my behalf and suggest that if he finds my expenses excessive, perhaps he would take all my personal property in part payment and house me wherever he finds the most convenient. I can reduce my household; all I require are at least two maids, my confessor, a physician and an apothecary. If he still finds that too much then inform him that I will willingly go about the world and beg for alms for the love of God."

As her attending ladies broke into a spontaneous round of applause, William bowed deeply and left to do her bidding.

The following month, without the King's direct answer to her chamberlain's letter Catherine was ordered to move herself and a greatly reduced household to a small fortified manor house known as the palace of Buckden in Cambridgeshire. That she would take her confessor, her apothecary and her physician was non-negotiable, but she received instructions that her ladies could number no more than ten, meaning she would have to dismiss more than half of them. Not wishing to show favouritism, she let it be known that she would retain the ten ladies and maids with the longest service.

As a relative newcomer to the Queen's service, Jane knew that her time was up. Reluctantly she packed her belongings, took an affectionate farewell of the woman she had come to love and respect more than her own mother, and travelled home to Wolf Hall.

Chapter Eight

It was a much-subdued Wolf Hall to which Jane returned in August 1533. Her father was largely absent, her mother was withdrawn and frequently tearful and the servants were sullen and much fewer than before she went away.
Jane found the running of the house and estate fell mostly to her, with some small assistance from her mother. She was the only daughter left at home now, Dorothy having recently married and moved away.
With both her younger sisters married, the shadow of notoriety hanging heavy over Wolf Hall thanks to her father's alleged affair with Edward's wife and her court career seemingly over, Jane could not see a lot to look forward too. Her future was as unclear as it had always been.

No suitors had appeared, either during her court life or in Wiltshire during her absence and it looked very much as though her mother's prophecy was going to come true and that she would remain a spinster.

Then suddenly out of the blue came possibility and hope. One morning, after having supervised the dairy duties, Jane was summoned to her mother's solar. Lady Margery appeared flushed and excited; as Jane entered the room she waved the letter she was holding and indicated that she should take a seat beside her on the ottoman.

"What is it mother?" Jane spoke impatiently; she had been hoping for some time to herself and suspected that her mother was about to speak of more household matters.

"This is from Sir Francis Bryan" her mother began. "The Dormers are looking for a wife for their only son William and he thinks that he can engineer a match between the two of you. You remember William?"

Jane screwed up her face, trying to think back. "Isn't he one of Edward's friends? I believe I remember him coming here a few times. I cannot say that I know much of the family however."

"Oh, make no mistake he comes from a good family" Lady Margery tapped her playfully on the arm with the letter as she spoke. "His father Sir Robert is a prominent member of the court, a member of parliament no less. He made his fortune as a wool merchant originally, I believe, and they are one of the richest families in England. It would be a great match for you."

"Anyone would think you were trying to get rid of me mother" Jane replied dryly.

"I just want to see you happy and settled, like your sisters. Are you prepared to pursue this match?"

Jane nodded. "More than happy. I cannot see the likelihood of me returning to court, not now she is Queen, so a husband would be the obvious solution. I doubt you want me under your feet for the rest of your days, do you mother."

Her mother squeezed her arm affectionately. "You will always be welcome here Jane, married or not. This is your home and I will always be glad to have you here."

Although she tried to appear aloof and disinterested, Jane was exultant at the thought of marriage to a wealthy heir. She almost wished that she was at court, so she could be party to the negotiations and maybe impress her future in-laws with her modest demeanour. Jane had become quite the actress and could assume whichever personality was expected of her at any one time. Occasionally her true nature peeped though, but mostly she could pass off any biting retorts as quick wit and ready humour.

Despite his pretended optimism, Sir Francis Bryan felt that his suggestion of Jane Seymour for the Dormers' son did not quite match up to their expectations. Sir Robert was stalling a little, saying that there were a great many other young ladies who were available and that they wanted William to be sure that the lady chosen was one with whom he could be happy.

In truth, many courtiers had daughters they would like to match with William; his family's wealth and connections were powerful incentives.

Bryan persisted in pressing Jane's suit so Sir Robert,

afraid of offending such a close friend of the King, agreed to sit down and talk terms.

Whilst there was no doubt that Sir Robert was master in his own house, when he acquainted his lady of the proposed Seymour match, she was horrified.

"Jane Seymour? She who has been overlooked by just about every family up to now? What age is she, twenty-five or so? Hardly a girl, and her best childbearing years already behind her. And that is before you consider the scandal her father brought down on the house with his ill-advised fling. It is a miracle that her mother managed to get those other poor girls as well married as she did. No, Jane Seymour is not a fit match for our son, the family is not prominent – at least not prominent for the right reasons, and what dowry has she? She is not an heiress. No, the Seymours are on their uppers and they seek to attach themselves to a wealthy family in order to pull themselves back up. Not my son, and not our family!"

Sir Robert was not taken aback by his wife's outburst for she did vent her feelings with monotonous regularity. He did not have the answer to any of her questions, if indeed they needed answering because it was clear that she was dead set against any such match.

He spread his fingers in the air apologetically. "Negotiations have progressed, I am not sure I can withdraw honourably now."

Lady Dormer glared at him. "Then leave it to me. Stall for just a few more days, I know how to stop this."

As soon as she could get away from court unnoticed,

Lady Dormer made straight for the Buckinghamshire home of her dear friend Lady Anne Sidney. Lady Anne's daughter Mary and William were much of an age and the two ladies had often casually discussed making a match between the two of them when the time was right. Lady Dormer decided that the time was most definitely right.

Lady Anne listened to her friend's story with mounting indignation. How dare those upstart Seymours bully their way into Buckinghamshire society by daring to put forward their spinster daughter.

Delighted to have an ally, Lady Dormer outlined her plan. The Dormers and the Sidneys would announce that a marriage had been discussed and settled between William and Mary when they were still in their cradles. It was only when the Sidneys heard that William was considering marriage did the Sidneys remind the Dormers that the matter had been settled long since.

Well satisfied, Lady Dormer returned to court and acquainted her husband with the story; there was no question of Jane Seymour marrying William because he had been unofficially betrothed to Mary Sidney since infanthood. Now all he had to do was tell Sir Francis that a longstanding arrangement had been forgotten but was now remembered and could not be broken.

Sir Robert, a skilled parliamentarian and courtier, broke the news to Sir Francis without delay.

Sir Francis, who knew a concocted story when he heard one, was deeply suspicious of this sudden longstanding arrangement and did not hesitate to say so. "Why then was it made known about the court that you desired a wife for William?"

Sir Robert employed his very best rhetoric. "My dear Sir Francis, as far as I was concerned we did! This arrangement with the Sidneys was made years ago when both were babes. You know how mothers like to plan ahead for their offspring, it seems that my wife and Anne Sidney did just that, agreeing that if both survived to adulthood, they would marry. She may have told me, I don't remember. It was only when the Sidneys heard that William was looking for a wife that they reminded us of it."

"Then that is regrettable for Mistress Seymour, but if arrangements are in place, I most reluctantly withdraw my kinswoman's suit." Inwardly he cursed that he had not thought to get Sir Robert to sign an approval for the betrothal with Jane.

"I am sorry that we have wasted your time." Sir Robert, knowing the danger was past, was prepared to be friendly and affable. "It seems that the marriage is already arranged and will take place next month."

Sir Francis bowed. "Then may I offer my very best wishes to both your family and the Sidneys, along with my fervent hope that the two young people will have a long and happy marriage."

Without delay, Sir Francis started out for Wolf Hall. This was news which had to be delivered personally and not by letter.

Lady Margery, who had been waiting impatiently along with Jane for any news, was not expecting a visit, and wondered if the reason was that the tidings were not good. She received him alone, although sent a servant to find Jane.

"Lady Margery" Sir Francis swept aside his feathered

hat as he executed an exaggerated bow. "I trust I find you well?"

"You find me impatient" she replied. "Impatient for news."

His smile faded. "Alas, the news is not good. William Dormer is to marry Mary Sidney next month."

"Mary Sidney?" Jane had come into the room in time to hear all. "How did that come about?"

"It seems that they have been unofficially betrothed since childhood. Indeed, so much time has passed that the Dormers had all but forgotten, until Lady Sidney reminded them."

Jane's carefully constructed mask slipped. She snorted in a most unladylike fashion. "Is that so? How very convenient and what accomplished liars the Dormers must be."

"Jane…" her mother tried to intervene but Jane ignored her.

"And you Sir Francis" Jane turned on him angrily. "How dare you presume to raise my hopes so, only for me to be cast aside like a woman of no significance. I have feelings you know, and now it seems I am destined to live out my days here in obscurity, without hope of advancement, because once this story becomes public knowledge I will be a laughing stock."

"It is most unfortunate Mistress Jane" he began.

"Unfortunate?" she raged. "This is not mere misfortune, you have mismanaged my case sorely and now you will ride away back to your fine court life and leave me stranded here to pick up the threads of my futile and worthless existence!"

He exchanged rueful glances with Lady Margery and shrugged apologetically. Jane turned her back on him. "I would rather you were out of my sight, get you gone."

Knowing when he was beaten, Francis bowed to Lady Margery and to Jane's back and began making his way out of the chamber. Then on the threshold he paused and turned back. "My kinswoman, the new Queen is finding it lengthy and difficult to gather ladies about her whom she can trust. May I perhaps put your name forward?"

Jane spun round. "Anne Boleyn?" she sneered. "That jumped up concubine. Why would I even want to be in the same county as her, let alone serve her?"

Sir Francis shrugged. "Why indeed, if you feel so strongly. But it would be an advancement for you of sorts; she is always looking for ladies to fill her household and at the moment she is at a low ebb?"

Jane was immediately interested. "Oh, why so?"

"I think the King becomes less enamoured of her the longer the marriage goes on. Before their marriage he could not get enough of her, but now... And since she only managed to produce a princess last September rather than the longed-for prince, his eye wanders a little I think. Her tempers are quick and uncertain and there is no doubt that she can be a difficult mistress. But if she likes you, you'll not find a kinder one."

Jane thought hard. Much as she disliked the new Queen for her treatment of good Queen Catherine, what better place to be to extract a little revenge than in her inner circle? If she were clever, who knew what mayhem could be wrought! Her mind made up, she smiled slyly. "By all means, mention me to the Queen. If she wishes me to serve her, then I can be available with immediate effect."

Chapter Nine

As Jane was familiar with the ebb and flow of court life in a Queen's household, she slipped seamlessly into Anne Boleyn's service. Anne had welcomed her warmly and made sure her ladies had helped her settle, but despite this, Jane looked upon her new mistress with suspicion and dislike, carefully masked by her adopted persona of demureness and obedience.

Anne, only too aware that already the King's eye was wandering, could see no threat in this pale faced newcomer. She was so quiet and mouse-like that often it was easy to forget that she was even in the same chamber. However before long, Anne came to realise that Mistress Seymour was not all she tried to convey.

The January weather was bitter and try as she might, Anne could not drive the cold from her bones. Even seated before a roaring fire she shivered, despite the ministrations of Lady Lee, her closest friend and ally.

"Your Grace, drink this." Margaret Lee handed Anne a golden goblet filled with mulled spiced wine.

"Thank you, Meg." Anne's cold fingers closed gratefully around the warmed metal. "I know not why I feel the cold so. It is like there is a lump of ice inside me spreading its icy fingers throughout my body." In a few most unladylike gulps she drained the goblet and held it out to Meg.

Lady Lee took the goblet from her and chafed Anne's cold hands in an effort to restore some warmth. "You should dress more warmly" she chided. "Let us take you to your bedchamber and change your gown for something heavier to counter this chill."

Anne shook her head. "No, I do not wish to move from the fire. Pay no heed Meg, I am sure that sooner or later all will be well."

"Be that as it may" Meg tucked a rug around Anne's legs as she spoke, "but you should not ignore such symptoms. You must have caught a chill and I should summon your physician without delay."

"Leave it." Anne caught hold of Margaret's wrist as she turned to go. "A few hours either way will not hurt; if I am not restored by this evening I will see him."

Jane stood in the shadows at the back of the chamber watching the exchange with disgust. What a child she was, whining about feeling chilled in a chamber which was as hot as the fires of hell. Perhaps a sojourn in some of the cold and windy houses which poor Queen Catherine had been forced to inhabit due to the concubine's conniving might teach her what cold and discomfort felt like. Lady Lee was clucking around her like a mother hen, trying to persuade her to take to her bed all the while encouraging a page to build the fire up even higher.

"You, girl."

Jane jumped guiltily, catapulted out of a daydream where she was imagining the concubine dead and Queen Catherine restored to the King's favour.

"Yes, you." Margaret Lee was staring at her. "Can you not manage to show at least a little concern for the Queen's Grace? Fetch her warmest cloak from the bedchamber, the one with the fur lining."

Mutely Jane bobbed her head in acknowledgement and scurried into the inner chamber, where the Queen's great bed with its rich hangings dominated the surroundings. On her way to the coffer under the window in which the Queen's outer garments were stored, Jane's attention was diverted by her own reflection in the Queen's huge and magnificent looking glass. Made from the finest Venetian glass and surrounded by an ornate carved silver frame, it was by far the grandest thing Jane had ever seen. She had seen it before of course, but it was usually screened by the many ladies engaged with completing the Queen's toilet, and to see it standing there in all its solitary glory all but took Jane's breath away.

Fascinated, the cloak forgotten, she moved closer. Never before had she seen herself in such a large looking glass, so spun herself about, studying her reflection from every angle. She could happily have stayed there for hours but a commotion in the outer chamber reminded her of her task so she tore herself reluctantly away to rummage in the coffer for the fur lined cloak.

This she had not seen before and it was almost as glorious as the looking glass. Made from the heaviest velvet she had ever handled, it was overstitched and embroidered with the Queen's heraldic falcon. The lining was of thick sable, smooth and luxuriant. Darting a glance at the slightly open door, Jane carefully draped the cloak around herself and went once more to stand in front of the looking glass. Anyone could look like a Queen wearing this, she decided, turning this way and that, enjoying the drape of the heavy fur about her body.

"What do you think you are doing?"

At the sound of the Queen's voice, Jane spun round in horror, dropping the cloak to the floor.

"How dare you!" Anne, seemingly miraculously restored, strode towards her and stooped to pick the cloak from where it had fallen. Behind her, other ladies crowded in at the door, alerted by the Queen's raised and angry voice. Meg Lee pushed her way through and came to the Queen's side. "What is it? What has Mistress Seymour done?"

Anne half turned towards Meg. "I found her dressed in my cloak, flaunting herself before my looking glass." Turning again to Jane she continued. "Is this how you conduct yourself in royal service, trying on whichever of the Queen's clothes takes your fancy?"

Margaret Lee stepped forward and grasped Jane roughly by the arm. "Get yourself out of the Queen's sight and to your chamber. There, think long and hard about your behaviour and whether you are suited here. Tomorrow, you will apologise to the

Queen for laying hands on and wearing what does not belong to you. Do I make myself clear?"

Jane nodded sullenly, curtsied to the Queen and almost ran out of the chamber, only to collide with the man who stood just outside. "I am so sorry!" Jane's hands flew to her face in horror, then as her gaze travelled up his mountainous frame and to his face, she realised it was not just any man she had almost knocked flying, it was the King himself.

"Your Grace!" Jane sank low to the ground in a curtsey so deep, she half wondered if she would be able to get up again, her knees were trembling so.

"No harm done." To Jane's relief, he did not sound angry. "Rise now, Mistress…?"

"Seymour." Jane got to her feet as elegantly as possible. "Jane Seymour."

"Ah!" The King evidently knew of her. "Edward's sister? I heard you were come to court. I bid you welcome, although it sounds like you have managed to get yourself into trouble."

On her very best demure behaviour, Jane pulled the most contrite face she could muster. "I am afraid I am guilty of being unable to resist trying on the Queen's most beautiful cloak. I fear she is very angry with me."

Oh, not such a very treasonous act surely?"

"I fear the Queen thinks so. I am banished to my chamber to reflect on my transgression."

"Worry not. The Queen's anger burns hot for only a short while. She will soon forgive you."

"I do hope so Your Grace." Jane looked up into his face and risked what she hoped was a charming smile.

"Run along then and leave the Queen to me." He watched her go with a certain appreciation, impressed by her honesty and dignity.

He turned as the Queen, reunited with her cloak, entered the chamber with her ladies trailing behind her. Striding up to her, he looked down into her face and rubbed her arms gently. "Sweetheart, I hear you are unwell?"

"Tis nothing" Anne waved her hand dismissively. "I just feel chilled to the bone for some reason."

The King's face brightened and hope shone in his eyes. "Sweetheart, do you think you may be with child once more?"

Anne looked taken aback, but she gave his question a few moments thought. "It is always possible" she admitted. "Although I confess that I have never heard that feeling excess cold is a reliable symptom."

"You must take care" he told her earnestly. "Take no risks and rest until this chill leaves you. I will come and see you tomorrow and maybe you will have good news for me!"

Anne managed a small smile as he kissed her soundly and took his leave. Her face was agonised as she turned towards Meg. "How am I supposed to be able to confirm or deny if I am with child in the next twenty-four hours?"

"Hush Anne. Worrying about it will not change anything. Do you think it may be so?"

Anne considered, then grimaced. "Possibly. It certainly would not be for want of trying!"

"Your courses are due soon?"

Anne screwed up her face in an effort to remember. "Maybe within the next fortnight. I suppose if they do not appear then I will have the answer the King most desires."

"Dearest Anne, let us hope."

Chapter Ten

Jane, sitting alone in her shared quarters late in the evening, was startled by a sudden pounding on the door. Reluctantly she prised herself from her seat and went to see who it was. Opening the door slowly, she was alarmed when the shadowy figure outside roughly pushed the door wide and forced his way into the room.

"Edward!" She was relieved to see it was her brother. "What is this? What have you been about sister? I looked for you at supper and one of the maids said you were sent to your chamber for bad behaviour. Just when it seems our family could be brought no lower, you find fresh ways to disgrace us even further. Don't you think enough is enough?"

"If you will let me speak then I will explain!" she snapped. "I was sent to fetch the Queen's cloak from her bedchamber. I had not seen it before and found it particularly beautiful, so I momentarily tried it on before her looking glass, that is all."

Edward listened with a rising disbelief. "That is all? Are you totally stupid, hopelessly vain, or both? Servants do not try on the clothes of their betters and prance around a royal bedchamber! What were you thinking?"

Jane stuck out her lower lip in a childish pout. "I did not mean any harm. Had the King not arrived and the Queen become anxious for her cloak, I would not have been caught."

"Being caught or otherwise does not excuse your actions. The King also knows about this?"

"Oh yes. He asked me what I'd done and I told him. He was very kind and understanding and told me the Queen would soon forgive me."

"Was he by God!"

Jane smiled smugly and a germ of an idea began to hatch in Edward Seymour's large and capable brain. His temper softened and he began to see Jane in a new light. "Since you appear to have made a friend in the King, I suggest you continue to charm him if and when you can. It may be that you can gain an advantage for our family in so doing."

"How? How can I gain an advantage?"

"I do not know for sure, but it is worth pursuing because our beleaguered family name sorely needs bolstering. As to how we achieve this… I will need to speak to some of my like-minded confidantes." Without a further word, he left the room, slamming the door behind him.

Jane ran to the door, opened it and called down the passageway to his retreating figure. "Edward! What

do you mean?"
In answer, he turned briefly, finger to his lips, before striding on.

The next day, Jane fell on her knees before her royal mistress and humbly begged her pardon for her thoughtless actions the day before. Tempted as she had been to just resign her position and get as far away from Anne Boleyn and her lackeys as she could, her brother's words of the previous night intrigued her. Maybe she had been brought here for a reason, to restore her family's good name. She could not see immediately how this could be achieved, but Edward was clever. He would come up with a plan, she was sure.

Anne Boleyn spoke the words of forgiveness over Jane's bowed head without any real conviction. She had been told of the King's gentle words with Jane, and of his appreciative glance at her as she left the chamber. Although she could not think for the life of her what interest Henry could possibly have in such a pale, long-nosed nonentity as Jane Seymour, the situation needed her close attention.

Jane found very little opportunity to even see the King over the following weeks, let alone speak with him. The Queen was still out of sorts and shunned any public court events. On the occasions that the King came to the private chambers, Jane invariably missed him, having been sent on some errand or other by Lady Lee.

She began to believe that the Queen was purposefully keeping her away from his gaze.

She did not seem so particular about her cousin Madge Shelton though. Madge did not have a full-time court position but always seemed to be closeted with the Queen. Jane did her best to find out what it was that they discussed so avidly, but every time she drew near enough to make out a word or two, the Queen would lift her head and fix Jane with a stare cold enough to kill her stone dead.

Eventually the news filtered through the court that the King had taken a mistress and that mistress was none other than Madge Shelton. The King seemed blissfully happy and content and strangely enough, so did the Queen. Jane later confided in Edward that she believed that the Queen had purposely pushed Madge under his nose to divert his attention from any other lady, herself included. Edward seemed to find her theory hugely amusing. "When you say 'any other lady', do you mean yourself?" He guffawed loudly. "You honestly believe that the King was set on making you his mistress?"

Jane was deeply insulted. "Why not?" she hissed. "He was obviously looking for someone to while away a few hours with, so why not me?"

"And you think that the way to clear our family name is to sleep with the King. Is that what you want?"

"Of course not. I do not intend to demean myself in such a way. Not with the example of the present Queen before me."

"How so?"

"She was but a humble maid of honour herself until the King's eye alighted on her. She refused his advances and see where she is now."

Edward laughed again. "So, you're aiming to be Queen now? It seems I am not the only member of this family with wild ambitions."

"Not so very wild brother. Think for a while of his current favourite Mistress Shelton. She may be a little younger than me, but she has the same pale skin, blue eyes and yellow hair. Perhaps the King looks for an antidote to his tempestuous black-haired wife and seeks pale and gentle rather than brunette and stormy."

He was silent for a while, considering her words carefully. "There could be something in what you say sister. For now, charm him if and when you can. I will try to gauge the mood of both the King and those very close to him".

The ambitions of both Seymours were to be summarily reined in. As the spring approached, the King's attention was taken up on two fronts. The most important state matter was the ongoing dissolution of the monasteries. The King's break with Rome and the establishment of the Church of England was not popular with many, and the King's council advised him that many religious houses would remain loyal to the pope.

At the beginning of the year, crown representatives were sent to all religious institutions to check on their standards; to look for evidence of scandal and mismanagement of funds which would be ample excuse to close them down. At the same time, a careful assessment was made of each house's wealth and property.

It was not a popular move and many monasteries and convents were as obstructive as they dared,

some squirreling their gold, jewels and other wealth

out of sight of the commissioners' eyes. As the reports began to make their way back to the King, he was astounded at the wealth which lay in even the humblest of houses and ordered Cromwell to look into ways in which he might acquire these riches without seeming to just take them. His treasury no longer contained the huge wealth amassed by his father and he saw the monasteries as a convenient means to top up his dwindling assets.

On a personal level, he was still involved with Madge, but also distracted by the announcement of Anne's latest pregnancy. The bizarre symptoms she experienced in the winter months were indeed an indicator of her condition and although she was still in the early stages, the King was once more expecting all to proceed towards the successful delivery of his male heir.

Despite her best efforts, Jane was unable to even manage to be in the same room as the King, let alone make any eye contact. Anne was sickly still and kept mostly to her chambers. The King, who despised all kinds of sickness, even when he was the direct cause, only visited her at night before retiring, long after Jane's duties were concluded.

Her brother was frustrated at her lack of progress but used the time to plan and plot with his close friends. Chief amongst those was Sir Francis Bryan who although being a cousin of the Queen, had come to be resentful of the influence she had over the King.

When Edward confided to him the King's fleeting interest in Jane and explained her theory that the King, tired of the Queen's temper and tantrums was looking for a more peaceful and obliging companion, Sir Francis saw his chance to become even more influential at court through the Seymours. But his first task was to disassociate himself from the Boleyns.

The opportunity soon presented itself. He got into an argument with the Queen's brother George over the most trivial matter. Neither man would back down and it was left to Anne to try and smooth things over. When Sir Francis would not oblige, Anne came down in favour of her brother, giving Francis the perfect opportunity to distance himself.

As soon as his falling out became common knowledge, his brother in law Sir Nicholas Carew, a staunch catholic and supporter of Queen Catherine, took him under his wing, firing him with the ambition to bring down the upstart Boleyns and set up a malleable Queen in Anne's place who would gently lead the King and country back to the catholic faith. Edward Seymour also held similar ambitions and the three of them began conspiring to bring their ambitions to fruition. They had no illusions about the difficulty or complexity of their task. Jane Seymour was to be the bait, but would the King rise to that bait?

Meanwhile Edward Seymour was quietly furthering his own ambitions. Having been unattached since the scandal of his first wife's alleged affair with his father, he had for some time been looking for another wife as ambitious as he and now he had found the ideal lady. The only complication was that his first wife was still living and there had never been a divorce between them.

Anne Stanhope was a wealthy young woman in her own right and sole heiress to her father's
considerable fortune. She was a strong-minded

character and had firm ideas about what she required in a husband. Edward Seymour, she was sure, would go far and with a good wife behind him who knew what he may achieve.

He and Anne Stanhope had already contracted to marry when Catherine Fillol died quietly, and some said, quite unexpectedly at her home in Devon.

They married without fuss and Edward took steps to make sure that the children his first wife had borne would inherit none of his monies, titles or properties. All of this was reserved for the children he intended to have with Anne.

However, with their mother dead, John and Edward reverted to his care; no matter what their true paternity, they were born during their parents' marriage and as such were his responsibility during their minority.

Anne Stanhope, not surprisingly, wanted nothing to do with them, so the children were entrusted to the care of servants answerable to Edward and brought up quietly at one of his more remote estates.

Chapter Eleven

In June 1535 the most prominent victim of the newly passed Treasons Act was brought to trial. After the Act of Supremacy in 1534 which stated that the King was the head of the newly created Church of England, a further act was required to deal with all those who would not take the Oath of Supremacy and continued to support Queen Catherine and the Princess Mary. The Treasons Act did all this and much more.

Bishop John Fisher had stubbornly refused to accept the King as head of a Church of England. He believed that no man, King or not, had the right to establish a church outside of the catholic faith and attempt to force the populace to accept it.

On Thursday 17th June he was accused of treason and found guilty, sentenced to be hung, drawn and quartered at Tyburn. A huge public outcry followed this sentence so in an attempt to appease the masses, the King commuted the sentence to that of beheading on Tower Hill.

Five days later in the face of huge public shock and disapproval, the sentence was carried out.

The shock was felt just as keenly at court; catholic sympathisers kept a very low profile and Edward Seymour advised Jane to make no attempt to speak with the King unless he spoke to her first. She was told to appear quiet, demure and obedient at all times and to hope that this might draw the King's eye to her.

A few days after Fisher's execution, the Queen fell ill, complaining of pains all over her body. At first the physicians maintained that her discomfort had nothing to do with her five months pregnancy and that she was merely suffering from anxiety. Anne however had feelings of great foreboding, both for herself and her child and took to her bed. The King had finally tired of Madge and given her a generous gift of money with which to attract a husband and make a new life for herself. With the King not amorously occupied, Anne feared he would look around for another diversion, especially whilst she was not in a position to either entertain him or keep him company.

Anne was still convinced that Jane Seymour could prove a rival, so she made sure that Jane was always on duty in her bedchamber during the day and

tucked safely up in her shared quarters with the other maids at night.

Jane suspected Anne had an ulterior motive; it certainly was not because she was fond of her that she kept her so close. She was uncomfortably aware that the Queen's eyes followed her almost constantly whist she was about her duties and the knowledge made her both angry and elated. Angry that her little plan was no longer a secret and elated that the Queen took her so seriously as a potential rival.

"Fetch water Jane, and bathe the Queen's brow" Lady Lee directed, having seen how Anne seemed loath to let Jane out of her sight.

Jane did as she was bid and seated herself beside the Queen's bed, wringing out the cloth in preparation.

"Do not think that I do not know what you are about, you sly slut" Anne whispered maliciously.

Jane folded the cloth neatly and placed it gently on the Queen's forehead. "I am sure I do not understand your meaning Your Grace" she replied pertly. "I think you speak out of delirium."

Anne irritably swept the cloth from her forehead, wishing she could reach up far enough to slap the girl's pasty face. "I know you plot with your brother and his sympathisers, and when I tell the King he will have all of you arrested and taken to the Tower."

Jane patiently rinsed and wrung out the cloth before replacing it on Anne's brow. "Your Grace, you know not what you say. There is no plot, all is well."

"All is not well" Anne gasped. "You and your catholic friends seek to oust me and set up a puppet queen. Are you the puppet Jane? Are you so stupid and pliable to allow yourself to be so used?"

On the pretext of smoothing Anne's pillows, Jane leaned across the bed and put her face close to the Queen's. "I am not so stupid and pliable that I cannot see that the King is sick of you; he only pretends he cares because you carry his child. See what will happen if this pregnancy fails, I guarantee that it will be the beginning of the end for you and that aspirational nest of vipers you call your family." With a sweet smile, Jane sat back and began using the cloth to dab the Queen's face.

"Go away Jane. Meg! Meg! Come quickly."

Lady Lee was there in a trice, waving Jane away from her seat at the side of the bed and bending close to Anne, straining to hear her low words. Jane put her bowl and cloth on the side table and went to sit a little away from the bed, but in a good enough position so that she could see all that was happening around the Queen.

As Lady Lee's eyes flicked briefly towards her, she wondered if Anne was confiding the details of what she suspected, but it soon turned out that it was something far more serious.

"Fetch Doctor Butts!" Meg Lee issued the order loudly and to no-one in particular. After a second's delay Margaret Douglas hurried to find him.

Aware that Jane was watching on with great interest, Lady Lee drew the curtains closely about Anne's bed. Even disliking Jane as she did, Anne was distressed when she could no longer see her. "Watch Jane" she begged Lady Lee. "Do not let her leave this chamber."

"Anne there are more important things afoot here than the whereabouts of one of your maids. Tell me, is it the babe?"

Anne's eyes filled with tears as she nodded mutely.

"Doctor Butts will be here any moment. It may yet be nothing to concern yourself over".

Doctor Butts did indeed arrive promptly but even his undoubted skills could not halt what had already begun. Shortly before midnight, Anne gave birth to her stillborn son.

Jane, even with ample opportunity to escape the Queen's chamber whilst she and Lady Lee were distracted, stayed in her seat. Each time the Queen screamed in her pain and distress, Jane smiled to herself and hoped for a bad end both for the Queen and the child. That would teach her to presume to oust the true Queen and arrogantly assume that she would succeed where Queen Catherine had failed.

She felt no pity when she saw the midwife carry out the dead child, wrapped hastily in linen, and she certainly felt nothing but savage elation when the bed curtains were finally tied back an hour later, revealing the dishevelled Queen sobbing into her pillow.

Then it occurred to her that since the King had not been near, perhaps he was yet to be acquainted of Anne's latest failure. Rising to her feet and smoothing down her skirts, she approached Lady Lee who was standing by the fireplace in conversation with one of the midwives. Margaret stopped speaking as she saw her approach. "Yes Jane?" she asked curtly.

"I wondered if you would like me to go and alert the King to this... sad development?"

"Oh, you'd like that, wouldn't you Jane" came the weak voice from the bed. "Keep your distance from my husband. I am the only person who should acquaint him of this."

"As Your Grace pleases" Jane withdrew and regained her seat by the wall.

"Ladies" Margaret Lee clapped her hands to attract their attention. "Her Grace thanks you for your kind attentions this night but feels it is time you all went to your beds. I will sit with her until morning."

Jane tossed her head crossly and joined the exodus of ladies. She had been hoping to witness the King's furious outburst once he knew he had been denied a son yet again. Then she could have contrived to calm him and offer gentle sympathy, however it seemed that the opportunity would not be forthcoming. Not this time anyway. Looking over her shoulder at the weak and defeated Queen, Jane had a distinct feeling that there would be another time.

If Jane had been hoping for the King to stamp about the court, raging at his misfortune, she was to be disappointed. If Henry raged, he raged in private. If he blamed Anne, then he kept it to himself and was most courteous and gentle towards her in her obvious distress.

The day after the still birth, Lady Lee gathered all who had been present in the bedchamber the previous night, and all who knew what had transpired during it, and warned them that the King did not want the news to be made public. Looking around at everyone, Jane could not resist voicing that which she was sure everyone was thinking. "Why is this not to be spoken of? Surely all who knew of the Queen's condition will soon realise that she is no longer carrying a child?"

"That is the King's business and no concern of yours or anybody else's here. If you know what is good for you, you will never speak of this again. I warn you, do not disobey the King in this."

Jane was not good at holding her tongue, particularly if it was a piece of juicy gossip. At the earliest opportunity, she spoke to her brother.

"The Queen miscarried of a son last night" she announced, to not only Edward, but also his companions Nicholas Carew and Francis Bryan.

"Ah! I suspected something like that was afoot, but none of the Queen's women were prepared to speak of it." Francis was glad to have his suspicions confirmed.

"We are supposed to be keeping the information to ourselves. I asked Lady Lee how that was supposed to work; after all, everyone knew the Queen was expecting a child and when no child arrives, it will be obvious that she has lost it."

"I think it is more to do with John Fisher's execution than anything else" Edward spoke solemnly. At everyone's puzzled expression, he continued. "It is barely a week since the King had Fisher executed against the wishes of the people. Did God also disapprove? That is what the King will be asking himself now. If this miscarriage becomes public knowledge, the people will say that it is God's punishment on the King for executing Bishop Fisher."

"Remember, Thomas More is to go to trial next week" broke in Carew. "He is certain to be found guilty and go the same way as Fisher. It will be another unpopular move for More is much loved. The King is wise to keep out of public sight."

Chapter Twelve

The King had given Thomas More every opportunity to read the Oath of Supremacy, digest it, and agree to it. However, More was a man of conscience and could not agree verbally to that which his heart deplored, even though it would save his life. He would not even pay lip service to that which he felt was fundamentally wrong, even though his devoted wife and children begged him to agree to the King's demands and maintain his own beliefs in private telling him God would know what was in his heart.
Again and again they pleaded with him but he was resolute. His conscience would not allow him to agree to something he did not believe in.
His trial was a foregone conclusion as all present knew he would not try to defend himself or his actions. It took just fifteen minutes for him to be found guilty and his execution was fixed for July 6th on Tower Hill.

Due to yet more public unrest, the King decided that it might be better if he were out of London when More went to the scaffold. The court generally left the capital for a summer progress, so arrangements were made for that to commence on July 5th, the day before the execution. The only flaw in that plan was the condition of the Queen, who was still recovering slowly from both the premature birth and her immense disappointment.

However once acquainted with the King's plans, she shook off her misery and left her bed. To prepare herself for the arduous travel she began walking in the palace gardens and found her spirits much lifted by the exercise and good company of her attentive ladies.

Jane too joined in those garden ramblings. Not because she particularly enjoyed walking with the Queen but because the privy gardens were overlooked by the King's private apartments and there was always a chance that he may look out and see her. She took to hanging back from the main group, walking at a sedate and steady pace, hands folded across her stomacher with her head held high and eyes modestly lowered.

So immersed was she in her deportment and pretended dignity, that it was a moment before she realised another walked beside her. Annoyed that her solitude was compromised, she whipped her head around, a rebuke for the interloper on her lips which had to be hastily stifled.

"Why do you walk alone Jane?" the Queen's sweet voice indicated not concern but scorn.

"I enjoy being alone with my thoughts Your Grace."

"And what thoughts are these?"

"None that would interest the Queen's Grace."

The Queen stopped abruptly and Jane had no option but to follow suit. "I think I may find your thoughts quite intriguing; you underestimate yourself Jane. How well you play the part of ingenue, I confess I have never seen it done better. That you have ambition is clear; portray yourself as innocent and guileless all you like, I can see through it all."

Jane raised her eyes and met the implacable stare of her Queen, then risked a crafty glance up at the King's windows. He was nowhere to be seen.

"You see?" the Queen laughed and gestured towards her waiting ladies, only a short distance away and party to all that was being said. "Even when in conversation with me, she looks for royal appreciation from above. Well I am sorry to disappoint you Jane, but the King has gone hunting, so be as regal and dignified as you like, he will not be there to appreciate it."

Jane's face hardened and she did not even try to suppress the ready retort which rose to her lips. "At least I can be regal and dignified, not like you with your common ancestry and pretend airs and graces."

The Queen's hand shot through the air so fast, Jane barely saw it until it connected with her cheek. It was a stinging blow, amplified by the many and jewel encrusted rings which Anne wore. "Perhaps that will serve as a timely reminder that you do not presume to criticise your Queen. Mind your manners Jane or you will find yourself banished from court and sent home in disgrace." Surveying Jane's reddened cheek with evident satisfaction, Anne turned on her heel and continued along the path, her ladies trotting in her wake.

Jane's wish for solitude was summarily granted. Not one sympathetic glance came her way and no-one hung back to console her. In fact it was more than obvious from their ramrod straight backs that they all felt she had got what she deserved. Full of resentment, she stared after the Queen. One day very soon she would see that strumpet brought down into the gutter where she belonged.

Everyone enjoyed a royal progress, except perhaps those hundreds of servants whose task it was to see that everything was packed, loaded and carted. The King was no exception; much as he enjoyed his many London palaces, there was nothing quite like taking to the highways and byways of the English countryside benignly gazing down on the smiling faces of his subjects. Even better was the excellent food, accommodation and entertainment he received at every stop, and all at his host's expense.

The Queen too was glad to leave the smoke and stench of London far behind, along with her recent unhappy experiences.

Here was a chance to blow away the cobwebs, enjoy the fresh air and be invigorated. She needed to regain all her strength because it was imperative that not only should she get with child soon, but that the pregnancy should proceed safely to term and produce the longed-for prince.

Jane was amongst the entourage, rather too far down the procession for her liking and somewhat under horsed. She did not keep her own horse at court, few ladies of her status did, so she had to accept what was offered to her for such excursions. Most of the finer riding horses were allocated to ladies of high rank and all that was left for Jane was the choice between a very small palfrey which looked as though anything more than an eight-year-old child would cause it to drop dead in its tracks, and a sturdy white mule, similar to those which the late Cardinal Wolsey favoured. Jane chose the mule; at least it was tall and striking. It was hardly any challenge to her abilities as a horsewoman, but at least her gown would not be at risk of dragging on the ground.

At sounds of hilarity from further up the procession, she craned her neck in an effort to see what was going on. The King was guffawing loudly at something; his voice was unmistakable, as was the volume he generally employed. The Queen was beside him and appeared equally amused; it seemed that all was well between them again as he grabbed her hand and kissed it gallantly.

Jane sniffed disdainfully and averted her eyes. She was not sure how to proceed under the circumstances; Edward was occupied elsewhere and was not in the party. Sir Nicholas Carew and Sir Francis Bryan likewise. Her last instructions had been cryptic; draw attention to herself by not drawing attention to herself. That was all very well at court, where the day to day activities were often humdrum and predictable, but a royal progress was anything but.

As the royal party made its way over the border from Surrey into Hampshire, the skies overhead began to darken. It was not long before the first raindrops began to fall and the order went out for all haste to be made towards their first stop in the county, a fine manor house just north of the market town of Alton. As the rain began to fall with more purpose, those on horseback forged ahead of the pack mules and carts, eager to reach shelter.

The manor house was a large and ancient building, half fortified and half domestic dwelling. The King and Queen were to lodge in the tower which formed most of the west wing, with their personal servants close by in apartments which led off the adjoining gallery. The rest of the entourage was scattered haphazardly throughout the building, but there was room for all with space to spare.

Jane managed to claim sleeping quarters which were but a stone's throw from the royal bedchamber and it was she who was called to help Lady Lee prepare the Queen for bed. Cheeks flushed with excitement, Jane moved timidly across the threshold of the large circular room and joined Lady Lee, who stood behind the Queen, she being seated in front of the looking glass Jane so admired.

As Jane stared into the glass, Anne raised her eyes and stared back, her face expressionless.

"Turn down the bed please Jane." Lady Lee did not look towards her as she spoke, her attention was on her own task of brushing the Queen's long and luxuriant hair.

Jane obediently turned down the sheets, plumped up the pillows and smoothed the fur coverlet before rejoining Lady Lee at the mirror once more.

"Thank you, Meg." The Queen spoke at last. "Jane can take over now, you may retire."

Lady Lee looked perplexed at her sudden dismissal, but handed Jane the hairbrush and took her leave as directed.

Jane was equally bewildered at being assigned to this most personal service. The hairbrush was long,

narrow and heavy, with an ornate silver back not unlike the looking glass frame. As Anne sat patiently, watching her every move, Jane grasped the brush firmly and began rhythmically brushing Anne's hair from root to tip. It was a backbreaking task, with hair as long as hers. Although Jane was not very tall, even she had to stoop to complete each brush stroke. After about two dozen long strokes, Jane's face began to redden and her breathing became shallow and rapid.
"Goodness me Jane, you are most unfit to be so out of breath so soon" Anne observed. Her smile, although seemingly genuine, did nothing to mask the dislike in her eyes.
Jane decided to be reserved and subservient. "It is an honour to so serve Your Grace" she murmured, impressed despite herself, with the thickness and vivacity of the shining black hair she held in her hands. It almost had a life of its own; the ends would curl unbidden around the brush.
 Jane had a sudden vision of that same hair snaking around her own neck and choking the life out of her. Alarmed, she gasped and looked into the mirror at the Queen to see if she had heard. The Queen gazed steadily back at her, the half-smile on her face led Jane to believe that she was imaging the same scenario.
Warming to her task, Jane brushed on, starting a little as the bristles passed over her own hand. They were sharp and unforgiving but since the Queen's hair was so thick, she was untroubled by them. Ever resourceful, Jane lifted Anne's hair and proceeded to brush it from underneath, daringly bringing the
brush a little closer to the Queen's neck at the start of every stroke. Anne was relaxed, her eyes almost

closed in her enjoyment. With the Queen's guard down, Jane took her chance, viciously dragging the bristles across the Queen's neck before dropping the brush and leaping away in apparent contrition as Anne leapt to her feet with a shrill shriek.

Immediately the door opened and the King hurried in. Without so much as a glance at Jane, he went quickly to Anne and took her tenderly in his arms. "What is it sweetheart?" he murmured. "You cried out, has someone hurt you?" His menacing glare swept around the chamber and fastened on the only other person present, Jane.

Jane immediately dropped into a deep curtsey. "What have you done to your mistress girl?" he roared.

"Henry, Henry" Anne's fluttering hands on his broad chest diverted his attention back to her. "It was but an accident, I am sure. My maid was brushing my hair and scratched the back of my neck with the bristles."

"Let me see." He turned her around and lifted her hair. There were several bloodied scratches across Anne's white skin. He replaced her hair across her shoulders lovingly and then turned on Jane. "What way is this to handle your mistress? What have you to say for yourself?"

Jane sensed that his anger was real as she quailed before him. "It was an accident Your Grace, with the weight of the Queen's hair, the brush slipped."

"So it is the Queen's fault, is that what you say?"

With her hands covering her face, Jane dropped to her knees before him and burst into tears. Tears would melt him, she was sure.

But Henry felt no pity for the snivelling creature

before him. His beloved Queen had been hurt and she was the culprit. "Get yourself from our sight!" he roared, before turning once more to Anne.

Jane swiftly regained her feet and hurried to the door. As she closed it quietly behind her, she glanced back into the chamber and saw Henry lovingly lift Anne's hair aside and begin to kiss each and every scratch.

Chapter Thirteen

The following day, the Queen wasted no time in acquainting Lady Lee with Jane's latest misdemeanour. As far as Meg Lee was concerned, Jane had overstepped the mark for the last time. She told her that she was suspended from any duties about the Queen's person and if she knew what was good for her, she would keep a very low profile over the coming days.

Whilst Jane was not the slightest bit sorry for the injuries she had inflicted, she was very much afraid of what Edward and his cohorts would say when they heard that the King had raged at her. She had been urged to stay gentle and patient to attract his attention but instead had been caught scratching at his Queen like a common alley cat.

The hunting was good at Alton so the royal party stayed several days longer than originally planned. Whilst the King and Queen rode out every day together, Jane was not invited to be part of the entourage. Instead she was confined to the manor, employed with her needle under Lady Lee's eagle eye. She reverted to her childish sullen manner, snapping when spoken to and resenting every moment she was forced to sit and forego the pleasures of riding and hunting.

Her discomfort was only increased when her brother Edward called at the manor en route to one of his estates. With the court away from London and its normal routine, he felt that there was ample opportunity for Jane to make some real progress and he was anxious for news.

His page approached Lady Lee as the senior lady and informed her that Mistress Seymour's brother had arrived and would like to speak with her. Lady Lee was not fond of Edward Seymour and felt that the only reason he might want to see his errant sister was to conjure more mischief. However, she could think of no reason to deny him access to Jane so reluctantly gave permission for her to go down and see him.

Edward was pacing up and down the great hall in his usual impatient manner. "At last!" he exclaimed. "I had just about given up hope. Would the Queen not allow you to leave her?"

"The Queen is out hunting with the King. She can barely tolerate the sight of me" Jane retorted bitterly. "I am forbidden from attending her person after accidently scratching her with the hair brush."

"How accidently?"

"Alright, purposely scratching her with the hairbrush."

"Why ever would you want to do something like that?"

"Because I hate her!" Jane shouted, not caring who might hear. "I hate the sight, sound and smell of her. She counters everything I do. She knows, Edward. She knows I work to destroy her."

Edward shook his head sadly. "I am disappointed in you sister, I had thought you to possess more intelligence. You cannot openly defy the Queen and expect to succeed, you must employ patience and tact if you are to topple her."

"Patience and tact are all very well, but they will not get me noticed!"

"I think they will. How are the King and Queen together? Does she seek to tease and aggravate him? Are her tempers wild and uncontrolled?"

"She is as sweet and affectionate towards him as he is to her. They are like newlyweds, barely able to tolerate being apart."

Edward sighed. "That surprises me; I had expected him to be impatient and angry with her after her latest failure."

"If anything, he is even more devoted now than he was when she was last with child."

"Then now is not the time to make any strong moves. Listen sister." He took her by the shoulders and gazed down at her. "This honeymoon cannot last. Once they get back to London with all the distractions and court intrigue she will soon lose her sweet disposition, you will see.

The King will once more become engrossed in state matters and will grow ever more impatient if there is no sign of his prince. Let there be no more scratching and spleen between you and the Queen, you must rise above all that or you will come to be known as a troublemaker and may well find yourself ejected from the court."

Jane sighed and nodded. "I will do my best."

"I hear that if time permits, the party may well ride into Wiltshire and spend a few days at Wolf Hall. Should that come about, it will be your chance to shine."

"How so?"

"As the daughter of the hosts, you will naturally help to entertain the King. It will be your chance to impress him with your amiability and your demureness. Success at Wolf Hall may have long reaching consequences once back at court. As soon as the Queen reverts to her sarcastic, tempestuous self, he will remember your gentle manners and quiet ways."

In the middle of September the royal party moved on to Winchester where they saw three new bishops consecrated in the cathedral. Edward Fox to Hereford, John Hilsey to Rochester and Hugh Latimer to Worcester. The Queen had a particular fondness for Latimer, the reformed papist who had wholeheartedly embraced the new learning and supported her quest to introduce a reformed faith. She had campaigned for his elevation to Bishop of Worcester and had paid his costs from her privy purse.

Following the ceremony, there was a celebratory feast after which the new Bishops spent some time alone with the King and Queen before going their separate ways to take up their duties in their new diocese.

Jane looked upon the proceedings with distaste; like everyone else she was forced to appear to conform to the new Church of England and its ritual but at heart she was, and always would be, a catholic who accepted no jurisdiction other than that of the pope. However, that was a dangerous stance in Henry's new England and those who spoke out against the protestant faith tended to meet an untimely end.

After leaving Winchester, they rode north to Andover and stayed at a modest sized country estate which struggled to accommodate them all. Due to the cramped conditions they only remained there for two nights. During that time, Jane barely glimpsed the royal couple. The King spent his time out hunting with his host Lord Anstey whilst the Queen spent time indoors with Lady Anstey and her large and engaging family. Jane was still not allowed anywhere near the Queen and spent her time quietly sewing, giving her ample time to plan her next move.

As Edward had predicted, the party headed over the border into Wiltshire and made for Wolf Hall. Jane had not been home since the beginning of the year and hoped that it would be a happier household to which she returned.

On the surface it seemed so. The King, who preferred not to see anything which would spoil his happy mood saw only that Sir John and Lady Margery were standing outside, along with their senior staff, waiting to welcome him.

He did not notice how Lady Margery took care to leave a goodly distance between herself and her husband, or her stiff and unnatural smile of greeting. Sir John seemed a little more relaxed, clearly delighted that the King chose to honour him by paying a visit.

Jane summed the situation up at a glance. Her mother and father were doing their best to put on a display of marital harmony for their monarch when in fact it was clear that they could barely tolerate being in each other's company.

The King, after helping the Queen to dismount, gave Sir John a bear hug which almost took the breath away from the smaller man. He greeted Lady Margery then proceeded to walk to the house, his arm slung around Sir John's shoulders.

The Queen, more perceptive, recognised the other woman's discomfort and spoke to her quietly before the two of them turned to follow the men inside. This was the signal for a frantic scramble as the accompanying ladies and gentlemen hastily dismounted, anxious to get inside and enjoy the refreshments, leaving their animals wandering around the courtyard, reins dangling, pursued by hapless grooms and stable boys. Minutes later the convoy of carts and pack mules arrived, adding to the general melee.

Jane followed a little more slowly, in no hurry to reacquaint herself either with the building or the people it housed. Once in the hall, she glanced up the staircase before moving on towards the area her mother liked to call the great hall.

Really only a high ceilinged modest sized space, nonetheless it was the largest chamber in the house and judging by the noise emanating from it, was where most members of the party were to be found.

It was the busiest she had ever seen it, she mused, as she crossed the threshold. The King was holding court with Sir John and cluster of gentlemen over by the hearth, the Queen sat a little to the side in earnest conversation with Lady Margery whilst the rest of the party ranged about the chamber, helping themselves to the various cakes, pastries and fruit set out on long low tables. The wine was flowing freely and there was much jesting and jostling.

Jane could picture the scene in the huge kitchen as the servants toiled over the preparations for the huge banquet which would follow later in the evening. She wondered if she should go down and check on their progress; her mother may well have it all under control but it wouldn't do any harm just to look in. It was important that the King remembered his visit to Wolf Hall for the calm dignity and efficiency of the daughter of the house, not for the inadequacy of its kitchen.

Her mind made up, she walked quickly down the narrow passageway, took a shortcut through the pantry and still room and entered the kitchen through the side door next to the spit. Cook was standing there watching over the huge roast and gave a squawk as Jane suddenly appeared.

"Great goodness, Mistress Jane! You gave me such a turn."

"Cook." Jane nodded her head curtly in acknowledgement. "I came to see that all the

preparations were going well for the banquet this evening?"

Cook blew a stray strand of hair from her eyes and turned to face Jane, her hands on her ample hips. "If you would care to inspect the counters" she gestured into the heart of the busy kitchen as she spoke. "I think you'll find that everything is in order and running to time."

"Good." Other than flicking a glance in the direction of cook's outstretched arm, she made no move forward. "I will let Lady Margery know you have everything in hand." Without waiting for any reply, she disappeared silently the way she had come.

Cook looked after her, shaking her head. Being at court had certainly altered Mistress Jane, she was haughtier and more patronising than ever.

Jane retraced her steps until she was once more on the threshold of the great hall. Seeing her mother walking along the line of tables making sure there was still plenty of food left, Jane made her way across the room towards her. Seeing her approach, Lady Margery turned to meet her. "Jane. I had thought you were not of the party; I looked for you but could not see you."

"Oh, I was well down the pecking order. You and father were already inside with the King and Queen when I dismounted. I have just been down to the kitchen to check on preparations for the banquet. It seems all is progressing well."

Lady Margery's hand fluttered to her chest in a gesture of relief. "Bless you Jane, that was to be my next task."

"Pleased to be able to help, mother." Looking around at her father, now talking to both King and Queen, she continued, "how is father?"

Her mother grimaced. "Much the same. Trying to carry on as normal when I cannot think that anything will ever be normal again."

"He still denies any wrongdoing?"

Lady Margery nodded. "He says it was all Edward's fabrication just to get rid of his wife."

"And was it?"

"Well, you know Edward. He'll stop at nothing to get what he wants." Lady Margery's expression was sad and wistful. "If it was his doing, then I hope he can live with himself for virtually destroying what was a good marriage. I just hope he keeps out of your father's sight whilst he's here today."

"Edward is here?"

"Yes. He arrived a few minutes ago; just a brief visit on his way back to London. He'll be gone by early morning." Lady Margery looked around vaguely. "Thomas is here too, somewhere."

Jane wasn't interested in her brother Thomas, she wanted to see Edward. "Where is Edward, do you know?"

"No, I don't, I'm sorry." Lady Margery then turned back to the tables and began arranging more platters.

Jane left her to it and began making her way around the chamber searching for Edward. Her quest was interrupted when Lady Lee caught her eye and beckoned her across. "I have been looking for you Jane, even though you are not in close attendance on Her Grace, I need to know where you are at all times."

"I do apologise Lady Lee" Jane was all sweetness and politeness. "As you know, this is my family home and I was helping my mother with the arrangements for the banquet."

"Ah, of course." Meg looked at her calculatingly. "In that case, why don't you continue with that. I am sure your dear mother would appreciate all the help she can get."

It was just what Jane wanted to hear. Bobbing a respectful curtsey, she took her leave and resumed her hunt for Edward.

After a long and frustrating search, she finally came across him in her father's library, deep in discussion with two men she did not know. Uncertain whether to approach him and risk his anger at the disturbance, she hovered in the doorway.

Although out of Edward's direct line of vision, some sixth sense told him she was there and he looked up. "Ah, Jane." He waved his hand, indicating she should come closer. "We were just talking about you."

She was intrigued. "About me?"

"Indeed." The taller of the two men spoke, although both were regarding her with great interest.

Jane looked from one face to the other then turned again to Edward. "Are you not going to introduce me to your friends?"

"It is better that you do not know who we are." The second man spoke in a foreign accent. "We are interested in restoring the true faith to this God forsaken realm and we think that you can help us achieve that."

"Oh yes?" Jane tucked her hands inside her sleeves and tilted her chin upwards, assuming a haughty expression.

All three men laughed. "Ah yes Edward" said one. "She will do very well."

Jane did not like the way the strangers looked at her and began to frown. "Edward, will you please tell me what is going on?"

"Later" he waved his hand at her vaguely. "Jane, will you wait outside please?"

She was mortified. "Outside? This is as much my house as yours, how dare you order me about like one of your lackeys!"

"This is in your best interests. You do not want to be compromised. Outside. Now."

Much as she objected to being ordered about like a naughty child, she sensed that the strangers were important men, so dropped a respectful curtsey to them and took up a seat outside the room. She left the door open a crack in the hope of hearing some snippet, but their voices were low and their words indistinct.

It was not long before Edward ushered them out. They bowed to Jane as they passed and hurried down the back staircase, presumably so they would be able to leave unseen. "Wait there Jane" Edward called. "I will return once I have seen these gentlemen on their way."

Shortly afterwards, he returned, striding jauntily up to her and indicating that she should once more go into the library. "What is all this about Edward?" she demanded, once he had carefully shut the door and come to stand before her.

He pulled on his beard thoughtfully. "I do not want to say too much" he began. "The less you know, the better it will be for you. Have you heard of the imperial party?"

She thought for a moment and then shook her head. "No."

"Good. Now forget I ever mentioned it."

A sudden thought gripped her. She moved closer to him and lowered her voice. "Do you plot against the King?"

Edward laughed. "Heavens no. It is the Queen we

wish to topple. If she goes, in all probability the reformed faith will lose momentum and the King can be gently directed back to the old ways."

"So how I am I supposed to help your cause. Poison the Queen?" Jane's voice had grown gradually louder causing Edward to put his hand over her mouth to hush her.

"Hold your tongue or you will have us both in the Tower! No, we can achieve our aim without risking all. There is now more than one faction working against the Queen and all she stands for and we all plan to work together to achieve our end. For now it has been agreed that we continue with our original plan, for you to lure the King and to make him come to believe that you would make a far better Queen and mother to his children than the witch he has tied himself to."

"But that may take years!"

"No" he insisted. "It will not. Remember, the King is in our father's house. As I told you before, you can help entertain him and make him notice you by being a direct contrast to the Queen. If she is quiet, you can be animated. If she is temperamental and rude, you will be virtuous, quiet and obedient. He cannot fail to notice you."

Chapter Fourteen

Despite the best efforts of the kitchen, due to the sheer quantity of food, the banquet started later than anticipated. Lady Margery was anxious at the thought of keeping the King waiting, but he was in such a good mood he barely noticed the delay.
Jane, determined on making herself as prominent as possible, made a great show of standing to the side of the great hall with the Steward, inspecting all the dishes as they were brought from the kitchen and directing them up to the King's table.
She contrived to be dignified yet animated and was delighted when a quick glance at the top table revealed that the King's eyes were on her. Just as the Queen's eyes were on the King.
As Henry wrenched a capon apart, he leaned over to Sir John and asked who the very efficient lady was, who stood with his Steward directing proceedings.

Sir John, who had not until that moment even realised Jane was present, was pleased to confirm that it was his eldest daughter.

The Queen, who had been listening to their exchange, wryly commented that it was the same girl who had carelessly scratched her with the hairbrush earlier in the progress.

"Indeed?" The King wiped at his greasy mouth with his sleeve and reached for more meat. "I would not have recognised her from that night, but then she was somewhat distressed and snivelling as far as I recall."

"I too was distressed" Anne reminded him gently.

"Of course, of course" The King patted her hand affectionately whilst the Queen grimaced at the greasy marks he left on her skin.

"You have a gem there Sir John" he shouted, gesturing towards Jane. "I find it remarkable that some young man has not swept her away."

"Not as yet Your Grace, but I hope there is still time."

"What age is she?"

Sir John looked perplexed and glanced across at Lady Margery for support. "She will be twenty-seven years old in a few months Your Grace" Lady Margery stepped in to cover her husband's embarrassment. "I am afraid that the ages of our children are not something of which Sir John keeps a tally."

"You have a large family, do you not?" The King darted a sly glance at Anne before directing the question towards Lady Margery.

"Indeed, Your Grace, we have been much blessed."

"Ten, is it?"

"I had the great fortune to give birth to ten children, yes. Five boys and five girls, although four of them did not survive to adulthood."

The King looked thoughtful and not a little envious. "Five boys eh? Perhaps I should have married you Lady Margery!" The King was evidently pleased with his jest and laughed heartily, whilst both the Queen and Lady Margery looked embarrassed and uncomfortable.

Meanwhile Jane, having seen in the first half dozen courses, decided to make herself known to the King. Etiquette said that she should first be formally introduced, but she decided that here in her father's house, it was for her to do as she saw fit. After smoothing her skirts and putting her hands up to make sure her hood was properly placed and straight, she made her way towards the top table.

The King, engrossed in conversation, did not notice her approach. The Queen, who had been watching her closely, tensed and turned on the full force of her baleful glare.

Upon reaching the King's table, Jane stood quietly in front of him until he finished his conversation and noticed her presence.

"Jane Seymour, Your Grace" she murmured as she sank into a deep curtsey. "I am the eldest daughter of the house. I trust that all has met with your satisfaction thus far?"

"Indeed it has Mistress Seymour and I thank you for your close attention to our comfort. I have noticed you, inspecting the quality of the dishes and directing the service. Your domestic accomplishments are much to be admired."

Uncomfortably aware of the Queen's eyes boring into her, Jane kept her gaze on the King. "I thank Your Grace for such kind words" she replied. "I will endeavour to ensure that the remainder of your stay here is equally satisfactory. If Your Grace should require anything, anything at all, you have only to send for me and I will personally ensure that you are well served."

"Why thank you Jane, we will remember that, won't we sweetheart?" He picked up Anne's hand and pressed it to his lips.

"You are most hospitable Jane." By the look on Anne's face, it was all she could do to force out those few words. If looks could kill, thought Jane, I would be stone dead.

The King was still looking closely at Jane. "I think we can forget that most unfortunate incident of a few days ago, can we not sweetheart?" He turned to Anne as he finished speaking and beamed happily at her.

"As you wish" she murmured, averting her eyes.

"And Mistress Seymour can once again be part of your inner sanctum? With so many obvious talents, it seems wasteful for her to be ostracised."

Jane turned towards Anne, seeing how she fought with her emotions. She was hoping for one of the Queen's spectacular temper tantrums which would reinforce in Henry's mind how dignified and demure Jane was in contrast.

However Anne would not oblige and instead smiled benevolently at Jane and told her she was more than welcome to resume her duties as before.

Crushed, Jane took her leave. The Queen may have won that particular exchange, but Henry had noticed her and said he was appreciative of her talents. It was a start.

The royal party stayed a full week at Wolf Hall. Jane continued to ensure all ran smoothly and was frequently complimented for her efforts by an appreciative King although was not able to see him other than in a large company. She had been hoping to engineer a private meeting and charm him with her directness and simplicity, but the Queen was deeply suspicious and used all her wiles to ensure that he rarely strayed from her side.
After the party left Wiltshire, they rode back over the border to Berkshire and spent another three weeks enjoying the hospitality of various estates as they wended their way slowly back to Windsor.
Remembering Edward's words about how he expected the Queen would revert to her caustic self once the court had reassembled, Jane watched and waited, hoping that some opportunity might present itself.
The Queen had indeed accepted her back into close personal service but said very little to her, instead spending much time whispering in corners with the ever-present Lady Lee. Jane thought how much easier her task would be if she too was a confidante but despite behaving herself and displaying her sweetest disposition, the Queen continued to keep her at arm's length.
Almost a month after their return, Anne triumphantly announced that she was once again with child and that the birth was expected in June.

"It is a blow, I'll give you that" Edward told her, as

they discussed the Queen's condition. "And if she does contrive to give birth to a prince then that will be that. The King would never displace the mother of his son."

"Then we must work towards ensuring that she loses this child as she did the last. It is evident that she does not carry well. A few upsets and who knows what might come to pass." Edward looked at his sister in surprise. He knew she could be as cruel and ambitious as himself but wishing death on an innocent child seemed unnecessarily callous. His own wife had recently lost their first child and he was only too painfully aware of what a devastating effect it could have on both mother and father. However, where ambition was concerned, there was no room for sentiment and it was clear that they could not risk the Queen carrying to term and potentially producing a prince.

Jane was thinking hard. "Now I am back in the royal chambers I may be able to contrive something. The King knows me and is kind to me which makes the Queen insanely jealous. Added to that is her worry of miscarrying or premature delivery. She cannot control her emotions at the best of times let alone under so much strain so I will try to goad her rage as much as possible. If I can do it in the King's presence so much the better; I can be all calm reassurance whilst she will be the harridan she always is."

Goading Anne was a lot more difficult than Jane anticipated. If she was worried about the pregnancy then she did not show it and remained uncharacteristically calm. From the outset she took no risks, rested every afternoon and retired at a sensible hour unless there was an occasion which demanded her presence. The King was pleased to see how careful she was being and took to spending the afternoons with her, sitting by her bedside talking or reading to her. Jane managed to find excuses to waft through the chamber quite frequently, but the King's eyes rarely strayed from his Queen or the book he held.

In early December there was news from Buckden, where the former Queen still resided quietly with her much-reduced household. The ten ladies she had originally taken with her now numbered only three. Catherine had been experiencing severe chest pains and had been confined to bed by her physician where she was supposed to rest and eat nourishing food. However Catherine felt so ill, she had no appetite whatsoever and grew weaker by the day.

The Lady Mary wrote urgently to her father begging leave to visit her mother but the King would not even consider allowing such a thing. He refused to believe that Catherine may be dying and was sure it was just a ruse for the two to get together and plot against him.

The Spanish Ambassador also craved permission to visit Catherine, and not wishing to anger Catherine's nephew the Emperor any more than he had done already, Henry granted leave for him to go to Buckden the week following a rather muted Christmas celebration at court.

Jane wished she could have gone to see Catherine too, but devoted as she was to her former mistress, the stakes were too high for her to be absent from court at that time. She felt immense pity that Catherine had been brought so low and prayed for her recovery, wondering how she would react if she knew that Jane sought to avenge her suffering by replacing Anne at the King's side. She resolved to wait until the King was to be absent from court for several days on a hunting trip or similar, then travel in all haste to Buckden and acquaint Catherine of how hard she worked to bring down the concubine.

But Jane was never to see Catherine again. She died just a week into January after writing a final letter to Henry, the man she always maintained was her lawful husband and thus she his Queen. He read the letter in private before taking it to show Anne. Both struggled with their emotions at the death of the former Queen; Henry because he had once loved her, and Anne because one of her safety nets was gone. Even if their marriage had hit unsurmountable difficulties, she knew Henry would never leave her because if he did, he would have been forced to take Catherine back. Now Catherine was dead, Anne was the only Queen living and more vulnerable because of it. Now it was even more imperative that she produced a healthy prince; only his birth would make her unassailable.

Chapter Fifteen

On the evening following the news of Catherine's death, the King ordered that the court celebrate his deliverance from the threat of the Emperor's might. Whilst Catherine lived, Henry had been afraid that the Emperor might mount a military campaign against England in support of his aunt. Now she was gone, so was that worry.

Jane was disgusted to see the court en fete. Everyone was expected to join in and make merry or risk the King's wrath. His eagle eye was everywhere and he missed nothing. He knew who the closet supporters of Catherine and Mary were and he made a point of seeking them out and insisting they displayed a joy they did not feel.

As if the forced merriment was not bad enough, the King was dressed all in yellow, generally accepted in England as the colour of joy and happiness. The Queen, who appeared late, was also head to toe in yellow. Taking her hand, the King addressed the assembled throng. "Friends, we are all come together this night not only to celebrate the removal of the threat of war, but also to pay our respects to our dear departed sister in law the Dowager Princess of Wales. In seems appropriate that here in England, yellow is the colour of joy, whereas in Spain it is the colour of mourning. Make merry my friends for there is much to celebrate!"

A polite round of applause greeted the King's speech after which he led the Queen in some of the slower dances before escorting her back to her chair, handing her wine and refreshments and insisting that she sit still and rest for the remainder of the festivities.

Jane, not required to attend the Queen that evening, had been partnered in the first two dances by her brother Thomas but since then had been overlooked by all the young gentlemen and had stood quietly at the side, watching the merriment.

Amongst all the noise, colour and movement, it was her very stillness which drew the King's eyes to her. After a sideways glance at Anne, who was occupied in conversation, he stepped down from the dais and wove his way across the floor towards her. Jane knew he was approaching, but nonetheless pretended to be surprised, placing her hand to her chest as if in shock before sinking gracefully to the floor. "Rise, Mistress Seymour." The King extended his hand to assist.

"I thank Your Grace." Jane managed to infuse a breathy, humble quality to her voice as she straightened and looked boldly up at him.

"You are an oasis of calm in this raging torrent of noise and activity" the King told her kindly as he gestured towards the dancers and musicians. "You do not like to dance?"

"Indeed I do, Your Grace. But I also enjoy observing and thinking quiet thoughts."

"You really are most admirable in every way, Mistress Seymour. May I tempt you on to the dance floor or would you prefer to remain here?"

"Your Grace, I would never pass up the chance to partner an acknowledged master of the dance."

It was just the right thing to say. The King beamed, caught hold of her hand and led her into the midst of the throng.

On the dais, the Queen had seen all of their exchange, despite pretending to engaged in conversation. As the King took Jane into his arms, Anne slammed her wine goblet down on to the table at her elbow. Those about her looked around in surprise, but Jane and the King were oblivious to her fury as deep in their own conversation, they moved gracefully around the floor. Jane was not a particularly proficient dancer but she managed to keep in step and made sure to smile up into his face at every opportunity whilst performing her steps with exaggerated care.

As the dance concluded, the King gallantly kissed her hand, led her back to where she had been standing, then began to make his way back to the Queen, every so often stopping to exchange a few words with friends and acquaintances.

As he reached the dais, the Queen stood up suddenly, the platter of fruit which had been on her lap, clattering to the floor. "Do you seek to make me jealous?" she hissed, without any preamble.

"Of course not sweetheart" he blustered. "I simply selected Mistress Seymour as a dance partner because I spied her standing all alone."

"And why do you think she is standing alone, all wistful and virtuous?"

The King opened his mouth to speak and then shut it again. It was clear Anne was teetering on the edge of one of her hysterical outbursts and he did not want to make it any worse by saying the wrong thing in public. As it was, a large number of people were watching their exchange with great interest.

"I'll tell you why" she continued. "Because she knows that it is the best way to draw attention to herself. And also because she has no friends and not a man in this room save her brother had offered himself as a partner. Until you."

The King's eyes darted from side to side as he sought a way to calm her. Great fearsome monarch that he was, she had always had the power to make him feel like an insignificant schoolboy.

"Sweetheart" he began in his most conciliatory tone, "remember …. "

"If you say 'remember the child' I swear I shall strike you" she screamed, raising her hand as if to do just that.

None too gently he caught hold of her raised arm. "And you Madam should remember that not only am I your husband but your King and if you should be so foolish as to strike me in front of this company I will have no alternative but to send you to the Tower to cool your heels."

Shocked at the venom in his voice, she paled visibly before crumpling back into her chair, sobbing hysterically. Henry watched her for a moment before patting her shoulder awkwardly and gesturing to her ladies to take her to her chamber. "I will come and see you anon" he called after her.

Jane smiled with satisfaction; since she was not in attendance on the Queen that night, she would be able to stay. Watching the weeping Anne being hurried away she felt no pity and formed the opinion that a woman with a sick and sallow complexion such as Anne's should never under any circumstances wear yellow.

Expecting that the King would once again seek her out, Jane remained where she was, aloof and still. But to her disappointment he did not dance again, remaining slumped despondently in his chair, gnawing at the side of his thumb. He refused any further food and drink and within the hour, retired from the company, directing as he left that the merriment should continue in his absence.

Professing concern for Anne's wellbeing, the King hurried to her chambers, only to be stopped on the threshold by Lady Lee. "The Queen has taken a sleeping draught and is resting quietly now" she informed him.

"And is all well?" He did not mean just with Anne, he was even more concerned for the welfare of the child.

"All is well" confirmed Lady Lee, well aware of his meaning. "If anything should change, I will see that Your Grace is informed immediately.

Henry was thoughtful as his gentlemen prepared him for an unaccustomed early retirement. He loved Anne, of course he did, but what if this pregnancy came to nothing like the last? How long could he continue waiting and hoping? He was getting no younger and neither was Anne. Already her childbearing history was distressingly similar to Catherine's and how many years did he waste trying and hoping with her? Was God again showing his displeasure with his chosen wife by blighting his seed?

Once in bed and alone, Henry propped himself up on his pillows and tried to find answers to his many questions but found himself instead answering those questions with yet more of the same.

Then he thought of Jane. Calm, dignified Jane. She could be a Queen beloved by the people, no doubt. Whereas Anne was hated because not only was she from what was seen as an upstart family, the people believed she had forced good Queen Catherine in to a lonely exile and premature death. But would Jane prove fertile or would a relationship with her just become a repeat of what had gone before? There was only one way to be sure and that was to try her out.

Henry smirked to himself; he loved the thrill of the chase. He was sure that faced with his indisputable manly charms, Jane would jump only too willingly into his bed. Then if she should prove fertile and Anne fail to see her pregnancy through, it would plainly be God's will that he replace one with the other.

There was only one obvious flaw to that eventuality; Jane would no doubt make an excellent Queen but was she wifely material? Try as he may, he could not find himself excited by the thought of Jane, whereas Anne… Even now, when she berated and screamed at him in public, all he wanted to do was be with her. He would leave it to God, He would show him the way to proceed.

Heaving himself out of bed, he lumbered across the room to the little cabinet in which he kept his most precious possessions. Inside were small pieces of jewellery and other mementos of his adored mother, a jewelled wristlet which had once been his brother Arthur's and a velvet cap which had once adorned the head of his legendary grandfather Edward IV. It was also a place where he kept items which could be used as gifts. Gifts which could bestowed quietly and discreetly without the need to trouble the court jeweller and draw attention to something he would prefer to keep between himself and the recipient.

Opening a small secret drawer inside the main compartment, he drew out a large ornate oval golden locket on a fine gold chain. The front of the locket was set with seed pearls and tiny emeralds and opened to reveal a small portrait of himself. He opened it and studied the portrait; it was a flattering likeness, made perhaps when he was younger and lighter of build. He snapped the locket shut and weighed it in his hand. It was a fine and expensive piece of jewellery and he would present it to Jane, he decided. As soon as he could get her alone he would offer it to her and hope that she understood that in return she would have to offer herself to him.

Keeping the locket in his hand, he climbed back into the great bed and slid his prize under the pillow. Tomorrow he would tuck it into his doublet and wait for his chance. He already liked Jane and in time could learn to love her, he was sure of it.

Chapter Sixteen

Had Jane been aware of the King's thoughts as he settled himself down to sleep, she may have had a better night herself. As it was she tossed and turned, worried and fretted, then finally began to doubt that she could live up to her brother's overwhelming ambitions.

Despite paying her attention the night before, the King had gone scuttling back to his Queen as soon as was decently possible. How could she even begin to come between such a couple?

The next morning she was in attendance on the Queen bright and early as was required. Anne, seemingly fully recovered in both body and mind from the night before, sang a pretty French ditty to herself as Margaret Lee tended to her coiffure and secured the French hood firmly on her head.

"Thank you, Meg." Satisfied with her reflection, the Queen stood up, stepped away from her mirror and began the short walk to her presence chamber. Seeing Jane, even whiter than usual and with dark shadows under her eyes, caused her to stop.

"Jane."

"Your Grace."

"Are you unwell? You look out of sorts."

"I thank Your Grace for your concern, but I am in good health."

"Then you had a late night?"

"No Your Grace, I was in bed early." Jane smirked, hoping the Queen would worry that she had not slept alone, but nothing could lower Anne's spirits. It was the first morning that she had not felt nauseous and she took it as a sign that all was progressing well.

"Very well. If you believe you are fit enough to carry out your duties, then I will take your word for it. But if you feel in any way unwell, Lady Lee will give you leave to go and rest."

Jane curtsied. "Your Grace is most kind."

"Her Grace is most anxious to be rid" murmured Anne to her closest ladies as they moved on towards her presence chamber. They tittered unkindly and looked back at Jane, who had not heard the Queen's comment and wondered what had been said.

Just as Anne crossed the threshold, she met the King coming the other way. He strode quickly to her, took both her hands and pressed them to his lips. "How are you today?" He looked closely at her and rejoiced in the signs of her obvious good health.

"I am feeling very well; very well indeed!" she exclaimed, her eyes sparkling.

"God be praised" he replied fervently.

Flashing him her brightest smile and blowing him a kiss as she walked on, Anne proceeded grandly into the chamber where she was immediately absorbed into the press of the day's petitioners.

Henry watched her go, smiling to himself, then turned and saw Jane approaching. As he saw her white face and shadowed eyes, his smile died on his lips. "Why Mistress Seymour, you do not look well."

She wanted to snap back but knew she had to maintain her calm and dignified façade. "Your Grace is most considerate, but your concern is misplaced. I am perfectly well, I just did not sleep well, that is all."

He said nothing but raised his eyebrows questioningly.

"I was troubled" she told him. "I find myself in a quandary and know not which way to turn."

"Why Jane" he stepped closer, his concern clear. "What is amiss? You may tell me all."

Jane looked away, her downcast eyes masking her triumph at his obvious care for her well-being. "Matters of the heart Your Grace," she whispered softly.

"Ah." He took a step back so he could better study her face. "I confess similar thoughts have kept me awake for many a night over the years. Will nothing lift your mood and make you smile?"

"Only the resolution of the problem" she replied, keeping her eyes downcast.

Suddenly remembering the treasure tucked in his doublet, he casually turned his back on his waiting gentlemen and pulled the locket from its hiding place. Holding it by the chain, he held it out to her.

Jane's eyes gleamed, like any woman she loved jewellery, and this was obviously an expensive piece, finely made and very decorative. Although she itched to snatch it from him, it was not what a virtuous maiden would do. It was clearly a bribe and she had to acknowledge it openly to him as such.

"It is a most beautiful piece Your Grace" Jane kept her hands carefully folded on her stomacher. "Is it for the Queen?"

"The Queen?" He seemed surprised. "No, the Queen has many jewels and is not in want of more." Keeping his eyes on hers, he carefully opened the locket and showed her the portrait inside.

"Oh, Your Grace is so handsome" she exclaimed. "It is such a good likeness."

Henry puffed out his chest a little more. She thought him handsome. He found himself liking her more and more.

"This is for you Jane" he told her softly. "Something to remind you of me when we are apart. And I wonder if it may resolve your little problem?"

She bit her lip and fluttered her eyelashes. "Your Grace, handing such an expensive gift to a humble maid of honour can only mean one thing."

His eyes twinkled. "And what might that be?"

"You wish me to become your mistress."

He was taken aback by her directness and spluttered a hasty reply. "That would be for you to decide Jane, I would not think to force you into anything which was distasteful to you."

"Never distasteful Your Grace" she replied earnestly. "But for one such as I, with no suitor and only her virginity to recommend her, it may be a foolish and indelicate step."

The King sighed deeply, took her hand and pressed the locket into it. "It is yours to keep whatever you decide" he told her with great sincerity. "But I must away now before suspicion should fall upon us."
Jane watched him stride away, almost hugging herself in her excitement. Edward would be very pleased for she was on the road to greatness.

Jane kept her secret to herself for the rest of the day. Attending upon the Queen gave one very little time to oneself and it was not until she was in her bed that she had a chance to thoroughly examine the locket by the light of her spluttering candle and again reflect upon its significance. But what to do? Hold out like Anne had done and hope he offered her marriage? She was not sure that she could keep his attention for long without making the ultimate sacrifice; she was not naturally amusing or well educated like the Queen. If she did give in and by chance become pregnant, what then? If the Queen were to miscarry, then it would force his hand, but if Anne were to deliver a prince, the King would stay with her. In the meantime, she, Jane, would be shuffled off to the country to give birth to her royal by-blow and then left to rot in obscurity no doubt whilst the child, if it were a boy, received all manner of honours and titles befitting the bastard son of a King.
She wished Edward were at court to offer her some guidance, but he was not. She would have to make up her own mind and play her own game as best she could.
As she dressed the next day, she slid the locket from under her pillow and clasped it about her neck.

Her gown was dark green and the locket with its tiny emeralds and pearls became her very well. She noticed the other maids glancing at it enviously as they all got ready, but none approached her to ask about it.

Lady Lee also noticed it immediately she entered the Queen's bedchamber but also said nothing.

Anne's mood was not so sunny as the day before and she irritably slapped at the maid who was lacing her gown, complaining that she did it too tightly and too roughly. Lady Lee stepped in to smooth things over and soon the Queen was properly dressed for the day although still complaining of discomfort.

It was as she turned to leave the bedchamber that Anne saw the locket. In fact, she noticed the locket before she noticed whose neck it adorned. Curious, she went over to her. "That is a very fine jewel you have there, Jane. May I see?"

Jane covered the locket with her hand, protectively. "Thank you, Your Grace."

Anne was very close to her now and she made Jane nervous. "May I ask where you got it?" she asked in her most honeyed tone.

"It was a gift Your Grace, from a very dear friend."

"Ah, was it indeed." The Queen nodded, her eyes still on the jewel partly hidden beneath Jane's hand. "It is a locket is it not? Is there perchance a portrait inside?"

"I confess I do not know" Jane replied airily. "I have not opened it as yet."

Anne's brow creased in confusion. "Have you not? I find that strange; to receive a locket from a dear friend yet not be bothered to look at what may be inside?"

She looked round at her ladies for confirmation. "It rather suggests to me that you know very well what is inside yet you do not wish to tell me."

"Why would I lie to Your Grace?"

"Because it comes naturally to you perhaps. And why wear such a sly smug expression? This generous friend must be very rich and influential to be able to favour you so."

Jane smirked. "I suppose he is."

Anne appeared to have tired of the exchange and began to turn away. Jane, thinking the danger was past, released her hold on the locket, only realising her mistake too late.

Faster than a cobra's strike, Anne's hand shot out, grasped the locket and wrenched it from Jane's neck. The gold chain, delicate as it was, resisted the initial tug and only snapped when Anne yanked at it for a second time.

Jane cried out in pain and put her hands to her neck, rubbing at the angry red streaks which were fast appearing.

The Queen deftly opened the locket and found inside what she half expected she would, her husband's portrait. She stared at the portrait for a long time then snapped the locket shut. After examining it closely and turning it over and over in her hand whilst the broken chain twisted and glinted dully in the light, Anne raised her eyes to Jane's face and looked hard at her, for the first time truly assessing the woman who seemed determined to become her rival.

Gesturing towards Jane with the locket Anne asked sweetly "Do you really believe this is anything other than a mere trinket designed to lure you into the

King's bed for a night or two? Do you honestly believe that he would ever be seriously interested in you?"

Jane raised her chin and stared back haughtily. "I do. And he is".

Anne threw the locket into a corner of the room and turned her back, saying "Go away Jane, you're deluded. Get back to your father's house and consider if your behaviour is appropriate to a Queen's servant."

"The King will not allow me to leave court" Jane retorted. "He values my counsel and company too highly."

Anne rounded on her, her expression savage. "I am the Queen here and you are my servant, bound to me. It is my orders that you follow, and I say get you to Wolf Hall and do not come back unless I send for you!"

For a moment Jane stood her ground, unsure of what to do. Then looking around at the faces of the company, many wearing expressions equally as hostile as the Queen's, she made the decision to withdraw graciously. With as scant a curtsey to her mistress as she knew she could get away with, she left the Queen's chamber and headed straight to the King.

Chapter Seventeen

At first he seemed nowhere to be found. Frantically she ran up and down the various passageways which connected the Queen's chambers to the King's and eventually came upon him climbing back up the stone steps which led down to the armoury.
"Your Grace!" Jane was so flustered, she all but threw herself into his arms.
"Jane? What is amiss?"
"It is the Queen…" Jane was about to continue when a look of horror passed over his face. "The Queen? Has something happened to her or the child?"
"No, no" Jane flapped her hands in agitation. "As regards health, she appears well, it is her temper I fear."
The King sighed deeply. "What has happened? Tell me all."

"I wore the locket today; it was so beautiful I could not bear not to. The Queen saw it immediately and quizzed me as to its origin."

"And what did you say?"

"I told her it was a gift from a very dear friend. She then asked if there was a portrait inside and I dare not tell her there was so I said I had not opened it to find out."

The King groaned. He had already noticed the red marks around her neck and knew what was to come. "I imagine she did not take it well."

"Your Grace she behaved like a harridan! She ripped it from my neck, raved at me and told me to leave court and go back to Wolf Hall." Jane was enjoying herself now, subtly enhancing her story to wring a little more sympathy from him. "I told her that you would not allow it; that you valued my company and my counsel far too much."

"That was not a wise move Jane." The King's expression darkened as he looked at her, causing Jane to back away. "It was foolish to so anger the Queen, especially in her delicate condition. You could have put my son in peril."

"But you gave me the locket so that I should wear it, did you not?"

"Indeed. But not during the day. It is too ornate for everyday use. It is something which should only be worn on a special occasion. She would not have questioned it had you worn it on one of your free evenings about the court. I had thought you would have realised that."

Jane thought quickly. She was losing ground, she needed to think of something quickly to reinstate herself in his affections. "Your Grace" she stepped forward, placed her hands on his chest and looked up at him appealingly. "It is by far the most beautiful piece of jewellery I have ever seen, let alone owned. And it carries a portrait of you, my most gracious lord. I could not bear to be parted from it."

As she hoped, his expression softened immediately. "That is understandable. Worry not, I will smooth this over with the Queen once I have given her a while to calm down."

"Should I leave court as ordered?"

"No of course not." He lifted her hand to his lips as he spoke. "You spoke truth when you said that you are needed here. I still have every hope that you will find it in your heart to grant me that which I most desire."

Jane averted her eyes and blushed, causing the King to become even more smitten. "Keep yourself out of sight for the rest of the day and resume your duties tomorrow. I will have spoken to the Queen by then and all will be well."

Once alone, the King dithered as to whether he should leave Anne to recover her temper for an hour or two or whether he should just go and confront her. For a man who ruled his kingdom with a rod of iron and who was strong and decisive in all matters political and domestic, in the face of warring females his good sense deserted him and he floundered.

He knew he could never settle to the days affairs with such a task hanging over him so he decided to get it over with and go and face the dragon in her den. And she would be breathing fire, of that he was certain.

The first thing he noticed when he approached her chamber was the silence emanating from within.

Even if there had been nothing wrong that he knew of, the silence would have alerted him to a potential problem. Anne loved music and activity and shunned quiet and seclusion.

Taking a breath, he opened the door and went in. She was sitting in her chair of state facing the door. It was immediately clear to him that she had been waiting for him and no doubt had expected him long before. Her ladies were huddled in a corner, pretending activity with their embroidery frames but in reality waiting for the storm to break.

"You took your time" she barked, in a voice which brooked no apologetic response.

He spread his hands in mute acceptance. "I would have come to you sooner, but there were matters I had to attend to first."

"Ha. The bleatings of that wench Seymour no doubt." She looked away from him and began tapping her fingers on the arms of her chair in agitation.

"Sweetheart..." he took a step towards her but she held up her hand imperiously.

"Do not presume to call me sweetheart when no doubt the same word has been dripping from your lips and into the ear of that whey-faced sheep."

His anger began to mount. "I would never..."

"But you would" she hissed. "And no doubt you have. Leave me, I have nothing to say to you." Rising from her chair, she turned her back to him and stood staring out of the window.

Henry glanced across at her ladies and glimpsed the rapt expressions which were rapidly hidden by their bent heads as they resumed their sewing.

"Ladies, if you would leave us please." They jumped

at the sound of his voice but immediately left their activities and did his bidding.

Once the door had closed, he turned once more to Anne. "Come here" he said in his most conciliatory manner. "Let us talk."

"Talk of what? Your latest love interest? Or perhaps you want my advice on the ultimate gift, the one which will make her fall willingly into your bed?"

"You know I love only you." He crossed the chamber in quick strides and turned her to face him. As he tilted her face up to his, he saw traces of tears on her cheeks and silently gave thanks. Once the tears came, she was generally easier to deal with. It was her cold anger and hot temper he feared most.

"Sweet Anne, I hate it when we quarrel. How can you doubt my love for you when I waited all those long years to make you mine and defied the whole of the world to achieve that?"

She sniffed disinterestedly. "And no doubt you sorely regret it now. All that time wasted when the love of your life waited just a few counties away at Wolf Hall."

"Yet here I stand with you. And this is where I want to be." Hesitantly he took her into his arms and breathed a sigh of relief as he felt the stiffness in her body begin to lessen.

"The locket...." she began, her voice muffled against the heavy brocade of his doublet.

"Anne." He loosened his hold so he could look down into her face. "It was nothing. The girl was hospitable at Wolf Hall and is pleasant to talk with, that is all. It was a spur of the moment thing and you know how I like to give spontaneous gifts."

Anne frowned. The jewel was not a frippery; it had no doubt been a considerable expense. Whilst Henry could be very profligate with money, he rarely gave spontaneous gifts of expensive jewellery. She decided to leave the subject of the locket and voiced another concern which had recently been occupying her mind.

"You know there are factions at court working against me?"

He looked aghast, then hurried to reassure her. "Petty plots cannot hurt you sweetheart, and should anything come to my attention, then by God my actions will be swift and pitiless. To work against the Queen is to work against the King and I will brook no interference."

"And you are aware of the purpose of their scheming? It is to sweep away the new religion and me with it."

"That cannot happen!" he blustered.

She shook her head pityingly. "Open your eyes Henry, your court is a hotbed of plots and counterplots hatched by catholic sympathisers. Do you not think that Mistress Seymour may be their pawn?"

It had crossed his mind, but he preferred to believe that Jane was smitten with the man rather than the religious conversion of King and kingdom.

"She is a simple girl from a loyal family" he began. "I do not believe that she would allow herself to be used in that way."

"Edward Seymour is an ambitious man, as is his brother. Can you not at least admit the possibility of some sort of grand scheme?"

He shook his head. "Edward is loyal to me and

therefore to you. He knows that if I suspected him for a moment, it would not be long before his head was parted from his body."

She decided to believe him and trust that he would protect her from her enemies. "Very well." She took his hand and kissed it fervently. "Then we are friends again."

If she saw the relief in his face, she made no comment. "I assume I am required to welcome Mistress Seymour back into my service as if nothing had happened?"

"It would be a favour to me. I do not wish to have the girl sent home in disgrace when she has done nothing wrong."

Anne looked sceptical. She could provide a very long list of things Mistress Seymour had done wrong. But for now she would bide her time.

Chapter Eighteen

The next day Jane presented herself for service expecting a tirade of abuse or biting sarcasm at the very least. However to her surprise, the Queen treated her much as she always had, with distance and icy politeness.

The locket still lay in the corner of the chamber; Jane's eyes kept straying to it but she dared not pick it up. Every time she thought there might be a chance to casually pass by and snatch it quickly she caught the amused eyes of the Queen watching her every move.

Her chance came when the Queen moved into her presence chamber to hear the day's petitions. Jane ensured that she was right at the back of the queue of ladies and managed to sidestep and scoop up the locket without anyone noticing. For safety she tucked it into the front of her bodice, gasping as the cold metal pressed against her warm skin.

When the Queen returned to her chamber much later, her eyes immediately went to the empty corner and then to Jane, who stared back with all the innocence she could muster. They both knew what had occurred, but the Queen did not mention it and Jane resolved to keep the locket away from the Queen's gaze when and if she ever wore it again. She thought it wise to keep it safe within her bodice every day as she would not put it past Anne to have it secretly removed from her possessions whilst she was busy about her duties.

The Queen was feeling well and she was feeling positive. Her pregnancy was advancing and with every day which passed she found herself daring to hope that finally and after so much heartbreak, all would be well. Her body was beginning to change; she was naturally so slender that even at such an early stage, the roundness of her stomach proclaimed her condition.

Henry was attentive and forever grateful that she had been so forgiving over his flirtation with Jane. Because he insisted to himself that it was nothing more; Mistress Seymour had simply been a diversion from his worries over the condition of his dearly loved wife.

He had almost convinced himself that Jane meant nothing to him when he came upon her tidying the Queen's clothes in the bedchamber. Jane was entirely alone and the King looked around in surprise.

"Where is the Queen?" he asked

"Your Grace" Jane curtsied low. "Her Grace takes a little exercise in the gardens today."

"Then I hope she is well wrapped against the cold." The King stalked to the windows and looked down on to the privy gardens. He could just see Anne and her ladies at the far end by the sunken garden. She was indeed well insulated against the chill weather, swathed in furs. Meanwhile Jane carried on lifting and folding gowns before packing them securely in the lavender strewn coffer at the foot of the bed.

He turned and watched her, diligently performing her duty. "Has the Queen been kind to you of late?"

Jane straightened. "You mean after the business with the locket?"

He looked down at the floor and nodded. "Yes, the locket. In hindsight I was unwise to give you such a distinctive and rich jewel."

"I am so glad you did!" Jane went to him, smiling. "I have it well tucked away now and she will never find it."

"How can you be so sure?"

"Because I keep it with me at all times." Provocatively she stroked the low neckline of her gown. "Unless of course she decides to divest me of my clothing!"

The King's eyes gleamed as he pictured his gift, nestling against her soft white breast. "Let me see" he demanded, moving closer.

Jane squealed in surprise. "Your Grace, that would not be seemly."

"Leave it to me to decide what is seemly and what is not." Before she had the chance to object, he lifted her effortlessly off her feet and carried her over to Anne's chair. Levering himself down in to the narrow seat with some difficulty, he held her captive on his lap.

Jane giggled nervously. "Your Grace, what if someone should see?"

"I care not. Now where does that locket hide." He began to inch his fat fingers under the tight bodice of her gown. Jane was quite delighted at the attention here in the Queen's own bedchamber. There was every chance that their interlude might lead to discovery.

He was oblivious. "Now, is it here?" His fingers inched downward. "Or here?" He moved them across. "Or are you being deliberately provocative and have in fact secured it in your nether garments?"

Jane giggled as his fingers began to hitch up her skirt, inch by inch. "Provocative Your Grace? I?" She nuzzled playfully into his neck whilst he, encouraged by her brazenness prepared to take even more liberties. So engrossed were they in their licentious fumblings that the commotion in the outer chamber went unnoticed.

It was only when the door flew open and Anne and her ladies tumbled in, rosy-cheeked and

laughing together, that the guilty couple froze.

There was silence as Anne took in the scene, her mouth agape. Henry, aware that he was thoroughly caught out and that this time his actions could not be easily explained away, stood up abruptly, tumbling Jane from his lap. Jane sat upright on the floor, pulling her disordered garments together, a half smile playing about her lips.

Stepping forward, Anne bent and slapped Jane soundly and was just about to do the same to Henry when he deflected her blow. "Mind what you do Madam" he reminded her. "Remember before all else I am your King. I am your husband second."

"You are no more than a lecherous pig!" she shrieked. "All that comfort and reassurance so recently given, then I come home to this?"

"I am a man" he reminded her. "And a man will take comfort where he can if his wife will not provide it."

"Is that so?" The rising hysteria had been replaced by icy calm. "Then is that so for a wife? That she may play the coquette with any man who pays her attention because her husband is occupied elsewhere?"

"You know that is not so" he told her primly. "A wife who behaves thus is little more than a whore and deserves not only humiliation but a whipping."

"But a man may go where he pleases even though his wife is bearing his child? A man who professes undying love yet lays hands on the first slut to give him the eye? I mean you, Mistress Seymour!" Anne turned on Jane so suddenly that she jumped in alarm and edged closer to the wall for protection. "Look at you, all assumed decorum and virtuousness. Where is that famed modesty now? If I had not returned, where would this interlude have led? Would you so far have forgotten yourself that you would seduce my husband on my own bed?"

Jane sat up a little straighter. "I confess I was enjoying His Grace's attentions. If he had led, then yes, I would have followed."

"You do not even attempt to deny it?"

"We must all obey the wishes of our King" Jane retorted smugly, getting to her feet.

"And also of our Queen." Anne advanced towards her menacingly. "Now hear this. You will go straight to your quarters and pack your belongings. You will then beg a horse from the stable and get yourself back to your father's house. I never want to set eyes on your goggle-eyed, sly little face ever again. Do I make myself clear?"

"Perfectly, Your Grace" Jane tossed her head arrogantly. "But I fear that the King will countermand your order. He after all is master in his own house."

The King stepped between the two warring women fearing Anne would tear Jane limb from limb.

"Get you gone" he jerked his head at Jane. "I will speak with you later. Ladies, you also should leave your mistress now."

When they were once more alone, Anne began to laugh. "So here we are again. How do you propose to explain this away?"

"I cannot and I will not" he snapped. "Perhaps it is time for you to close your eyes to my actions like your betters have done before you and concentrate on seeing my son safely into this world."

"Is that so?" she taunted. "Then I am just to you what I have always suspected. A brood mare. Just a convenient vessel to grow your children."

"And like any unsuccessful brood mare you face destruction unless you fulfil your purpose."

"Ah". She stepped away from him, pulling her furs more closely about her body. "So it is official then. If, God forbid, I lose this child, or even if it is born female, you would look to be rid of me."

He suddenly feared for the welfare of the child she carried as her face paled and she swayed slightly.

"You should rest" he caught her to him and spoke earnestly. "There is no need for you to worry. This is but a silly misunderstanding. You are my Queen and you will shortly be the mother of my son, please

God. Do not fret further and jeopardise all."

Angrily she shook off his restraining hands. "And in the meantime, you will continue to contrive to seduce Mistress Seymour no doubt. I take it that you will countermand my order to have her removed?"

"I am sorry Anne, I do not have to explain myself to you. Jane keeps my mind occupied and reminds me that I am not just a King, but a desirable man."

"You, desirable?" She laughed coldly. "All you are to Mistress Seymour is a means to foist her detestable religion on this country. Oh, and I think she would quite like to be Queen as well, but don't think she will ever bear you a prince. Her best child-bearing years are already behind her."

"I think you will find that she is younger than you yourself" he pointed out.

"Yes, and look how successful I have been" she retorted bitterly. "And if Mistress Seymour has her way, this child will go the way of the others. Ever since we returned from progress, at every turn she has sought to enrage and humiliate me, and you do nothing to dissuade her. Do you two plot together? Have I been nurturing a pair of vipers even as I contrived to make her welcome and be a good wife and Queen to you?"

"That is a preposterous theory and one which does you no justice. Believe me Madam, I do not need to plot to have you removed should I wish. That can be achieved just like that!" He snapped his fingers in her face.

"Well then that is a comforting thought for me to muse on. My husband can bed whom he pleases whilst I play the mute pregnant wife grateful for his smallest attentions whilst he heaps humiliation upon me."

"If that is how you see it." His voice was cold.

"It is how it is" she retorted. "And you do not care enough for me to even hide your infatuation from the court. All my ladies saw what went on here today and I have no doubt that by now the news travels to every corner of the land."

He shrugged. "Be that as it may. You know your duty and I suggest you retire to your bed and make sure that your venom has not disturbed my son."

He stamped his way out of her chamber, almost as though it was he who was the injured party. Anne placed her hands over the child in her womb and prayed fervently for a happy outcome but could not shake off her sense of darkness and doom.

Chapter Nineteen

Jane was cock-a-hoop as she gave her account of the afternoon's events to her brother Edward, who listened with rapt attention.
"He could not keep his hands from me" she crowed. "Had we not been disturbed, who knows where his attentions may have led."
"Do not give too much too soon" her brother urged. "Remember, above all it is the chase he enjoys the most. He tends to discard that which is too easily won. Remember how the Queen kept him dangling for all those years; she would never have come to the throne had she bestowed her favours from the beginning."
"Fear not, I know what I am about" Jane told him arrogantly. "I will know when the moment comes to submit."

"Then you would not wait until marriage? Or the promise of marriage at least? You must tread carefully sister, one false move at this stage could jeopardise all you have achieved thus far."

Jane weighed his words carefully before replying. "These are different times. Although the situation appears similar as before, when that witch lured him from Queen Catherine, I believe it now requires a different approach. A good many years have passed and whereas he was impatient for his son then, he is verging on desperate now. It is more than two years since the Queen produced a living child and since then every hope has been dashed. Even if she bears a living male child, there is no certainty that it will live. What better than for the King to already have a substitute queen in place, one who has proved that she can conceive?"

Edward shook his head disapprovingly. "That would be a dangerous game to play. You could end up as yet another one of the King's discarded mistresses with a ruined reputation and possibly with a child to raise."

"You should know that any goal worth reaching has risks. The greater the risk, the sweeter the achievement. So what for my reputation? It is clear that the world at large believes that I am not marriageable. Even our mother maintains that I am for spinsterhood. If I become another discarded mistress, what of it? I will have lost nothing because I have nothing to lose."

"But you should remember the wider cause" he reminded her sternly. "If all becomes lost, it is not just your personal failure. A great many powerful men have thrown their lot in with ours and they will do whatever it takes to avoid exposure. If you fail, and our plot should become common knowledge, then they would have no compunction in offering our names to the King as conspirators who worked to destroy his Queen."

"Fear not brother" she waved away his concerns. "The Queen becomes more fragile of mind with every day that passes. Her tempers cannot be good for the child and I feel sure that matters will shortly come to a head. For now, you must trust me."

January 1536 was a particularly cold month. Although no snow had fallen, the land lay swathed in frost and ice making the highways and paths treacherous for both man and beast. Despite her avowed love of fresh air and exercise, even Anne gave up her daily walks for fear of falling.

The King too missed his exercise. Always a heavy man, forced inactivity caused him to pile on even more weight which in turn only increased his bad temper. Finally he could bear it no more and announced his intention to ride in the tiltyard that morning. Anne was concerned and told him so.

"Your Grace, surely you risk injury or worse, riding whilst the frost is heavy upon the ground?"

Henry, buoyed up by the expectation of exercise and a little healthy competition, countered her good naturedly. "Worry not sweetheart. I have ordered that the tiltyard be well sanded, all will be well."

But Anne did worry. She was aware that the vultures were circling and that all depended on her ability to bring her pregnancy to a successful conclusion.

However should some calamity befall the King, her only protector, then she had no illusions about what her enemies would do to her. One thing would be for certain, her child would never be born.

Gently she chided him. "Make sure you dress warmly and take no risks."

"Sweetheart" he held her briefly to him before releasing her. "I can only wear the usual protection beneath my armour, or would you see me don woollen hat and fur cape also?"

She smiled, picturing Henry in full armour with woollen hat set at a rakish angle on his helmet. "Just keep yourself safe, that is all I ask."

Jauntily he kissed her hand as he departed. "I will. For you."

She had no premonition of doom that bright morning, as she watched him go. She told herself that he would not be foolish and that as an experienced horseman and jouster, he would not put himself or his mount in danger.

Jane, standing quietly to one side, felt somewhat aggrieved that his eyes had not sought her out, but her hurt feelings were more than offset by the obvious agitation of the Queen.

Anne's agitation only increased as the morning drew on; she could settle to nothing and paced relentlessly. Jane, plying her needle, had one eye on the linen and one eye on the Queen, whilst keeping alert for any sound outside.

Finally as the dining hour approached, there was the sound of many booted feet climbing the stone stairs to the Queen's chamber. Quickly Anne made her way to her chair; it would not do for Henry to find her standing and fretting. The ready smile on her lips died as the door burst open to reveal not Henry, but her uncle of Norfolk, accompanied by half a dozen of his men. In that brief second, two thoughts jostled for precedence in her brain. Was this arrest, or was it news of the King?

As she half rose from her seat, Norfolk blurted out. "Niece, brace yourself. The King has fallen from his horse and cannot be roused. We fear he is dead."

Wordlessly Anne extended her arm out to Lady Lee, who gently set her back down in her chair. "No." Anne tried to rise. "I must go to the King."

"You would do well to remain here and protect the heir to the throne" Norfolk told her shortly. "I will see that you are informed of any change."

As some of her ladies began to wail quietly, Anne stared into the middle distance, her stricken face reflecting her shock and fear. It was as she had always feared, the King would die and leave her vulnerable and alone. Protectively she folded her arms across her belly, leaned forward and began to weep softly.

Jane stood nearby, wide eyed and panicked. It was not so much concern for the wellbeing of her King, but concern for her ambitions and all the efforts she had made thus far. Would it all be for nothing?

Twice during the following hours Anne went to the King's chamber only to be turned away at the door and urged to remain optimistic and calm. There was no change they told her, but the King still breathed.

By suppertime, she had taken to her bed, Lady Lee firm but insistent that she lie still for the sake of her sanity and the child's wellbeing. A constant stream of ladies was dispatched to the King's chamber in search of news, and finally, a positive message was brought back.

Mary Zouche, her face alight with joy, approached

Anne's bedside and shyly took the hand which restlessly plucked at the fur coverlet. "Your Grace" she whispered. "The King has awoken from his daze and sits up in his bed."

Anne turned her head on the pillow to look at Mary. "Truly?" As Mary nodded her head earnestly, Anne began to sob with relief. "I must go to him." She began to struggle to sit up. "He will expect me to visit him."

"No, Your Grace he will expect you to be resting. Once the night has passed, he will be glad to see you." Lady Lee gently placed her hands on Anne's shoulders to underline her advice.

"You're right Meg, of course you are, but will you please get a message to the King telling him I thank God for his deliverance?"

"Of course." Lady Lee looked about her and spied Jane standing by the door. "Jane will take the message. Jane?"

Jane moved gracefully towards the bed and curtsied to Anne. "Your Grace?"

Anne repeated her message, Jane nodded and left the chamber. But instead of delivering the message, she spent the following minutes walking aimlessly around the palace corridors before returning to the Queen's bedchamber. "Is all done?" Anne asked, as Jane appeared.

"Indeed Your Grace. I gave the message to one of his gentlemen who said it would be conveyed directly." Jane told her lies shamelessly and with perfection.

Anne nodded. "Thank you, Jane."

The next morning, Anne found herself too weary to rise and decided to keep to her bed for a few hours more. She was reading quietly when the King made a sudden appearance, limping profoundly and with a face as red as that of his velvet surcoat. "Your Grace!" Anne sat up in surprise. "I had not been informed that you were up and about."

"It is as well I am then Madam" he snapped. "Since it appears that you have so little regard for my wellbeing that you do not bother to send me a message or rise from your bed to visit me."

"I did send a message!" Anne protested. "As soon as I was informed that you had woken, Meg sent Jane to your chamber."

"Oh yes?" The King's head whipped around, his eyes scanning the ladies present until he found Jane.

"Mistress Seymour? I saw you not last evening."

"No, Your Grace" Jane stammered. "I did not enter your chamber but gave the message to one of your waiting gentlemen."

"Which one?"

"I confess I do not know his name."

The King snorted and turned once more to Anne. "I received no such message. I felt abandoned Madam."

"That was not my intention" she soothed. "I wanted to come to you myself but was advised to rest since the news of your accident shocked me greatly. My uncle Norfolk is not the most subtle of men."

"Did he break it to you harshly?"

"He told me you were feared dead with no preamble whatsoever."

The King guffawed. "That is what happens when a soldier does the task of a courtier! I trust you are recovered now?"

"Seeing you thus has put all my fears to rest. How did you come to fall from your horse?"

The King scratched at his head absent mindedly. "I cannot say that I remember exactly what happened I ended up with my face in the sand and the horse fell on top of me. The horse was unharmed but they tell me I was unconscious for more than two hours and insensible for several more."

" What injuries have you?"

"My leg was gashed and pains me greatly, but other than that nothing more than a large collection of bruises the size of a man's hand."

"Poor Henry." Anne reached up and stroked the side of his face tenderly. "Once I am feeling better I shall tend to your injuries personally."

The King beamed. "I shall look forward to that. But for now, you take as much rest as you need and I will see you again soon." After leaning down and kissing Anne gently, he limped from the chamber.

Jane watched him go with hot resentment. Once again, he had virtually ignored her and it was all about Anne. Always Anne.

Chapter Twenty

Over the next few days, the King steadily mended. Although his limp failed to improve significantly, the bumps and bruises pained him less thanks to the herbal ointment his physician blended for him.

Jane constantly conspired to accidentally meet him around the palace and succeeded on several occasions but other than a polite greeting, he remained frustratingly aloof, his mind evidently on other matters.

Anne however, was out of sorts again. She thought she had recovered from the shock of the King's accident but could not seem to put her mind to anything and was suffering from vague aches and pains of her own. Nothing distinct or even dangerous, at least according to her physicians, but despite all assurances, she was beset by nagging feelings of doubt and impending doom.

In the early hours of Wednesday morning, Jane was asleep in the Queen's antechamber with several other maids. Those whose duty it was to dress the Queen in the morning often slept in the next chamber; they were also available should the Queen require anything in the night.

Jane was dreaming about Anne. The Queen had once again found her and the King together and was standing in front of them screaming over and over. It seemed to be going on for ever and Jane tossed and turned restlessly before stirring at the sound of movement nearby.

The Queen was still screaming; it was not a dream and all about her the other maids were jumping from their truckle beds and hastily throwing on robes. Jane did likewise then followed the others into the Queen's bedchamber.

By the light of a single candle they could see Anne sitting up in bed, her hair disordered, her eyes wide and frantic, holding in front of her hands which were covered in blood, all the while screaming hysterically.

Margaret Douglas reacted first. "Jane, fetch Lady Lee. Nan, run for the Queen's physicians. Quickly!"

More lights were brought and physicians converged upon the chamber from all parts of the palace, but it was no good. After the briefest of labours, the Queen brought forth a dead child of about fifteen weeks gestation. It was well formed, apparently healthy, and male.

Try as she may, Jane could not initially feel the elation that she expected she would feel. Yes, the outcome had been all that she could possibly desire, but she knew that those screams and all that blood would stay with her for a very long time. It had been a sobering thing to witness, and even as she helped wash the Queen and freshen the bed, she felt too numb to be anything but coldly efficient. The feeling did not last of course; as the implications of the Queen's latest miscarriage became clear to her, she began planning her next move. The King's rage was going to be even greater than the last time and she would need to be a calm and soothing influence to get herself noticed in the Queen's chamber. A lot depended on how Anne reacted. If she dissolved into tears and melted the King's heart, he might well be overcome with emotion and console her. But if she met rage with rage, then things might be said between them which could never be taken back or forgiven.

Through her pain-filled haze of misery and fear, Anne became aware of a different touch on her brow. The cloth was rough, the touch uncaring; these were obviously not the ministrations of her faithful Meg Lee. Slowly she opened her eyes to a blurred figure standing over her and as the picture focused, she saw it was Jane pressing rather too hard on her fevered brow, a triumphant smile on her face.

"Your Grace." Jane removed the cloth, rinsed it in the silver bowl on the side table and after a rudimentary squeeze, slapped it back onto Anne's forehead. Anne winced, moaned and closed her eyes once more.

Glancing around surreptitiously, Jane noted that no-one was close enough to pay any heed to what she was doing or saying, but to make doubly sure, she bent over the bed and put her mouth to Anne's ear. "You have just destroyed the King's son thanks to your hysterics and black temper" she whispered.

"You are finished. It is likely he will never come near you again and seek to put you away, as you ensured he did with Queen Catherine. Everyone hates you, it would have been better for you had you died in childbed."

She jumped as Anne suddenly opened her eyes and clamped her hand on to Jane's wrist. Jane straightened, aware that eyes were now upon them and set about trying to break free of Anne's grip, which was surprisingly strong for one so weakened after such an ordeal. Loudly she said "Please let me go Your Grace. You are delirious, you know not what you are doing."

Anne half raised herself, causing Meg Lee to step forward to support her. "I know well what I do, as I think you do too Mistress Seymour. You think to replace me in the King's affections, you with your milksop face and deceitful demeanor. He would not consider you for one moment, not even for dalliance." Exhausted she fell back. Margaret Lee tucked the sheets neatly around her shoulders, all the while looking accusingly at Jane.

Jane stepped back, sneering "Are you sure about that?" As Anne turned her head on the pillows, gathering herself for another attack, Jane put her head on one side, adopted her most pitying expression and raised her hand to her stomach, caressing it lightly. "The deed is done and you are no longer of any use." Not stopping to see Anne's reaction, or that of the other bystanders, Jane turned on her heel and flounced from the chamber. The deed was most definitely not done, not yet, but Jane did not anticipate too much reluctance on the King's account.

The King was not informed of Anne's miscarriage until he woke the next morning. With a howl of rage, he pushed away the attentions of his gentlemen and barber, hastily donned a full-length fur lined robe, took up his walking stick and limped angrily towards the Queen's bedchamber.

Anne, who had only fallen into a restless sleep a few hours earlier, was abruptly awoken by the sight of the unkempt King standing over her bed and berating her. Biting her lip, she let him finish his rant before weighing in with her own opinions.

"This is what happens when you dally with your latest amour under my very eyes and in this very bedchamber" she shouted. "I had barely recovered from that shock when you ill-advisedly decide to practice your jousting in dangerous weather conditions and suffer a terrible fall. How could any wife fail to be frantic when you lay so close to death for so many hours, especially after having the news broken to me in such a callous manner?"

"These are nothing but excuses" he spoke quietly now and with real malice. "You have destroyed yet another boy with your bile and tantrums. You are both an unfit mother and an unfit wife. A Queen who cannot bear children is of little use dynastically. I have given you chance after chance yet you throw it back in my face each time. All those years and all those promises, and what do I get? One female child. I am minded to end this here and now!"

To emphasise his words, he struck the floor sharply with the stick he carried. Anne shrank back against her pillows, half expecting that she would be struck next. Seeing her fear gave him savage satisfaction.

"You may be sure that if striking you would avail me anything, then I would do it. As it is, you are not worth my efforts."

Anne tried again. "This is just misfortune. We are still young Henry, we have proved we can get children. In time, all will be right."

"We do not have time!" he shouted. "And we neither of us are so young that we can risk another decade of fruitless endeavour. God does not look kindly upon this marriage and the death of my sons proves all. I suppose you are aware that this is the day of the funeral in Peterborough for the Dowager Princess of Wales? How much clearer can God's message be? You are denied my child on account of your cruelty towards the late Princess!"

Anne had forgotten that it was the day of the funeral but decided it was not wise to be drawn into a theological debate whilst the King was in such high temper. "When I am recovered from this, we can try again. By this time next year we will have our prince." Anne pretended confidence she did not feel.

The King looked at her coldly. "I am not minded to ever come near you again. It is a pointless exercise which leads only to misery and death. This was your last chance and I am telling you here and now that you will get no more boys by me."

Anne tried to placate him. "You are speaking from rage and disappointment. That will pass. Look at how bright and clever our daughter is; think of the son we could make together."

"For many years I have been dreaming of the son we would make together, but my misfortune has been to see those sons brought dead into the world before their time. Enough is enough. I refuse to allow you to placate me or murder any more of my children.

When you are up, we will talk, for now, I take my leave."

Anne watched him go then turned to her dearest friend Meg. "Meg, what am I to do? You heard him, he wants no more of me. I am so afraid."

"Your best course of action is to rest and regain your vitality" Margaret advised. "You know how to charm him; there is no another woman who can fascinate and lure him like you can. He will calm down and realise that this was not your fault, and it was merely a chain of unfortunate events which brought you to this."

Anne wiped her eyes. "Do you really think so? What of her? You heard her inferring that she has already shared the King's bed and may even already carry his child." Anne nodded towards Jane, who was in the ante chamber, pretending not to hear, when both knew that she could.

"You know how she lies. To my certain knowledge she has not spent any significant time alone with the King. Even if she can attract him, she will not hold him for long" Meg soothed. "Once you are back to your sparkling best, he will forget that he ever set eyes on her."

Jane straightened from her duties in the antechamber and shot both Anne and Meg a withering look. Soon they would see just what they were up against. She decided that it was time to make her move.

Chapter Twenty-One

Anxious as she was to make headway with her plans, even Jane knew that to approach the King at that moment, whilst he was angry and looking to apportion blame, would be foolhardy. Instead she quietly carried out her duties, aware that the Queen heartily wished that she were anywhere other than in close personal contact.

Eight days after her miscarriage, Anne left her bed and eased herself back into the rigours of court life. Her pretended vivacity only accentuated her lacklustre eyes and sunken cheeks.

The King did not actively seek her out, but when they were required to appear together there was no indication in his manner that he had anything other than right and proper husbandly concern for his wife following her traumatic ordeal. His leg still had not properly healed and although he was able to discard his stick, he walked with a pronounced limp and his temper was all the more uncertain because of it.

Whenever she was able, Jane saw to it that she stood in a prominent position behind the Queen, so that should the King look in that direction he could not fail to see her downcast eyes and modest demeanour. It was Jane's bad luck that the King's eyes rarely travelled towards his wife so her efforts were largely unnoticed.

After almost a week of being ignored, Jane decided to contrive to see the King alone in his chambers. She chose a day when her duties were not due to commence until the evening and planned her approach carefully. She knew that the King would be closeted with Cromwell in the early part of the day and that when Cromwell left the King's chamber, there was a chance he may be alone until his gentlemen came to enquire whether different dress was required for any afternoon activities.

On the pretext of running an errand for Lady Lee, Jane extricated herself from the gaggle of ladies who still occupied their shared quarters and made her way to the corridor which led to the King's privy chamber. Once there, she secreted herself as best she could in a small alcove which had a convenient curtain for her to wait behind.

Time passed so slowly that Jane was beginning to think that she had made an error. Surely Cromwell should be taking his leave by now? Or perhaps he already had and even now the King was preparing to leave his chamber bound for some other appointment. She was on the point of leaving her hiding place when the privy chamber door opened and Cromwell backed obsequiously across the threshold. She could not hear what was said, but she did gauge from the King's tone of voice that he was in a reasonably good mood. Patiently she watched Cromwell until he was out of sight, then prepared herself for the next obstacle, the King's guard.

The guards were not yet aware of her presence because her alcove was conveniently out of their sight. However, if either of them was looking her way when she broke cover, there would be questions asked as to why she lurked as she did.

Flattening herself against the wall, she risked a glance in their direction; they appeared to be looking straight ahead so now was the moment. Silently she stepped into the passageway then walked slowly towards them, head held high. As she reached them, they blocked her access to the door and asked her what business she had with the King. In her haughtiest voice she informed them that she brought a message from the Queen and advised them not to hamper her on pain of the King's displeasure.

Without asking for further clarification, they opened the door and granted her access.

The King was standing beside a table looking at large roll of parchment. He did not look up immediately, only when he had finished reading. His surprise was evident when he saw who it was. "Jane! Do you bring a message from the Queen?"

With a hasty look over her shoulder at the closed door, Jane boldly approached him, curtsied, and said "Not as such Your Grace, although I am sure that if she knew I was here she would send you her greetings."

"Your mistress does not know that you contrive to be alone with her husband?"

Jane was all innocence. "I am not sure that I contrived this meeting as such, but I am off duty and this time is my own. I wanted to know how you were after your accident and the Queen's loss of your son."

Henry's face was solemn. "And you think it your place to simply arrive here to ask me that?"

"It is the duty of every one of the King's subjects to be concerned for Your Grace's health and well-being. However I wanted you to know that I am especially mindful of your troubles and I wanted to offer you what consolation I could."

The King's expression brightened immediately. "Is that so?" He replaced the parchment on the table and came towards her. "And what form will this consolation take? Tell me, I am all ears."

Jane looked up at him with her very best expression of innocence. "I am Your Grace's to command. I will go where I am needed."

As his affable smile was slowly replaced by a lecherous leer, Jane swallowed hard and smiled back tremulously. She did not need to pretend maidenly modesty for she was absolutely terrified of what was to come.

"Come then Jane." He took his feathered velvet cap from his head and threw it on to a chair before taking her hand. "I am in sore need of much consolation and I believe that your womanly wiles can restore me."

Slowly he drew her with him towards the bedchamber. After a moments hesitation she
followed his lead with downcast eyes and flushed cheeks.

It was not an experience she was ever likely to forget, she decided, as she left the chamber some time later under the knowing glances of the King's guard. And however much she envied the Queen her throne, her jewels and her status, she very definitely did not envy her marital duties.

Aware that her recent experience was most likely written all over her face and that her clothing was not in the required order for her royal duties, she sneaked back to her quarters by the most secluded route possible. Delighted to find the chamber deserted, she changed her crumpled gown, washed her face and brushed her hair. Peering into her tiny looking glass, the face which stared back at her was full of triumph. She, Jane Seymour, the mistress of a King! However much she wanted to hug that information to herself and revel in it, the time was approaching for her to present herself to the Queen. Wondering how she was going to explain away her sparkling eyes and high colour, she took as much time as she dared before approaching the Queen, hoping that a sedate pace and calm deep breathing could disguise her activities.

The Queen was being dressed for supper and looked upon Jane coldly. "You are late Mistress Seymour. What have you been about?"

"I have been sorting and tidying my possessions Your Grace. I apologise for my lateness, I forgot the time."

"It is a long time since I have seen anyone so flushed and excited as a result of such mundane activity."

The Queen spoke wryly, causing some of her ladies to titter.

Jane longed to reveal all and wipe the smile from Anne's face and met her gaze challengingly. Anne stared back; the Seymour was hard to read but she thought she detected something which had hitherto been missing. The girl had always been haughty and smug, but something out of the ordinary had taken place, she was sure of it. Anne blinked and looked away. If it was what she suspected, then all would become clear once the King joined them for the meal.

The King generally enjoyed his public supper but on this occasion he did not appear and sent a message to the Queen explaining that matters of state kept him occupied and he would eat privately in his chamber. It was not the first time this had happened so to Anne it was nothing out of the ordinary, but his non-appearance caused panic in Jane. What a fool she had been; she had submitted to the King and now he was not even going to bother to come down for a meal at which he knew she would be present. Now he had got what he wanted, was she surplus to requirements? Had she overplayed her hand and made a fatal mistake? Her head swam and her stomach churned. She had been a stupid, arrogant simpleton and once Edward and his supporters heard what she had done they would be furious.

Desperate for some guidance, she went to those chambers which Edward occupied when he was at court and found his wife at home. She and Jane were alike in many ways, both bossy, demanding and haughty. Each recognised the other for what she was and what existed between them was not exactly friendship, more a healthy respect.

As soon as she saw Jane approach, Anne Stanhope Seymour's face was agog with excitement. Taking hold of her sleeve, she all but dragged Jane to a quiet corner. "Tell me Jane, is it true." Her mouth was agape, waiting for the juicy gossip.

"Is what true?" Irritated, Jane smoothed her crumpled sleeve. "I know not what you mean."

"It is all over the court that you are the King's new mistress!"

It was Jane's turn for a gaping mouth. How could it possibly have got around the court so soon after the deed was done? She decided to brazen it out, just in case her sister in law was somewhat over egging the pudding.

"All over the court? Where did this rumour start?"

"You said it yourself, in a manner of speaking, after the Queen's childbed! Many heard you and it has been repeated everywhere."

Jane thought hard, what exactly had she said? She shrugged helplessly and gave her sister in law the full force of her most innocent expression. "I can only think that I made a comment which has somehow been misinterpreted" she said at last. "You know how easily gossip spreads in a place such as this. I had no idea that a casual comment I made weeks ago had sparked the rumour mill."

"Then it is not true?" Anne's face fell in disappointment. "I was hoping for some details."

Jane grimaced. "Details? I would never be so indelicate as to discuss such a private undertaking."

Anne sighed, and patted her shoulder consolingly. "Never mind then my dear. I should however say that I do know what is afoot. Edward has told me all."

"Really?" Jane looked unconvinced. Edward could keep secrets like no-one else and it seemed hardly possible that such a political animal would confide all in an acknowledged gossip such as his wife.

Anne smiled superciliously. "I do not allow him to keep secrets from me. To be a good wife, one needs to share one's husband's hopes and aspirations."

"Should I ever become a wife, I will remember that" Jane retorted. "Now, when is Edward next at court? I need to speak with him."

"I expect him late tomorrow. Is there perhaps a message I can give him?" The look of avid curiosity on the woman's face was almost comical, Jane thought.

"No message" she said airily. "He need only know that I wish to see him."

"Very well." Anne was visibly deflated. "But remember that if there is anything you wish to confide in me, I am a willing listener. Anything. Anything at all." She looked at Jane hopefully. "Remember I am a woman of the world and would be able to offer guidance in many matters."

"Thank you dear Anne, I am truly grateful." Jane took her leave, feeling she had managed a very narrow escape. If she had ever thought the Queen was able to see into her thoughts, then Anne Stanhope Seymour may quite possibly possess the gift to see into her soul.

Jane wished that she could make a friend and confidante of the woman, but with a tongue as loose as hers, no doubt all her business would be all over the court before an hour had passed.

Chapter Twenty-Two

The King did not appear at all the following day, seemingly closeted in his chambers with Cromwell and his minions. Jane had hoped for a summons from him, or at least a message asking how she fared, but the silence was absolute.
Desperate to talk to somebody, she called at Edward's chamber late in the evening, hoping that he would have arrived. When he opened the door, she all but fell into his arms.
"What is it sister" he questioned, pushing her none too gently away and standing her firmly on her feet. "Do you have news?"
Jane opened her mouth to reply, then wondered if other ears might be listening. "I need to speak to you alone" she confided. "Where is your wife?"
"You may speak freely, she is not here."

"Are you sure?" Jane pushed past Edward and glanced around the chamber. She would not put it past Anne to secrete herself somewhere, so desperate had she been to learn the nature of the conversation she wished to have with her brother.

"Quite sure." Edward looked at her quizzically. "Sister, are you quite well? You seem… out of sorts."

"As you would be had you spent much of yesterday afternoon in the King's bed!"

"So, the deed is done?"

"Oh yes" she replied bitterly. "Well and truly."

"It was not a pleasant experience?"

Jane was shocked. "I am not going to discuss such delicate matters with you, my own brother! But I confess, I am worried I have made a mistake."

"How so?"

"I had expected the King would at least contact me today, maybe even invite me to his chamber again, but I have heard nothing. Is it for me to approach him, do you think?"

"No! Do not on any account attempt to contrive a meeting. Remember, the King loves the chase. Rest assured he will be thinking of you, wondering if you felt he had measured up to your expectations. Remain aloof until he makes contact with you. He will, I guarantee it."

"How can you be so sure?"

"Because I have it on very good authority that the King has been closeted with Cromwell today not just on general matters of state, but more specifically on the subject of his marriage to the Queen."

"You think he means to remove her?"

Edward nodded. "That would be my guess, yes. But he needs to consider carefully how it will be done.

He all but tore the world apart to marry Anne Boleyn yet she is still widely regarded in Europe as merely a concubine. Now Catherine is dead, my thinking is that he will seek to annul the marriage so that he can make a new marriage which will be legitimate in all eyes."

"Does he have a bride in mind?"

"That is up to you." Edward took her firmly by the shoulders and gazed earnestly into her face. "Dynastically, no doubt a foreign princess would be good for the country, but the King needs to made aware that his people would desire a queen from amongst themselves, with good English blood. You need to put yourself forward with care and tact and remain demure and dignified at all times. As soon as the Queen learns what he is about, all hell will break loose. Remember what I told you before, always be a contrast to her. He finds her hysterical tempers hard to deal with and very taxing; let it be to you that he comes to be soothed."

"And by soothed, you mean …"

"Whatever it takes. On no account play the temptress, always maintain a virtuous hesitancy."

"Not so very easy when virtue has flown out of the window!"

"Always be ready to do his bidding and make sure you show due humility and gratitude for every attention he shows you. As you become closer, if necessary I can tutor you in what to say to make him think that he need look no further for a new wife."

Jane pulled at her lip thoughtfully. "It was all so easy thinking of marriage with him…before. Brother, I do not know that I have the stomach for it."

"You have come too far to turn back. He is on the hook which you have yourself baited. You cannot let him wriggle free at this late stage. Think of the family honour and reputation which our father ground so thoughtlessly into the dirt. You are in the position to restore us to glory. Many important people are relying on you to achieve what a few years ago would have seemed impossible. To prise the King away from the avowed love of his life and take her place."

Jane felt buoyed up by the power and passion of his speech. "You give me the courage to go forward, brother but I will need you close by my side if I am to achieve this."

"I can arrange to be around the court for the next few months. By then, we should have a good idea which way the events will turn. All you have to do is play sweet, innocent, demure and loving. Do you think you can do that?"

"If I have to" she sighed. "I wish I could find it in me to love him, but I confess I do not. The only thing about him I find remotely attractive is what he can do for me and our family. He is old, he is fat and his breath stinks but if he makes me Queen then I can keep up the pretence for ever if need be."

"Good." Edward nodded in satisfaction. Now you have aired your thoughts to me, never again voice any criticism of the King. Remember, walls have ears, particularly in a place like this where everyone is out for themselves."

"I will remember" Jane promised, before changing the subject. "Edward, when I spoke to your wife, she urged me to confide in her, saying that you had told her everything. Is that so."

"Did she by God" Edward laughed hollowly. "Dear sister, you know my wife as well as I do. Never entrust any confidential information to her because it will not remain confidential for long."

"Then she does not know the details of our plan?"

"Oh, she knows some of it" he admitted. "She has wheedled certain things out of me and I suppose you could say that she knows the gist of the plan. But I have impressed on her that should she leak anything in the wrong quarters, it will mean certain imprisonment and death for her. As a woman who has no wish to give up on life and the good things it offers I believe that she would not broadcast anything abroad. She wants to see the Seymour fortunes restored as much as any of us and she would not do anything to jeopardise that."

Over the following days, Jane's mind was put at rest by the way the King frequently singled her out for conversation and whenever possible, contrived to be alone with her so that he could kiss and caress her. What the Queen did not see was soon reported back to her and she knew that finally she needed to take Jane seriously. There was no doubt that she had a rival now.

Within a week of her and the King first becoming intimate, Jane found herself sharing a private supper with him in his bedchamber. Remembering her brother's words, Jane did all she could to charm the King and bolster an ego which seemed sorely in need of a little bolstering. She could not yet manage him the way the Queen could, but she had learned a lot from watching her.

When once more she found herself in the King's embrace she displayed just enough maidenly reticence to captivate him and more than enough humility and gratitude to beguile him.

"It is long since I have felt this close and comfortable with a woman" the King admitted to her later. "You soothe me like no other."

"I only wish to serve Your Grace" Jane replied primly.

"And it does not cause trouble between you and the Queen?"

Jane considered. "She behaves no differently towards me, yet she must be aware of the time I spend here with you."

"Indeed she is!" The door had opened so silently, neither had heard it. The Queen stood on the threshold, wearing a ravishing gown of midnight blue silk which Jane had not seen before. The colour greatly flattered the Queen's complexion and the sheen of the material brought out the highlights in the raven tresses which lay unbound across her shoulders.

After a sidelong glance at the King, Jane remained where she was, not rising to curtsey. He also remained in his seat gazing at the vision before him; it was many months since he had seen her looking so beautiful. Jane had been expecting him to rage, to tell the Queen to leave them in peace, but instead he got to his feet and moved slowly towards her, his velvet slippers making no sound, despite his pronounced limp. Jane felt as though she were watching a play as the two main characters faced each other. Instead of shouting and screaming at him, she smiled alluringly. Her eyes were warm and inviting as she moved closer and put her arms around his neck; Anne had very clearly come to get her man.

Jane did not know where to look; she could feel the flush of embarrassment spreading across her face, neck and chest. With an unladylike snort of outrage, she leaped to her feet, expecting one or other of them to turn to her. But they appeared to have forgotten she was even present. Boldly Jane approached the King and touched him on the arm. "Your Grace?"

He did turn to her then, but his eyes were glazed and it was clear that Anne had woven her magic once more.

"Good night Jane" he murmured. "If you would be so kind as to close the door on your way out…"

Jane did not just close the door, she slammed it as hard as she possibly could before stamping her way back to the maids quarters. Her mind was in turmoil; had he not been telling her how comfortable he felt with her, and how she soothed him? Then as soon as that temptress made her entrance, everything changed and she was dismissed as though she were nothing.

It was no good, she just could not compete with Anne. What man wanted to feel mere comfort with one woman when another offered him untold delights? As she passed the great hall, a man stepped from the shadows and grasped her wrist. With a howl of rage, Jane shook him off, before recognising one of her supporters, Sir Nicholas Carew.

"Where is the Queen?" he hissed urgently. "One minute she was here, the next she had vanished.

"She is with the King" Jane retorted bitterly. "Acting the seductress. One look at her and I was forgotten."

"Be of good cheer" he urged. "Matters are

proceeding apace and I guarantee that the siren will have few more opportunities to outshine you."

Jane was intrigued and moved closer. "What have you heard?"

"It is better that you remain ignorant. When the King acquaints you with the facts, your surprise will be genuine."

"But she will surely do all she can to hold on to her position. Having witnessed how easily she can charm the King, how will he be persuaded to give her up?"

"Cromwell is building a convincing case, and has been for some months. Even before the Queen miscarried he was compiling interviews and evidence against this day. He knows the King better than any man, and his position depends on him anticipating his desires. Fear not Mistress Seymour, the prize is within reach. Do not reproach the King for his inability to resist the Queen's wiles. Her foul temper is sure to resurface again soon so just continue to be the gentle soothing companion that you have been hitherto, and he will soon find his way back to you."

"I gather you spoke with Sir Nicholas?" Edward Seymour fell into step and walked alongside his sister as she trailed after the Queen in the privy garden a few days later.

"I did, and found him greatly reassuring. I was angry at being overlooked for the Queen and he helped me realise that the King is having just a momentary lapse. Once the Queen loses her sweet temper, he will soon call for me again."

"Indeed." Edward nodded wisely. "Sir Nicholas

gives good counsel, all that is needed from you is patience."

"I am becoming expert in the art of patience" Jane replied. "After all, time is on my side."

"When the King calls you back, I would advise that you refuse to dine alone with him unless you have a chaperone."

"For what purpose? Will that not destroy any amorous intentions?"

"Chaperones can be dismissed at any time. The important thing is to impress upon him that you do not intend to be regarded as merely a plaything. This will send a message both to him and the wider court that you have standards and that you intend to be taken seriously."

"Very well, if you think that is a wise move then of course I will comply."

"Choose a member of the family as chaperone" he advised. "I am sure my wife would be more than delighted to help."

Jane laughed. "It would surely be a most satisfactory arrangement for her!"

"You also need to drop certain things into your conversation with the King; for instance that his marriage is detested by the people and that many believe it is not lawful."

"But will he not think that I am merely out for my own ends?"

"Not if some of our supporters are present. Some of them are titled and extremely influential; their agreement will help to keep the seed of doubt in the King's mind active and flourishing.

"I will try" she told him. "Although up to now I have only seen him alone. Should I mention it when I next see him?"

Edward shook his head. "No, for the words to find their mark they need to be backed up by others whom he respects. Wait perhaps until the next court function; the King will surely select you for the dance. Our supporters can easily arrange to be close and will heartily agree with all you say."

Chapter Twenty-Three

Jane found it enormously difficult to ascertain exactly how much the Queen knew of her relationship with the King. She made absolutely no mention of the previous night whereas Jane expected a few acidic comments at the very least. The Queen seemed reassured by the ease with which she had edged Jane from the King's mind and confident that she had beaten back her rival.

Anne however was not as confident as she appeared. It would take more than a new dress and a practiced seduction technique to keep the King's eyes purely on her. She could not understand what it was about Jane Seymour which attracted the King. Such a pale, shrewish face and not a particularly comely figure to boot. Neither could it be her wit or sparkling conversation because she appeared to possess neither. Perhaps it was her virtue which was the challenge? None of her spies could tell her if the King had charmed her into his bed although Anne herself thought not. Why would she submit when she had Anne's example before her, showing that the way to reach the glittering prize was to hold back?

Jane was certainly spending plenty of time with the King because she was frequently missing from her duties, not that a lack of Jane bothered Anne, it was what the little minx was doing in her absences which concerned her the most. Of course she could complain to the King at Jane's absence and make a scene, but surely that would be playing into her rival's hands and Jane seemed to have the upper hand already without Anne assisting her in any way. Perhaps it was best to just watch and wait.

It had been some weeks since the King had been present at any of the post-supper entertainments, but as Edward confided to Jane, he would that evening.

"He has paid me little attention of late" Jane complained. "He waxes and wanes so, I never know where I am with him."

"He has a lot on his mind. Remember, if you should dance with him tonight, it will be the ideal opportunity to further damage the Queen in his eyes."

"If he dances with me at all! I am wondering if I was just a diversion to make the Queen jealous."

"Never think that. If he has been lacking in attention to you, it is just a device to throw the Queen off the scent."

"I haven't even had the chance to insist on a chaperone because I have not dined alone with him for weeks."

"When last did you share his bed?"

Jane flushed. "I do not know! I do not keep a tally. Two weeks, maybe three."

"Perhaps he fears discovery. Keep faith, let him set the pace without pressing your own agenda."

The King and Queen came in to supper together. After gallantly assisting her to her seat, the King remained standing for a moment, sweeping his eyes around the long tables. When at last he located Jane, seated with members of her family, he inclined his head regally before throwing himself into his own chair.

The Queen, ever watchful had followed his gaze, and her own hardened at the brief exchange between them. She wore yet another new gown, this time a vivid scarlet, with pearls at her ears, neck and in her hair. The moment the King sat down, she engaged him in conversation, attentively listening to his replies and striving to ensure his eye did not wander.

Jane was hungry, at least she thought that was the reason for the strange feeling in her stomach and the slight dizziness. However as soon as the dish of mutton was set before her swimming in its own grease the vague feeling of discomfort quickly became rising nausea. Hurriedly she rose from her bench and made her way quickly from the great hall, hoping no-one other than those seated close by had noticed her haste.

The King had, and the Queen also. "Mistress Seymour appears to have had something which disagrees with her" she commented lightly, shooting a sidelong glance at the King, who stared after Jane thoughtfully.

On her knees in the privy, Jane retched and vomited alternatively. Every time she pictured the plate of mutton, she retched again. Finally, when it seemed that she had vomited back every meal she had eaten for the past week, she got to her feet and leaned weakly against the wall. When her legs finally seemed ready to carry her, she made her way slowly to her quarters and after the briefest of preparations, fell into her bed. There she lay with her eyes closed waiting for sleep to come for she felt greatly fatigued. Suddenly instinct and realisation combined, causing her eyes to fly open. Her relationship with the King had begun, how many weeks ago? The exact duration escaped her but it had to be six or maybe even seven weeks. Her courses were overdue, and that was something which had never happened before. She could hardly dare admit it to herself, but it seemed that already she carried the King's child.

When the other maids came to their beds much later, they passed Jane's truckle bed and stared at her curiously. She was fast asleep, smiling contentedly with no trace of sickness about her.

She felt much better the following morning and prepared herself for duty in the Queen's chamber. Other than a very searching look when she appeared, Anne said nothing to her, although the other maids whispered incessantly with their hands held to their mouths. Jane, used to being left out of any confidences, ignored them all and set about doing what she had been directed to do.

As soon as she was able, she slipped away and made her way to the King's chamber. She didn't care who was with him or what he was doing, he had to be told her news.

The King was deep in conversation with Thomas Cromwell when she edged hesitantly into the chamber. He looked up, irritable at the intrusion, only to break in to a huge smile when he saw it was her. "Ah, Mistress Seymour. Come in, come in." He waved her closer. "Thomas, my good friend, Mistress Seymour no doubt brings me a message from the Queen. If you would be so kind as to return later, we will conclude our business then."

"But of course, Your Grace." Thomas Cromwell bowed low and rapidly made his exit.

"Now then Jane." Cromwell had barely closed the door before the King beckoned Jane to him. "What is it you want to tell me? You are not ill I hope? I saw your hasty exit last evening."

Jane had been wondering how best to break the news, turning different scenarios over and over in her mind. In the end, she decided to tell it simply and directly. "It is early yet, but I believe I am with child."

"Jane!" He caught hold of her, lifted her off her feet and swung her round in exultation. "How long before you are certain?"

She shook her head. "I don't know. This is all very new for me and I have confided in no-one but you. Perhaps another few weeks?"

"It is everything I had hoped for" he told her
earnestly. "For some time now I have been concerned about the validity of my marriage. I believe that the Queen and I have displeased God and that is why He has denied us children."

Jane thought of the Princess Elizabeth, robust and healthy, but kept her thoughts to herself.

"Your news has but reinforced my belief" he continued. "This is God's way of telling me that I must dissolve my present marriage and take a new wife. And if you truly carry our child, then it is surely God's will that I make you my Queen."

Jane was feeling sick and dizzy again, not just due to her condition, but because of the dazzling possibilities opening up to her.

"We must keep this between ourselves for now" he urged, placing a gentle hand on her stomach. "Everything must stay as normal as possible until we are sure of this child, then I can make my move. Until then it would be best if we do not see each other alone, but let me know as soon as you can if there is to be a child or not. Just a nod or shake of the head will suffice."

To carry on as normal was more easily said than done, especially under the watchful eye of the Queen. Anne noted that suddenly Jane was turning up each time she was due for duty, whereas in the previous month she had only appeared about twice a week. This she took to mean as a sign that the King had already tired of her and may be looking around for another lady to court. Feeling secure in her position for the first time in a very long while, she too began looking about, trying to locate the King's next likely quarry.

Jane was all but bursting with her secret. She desperately wanted to confide in someone, even her sister in law, but dare not. For the first time in many years, she wished that she was close to her mother.

She could have gone home to Wolf Hall and asked for her advice on how to be sure that a child was on the way. But since that was not an option she would just have to keep her own counsel and wait for her body to confirm her suspicions. She supposed that should she miss her March courses also, then that would be all the confirmation she needed.

She all but held her breath as the due date approached and then passed. Even so, she could scarcely believe it but by 31st March she was sure. As the King came into supper that evening, she caught his eye, smiled and nodded. She saw by his expression that he understood her and all around him must have been astounded by his unbridled joviality that night. She saw the Queen lean in and whisper something in his ear, and for answer he kissed her hand but said nothing. Jane had no notion what had passed between them, but for the rest of the evening the Queen was in a foul temper and shot both her husband and Jane many suspicious glances.

Chapter Twenty-Four

Things suddenly began to happen very fast. The King immediately wanted to resume their intimate uppers, so obedient to Edward's bidding, Jane suggested that to demonstrate she was no passing fancy but a treasured companion, a chaperone should be present. The King was a little taken back, but hastily agreed. Anything to keep her and that precious child in her womb happy. Anne Stanton Seymour was only too delighted to sit quietly in a corner whilst Jane and the King ate and talked, and obligingly melted away when the King motioned for her to leave.

At the next court entertainment, the Queen retired early in yet another fit of jealous pique, leaving the King free to dance with Jane as and when he wanted to. At the end of a pavane, whilst she and the King were standing amongst the other couples talking, Sir

Nicholas Carew contrived to stand within earshot. As Jane commented lightly to the King that she felt that the Queen had retired because she was becoming aware just how much she was disliked, Sir Nicholas broke in. "Indeed Your Grace, I was only in the streets today and heard the townspeople speaking against the Queen and questioning whether her marriage was even lawful since Queen Catherine had still been living at the time."

Normally any mention of his marriage, especially its lawfulness threw the King into a fearsome rage, but in response to Sir Nicholas he merely nodded thoughtfully. Jane caught Sir Nicholas's eye and saw his almost imperceptible nod of approval.

Apart from her increased social prominence, Jane saw other advantages to being the puppet of influential backers. In response to her casual complaint that her wardrobe was not extensive enough or grand enough to support her new eminence, there suddenly appeared enough splendid clothes and jewels to satisfy almost any woman's whim. With the gowns came a selection of the French hoods so beloved of the Queen. Determined to keep herself distinct, Jane sent them all back and demanded that the traditional English gable hood be supplied instead. Old-fashioned it may be, but it would ensure

she stood out in a crowd. Only the more ancient ladies of the court still wore the gable hood and they were generally not present during late night entertainments.

In order to accommodate her new wardrobe and burgeoning jewellery collection, the King arranged for Jane to have a suite of apartments of her very own. At the same time, she was relieved of her duties to the Queen as neither woman could bear to be in close proximity to the other.

She was only too pleased to be able to leave her shared quarters, having made no friends amongst the other maids. She was packing up what few possessions were left, watched by some of the junior maids when the King's messenger appeared on the threshold. He lingered there, looking uncomfortable at the thought of crossing into a female dormitory, and coughed loudly to attract Jane's attention.

As she turned her head and saw him, he gestured her closer. "Mistress Seymour" he began, "I bear a gift from the King." He then handed her a heavy purse and a letter.

Jane suspected that the purse was in payment for services so far rendered and the letter most likely made reference to the forthcoming child. As she and the King had been very careful to keep their public association within the accepted bounds of courtship, it was clear what the gaggle of observers believed the purse and the letter to represent. "The King wishes to persuade you to be his mistress" said one boldly. "The letter is the request, and the purse is payment."

Jane saw her opportunity to bolster her reputation as an honest and virtuous gentlewoman. Throwing the other maids a horrified look, she raised her hands to her face in apparent confusion. "This surely cannot be so" she exclaimed. "That I should be so compromised in front of witnesses!"

She kissed the letter then handed it back to the

messenger unopened, along with the purse. She then threw herself to her knees before him, causing him to step back in alarm. "Please thank the King for his generous gift and tell him that I have no greater riches in the world than my honour and I would not injure it for a thousand deaths. Tell the King that if he is disposed to make me a present of money, let it be when God enables me to make an honourable marriage."

The messenger nodded in confusion and walked quickly away, leaving Jane still on her knees and the other maids open-mouthed at her refusal of the King's apparent request. It was a master stroke, publicly executed. Jane had demonstrated to all present not only how virtuous she was but that she was hoping for a husband. In not opening the letter, she had saved her secret from potentially becoming public knowledge and maintained her assumed modesty.

Meanwhile the messenger found his steps slowing significantly as he approached the King's chamber; there was no doubt that he was going to be mightily displeased to receive Mistress Seymour's response.

The King was with his councillors but had requested that the messenger return immediately he had seen Mistress Seymour. As soon as he spotted the man hovering at the door, he strode quickly to him, his limp scarcely evident in his haste. "What news?" he barked. In answer, the messenger mutely held out the unopened letter and purse, which the King took, his disbelief plain. "What means this?" he demanded.

"Your Grace, the lady begs me to inform you that she has no greater riches than her honour and she would not injure it for a thousand deaths. And that if you wish to make her a present of money, let it be when she is to be wed." He cringed, expecting an outburst at the very least, a blow at worst. To his absolute surprise, the King grinned, pressed a coin into his palm and dismissed him.

Turning back into the room and rejoining his waiting councillors, the King tossed the purse carelessly on to the table and gestured with the letter. "Here it is gentlemen" he announced. "Proof positive that the lady is virtuous and humble and very much suited for the high position to which I seek to raise her."

The councillors exchanged looks between themselves, all wondering exactly how an unopened letter and full purse proved anything. The King intercepted their glances. "I see your confusion gentlemen. Shall I just say then that there are certain events known only to the lady and myself. Had she sought to deny her elevation, she would have taken the purse and quietly disappeared. Rejecting it proves that she stands with me on this matter."

The councillors were still none the wiser, but to avoid angering the King they nodded and smiled as though they completely understood.

As blustery March gave way to a mild and warm April, the King made sure to only be seen talking with Jane in public, although they continued to meet in his chambers late at night under the watchful eye of Anne Seymour. He had become increasingly anxious about Jane's health and one day suggested to Anne Seymour that he would prefer it if she and her husband would move into the rooms currently inhabited by Thomas Cromwell.

Cromwell's rooms were far grander than hers and Edward's so she was more than happy to agree without even asking to consult with her husband. "Will Master Cromwell not mind moving out in order to accommodate us?" she questioned.

"He'll go where I tell him to go" growled the King. "There is also another reason for my request; I will be able to meet Jane whenever I please without her having to be seen going in to my chambers. There is a secret passage which runs between those rooms and mine. No-one will question Jane's regular visits to her family and once inside, I can come to her or she to me."

Delighted to be privy to such information, Anne Seymour nodded her understanding. Jane's condition was still a secret, even from her family, and although his reasons for moving the Seymours into rooms adjoining his were exactly as he had told Anne Seymour, easier and more frequent access to Jane would allow him to keep an eye on the progress of the child.

As the King had predicted, Cromwell was happy to make way for the Seymours. So what if he had to walk a little further to meet with the King, that was more than made up for by not having the King appear suddenly in his rooms at all hours of the day and night.

After a few weeks of living in their new accommodation, Anne Seymour came to hold views similar to Cromwell's; it was disconcerting to have the King of England just appearing whenever he felt like it. Should Jane be delayed, which she often was, wanting to make sure that she looked her best, it fell to her to keep the King entertained and she found it difficult to know what to say to him. If Edward was there, then he took on that task, but all too often he was absent, leaving her to provide the necessary hospitality.

Once Jane arrived all was well, although she wished that the King would speak up a little when they were in conversation. Jane always said much the same things, but often the King would lean in and talk to her so earnestly that Anne longed to catch the gist of the conversation.

The King was aware of Anne Seymour's reputation and if Jane had any other female relatives at court, he would have pushed strongly for them to act as chaperone instead. But Jane's sisters were not at court and the only other close family member frequently present was her brother Thomas. However Thomas did not have a wife and looked in no hurry to acquire one.

The King's hushed tones were reserved for when he spoke to Jane about her condition, although he contrived to phrase it as though he were simply enquiring after her health. Jane generally told him she was well, and every time he met with her and she replied in that vein, he became more and more certain that she would be successful in bringing the pregnancy to term.

The Queen was now marginalised; all but her closest friends were flocking to pay court to Jane. Anne no longer dined in public but always in her chambers. She was becoming reclusive, expecting arrest at any moment and hoped that by keeping out of public gaze and not competing openly with Jane, she would buy herself enough time to think her way out of her predicament.

Meanwhile Jane was thoroughly throwing herself into her placid and demure persona, listening attentively to all that the King said whilst she sat primly in her chair, hands resting quietly in her lap; always the contrast to the Queen who never could resist airing her opinions.

During one such meeting, after she had listened patiently to all his problems and offered her own gentle solutions, he startled her by pulling her to her feet and asking her humbly if she would consider becoming his wife when he was free.

It was said loud enough for Anne Seymour to hear, whose needle remained poised in mid air whilst she kept her eyes downcast, desperately straining her ears for Jane's reply. "I would be honoured Your Grace" Jane whispered.

Anne Seymour resumed her needlework, a smile of satisfaction upon her face.

Chapter Twenty-Five

"I want it done now, Cromwell!" The King thumped on the table with his great fist, causing candlesticks to fall and parchments to roll.

"It must be done properly Your Grace. These things take a certain amount of time." Cromwell occupied himself righting candlesticks and gathering up the fallen papers.

"I do not have time."

Cromwell straightened abruptly and stared at his King. He was a perceptive man who knew the whims and desires of his master. "Mistress Seymour is with child?"

"She is. I want this child born in wedlock Thomas, I do not want any aspersions cast as to its legitimacy."

"May I ask when the child might be born?"

The King looked vague. "She thinks towards the end of the year, November maybe. But I want this business over and done with before her condition becomes common knowledge."

Cromwell grimaced. If Mistress Seymour was already approaching her third month, then he had very little time left to achieve the impossible. But then the impossible was his speciality; he had done it before and he could do it again. "Very well, Your Grace" he spoke slowly, choosing his words carefully. "I will expedite matters and will push for a conclusion over the next few weeks."

"Is the evidence against the Queen sufficiently compelling?"

"It will be, Your Grace. I guarantee that it will be."

The King was fractious and Jane was getting more anxious with every day which passed. It was so hard to keep that calm and placid exterior when inside she was screaming. Even though she was now set on a course which would change her life, she could not help thinking of those who had gone before her. Queen Catherine, a devoted wife for over twenty years, swept aside and left to die in exile. The present Queen, whom he had loved for over ten years, about to be toppled from her throne. How that might be achieved, Jane didn't particularly care, so long as it was done quickly and before her secret became known. But in a few years, might he be seeking to do the same to her if she couldn't birth a male heir? It was a sobering thought and one which she could not push from her brain no matter how hard she tried. It was all very well being the interloper but once one had taken centre stage there was no escaping the eventual fate. Produce a son, and all would be well. Fail, and the consequences did not bear thinking about.

Her growing feelings of unease were only enhanced when a few days after the King's proposal, they had their very first serious disagreement. Of course there had been minor squabbles in the past, but most had only flared up when Jane had forgotten herself and instead of meekly accepting the King's will had attempted to put forward her opinion. On each occasion she had realised her mistake and quickly backtracked, marvelling as the King became instantly calm once he was unchallenged. This latest discord was caused by Jane raising the subject of the Lady Mary. "Your Grace, with the Queen in virtual seclusion, might not now be a good time to welcome the Lady Mary back to court and make all right with her?"

She should have been alerted by his response, which was not to look at her or alter his expression. "Why would I do that?"

Encouraged, she went on. "Because all danger to her is past, the Queen's threats cannot hurt her now."

"The Queen's threats were never more than just words. Despite some reports that she wanted to have Mary poisoned, all she wanted in reality was to have her here and perhaps make a friend of her. But to do that, Mary had to accept that her mother's marriage to me was invalid because it contravened holy law, and that is something which she still refuses to agree to."

"I may be able to talk her round" Jane wheedled, as she moved closer, placing a gentle hand on his arm.

Angrily he shook her off. "Enough!" he barked.

"Mary knows what she has to do if she wants to be accepted back at court, but she continues to defy me.

You, Madam are a fool to think you have any chance in changing her mind. I would suggest that you save your efforts and instead solicit the advancement of any children we may have together." Abruptly he got to his feet and stamped away, leaving Jane quivering both with anger and fear. How dare he speak to her like that when she was only trying to bring father and daughter together. Did he hold her in such low regard that he thought any of her poor efforts would but fall on stony ground?

Then her anger was replaced by that tiny worm of fear which had been pushing itself forward so frequently of late. He was becoming more distant and short tempered with her as the weeks went on. Did he not love her at all then, and only waited for the child to be born? Looking around her, she caught others eyes on her and was sure that they were thinking similar thoughts. Poor plain little Jane Seymour believed she had the King's love, but already he was tired of her simpering ways and low wit. Needing some time alone to think, she retired to her own chambers, turning away the ministrations of her waiting woman.

She was still very much in the doldrums when a visitor was admitted. "Sir Nicholas!" Jane was surprised to see him. "To what do I owe this honour?"

For answer Nicholas Carew pulled a small parchment from his coat and waved it at her. "The King wishes me to take you from court and entertain you at my estate in Surrey."

"Is this it then?" she wondered aloud. "He wants no more of me and sends me from his sight?"

"No, no" Sir Nicholas came closer. "It is quite the opposite; he does not want you present at upcoming events. There will shortly be a number of arrests and subsequent trials; the King feels that you would be better off well away from here."

"Not perhaps then because our relationship has become common knowledge and whatever is to happen may be perceived as him simply clearing the way?" Jane was angry at the thought of being sent away and spoke sharply.

He looked shocked and put his finger to his lips. "Better not to speak of it" he advised. "Just make yourself ready. We leave within the hour."

Jane had no alternative but to do as she was told. It was but ten miles to Beddington Park but even so, dusk was falling by the time Carew Manor came into view. It was a graceful red brick mansion with turreted towers crowning either wing.

She had been there for less than two days when news was brought that Anne's musician Mark Smeaton had confessed to adultery with her. Jane could hardly believe her ears. "Mark Smeaton? She never paid him any special attention even though he fawned like a lapdog at her feet. I cannot imagine that she would so lower herself to consort with the likes of him."

"It is not for us to comment, but to accept" Sir Nicholas warned her.

"He was tortured?"

"Most cruelly."

"There then is the reason for the sudden confession. Is this how it is to be then? Forced confessions from minions who have no wealth or family to defend them?"

"There will be others" he admitted, "some of them gentlemen I'll be bound."

"So she is to be charged with plain adultery?"

"Adultery is never plain or straightforward when there is royalty involved. Imagine if there had been a son from a union outside of marriage, that child would have grown up to inherit the throne. She will be accused of high treason."

Jane looked sceptical. "I have no love for the Queen but even I can see that these charges are fabricated. And if I can see it, then so will everyone else. Surely members of her household will come forward to speak for her and say that she never had the opportunity to so deceive the King?"

"Not if they value their lives, especially as some of her ladies have already corroborated the charges."

"All this to get rid of one wife and to marry another." Jane shook her head and gathered her furs more closely around her. "It is so simple for him, isn't it? He loved that woman to distraction yet see how easily he turns on her and directs Cromwell to concoct charges against her. How long before that is me, Sir Nicholas? How many years will I be allowed. Two? Five?"

"You will succeed where she has failed" Sir Nicholas replied firmly as he leaned forward to throw more logs on the fire. "I beg you to keep all I have told you to yourself as it is not as yet common knowledge. It was told to me in confidence by someone who very probably should have kept his mouth shut."

"Very well. Just one more question, when will the Queen be arrested for her part?"

"I understand that it will be some time after the May Day tournament at Greenwich."

"Good." Jane smiled with satisfaction. "I only wish I could be there to witness it."

Later that night, when inky darkness blanketed the Beddington estate from curious eyes, a hooded figure was admitted to the manor. Jane looked up in alarm as the tall figure approached her, thinking it was some assassin sent by the Queen. But as the hood was pushed back, she saw with profound relief that it was the King himself. "Your Grace! Thank God!" She ran to him and threw herself at his feet, grasping his hand and kissing his glove fervently. "I have been so afraid. I thought you wanted me away from you for ever". Her beseeching eyes met his amused stare.

"And why would you think that Jane?" He was quickly divesting himself of his outer garments, anxious to sit with her by the fire and take refreshments. "Do you perhaps have something to hide which may prompt me to take such steps?" He was clearly teasing her, but Jane did not recognise the jest.

"Of course not" she retorted hotly. "But I was greatly distressed to be sent from the court without so much as a kindly word from you."

"Did Sir Nicholas not explain to you?" he flicked his eyes towards Sir Nicholas before draining the goblet and holding it out for a refill.

"Only that I had to be away during upcoming events."

He nodded. "And so you do. Fear not, it will not be for very long."

"What is going to happen?"

"There have been arrests, and there will be more arrests. Once the suspects have been interrogated it will be decided who will stand trial."

"And what of the Queen?"

"She is spending her last days as Queen, depend on it. But let us not speak of her." He leaned forward, took her hands and gazed earnestly into her face. "How are you? Are you keeping well?"

Sir Nicholas, looking on, noticed the King's intense expression and saw Jane's face flush as she considered her reply. As she guided the King's hand to rest gently on her stomach, Sir Nicholas turned away to hide his astonishment. The little minx was already with child!

"I am well Your Grace" she replied.

"Good. Good." Heaving himself to his feet, he began replacing his outer garments.

"You are going so soon?" Jane was dismayed at the briefness of their meeting.

"I have to. My men are waiting outside under the trees. We must not risk discovery. Farewell." He kissed her chastely on the cheek, nodded to Sir Nicholas, and took his leave.

When they were once more alone, Sir Nicholas stared at Jane speculatively.

"You play your cards close to your chest, Mistress Seymour. Despite being advised to keep yourself pure and hold out for marriage, you have somehow contrived to not only get yourself with child but also secure the King's promise. I am right, am I not?"

"Yes" she sighed. "You are right."

"It was a very brave move. Had you failed, this business would still be dragging on. Does Edward know?"

"He knows about my consorting with the King, but not about the child. I would appreciate it if that could remain so."

"Did you not think he would be dismayed to be so kept in the dark?"

Jane nodded. "He will be extremely angry and disappointed no doubt, but it is for the best. The fewer people that know the better; especially now with the Queen being somewhat hurriedly disposed of. You and I both know the reason; that this child may be born in legitimate wedlock, but it might harm the King's cause if the wider public knew he was devising charges against the Queen just so that may be achieved."

"So I not only have one charge but two" Sir Nicholas mused. "We must take very good care of you now."

Chapter Twenty-Six

"The Queen is arrested!" Sir Nicholas interrupted Jane's rest without compunction. "Also taken are her brother, Norris, Weston and Brereton. Wyatt was taken previously but has been released without charge."

Jane had been reclining on a day bed; now her condition was known to Sir Nicholas she could at last give in to her overwhelming fatigue. "Wyatt, released" she observed. "Cromwell has missed a trick there, of all people, he is the most likely to have cavorted with the Queen in their youth."

"He is much beloved of the King" Sir Nicholas replied. "Immediately on release he was sent on an errand abroad. It will all be over by the time he returns."

Who else did you say?" Jane raised herself up on her elbows.

"George Boleyn, Norris, Weston and Brereton."

"Well, well. Her brother and the King's closest friends. Whatever next."

"The trials are already being arranged. The Queen and her brother will be tried on the same day, the others the day before."

"Then I look forward to news of their condemnation." Jane laid herself back down and closed her eyes.

The Queen's alleged lovers were tried on May 14th and quickly found guilty of high treason, a crime which was punishable by death.

On the morning of May 15th, the day of the Queen's trial, Jane received a message from the King bidding her be of good cheer because she would be informed of the Queen's condemnation by 3 o'clock that afternoon. It was as Jane had suspected, the trial was merely a formality, the verdict had long ago been decided and lately confirmed by the condemnation of her supposed lovers.

Anne and her brother were duly brought before their peers and despite both speaking eloquently in their defence, were condemned to death. Sir Francis Bryan was dispatched to Beddington to convey the news to Jane. To hear that the Queen was to die gave her great satisfaction and she felt that at last Queen Catherine had been truly vindicated.

"You bear no sympathy for the Queen's fate?" After seeing Sir Francis out, Sir Nicholas had returned to Jane.

"None whatsoever" she confirmed. "I believe she has but reaped what she sowed. Never was a fate more deserved."

"I feel sorry for those condemned with her" Carew admitted. "Norris particularly for he is a fine and honourable man. I do not believe he ever committed wrongdoing in his entire life, and certainly not what he stands condemned for. He has always been deeply loyal to the Queen and now he will pay for that with his life."

"Worry not about them" Jane ordered. "We are on the brink of attaining all we ever wished for. Soon they will be disposed of and a new era will begin."

The King put it about that he was traumatised by the betrayal of his dearly loved wife and moved about in public with tortured expression and leaden footsteps. In private however, he was all joy and anticipation. At the same time, he ordered Sir Nicholas Carew to bring Jane a little closer to London. Beddington was too far for him to get to since the scandal had broken. Since Sir Nicholas now owned Thomas More's former home on the river at Chelsea, only a mile from Whitehall, that would be a more convenient meeting place.

Although Jane was glad at the prospect of being closer to the King, she complained at the inconvenience of being shuttled from property to property. "You know my condition Sir Nicholas" she whined. "Is it appropriate for me to sent hither and thither?"

"This will be your final move under my care" he promised. Your next move will be into the royal apartments. The King has directed me to request that you begin to make plans for your marriage."

The Queen's alleged lovers met their grisly fates on May 17th and later that day she was informed that her marriage had been annulled. Her own execution was fixed for May 19th. As Anne Boleyn made her peace with her Maker whilst she waited to be led out to the scaffold, Jane was finishing a leisurely breakfast ahead of an appointment with a gaggle of seamstresses. And as the Queen's bloody remains lay where they had fallen, watched over by her devoted ladies, Jane was holding huge swathes of fabric against herself and twirling in front of a looking glass, trying to decide which was the richest and therefore most suitable for her marriage ceremony. She spared not one single thought for her former mistress, only revelled in the fact that now nothing stood in her way.

As soon as the King had verbal confirmation that the execution had been carried out, he dressed himself in his finest clothes, entered his barge and hurried down river to Jane, anxious to bring her back to Hampton Court.

Jane was still with her seamstresses and clad only in her chemise. She squealed in surprise as the King entered the chamber unannounced.

"Your Grace! You catch me unawares!"

"So I see" he replied, his appreciation clear.

The seamstresses exchanged worried glances and then attempted to cover Jane modestly by draping fabric across her shoulders.

"No!" The King held up his hand, causing them to freeze like frightened rabbits. "Leave her as she is and go."

"Now Jane." Once they were alone, the King took her in his arms. "Tell me, is all well with my son?"

"I believe so Your Grace. Now the sickness is past, he causes me no bother."

"Then make the most of this quiet time because once he starts to kick, by God you will know that you are carrying a Tudor!"

"I long for him to kick" Jane confided. "I do not care what discomfort it causes, just to know that he is alive and healthy will outweigh any inconvenience."

"You are a born mother!" the King exclaimed.

Jane lowered her eyes modestly, not wanting to admit that she had not even the slightest maternal instinct and that her anxiety for the child was down to pure ambition to cement her place on the throne.

"You have chosen your wedding finery?" the King inclined his head towards the mass of materials and trimmings.

"Indeed. It is to be the brocade with the silver thread."

He nodded his approval. "A fine choice. Order it made up without delay for the ceremony will take place before the end of the month."

"The execution went as planned?"

"It did. I wonder you did not hear the tower guns?"

"I confess I did not. There has been much noise and merriment here today."

"I can imagine" he observed dryly, raking his gaze over the chaotic scene. "You will need to make preparations to move yourself and all this paraphernalia to Hampton Court as soon as possible. Our betrothal will take place there on the morrow."

Jane clapped her hands with glee, then before his horrified eyes, suddenly doubled up with pain.

"What is it?" He steered her carefully to a chair and knelt beside her, looking up into her face.

"Just a momentary pain" she told him, rubbing her right side gently. "I'm sure it was nothing, it has gone now."

"You must take care" he reminded her. "Perhaps you should see Sir Nicholas's physician, to make sure all is well?"

"No." She was very firm, causing him to get to his feet and glare down at her. "I do not want my condition known before we are wed. Besides, whatever it was passed in the blinking of an eye."

"This child's safety is paramount…"

"Yes, I know!" She jumped to her feet and faced him angrily. "Even as you speak of weddings and betrothals to me, it is clear where your real affections lie. Here." She struck her stomach as she spoke. "Do you even want me? Or just the contents of my womb?"

Henry was horrified. This harridan was not his gentle, placid Jane. He bit back an equally angry retort in consideration of both her condition and her recent discomfort. Surely her manner was purely down to concern for the child. He tried placating her. "You are worried for the child, of course you are" he soothed. "Take some rest now; you have had a busy morning and must be fatigued. I will return later this evening to escort you to Hampton Court."

She made no answer, simply glared at him. He kissed her hand hurriedly and made a hasty escape.

Jane scowled after him, rubbing absently at her side. If he was under the impression that she would agree to spending the rest of her life incubating his children, then he was much mistaken. If this child was a son, she would avoid his bed for as long as she could following the birth. With a prince in the nursery, he would never seek to displace her, so she could bestow her favours if and when she pleased. There would no longer be the need to play sweet, agreeable Jane, she could revert to being sly, spiteful, haughty Jane. As long as he had a healthy son, he would not care if she turned out to be the devil in disguise.

There was of course a chance that it would be a daughter, in which case she would have to keep up the pretence a little longer, but she was perfectly confident of producing a prince sooner or later. She came from a very fertile family; her mother had produced ten children with very little trouble although with child mortality being the way it was, nearly half of that brood did not see adulthood.

There was that pain again. Rubbing at it, she made her way towards the bed, climbed on and lay down. Perhaps she had tweaked something with all that twirling in front of the looking glass. She wondered idly if Anne's looking glass, which she had always so admired, would still be in the royal apartments. She must try to remember to ask about its whereabouts when she got to Hampton Court. As queen in waiting, surely it would now become hers. Holding that happy thought, she closed her eyes and immediately fell into a light doze.

Chapter Twenty-Seven

By supper time that evening she was dancing around the Queen's apartments in Hampton Court with sheer joy at what she had achieved and in so little time.

Her arrival at Hampton Court had caused quite a stir. No matter how hard the King had tried to keep their relationship quiet, it was clear by the curious crowds on the river bank that many were well aware that something was afoot. Although they had hated Anne Boleyn, the general populace was critical of her arrest and rapid execution and found the charges difficult to comprehend. Although the King had been careful to keep himself dour and miserable in public, the undoubted joy he was now exhibiting whilst riding up the river with Mistress Seymour told the people all they needed to know. He had done it again; removed one wife to make the way clear for another. He would not long remain unmarried.

She had already enquired as to the whereabouts of the looking glass and had been informed that all the late Queen's possessions were still in her chambers at Greenwich, apart from those items she had gifted to her loyal friends.

Jane insisted that even if the looking glass had been gifted, it had to be returned because it was clearly designed for the use of royal personages. The lord chamberlain baulked a little at her demands, telling her that the late Queen had every right to disperse her belongings where and to whom she liked. He did not personally know what had become of that item, it may well still be in the royal apartments and he would make the necessary enquiries.

Jane thanked him airily and dismissed him with a wave of her hand. Astonished at the high-handed behaviour of a former maid of honour who was not yet raised to the position she so clearly coveted, the lord chamberlain bowed politely and made a dignified exit.

As she was making preparations to retire for the night, the King appeared with much ceremony, clad in his nightshirt and gown. It appeared that he had every intention of spending the night with her. Jane however was not disposed to company, especially as she was not even betrothed, let alone wed.

Sweetly she asked him, as a special favour to her, if he would desist from coming to her chambers so dressed until after the marriage ceremony as she wished to keep her reputation intact.

The King's expression darkened momentarily as he was not used to being denied. Keeping her sweet smile, Jane placed her hand to her side and winced a little. She had no pain, but he was not to know that. Immediately he was all tenderness and concern.

"You must endeavour to get a good night's rest" he urged. "I am sorry to have disturbed you at this late hour, but I thought you may be in need of comfort. As it is, I see that all you require is peace and quiet. Our betrothal ceremony will be at nine o'clock tomorrow morning and I trust you will be fit and able to attend."

"I am sure I will." Jane curtseyed with the utmost respect and then stood patiently waiting for him to take his leave. "I will see Your Grace in the morning" she reminded him when he failed to make any move. Despite his apparent concern, he was clearly annoyed at being refused. After another moment's hesitation, he shuffled away without further comment.

Jane sighed theatrically then waved her ladies back and indicated that they should finish helping her prepare for bed. As Jane's own household was yet to be assembled, she had been assigned those women from the former Queen's dismantled household who did not mind where they served. Many of Anne's ladies had been close and valued friends and they had made it clear that they did not wish for a place with the new Queen. Jane was piqued by this. They had all treated her disdainfully during her time in service and she had been looking forward to getting a little of her own back. She would particularly have liked to have had Lady Lee in her employ, but Meg had gone back to her family and let it be known that she no longer wished to serve in the royal household. Despite the luxuriousness of her bed and surroundings, Jane found it difficult to sleep that night. Her mood ranged from confidence to uncertainty and instead of being able to take joy from where she found herself, her heart fluttered like a captured butterfly.

Consequently, she was not at her best the following morning and took no pleasure from the fine clothes in which she was dressed for the betrothal ceremony. Before meeting the King in the chapel, she sent once again for the lord chamberlain to ask about the result of his enquiries regarding the looking glass.

"Madam, I have just received word that the item you seek remains in the Queen's apartments at Greenwich. I have given orders that it is not to be removed under any circumstances." If he thought that would satisfy her, he was to be disappointed.

"Good." She tweaked at her gable hood one more time, then turned to him. "Kindly ensure that it is brought here without delay. I do not want it left at Greenwich, I want it here. Today."

Used to dealing with the King's sometimes unreasonable demands, the lord chamberlain was able to mask his annoyance. If she had but said last evening that she wanted it brought, then it would have been brought. As it was he now had to dispatch another messenger to pack the glass carefully and bring it to Hampton Court. "Of course Madam, I will personally ensure that you have it here before supper."

"No, you will have it here by this afternoon or the King will hear of your tardiness." Jane folded her arms and fixed him with an uncompromising stare.
"I will do my best Madam."
"Let us hope then that your best is sufficient. Do not fail me in this, I warn you."
"Madam." He bowed and took his leave, slightly affronted by her manner. The former Queen might not have been always easy to serve, but at least she had always been unfailingly polite to him and understood that everything took a certain amount of time to achieve. Not so with Mistress Seymour it seemed.
Jane walked to the chapel with the utmost dignity, attended by eight ladies. As the chapel doors were thrown open for her entry, the King, dressed all in white turned with evident delight to see her process towards him. Cranmer was to officiate and also present were her father and two brothers, plus about a dozen of the King's gentlemen. As she reached her family, she paused and smiled condescendingly as all three stepped forward and one at a time, kissed her on the cheek. After they had stepped back to their places, she remained in front of them, believing they had disrespected her new status. "I think you will find that it is now appropriate that you bow in my presence" she told them sternly. After exchanging glances, the three bowed in perfect unison as she, with a self-satisfied smile walked on to join the King. Taking her hand, the King led her forward to stand in front of Cranmer.
First, he blessed them, then began the ceremony.
"You have contracted to marry" he droned "and

stand here today to fulfil the first part of that contract to betroth yourselves one to the other. Do you both consent to proceed?"

Jane opened her mouth to reply but was thwarted by the King's quick response. "We do" he said.

Jane flushed, annoyed that she was not allowed to speak for herself.

Cranmer continued. "A betrothal is a promise to marry but in certain circumstances can be broken if one party is proved to be guilty of heresy, infidelity, enmity, wickedness or drunkenness. Or if either party is proven to be already married or has an existing contract to marry. Now, please join hands."

They turned to face each other and took each other's hands as Cranmer produced a heavy gold ring encrusted with rubies and emeralds. Placing it on a red velvet cushion, he offered it to the King, who after kissing it, placed it on the third finger of Jane's right hand, before pulling her towards him and kissing her on the mouth.

Cranmer beamed. "You are now betrothed, one to the other" he confirmed. "All that is required now are your signatures." He gestured to a side table, upon which rested a large sheet of parchment.

Henry scrawled his signature quickly and efficiently, whilst Jane took a little longer to form her letters. As she laid down the quill, the witnesses broke into a polite round of applause as she and the King exited the chapel and continued on to the King's privy chamber where refreshments awaited.

As Jane stood with the King, receiving the congratulations of all, her brother Edward motioned her to one side. Seeing the King was deep in conversation with her father, Jane joined him. "You have done well sister" he told her approvingly. "You have achieved all we ever dreamed for you. Now the next part of your task begins, to sweep away this hated reformed church and bring the King back to the true faith."

"Can I not have a moment just to enjoy my new position?" she replied peevishly. "Of course, I desire a return to the true church but if you think you are going to order around Jane the Queen in the same manner as you have Jane the sister, you can think again. I am not beholden to you for the position I now find myself in, I have achieved this myself and by my own ends. I would thank you to not only remember that but in future to be aware of to whom you speak. I will be your Queen and I thank you to treat me as one. I am no longer your sister, I have risen far above you and my humble origins and in future you will only address me by my royal title. Is that understood?"

"Perfectly." Edward made a mocking bow and turned to join his brother.

As Jane returned to the King's side, he turned to her. "Your father suggests that we spend a few days at Wolf Hall before the wedding. He wants to host a huge prenuptial feast for all your friends and neighbours. What think you?"

The last thing Jane really wanted was to ride all the way back to Wiltshire, but the King seemed so enthusiastic and it would be a wonderful opportunity for her to show off to all those who had predicted that she would never make anything of herself and would die a sad and lonely spinster. "I would like that" she replied, injecting as much enthusiasm into her voice as she could muster.

"Good." The King clashed goblets with John Seymour to seal the arrangement.

"How many guests would we expect?" she asked her father.

"Everyone within a fifty-mile radius will want an invitation; I would think upwards of five hundred might attend."

"And where exactly would you seat five hundred revellers? Surely the largest chamber within Wolf Hall is the great hall and you would struggle to seat even half that amount in there."

"I have already thought of that" he beamed. "You remember the thatched barn? It is three times the size of our great hall. Everyone could be comfortably accommodated in there."

Jane threw a quick glance at the King before replying scornfully. "The barn? You expect the King of England and his soon to be Queen to attend a banquet in a barn?"

"I think it an excellent idea" the King broke in. "I am assured it is a very pleasant barn and could be made quite comfortable with the addition of hangings and banners."

Jane looked unconvinced. "I do not think it fitting" she replied haughtily.

"But it is sweetheart" the King urged. "It is entirely fitting that you, a daughter of country gentry should celebrate in a farm building in the time-honoured way with your friends and neighbours. It makes no difference who your groom is, king or commoner, it is about tradition."

"Tradition? Who wants to celebrate in a building meant for animals and fodder. Can it not be hosted on a neighbouring estate? Tottenham perhaps?"

"It is appropriate that it be celebrated on your family estate and that is where it will be held." The King had tired of debate and wanted to reward his old friend John Seymour as well as uphold country tradition.

Jane sighed impatiently. "Very well then, Wolf Hall it is."

Chapter Twenty-Eight

As soon as was possible, Jane made her excuses to the King and sauntered back to her apartments. She felt sure the much-coveted looking glass would be waiting for her in her bedchamber.

It was not. Angry at what she perceived as a slight, she called in one of her waiting women and sent them to find the lord chamberlain and bring him to her. He was not to be found immediately and more than half an hour had passed before he presented himself before her, bowing stiffly.

"Do you have no care at all for my orders?" she raged. "I specifically told you that I wanted that looking glass here as soon as possible, yet it is not."

The lord chamberlain, not accustomed to being summoned and scolded over female fripperies, drew himself up to his full height. "If you remember,

Madam, you requested that the item be here by afternoon. To my certain knowledge it is still well short of noon and whilst you can be assured that the item is, or soon will be, in transit, I cannot comment on the favourableness of the tide to speed its delivery."

Jane pursed her lips and huffed. "I expect you to treat my requests with the same urgency as you would the King's. I gave you the order more than two hours ago!"

"With the greatest respect Madam, it should be remembered that Greenwich lies fifteen miles upriver. It will take the boatman more than two hours just to get to the palace. Then there will the time it takes to carefully pack the item. As you are aware glass is fragile and needs careful transporting. Add on to that the time for the return journey, and I think you will find that my estimate of a supper time arrival is quite accurate."

Jane stamped her foot childishly. "Then why did you not make that clear when I saw you earlier this morning?"

"Because Madam you seemed overwrought, and I thought it better not disappoint your expectations ahead of your betrothal ceremony."

"Overwrought? How dare you seek to pass judgement on my well-being. I have a good mind to speak to the King about your high-handed manner towards me and recommend that he remove you from your post."

"As you please, Madam. However, the King will understand that I am not in the position to work miracles; he will be aware how long it takes to travel from palace to palace and will be able to set your mind at rest that I have not in any way disrespected your position or the order you gave me. I dispatched a messenger within minutes of leaving your presence and the looking glass will be here as soon as is humanly possible."

In the face of such calm logic, Jane could not think of a suitably cutting retort, so contented herself with a haughty stare and a wave of dismissal.

It did arrive by supper time and Jane was so delighted with it that she would have preferred to remain in her bedchamber admiring it rather than go to the King's privy chamber to eat. But he was expecting her and became impatient if his food was delayed so she had no option but to join him.

He seemed in a very good mood, so she decided to casually test the truth of the lord chamberlain's statements. "Your Grace, how far would you say we are from Greenwich?"

"Greenwich?" he turned to her in surprise. "Why would you want to know that?"

"Oh. Just a minor disagreement with the lord chamberlain" she said spitefully. "I wanted an item brought from Greenwich to here, and he said that it was a very long way and would take hours."

The King nodded as he stuffed a large chunk of roast beef into his mouth. "He spoke truth. It is more than fifteen miles as the crow flies. One could ride there in quick time, but by river it would be longer, how much would depend both on the boat and the strength and stamina of the boatman."

"Then it could not be achieved in perhaps three hours?"

"Three hours?" He began coughing hard, having swallowed the beef before it had been sufficiently chewed. "I should think not. Whoever suggested such a thing?"

"Oh, no-one Your Grace" she said quickly. "I was just musing, that is all. I had not realised that Hampton Court was quite so far from London."

"It is, and that is the beauty of it." He took a large gulp from his over-sized goblet and wiped away the droplets that lodged in his beard with his sleeve. The disagreement you mentioned with the lord chamberlain, was it about the duration of the journey?"

"Indeed" she nodded her head regretfully. "I am afraid that as a mere woman I had no notion of the distances involved."

He laughed and patted her arm patronisingly. "Then perhaps it is better if you concentrate on your own little matter rather than bother your head with subjects beyond your comprehension." He gestured towards her lower body with his head as he spoke.

Jane flashed him a bright smile which became a scowl as soon as he turned back to his food. How dare he be so condescending and treat her as though she had no brain in her head.

They took their time on the road to Wiltshire, riding at an unhurried pace and making several overnight stops on the way. As they passed through the various towns and villages, many of the inhabitants came out to cheer their King and look curiously at the woman he would shortly make his Queen. Jane did not deign to remove her hands from the reins to wave at them as the King did, she merely inclined her head regally when she deemed it appropriate.

As they had on the last visit, her parents again stood together in the courtyard awaiting the royal party. Jane felt a surge of pride as she approached them with the King; no lowly maid of honour this time but a Queen in waiting. If she was expecting any change in their welcome due to her elevated status then she was to be disappointed. Her father greeted her with a kiss on both cheeks whilst her mother managed a weak smile and a brief hug. Neither of them showed the deference Jane had expected, but she decided not to make anything of it on this occasion.

Looking across the high wall to the farmyard, Jane could see the uneven roof of the thatched barn and wondered, not for the first time, how on earth it could be made into a banqueting hall fit for royalty. Her mother intercepted her glance and read her thoughts. "All will be well Jane, do not worry."

On the following day at the appointed hour, the several hundred guests arrived at Wolf Hall and were escorted to their seats at the long tables in the barn. When all expected had arrived, the King was notified that it was time for he and Jane to make their entrance.

Clad in her finest gown, Jane was relieved that her train would not have to drag across the mud and muck of the farmyard as a thick layer of clean straw had been laid down to form a wide path. All three sets of double doors stood open and from inside came the hubbub of conversation and music. Flags and streamers adorned the roof and fluttered gaily in the strong breeze which happily diverted attention from the giant muck piles which stood at either end of the building.

Trumpeters heralded their approach and all fell quiet within, as heads and necks craned for the best view of the royal couple. Entering through the largest set of doors on the far right, the King proudly led Jane the length of the entire barn to receive the congratulations and approbations of all present, whilst the musicians played music composed by the King himself. There was clapping and cheering from all present which did not cease until Jane and the King had taken their own seats at the top table with her family.

Jane looked around the old barn in wonderment. It had truly been transformed. The roof had been swept free of cobwebs and the detritus of many years and was decorated with bunting and streamers. All around the walls were beautiful hangings depicting scenes from both the bible and ancient mythology. It was not possible to see the old scarred wooden walls at all, everywhere there was sumptuousness. The floor had been cleaned and levelled and was scattered with many rich rugs, making it soft and warm underfoot. There was plenty of natural light due to the huge doors, but in case the festivities lasted on into the night, freestanding torches stood ready for lighting.

Jane's father had been watching her appraise her surroundings and leaned across to her. "I trust you are favourably impressed?"

"Indeed yes!" Jane was unusually animated. "I had doubted that this place would ever be suitable for such an occasion and I am happy to be proved wrong!"

"It has taken the servants many days of hard and dirty work" he told her. "But they have done you proud and are pleased to welcome you here as a future Queen."

Jane doubted very much that any of the servants would be falling over themselves to welcome her back as anything, but she could appreciate the effort it had taken. "Where have all the hangings come from?" she enquired.

"Some are ours, the rest have been loaned by our wealthier friends and neighbours. This has been a joint effort by the whole county. We are all hugely proud that you, a simple country girl, have been raised to the highest estate in the land."

The merriment lasted long into the night; there was course after course of the finest foods interspersed with entertainment from jugglers and acrobats and performances from accomplished solo musicians. The King was in his element, enjoying the lavish hospitality of the Seymours and their friends. He could have continued until daybreak, but beside him Jane was yawning discreetly and he did not want her to become overtired. Getting to his feet, he made a short, impassioned speech about the love he held for everyone present and his gratitude towards all who provided the wonderful banquet and entertainments. Finally, he persuaded Jane to her feet and presented her to one and all as their future Queen.

Chapter Twenty-Nine

Jane was not only tired, she was irritable. She had smiled until her face hurt at all manner of neighbours and acquaintances who had been reluctant to even give her the time of day when she was but plain Mistress Jane Seymour. It made her sick to her stomach to see the way they were prepared to fawn over her and compliment her now, no doubt hoping that she would recommend them to the King.
Exhausted, she turned towards her bed only to be distracted by a brisk knock at the door. Motioning to her ladies to step into the next chamber and give her privacy, she wrapped a night gown around her shoulders and opened the door herself.
The King stood on the threshold, beaming and dressed in his night attire. She could gauge his
intentions but pretended to misunderstand. "How kind of you to come down and bid me good night" she told him.

"Not only that" he told her jovially. "I come to spend the night with you."

Her look of horror had him open-mouthed. "It is unthinkable that you should seek to share my bed in my father's house!" she exclaimed. "It would not be seemly to be seen to condone the pleasures of the flesh before the marriage ceremony. Do you not consider my reputation at all?"

Henry had heard those excuses before. His expression darkened and his eyes narrowed. "I am becoming tired at your constant refusals of my company Madam. You seem all too keen to enjoy the advantages I can give you but strangely reluctant to bring yourself to offer me any nightly comfort. I do not forget how amiable and generous you were at the start of our relationship and it is clear that now you have my promise and my child you wish for no more of me."

"That is not true!" Jane quickly grasped his hand, fell to her knees and kissed it reverently. "Dearest lord, I do not seek to reject you, only to maintain my maidenly reputation until the marriage day. I could not in all conscience share a bed with you under my father's roof outside of marriage. Please tell me you understand?" She waited, eyes downcast, heart beating so hard she feared he could hear it.

"No, I do not understand" he said peevishly. "Your family know I intend to marry you and it is of little consequence to them whether I share your bed here or elsewhere. I am the King and therefore I do what I want, when I want, and I will have no one tell me nay."

Jane had not expected that response and did not know what to say next. She remained where she was, head bowed.

"Very well" he said at last. "Keep to your maidenly bed if you must but I will expect a change in attitude from you once we are wed."

In answer, she kissed his hand once more and got slowly to her feet. "Thank you, Your Grace," she said meekly, then slowly closed the door in his face.

Jane had not expected him to take her refusal too much to heart but it was clear at breakfast the following morning that he still held a grudge. His morning greeting was perfunctory and he did not look her in the face once. Whilst he chatted amiably enough with her family, he kept his back deliberately turned to her and quashed any attempts she made to join in the conversation. Jane decided to ignore his bad manners and sat quietly with her food. At the end of the meal, he rose and left the chamber with Sir John, again not bothering to say anything to her.

"You have had a disagreement" her mother observed when the two men were out of sight.

"How very perceptive of you mother." Jane adopted her most sarcastic tone in the hope it would prevent her mother from probing further, but Lady Margery was well used to such retorts.

"Is it anything I could help you with?" she persisted. "I am many years married and well used to being cut from the conversation over some trifling disagreement."

"You have not been married to a King though, have you. Let me assure you, I am walking a far more dangerous path. After all, father may have his faults, but he is not likely to have you executed on a whim."

Lady Margery was horrified. "It was that serious?"

Jane tried to backtrack, "No, not really. It was nothing and I am no doubt being over dramatic with talk of execution."

"Come." Lady Margery rose from her seat and held out her hand. "We shall go somewhere we can talk undisturbed."

Jane was directed to the window seat in her mother's solar. As Lady Margery took a seat opposite her, Jane said airily "I feel as though I am about to be interrogated!"

"Don't be silly child." Lady Margery's gaze was piercing. "I do not need to interrogate you, everything is there in your face for me to read."

"Oh yes?" Jane raised her chin a fraction and stared back. "And what do you see?"

"I see an unhappy, frightened young woman who wonders if she can fill the shoes of her predecessors."

Jane was taken aback. "I am perfectly confident I can be a far better wife and Queen than Anne Boleyn. Queen Catherine has left bigger shoes to fill, I grant you. But I am not unhappy, quite the contrary."

"And frightened?"

Jane opened her mouth to brazen it out, then realised that it was fruitless to lie. "A little" she admitted. "It is a lot to take on and I am only too well aware of the price of failure."

"When is the child due?"

"Who told you?" Jane burst out. "It is supposed to be a secret until after the marriage ceremony!"

"No-one needed to tell me child, it is there, in your face."

"That is ridiculous. You have lived in the country for too long mother, your wits are becoming addled."

"But I am right, am I not? And yes, I admit I have absorbed some country lore over the years, as would anybody. You cannot keep a secret like that from country folk, I wager most of the women in that barn last night guessed your condition."

"Then it is not a secret any more, is it." Jane crossed her arms and glared at her mother.

"Everyone who guessed would have been happy for you. You will be married in a few days and no doubt the pregnancy will start to show soon anyway. A child cannot be kept a secret for long, daughter."

"I suppose not." Jane relaxed a little and turned her head towards the window at the sound of galloping horses. She saw it was the King and some of his gentlemen, off on a hunting expedition no doubt, with no word to her or enquiry for her health.

"Do not worry" her mother soothed. "He will soon come round. There is nothing like a few hours in the saddle to lift the spirits. And he will not wish to prolong any bad feeling between you, not in your condition."

Jane's expression was sceptical. "He was most unpleasant last night" she confided. "He came to my room expecting to share my bed and I turned him away."

"Why did you do that? Your father and I would not have thought any less of you, not with the marriage imminent."

"Because I wanted peace" Jane explained. "Once we are married, I will not be able to sleep alone very often. Quite apart from his demands, which can be excessive, he takes up most of the bed, he snores and he sweats profusely."

"He is a man, Jane. And like all men, he can be

managed."

"Like you managed father over his affair with Edward's wife?" Jane sneered.

"That was a low blow Jane" her mother complained. "And one cannot manage a matter which one does not know about until after the fact." Lady Margery's distress was evident and Jane felt herself slightly ashamed at reminding her of it.

"I apologise mother, it was unfair to bring that up."

"It is of no matter" her mother leaned forward and patted her hand. "It is long over and poor Catherine has been in her grave these many months."

"So you forgive her?"

"Of course. She was never a threat to me and she is certainly no threat now. I refuse to let your father's foolish behaviour blight the rest of my life." Despite her bright tone, Lady Margery then fell silent and was clearly dwelling on unhappy memories. Then just as suddenly, she brightened once more. "Let us talk of happier matters. When will the child be born?"

Jane screwed up her face. "I confess I am not sure, but I think sometime in November."

"The King has not ordered you to see a physician?"

"No, he supported my wish that it be kept purely between us. Sir Nicholas guessed a few days ago, and if you are to be believed, half of Wiltshire also!"

"Oh, do not worry, by the time any news filters out from here, you will be married and your condition will be common knowledge." Lady Margery was quick with her reassurances. "You are keeping well?"

Jane tilted her head, considering. "I believe so. There was the sickness of course, in the early weeks, other than that, just the odd little twinge here and there."

"You have pain?" Lay Margery's concern was clear.

"Just here." Jane put her hand to her side. "But only sometimes, and it soon passes. But it is normal, yes? You must have experienced something similar?"

Her mother shook her head. "Not that I remember, and certainly not so early on. Later though, when the child is large there can be some discomfort and many a disturbed night."

"Oh." Jane looked down at her stomach and rubbed it gently. "Perhaps I should take extra care and see the King's physician if the pain returns."

Her mother nodded approvingly. "Yes, I think that would be advisable."

Lady Margery was correct in her assumptions regarding the King's mood. He arrived for an early supper in extremely high spirits, pulling Jane to him and kissing her soundly before he took his seat at the table.

"Was the sport to your liking?" she enquired, making no mention of his earlier sour mood.

"Indeed it was!" he exclaimed. "I had great success and I warrant that this house will remain well stocked with venison for many days to come."

"Congratulations Your Grace. Your horsemanship and marksmanship are second to none."

"Why thank you Jane." He caught hold of her hand and kissed it gallantly. "You pay a pretty compliment."

"Only where it is deserved Your Grace."

Seated close by, Lady Margery heard their conversation and was impressed by Jane's easy flattery. Whilst it might have sounded sincere to the King, she knew Jane well and immediately became aware of the underlying sarcasm. But it was the King's opinion which mattered, and for the moment it was clear that all was well between them once more.

Chapter Thirty

The royal party arrived back in London on May 29th and on the following day Jane and Henry were married quietly in the Queen's Closet at Whitehall; the transfer of the betrothal ring from Jane's right hand to her left hand sealing the marriage contract. There were few witnesses because the King had deliberately kept the exact time and place of the ceremony secret.

Jane was a little disappointed that she could not enjoy a public ceremony and impress a wider audience with her elegant wedding finery but understood that with the previous Queen so recently dead, discretion was needed to avoid any criticism being directed at the King for his haste in remarrying.

She was however delighted at the amount of property settled upon her on her marriage day. She was now an extremely wealthy woman in her own right, far more so than even her father had ever been. Jane determined to keep a close eye on her new assets and looked forward to exercising her talent for management.

After the ceremony was concluded, and before the party moved on to the great hall for the wedding feast, the King presented Jane with a magnificent emerald and pearl pendant to mark the occasion. It had been designed by Holbein, who had the same talent for design as he had for portrait painting. Jane was delighted with it and lifted her veil so that the King could fasten it around her neck.

"Not like the last pendant I gifted you, eh?" he whispered. "This one you can wear proudly whenever you please."

Jane smiled, thinking back to that other pendant, which now resided amongst her other jewels; what a furore that had caused. She had never seen the former Queen quite that angry before.

As she and the King processed grandly to the great hall amid the bows and cheers of the household Jane believed that life really could not be better. She had gained the highest status possible, had access to untold riches and carried the King's child. All that achieved in a few short months by a presumed nonentity from the wilds of Wiltshire. All those who had doubted her or crossed her in the past had better take care. She had power now, and she intended to use it.

As she took her seat at the top table, she felt a stabbing pain run along her abdomen. Knowing all eyes were upon her, she kept smiling and acknowledging the congratulations of those around her all the while breathing deeply and slowly in an effort to control the pain. Gradually it lessened and she began to relax and enjoy the feast, only to be struck with nausea at the sight of the candied fruits which were put before her. She began to feel light headed, the King's pendant around her neck seemed unbearably heavy, almost as though it were dragging her down into untold murky depths. Agitatedly she snatched at her goblet and hastily drained the contents in an effort to regain her senses. The King glimpsed her sudden movement from the corner of his eye and turned to her in concern. "Is all well sweetheart?"

In response, she shook her head and her eyes filled with tears.

"What is it, what ails you?" He put his arm around her shoulders and tilted her face so that he could see it. "Are you unwell? Is it…?" He left the sentence unfinished, as those around them had noticed something was amiss and were watching them with interest.

"I do not know what it is for sure" she whispered. "I feel nauseous and I have pains. Perhaps it is just the excitement of the day."

He looked sceptical. "Possibly. As soon as you get back to your bedchamber I will send Doctor Wendy to you. He will be able to set your mind at rest I am sure."

"But he will have to be told about …"

"Yes, he will. But he will be discreet or will have me to reckon with. Have no fear, everything will be as we wish it."

Rising to his feet, he motioned for silence. "The Queen is feeling the effects of the excitement of the occasion" he announced. "As her next few days will be full of official engagements and other tasks, I think it better that she should retire and get some rest."

Immediately all rose to their feet as Jane gratefully departed the hall and made for her chambers. As they seated themselves again, an excited hubbub erupted as all voiced their opinions to their neighbours as to exactly why the Queen felt unwell. It did not escape notice that during the upheaval, the King called a messenger over and sent him off on what appeared to be an urgent errand.

Doctor Wendy reached her chambers only minutes after Jane herself did. Sending her women away, Jane saw him in private. She told him of her pregnancy and of the pain and nausea she had been experiencing. His face grave, he directed her to lie on the bed and indicate where the pain was located. She pointed to the side and middle of her abdomen, then watched him anxiously as he gently pressed on the areas she had indicated.

"Does it hurt now?" He palpated the entire area, watching her face for signs of discomfort.

"A little" she admitted.

"And the nausea. Does it come and go or is it constant?"

"I had it in the very beginning, then it went away. It has only recently returned and tends to last for several hours before abating."

"I see. How many months pregnant do you believe yourself to be?"

"About three." His expression did not change as he pressed gently on her lower stomach. "I cannot feel your womb rising, which I would expect to at this stage. But it could just be that you are a little out in your calculations."

He straightened and began to rummage in his apothecary case. Bringing out a small brown bottle, he placed it on the table at the side of the bed. "This is a gentle sleeping draught, enough for two doses. For the next two nights, take it when you retire. It is not a strong concoction but it will ensure you get deep, undisturbed sleep. Rest as much as you can during the day and try not to worry. A positive frame of mind can work wonders."

"Can you give me nothing for the pain?"

"I would prefer not to at this stage, not until I can be sure of the cause. It could just be the normal cramping associated with the growth of the womb, in which case I can give you a potion to ease that sensation."

"And if is not normal cramping, what is it?" Jane struggled to sit up, her eyes wide with fear.

He saw her rising panic and decided to keep his theories to himself. "At this stage, it is more than likely to be quite normal" he soothed. "You must try not to worry and take things as easily as you can over the next few weeks. Now, I advise you to retire directly and take the sleeping draught."

After he left Jane, the doctor went straight to the King, who was waiting anxiously outside the great hall. "How is she?" the King gripped the doctor's shoulders rather too tightly for his comfort.

"She has told me everything Your Grace. I consider her condition to be slightly less than the three
months she estimates but that is not to say that she has made an error."

"But what of the pain she experiences?"

"I am a little concerned" the doctor said cautiously. "Again, it could be quite normal, but it could also be a warning that something is amiss."

"No!" The King wheeled away and clasped his hands to his head in anguish. "Can anything to be done to save the child?"

"If it is healthy, then there is every chance that these little problems will simply go away as time goes on. If anything is amiss with the foetus it will spontaneously abort no matter what I try to do. I do not wish to sound harsh Your Grace, but it is nature's way that only the strongest and healthiest survive."

"Yes, yes, I understand. In your opinion, if she is to miscarry, will be sooner or later?"

The doctor pursed his lips, considering. "I would say sooner, Your Grace. Equally, if the pregnancy is going to settle and continue, it might be better if the Queen is only subjected to light duties for the next week or so. I believe that the outcome will become clear within a month, maybe sooner."

"Very well." The King's expression was thunderous, and the doctor wondered if he had made a mistake in being quite so honest.

He tried again. "Your Grace, this is often the way with a first-time mother. Nature does not quite work as well as it should. However, it does not mean that there is not every chance of success the next time."

The King sighed deeply, then patted the doctor on the shoulder. "Thank you, I appreciate your honesty. I cannot say that I will not be devastated if all this comes to nothing but I can understand that some things are just not meant to be. Is she well enough for me to look in on her?"

"I would advise not, Your Grace. I have given her a

sleeping draught, and if she is not already asleep, then she will be so drowsy as to render conversation impossible. Better to wait until morning, then I can assess her condition after a good night's rest."

Jane was still in bed when the King called the next morning. "How are you today?" He quickly crossed the room and sat on the edge of her bed.
Jane moved her limbs experimentally then eased herself up into a sitting position. "I feel quite well" she announced. "The sleeping draught certainly worked its magic, I cannot remember when I last had such deep and dreamless sleep."
"That is good." He got to his feet and stood looking down at her. "We were to go to Greenwich today so that you could begin to assemble your household. However, I have decided that we can delay that for another day in order to give you more time to rest."
"Thank you." She was grateful for the chance of a quiet day. "I am sure that I will be quite back to normal by tomorrow."
He leaned over and kissed the top of her head. "Let us hope so. At any rate, there is no rush to begin your queenly duties, they can be scheduled as and when you feel able to cope with them. We do need to proclaim you as Queen without too much delay
though; it doesn't do to keep the people in the dark about such things."
"Can that not be done here?"
"It is already arranged at Greenwich. I would not wish to change that."
"Very well." She lay back against her pillows and smiled weakly at him. "Greenwich it is. I will keep quiet today so that I will be completely well by

tomorrow."

"Good." He turned to go, still looking down on her. "Doctor Wendy will look in on you later today, as will I."

"I am grateful, thank you."

"Rest well." As he left the chamber, he blew her a kiss.

Jane wriggled back down into the bed and stretched like a cat. A whole day to do as she pleased without having to be serene and gracious to people she despised. What luxury!

Chapter Thirty-One

After her day's rest, Jane was ready to get on with the business of being Queen. It was decided that under the circumstances they would take the royal barge to Greenwich. There had been tentative plans in place for them to ride in order for Jane to be seen by her new subjects, but the King deemed that the barge would be smoother and less taxing for her.

At the appointed time, he handed her carefully to her seat under the canopy of state and sat down beside her with rather too much enthusiasm, causing the barge to rock a little, broad bottomed although it was. The King's bodyguard discreetly arranged themselves in the stern of the craft to even up the weight distribution. The King easily weighed four times that of his new wife and the river could be choppy at the best of times. It would hardly be the best start to their marriage if one or the other was bundled into the water.

Again, there were a good many people on the river bank to see their progress. Word got around quickly and most Londoners were aware that they now had a new Queen.

As the royal barge made its stately way along the river, the crowds lining the banks finally got their first proper view of their King's new wife. There were a few mumblings, but not many, some even cheered as the King and Queen glided past. Queen Anne had not been popular with the common people, but even they had been appalled by the speed with which she had been tried and executed. However, they were prepared to support their King's new choice, particularly if it meant celebrations in the streets at his expense.

"No oil painting, is she?" whispered one man to his neighbour. "Give the concubine her due, at least she was beautiful."

"She was a witch though." The man standing behind spoke up. "I heard that when they cut her head off, the glamour fell away and in reality she was just an ugly old hag; the beauty was just an enchantment she cast over all who looked upon her."

"Rubbish." Another joined the conversation. "That was just put about by Cromwell to make what they did to her seem just and deserved. I know which one of them I'd prefer to warm my bed!" This provoked much raucous laughter and good-natured jostling which attracted the attention of some of the King's guards, placed at regular distances along the barge route in case of unrest.

"Ssh." The wife of the first man put her finger to her lips and threw a cautious glance in the guards' direction. "Don't draw attention to yourself or you could end up like she did." All fell silent at that, and as one looked in the direction of the Tower, out of sight beyond the bend in the river but even unseen, an everlasting reminder of what happened to those the King wanted disposed of.

"At least he can be sure that this new Queen is no witch, look how plain and dull she looks, any enchantress worth her salt would change that."

"Aye" replied the other. "This one's as pale as death and likely about as much fun."

The King, who still had hearing as sharp as he ever had, heard the laughter drifting across the water from the crowds and waved out jovially. "See how happy they are to see you" he told Jane. "Wave to them, return the compliment."

Jane looked across at the little group and raised her hand disdainfully. She did not particularly want to engage with the rabble, dirty and disease ridden as they were, but worried the King might think her churlish if she did not make some effort.

As they neared Greenwich, the crowds were thinner and quieter. Most watched in silence as they went by and Jane felt uncomfortable at being so scrutinised. She did not look at them, but straight ahead, her eyes fixed on the Greenwich landing stage outside the royal apartments. She well remembered the last time she had landed there as a humble maid of honour new to the court. Sir Francis Bryan had been her escort on that occasion and he had hurried her from view as soon as possible.

Now she was returning to the same place as Queen and intended to make the most of the occasion.

As the barge approached the landing stage, their arrival was heralded by a fanfare of trumpets. The

King climbed carefully on to the steps and then held out his hand to assist Jane's safe disembarkation. She stood for a moment in almost the same place she had stood before, relishing her new position and the eyes upon her. Across the river she could see a few people cheering and waving their caps so she graciously inclined her head and waved. This caused them to cheer ever louder which she found deeply satisfying. Then that was spoiled when the King acknowledged them too; they cheered even louder for him.

No scurrying around the gardens to gain entry this time, they were admitted with due ceremony through the privy entrance below the royal apartments and eventually emerged from the grand staircase into the same passageway Jane remembered from her previous employments, with the King's apartments to the left and the Queen's to the right. He kissed her hand and indicated that she should proceed to her apartments by herself. "I have matters of state to attend to." He looked towards his apartments then back to her. "The lord chamberlain will be waiting in your presence chamber and after you have rested and taken refreshment, he will assist you with the business of assembling a royal

household." With that, he strode off, leaving her to make her way down the passageway herself. The guards saluted and opened the antechamber door at her approach, and there indeed was the lord chamberlain, anxiously pacing. "Your Grace." He bowed deeply. "The King has acquainted you as to my purpose here?"

"He has" she confirmed. "Although I do not see that I need help with choosing a household. Surely you can give me a simple list of positions I need to fill and leave me to get on with it?"

The lord chamberlain blanched at the thought of such a breach of protocol. "With the greatest respect Your Grace, it is not a question of choosing just anyone to fill a position, there are people who need to be accommodated because of their status. You may not know them and I need to direct you in this."

Jane looked at him with distaste. "I do not believe that it is your place to direct me to anything. I will decide who I want and who I do not want. Kindly provide me with a list of positions and if you insist, a list of those people I should include and the posts to which they would be suited. She nodded towards the papers in his hand and held out her own, wiggling her fingers to encourage him to hand over the parchments. He was deeply insulted at her refusal to listen to him and handed over the papers wordlessly.

"Thank you." Glancing down at them, she tossed them carelessly on to a side table and continued towards the watching chamber, dismissing him with a wave of her hand as she passed him.

As the doors closed, he scowled, turned on his heel and went towards the King's apartments. Henry was surprised to see him. "I had thought you would be closeted with the Queen."

"Your Grace, she will have none of me. She refuses my assistance and says she can do it all herself."

The King frowned. "You explained the protocol to her?"

"I tried to but she would not listen."

The King tutted in annoyance and glanced back at his work table, covered in papers he had to read, approve or otherwise, and sign. He did not have time to arbitrate. "The Queen is very new to such things" he began. "She has her own opinions on how she would like things to be done which necessarily have to be adjusted to fit in with our etiquette. Go back to her and tell her that I have ordered you to take on the task of assembling all of the household bar her ladies and maids of honour."

"With the greatest respect, Your Grace, I do not believe that she would listen."

The King let out a roar of exasperation, found a piece of parchment and a quill and wrote the instruction quickly and succinctly before scrawling his signature. "Here." He held the parchment out. "Take this and hand it to her. I think you will find that she will be a little more accommodating."

The lord chamberlain bowed low, greatly relieved. "I thank Your Grace for this intercession."

"Good, good, now go!" The King was anxious to get on with his own urgent business.

Jane was less than pleased to see the lord chamberlain again so soon. "What now?" she asked sharply.

"The King has advised that I am to deal with the bulk of the household appointments whilst you decide on your ladies and maids of honour." As she opened her mouth to air her views, he thrust the parchment at her. "Here are the King's written orders."

She read it quickly and then screwed the parchment up in exasperation. "He treats me like a child" she exclaimed angrily.

The lord chamberlain remained silent but could not help thinking that if she insisted on behaving that way then she could not really complain at being brought into line.

"I assume you went running to the King to tell tales?"

The lord chamberlain flushed angrily. "I merely informed him that you were reluctant to take my advice, that is all. He just happened to agree with me because he likes things done in a proper way."

"Which makes my opinions improper?"

"Of course not. It is understandable that you would have your own ideas about how to proceed and I am sure that you are well versed in household management. However, in a court this size, it is important that the right people are honoured, otherwise there are murmurings and upsets."

Jane was bored by the discussion. "Very well, do as you please. If you would kindly leave me now, I have other important matters to deal with." She gestured towards her bedchamber as she spoke.

From what could be glimpsed beyond the half open door, where an army of red faced pageboys appeared to be engaged in moving a lot of heavy oak furniture about, the important matters she spoke of were to obliterate the taste of the former inhabitant of those rooms.

"Your Grace." With a perfunctory bow, he took his leave, snatching up his papers from the side table as he did so. He cared not if she saw him.

Jane returned to the business in hand. "No, not there, over there" she ordered the two small boys staggering under the weight of the silver framed looking glass. "I want that against the wall at the foot of the bed. And that coffer, over there. And this cupboard, just here."

When all was done according to her orders, she stood looking around, considering whether it could be arranged any better. It was an improvement, but still not quite right. It was the bed. It was too big and garishly over ornate. "I want a different bed" she announced.

The gaggle of pageboys, none more than ten years old, looked at each other and then from the Queen to the enormous gilded four poster.

Jane sighed. They were clearly not strong enough to do her bidding. "You may go" she said abruptly, looking on in amusement as they scurried away like little mice. Scowling at the bed, she decided it would have to do until she could persuade the King to get her a replacement more to her taste.

Now she supposed she had better set about choosing her ladies. No-one other than her sister in law Anne Stanhope came immediately to mind, so she decided to enlist Anne's help in compiling a list of suitable list of ladies and maids. She did not mind who they were as long as they were from good families, would do her bidding without question and were not so beautiful as to divert the King's attention away from her.

Chapter Thirty-Two

There was one thing that could be said for Jane, when she set her mind to a task, she very quickly accomplished it. Anne Stanhope had been expecting an appointment from Jane and was very happy to accept a post as lady in waiting. She recommended some of her friends and acquaintances whom Jane was pleased to take.

There were one or two she baulked at, specifically those who had been close to Anne Boleyn. Margery Horsman for example had been a close friend of the former Queen and had been urged to give evidence against her. Although Margery refused initially, it was made clear to her that much advantage could be gained from doing as she was asked. In the end she complied, and so remained at court and in favour.

Then there was Lady Rochford, wife of the disgraced George Boleyn. She was another who gave evidence against both brother and sister. Both these ladies were experienced in the ways of the court and also somewhat plain. After her initial misgivings, Jane thought they would be ideal. They had once been loyal to the former Queen but had denounced her and helped in her downfall.

Most of the ladies chosen were already at court with their husbands and were more than happy to immediately wait upon the Queen so that she could speak with them to see if they would be suitable. Jane particularly liked the Countess of Rutland who was quiet, efficient and an expert in matters of court etiquette. She was also pleased to appoint the daughter one of Queen Catherine's former ladies, along with the daughter of the executed Henry Norris, Mary.

Eventually, between them, Anne and Jane appointed fifteen ladies in waiting and fifteen maids of honour, several more than either previous Queen had employed. Jane rather liked the idea of having a large entourage about her and was sure that the King would not raise any objections to either her choices or their numbers. Therefore, without consulting him, she immediately had offers of employment drawn up and sent to all along with their appointment for the official swearing in on the morning of 4th June.

By the time she joined the King for supper, Jane felt that she had achieved all that she had intended for that day. In answer to the King's enquiry about her chosen ladies, she was more than happy to announce that all was settled and the swearing in already arranged.

He looked at her in surprise. "You are most quick and efficient. Who have you chosen?"

As she reeled off the names, his expression turned from pride in her proficiency to astonishment at the sheer numbers. "Fifteen of each?" he spluttered. "That is a goodly number indeed."

"You do not mind?" she spoke softly, laying a cajoling hand on his arm. "Having had a somewhat isolated childhood, I will feel more secure having all these new friends around me."

He gazed at her intently, as if assessing her sincerity, then smiled. "If that is what you want, then that is what you shall have."

In answer, Jane smiled serenely. He was not so difficult to manage after all and she was learning fast. Suddenly she remembered the bed currently occupying most of her bedchamber. Touching his arm to regain his attention, she began "Your Grace, I would speak with you about the bed in my apartments."

"What about it?"

"I would have it changed for something more to my taste."

Astonished, he stopped chewing and turned to her. "A bed is a bed, is it not? Why would one be any different to another?"

"This one is enormous and gilded in a most vulgar fashion."

Leaning in to her, he spoke in her ear. But it was not the voice of a doting husband, it was the voice of a King about to run out of patience. "I would have you know that this vulgar bed you speak of was procured by me at great expense from France as a gift to my former wife for the birthing of our daughter. It is as queenly a bed as anyone could wish for and it will remain where it is."

"Then that is even more justification for its removal. I do not wish to sleep in a bed used by my predecessor in which to give birth."

"Yet you are more than happy to take her husband, her crown and use her apartments and other effects?"

Jane pursed her mouth in annoyance. "That is not the point" she insisted. "The bed is too big and leaves precious little room for anything else."

He paused, considering. "Granted, it was first placed in the lying-in chamber, which was a much larger room, but it has stood in those apartments ever since and I see no reason to have it moved again."

"But…"

"Enough Madam!" he spluttered. "You will use what you have inherited through your own wiles and be satisfied."

"My own wiles? What do you mean by that?"

Exasperated, he slammed his hand down hard on to the table top. "Will I never be free of prating women?"

"It was just a simple question." She spoke softly, hoping to mollify him.

"One of a long line of simple questions. I do not like to be so harried when I am at table and you are giving me indigestion with your constant demands." Abruptly he pushed his chair away from the table and stood up. "I am done here; you take as long as you please."

The King was obviously far more displeased with her than Jane realised because he kept his distance for the entirety of the following day. Absorbed with settling in to her new role, she missed his presence not at all and looked forward to the following day when she would officially be proclaimed Queen.

The following morning, her new servants assembled for their swearing in. Jane greeted each household member with a steely stare and listened carefully as they individually repeated the required oath. Some of the appointees she barely knew; these were those dealt with by the lord chamberlain on her behalf. She paid particular attention to her new ladies and maids; she had sent out an order to each regarding the standard of dress required. There was no room in her court for the French fashion. She decreed that all her personal female servants should dress in traditional English costume with gabled hoods which covered the hair completely. The ladies in waiting were required to appear in gowns of black satin or velvet with either tailored high necklines or modesty panels covering the chest. Maids of honour were expected to wear girdles of pearls numbering more than 120. Those with less pearls would not be admitted into Jane's presence. Like the ladies, they were also required to wear gowns which covered their chests. Those who did not comply would be severely punished. She would not condone flirtatiousness or unseemly behaviour in her unmarried maids, all were expected to be virtuous.

Once the swearing in was completed and the wider household had departed leaving just the ladies and maids of honour, Jane had one further statement to make, leaving them all in no doubt what was expected of them. "I expect you to keep your eyes downcast when in the presence of the King. If I see any of you attempt to catch his eye or lure him in any way, you will be instantly dismissed. Should he attempt to draw any of you into conversation, keep your eyes lowered, speak only when spoken to and make your excuses to leave his presence and continue with your duties as soon as is decently possible. Do I make myself plain and understood?"

All those present exchanged glances before nodding demurely as the Queen's eyes rested on each of them, one by one.

"Good." Jane was satisfied.

The King appeared at the appointed time and led Jane into the front courtyard of the palace where she could be seen by the public as well as those within the palace precincts. There, amid trumpeting fanfares, she was proclaimed as Jane, Queen of England with all due ceremony.

To celebrate the event Henry and Jane processed to the great hall and dined under a cloth of estate. Even though the King was gracious and considerate to her, Jane still sensed his resentment following their disagreement on the Friday before. Knowing that flattery was a sure way to appease him, she leaned sideways towards him and said softly. "Your Grace does much honour to me this day. I will do all I can to be worthy of your trust and respect."

"I am sure you will Jane." He did not look at her when he spoke and she had to strain to hear him over the general hubbub. Following his glance, she saw he was evidently admiring some young ladies newly arrived at court, all beautiful, richly dressed and well aware that the King's eyes were on them.

Jane bit back the comment she was tempted to make, instead making an effort to engage with the King's interest. "I have not seen those young ladies before today. How attractive they are."

"Indeed." The King's eyes remained fixed on them. "They are Sir Reginald's daughters." Looking towards the knight, the King raised his goblet to him and Sir Reginald followed suit. "They are just visiting for a few days, so no need to worry." The King drained his goblet and finally turned to look at her.

"Why would I worry?" Jane asked lightly. "I am your wife and your Queen and hope shortly to bear your child."

"As did others before you" he retorted irritably.

Jane decided to change the subject. "When does Your Grace wish for me to announce to the court that I am with child?"

"Hush!" he looked around anxiously to see if anyone had overheard and was reassured to see that they had not.

"Now we are wed it does not need to remain a secret" Jane insisted.

"I would rather wait a while" he replied. "Perhaps next month, when a decent period has elapsed. I do not wish it to appear that I got rid of a barren queen in order to set up a pregnant one in her stead."

"But you did just that." Jane was not one to mince her words.

The King sighed. "I also wish to make sure that this pregnancy will continue before I make it public."

"You think I will miscarry? Have you no faith in me?"

"Of course I have faith in you" he was quick to reassure her. "But you must admit that there have been problems and it would be better if we were sure that all had settled down before raising the hopes of the people."

Jane considered it was not so much the hopes of the people he was concerned about, more his own, but decided to hold her tongue for fear of angering him.

Following mass that evening, Jane was approached by the Imperial ambassador, Eustace Chapuys. She knew him by sight but had not been formally introduced so offered him her hand to kiss. Immediately he began speaking to her in French, a language she barely knew. Unable to reply to him in the same language, she was reduced to smiling and nodding helplessly as he continued on. Eventually the King noticed her confusion and went to her rescue. He could speak French fluently and explained to Chapuys that he was the first ambassador that Jane had encountered and that she was not familiar with the language.

Jane felt extremely embarrassed. It was true that she did not have much French but she did have a small understanding of the language. Granted she could not reply to Chapuys, but she did know something of what he was saying and felt that she did not need rescuing by the King and being made to look a dullard in front of the Emperor's representative.

Chapter Thirty-Three

"Your Grace seems discontented?" Cromwell missed nothing. He had expected to be dealing with a joyful newly married monarch but instead he was faced with a solemn face and dejected manner.

"I think I may have made a mistake Thomas. I have married in haste and may now repent at leisure."

"Your Grace, but yesterday you and the Queen seemed happy in each other's company; what can have changed so suddenly."

The King hesitated, trying to frame his dissatisfaction diplomatically. "Suddenly my court seems flooded with most attractive young women" he began. "I wish I had met them before I married and wonder if I was not too rash in my decision."

Cromwell smiled, he knew exactly which ladies the King was referring to. "You mean the daughters of Sir Reginald, I assume. I agree, they are all most beautiful and, I understand, wonderfully talented in music and dance."

The King's mood visibly plummeted even further. "And all much younger than my new Queen."

"Possibly a little too young" Cromwell replied. "Above all, our new Queen has dignity and serenity and is surely most excellently qualified to comfort and counsel Your Grace."

The King snorted. "Dignity and serenity? I grant you she can assume those qualities, but I assure you, underneath she is a very different woman to the one she portrays."

Cromwell was astonished. "I confess then, I was fooled. I thought her quiet, obedient and gentle."

"She can be. All that and much more. However, of late I have glimpsed little more than steely determination, ambition and haughtiness and I like it not."

"Perhaps she just needs time to adapt to her new position" Cromwell suggested. "I am sure that once she feels settled and secure, all will be well."

"I have one thing in mind which will raise her spirits" Henry crossed to his work table and tapped a sheet of parchment.

"Your Grace?"

"I will elevate her brother Edward and create him Viscount Beauchamp."

"That will please Her Grace mightily." The ambitions of the Seymour family had certainly not escaped Cromwell's notice. "I will attend to the letters patent immediately."

Delighted as Jane was with Edward's elevation, she found her first few days as Queen trying and exhausting. The King was in a difficult mood and she found it almost impossible to hold a conversation with him without it ending in a disagreement.

Every day seemed to herald a new pageant, and whilst Jane was overjoyed to be the centre of attention after so many long years in obscurity, she had begun having the pains again and feared that the constant activity was having a negative effect on the child. When she and the King had a quiet moment together, she mentioned her concerns and he promised that after the planned water pageant the following day, she would be able to have a few days rest.

The water pageant was to be the highlight of the festivities and had been meticulously planned. The river was a mass of barges; the lords and ladies headed the procession, followed by Henry and Jane, and then the King's guard bringing up the rear. They were to process from Greenwich to York Place where they planned to stay for at least a week. York Place was conveniently close to Westminster, where the King was to open parliament on June 8th.

There were many other craft on the river, some were small boats others were tall ships. As they passed the ships, every one let off a volley of guns. The banks were lined with people, all anxious to enjoy the spectacle, and all very appreciative of the King's gesture of allowing wine to flow freely amongst the populace. There was much cheering and applause and everyone seemed to be having a good time.

The King smiled benevolently at his subjects and encouraged Jane to do the same, but since she believed herself to be so far above them, her interaction with them was blighted by her high-handed manner. Luckily most were far too drunk on free wine to notice.

At Radcliffe, they slowed. The Imperial ambassador was on the banks standing under a brightly coloured open fronted tent emblazoned with the arms of the Emperor at the apex. On Chapuys's cue, two barges of musicians rowed out to the royal barge and serenaded them as they passed. Once the musicians finished playing, a forty-gun salute was then fired as the Emperor's salute to the new Queen.

On the approach to the Tower, another gun salute was fired. Jane marvelled at the efforts taken to make the grim fortress seem less forbidding; it was decorated with streamers and banners and one could almost forget what went on behind those walls on an almost daily basis.

London bridge was similarly decorated and yet more musicians serenaded them as they passed underneath.

Despite the smooth passage of the barge, Jane found herself completely exhausted from all the smiling and waving and was heartily glad when York Place at last came into view, although it was not a royal residence that she favoured. Anne Boleyn had spent a lot of time there and the royal apartments all reflected her taste and still had her crowned falcon badge hanging from the windows. It was almost as though she would suddenly appear and berate Jane for making free with her possessions.

Dismissing her women, Jane clambered on to the high bed and tried to rest, but only found herself becoming more and more uneasy. Gazing at the canopy above her head, there were the intertwined initials H&A embroidered repeatedly across the heavily decorated fabric. Turning her head towards the window only brought her predecessor even closer as the crowned falcon glared balefully at her. The other side of the chamber was no better; the carved oak table still held Anne's hairbrushes, cosmetics and perfumes.

Jane climbed off the bed and approached the table, fascinated by the phials of amber coloured liquid. Hesitantly she stretched out her hand and picked one up, feeling almost guilty as she eased out the stopper and put the phial to her nose. As Jane inhaled the musky rose perfume the late Queen always wore, suddenly it seemed as though Anne Boleyn was standing right beside her. She jumped, feeling the tiny hairs on the back of her neck begin to prickle, and gazed wide-eyed about her, almost expecting to see a shadowy figure close by.

As the door behind her opened, she gave a loud shriek and whirled around, one hand pressed to her heart, the other still holding the phial. The King stood there, puzzled at his welcome. "You should have knocked!" she insisted loudly. "My heart near stopped with fright."

"I am not accustomed to knocking on doors in my own property" he snapped. Then, as he detected the scent from the bottle and recognized it, he paled. "What are you doing?"

"Summoning the dead, seemingly" she replied flippantly, placing the stopper firmly back on the perfume phial.

"You should not speak of such things" the King seemed distinctly uneasy, looking around the chamber nervously, much as Jane had been doing. "I had not realized that so many of her things were still in here." His gaze swept across the littered table then to the badge at the window.

"I do not like it here" Jane said in a small voice, expecting that he would immediately switch into gallant, protective mode. "I fear her ghost watches me."

The King had not moved from his place on the threshold and seemed reluctant to go any further into the room, even though Jane was doing her best to convey that she needed comfort. "Come here, Jane."

Jane did as she was bid, approaching him with her very best wide-eyed and fearful expression. Putting his arms around her, he immediately hurried her from the room, firmly shutting the door on the memories of the woman he had once loved so passionately.

"There are other equally grand lodgings here that you can use" he told her, as they walked along the passageway. "I will have those other rooms cleared and made ready for you to use next time."

Within the hour, Jane found herself ensconced in chambers formerly used by Cardinal Wolsey. The King was right in that they were every bit as grand as those reserved for the Queen. They were most luxuriously furnished and appointed and bore no trace of the man who had occasionally used them. Once her belongings had arrived and been put away, she professed herself most satisfied with the new arrangements.

The following morning, the King went to Westminster to open parliament, leaving Jane to spend the day as she wished, arranging her new household and assigning various duties to all. It was late in the evening before he returned, although Jane knew better than to question how he had spent those hours following his business at Westminster.

As he had previously promised, Jane was then allowed to spend a leisurely week, running her household and taking as much rest as she needed. She also used the time to ensure that the lands and properties the King had granted her on the marriage day were being run to her exact specifications and dictated several letters to the various estate managers laying out exactly what she expected of them.

She had just finished dictating her final letter when one of her ladies came to tell her that Lady Lisle was outside and requesting an audience.

Jane did not know Lady Lisle but agreed to see her and rose to her feet as the woman approached her. Lady Lisle executed a perfect deep and most respectful curtsey, which immediately elevated her in Jane's estimation. "What can I do for you Lady Lisle?" she asked kindly.

"Your Grace, I have come to beg a place in your household for my daughter Anne."

"Indeed? Her name was not put forward to me when I was appointing my ladies and maids."

"No, Your Grace. She is at present in service in France, in a noble household just outside Paris. She will be returning to England next year and would be most grateful to have a place at your court."

Jane grimaced. No doubt Lady Lisle had sent her daughter to France in the hope that once returned she would be acceptable to the previous Queen. Jane had taken great steps to abolish all French fashions from court and the last thing she would countenance was a girl with a French education and the resulting manners.

"Lady Lisle, in all truth, I have no positions available at the moment, but tell me, how old is your daughter?"

"She is fifteen, Your Grace."

"That then rules her out. I will not employ any under sixteen years of age and prefer them to be a little older than that if possible."

"But Your Grace, Anne will be sixteen by the time she returns."

"That is as may be, but I cannot be expected to hold open a position for your daughter for the best part of a year, even if one were to become available, which is unlikely."

"May I perhaps approach Your Grace next year to enquire again?"

Jane was losing patience but had to admire the woman's persistence. "Another thing against your daughter is the very fact that she has a French education. I am trying to build a court based on traditional English values, namely modesty and dignity. There will be no place here for continental manners. By all means approach me again next year, but your daughter should be warned that should she be more French than English in her dress and attitude, there will be no place here for her no matter what her age or capabilities."

"I understand, Your Grace". Lady Lisle curtsied most respectfully and took her leave.

Chapter Thirty-Four

"Mary has written to me." The King tossed a large piece of parchment, closely covered in small black spidery writing at Norfolk. He caught it deftly and read it quickly.

"It seems a most respectful and daughterly letter" he replied cautiously. "She but congratulates Your Grace on his marriage and expresses a wish to see you both."

"I cannot see her whilst she continues to defy me!" the King roared. "I want you to ride to Hunsdon as soon as possible and make her see sense. I have made up this list of articles" he turned, selected another piece of paper and similarly threw it at Norfolk, "and I want you to get answers to all that is contained therein. Take as many members of the council with you as you think fit. I want this to be a deputation to put the fear of God into her."

Norfolk relished such a task and knew exactly which members of the council would have the required effect. "And if the Lady Mary still refuses to accept Your Grace as head of the church and persists in believing that her mother's marriage was legitimate?"

"Then use all force at your disposal. Threaten her, bully her, frighten her within an inch of her life if you must, but no physical violence, do you understand?"

Norfolk nodded grimly. As a practiced military campaigner and leader of men, he was a natural bully who had been known to cause even the most hardened of soldiers to weep as a result of his invective. He did not suppose that a mere girl would prove too much of a challenge for him.

At the very time that Norfolk and his selected councillors set out for Hunsdon, Henry and Jane were making ready to ride the short distance from York Place to Westminster Abbey to give thanks for their union. Attended by the whole court, they rode slowly through the narrow streets and were pleased to be well received and cheered by all. Upon reaching the abbey they processed grandly up the central aisle to the royal stall, walking behind a large ornamental bejewelled cross held aloft by the Archbishop.

The service was long and very solemn, but the King paid little attention; his thoughts were very firmly at Hunsdon and he wondered how Norfolk's celebrated intimidation technique would be received by his daughter.

He did not have long to wait. By early evening,

Norfolk had returned and was requesting an audience. Accompanied by those members of the council who had travelled with him, Norfolk approached Henry and Jane and bowed deeply.

"Well, what news?" The King was both anxious and optimistic. It was only when Norfolk straightened from his bow that the King read the answer in his expression.

"She refused to even read the list of articles, let alone acknowledge them. She has no care if she is denounced as a traitor to Your Grace. I must confess that I have never before encountered such a mulish and unnatural daughter. Her friends and servants rallied around her and even dared to call her Princess."

The King was almost purple with rage. Alarmed for his health, Jane stepped forward and laid a consoling hand on his arm. Irritably he shook her off and paced up and down angrily. "I want a list of those people who supported Mary today, particularly those who referred to her as Princess. It will be passed to Cromwell who will charge them all with treason and throw them in the Tower. Then we will see how obstinate she really is. If she persists with this behaviour then I will execute them all one by one and I will make her witness it all. And if that does not move her, I will find more of her friends and do the same to them. When all who have ever been close to her are dead, should she still defy me, then I will have no alternative but to condemn her to death also."

"Your Grace!" Jane was horrified at what she had heard. "Surely you would not send your own daughter to the block? Please, please be reconciled with her and forget your differences."

"Differences?" he roared. "You think this is just a minor disagreement between father and daughter? Then you are more of a fool than I ever thought. By the terms of the Act of Succession she is a traitor and therefore death would be more than deserved. I thank you to keep your nose out of my business and your trifling opinions to yourself. You are my Queen, not my equal, and do not presume to try to tell me how to deal with my own daughter. Is that understood?"

His outburst angered her more than frightened her, but she could see that there was just no reasoning with him when he was in such a temper. She bowed her head meekly and murmured "I understand, Your Grace".

"Good. Now get out and scuttle back to your women."

Outraged, Jane dipped a curtsey and stalked out, furious to be dismissed like a naughty child. Desperately worried for Mary although she was, self-preservation had to come first.

Jane was dreaming that she was in labour. The pain was excruciating but she knew that each agonizing spasm meant that her prince was closer to making his grand entrance into the world. Uncomfortable in her dream, she turned over restlessly in her bed, trying to break free of what was fast becoming a nightmare. As another pain ripped through her, her

eyes flew open. It had felt so real she almost believed it was really happening. Reassured, she was just closing her eyes when another pain gripped her, pain like she had never felt before. Her eyes filled with tears as she bit back a scream; there was no doubt what was happening, she was losing the child.

As the spasm eased, she called out for help, and was relieved when the first person to enter the chamber was her sister in law Anne.

"What is it Jane" she whispered urgently as she lit another candle. "Are you in pain?"

"Yes, a great deal of pain. Please send for my physician."

"Very well, I will rouse the other ladies to assist."

"No!" Jane was frantic at the thought of them all becoming privy to her condition. It needed to be kept within the family. "Just Doctor Butts. You can give him any assistance he needs."

It was all over within the hour. Jane bore the agony stoically and muffled her cries as best as she was able. Anne Stanhope, who had no idea that Jane was with child, watched on with mounting distress as the foetus was delivered, swiftly wrapped in a bloodstained sheet and hastily stuffed into the Doctor's capacious bag.

Anne offered what comfort she could and gently cleaned Jane and fetched her fresh nightwear before easing her back into her newly made bed. "I am so sorry" she whispered. "I had no idea of your condition and neither did Edward."

"The King wanted it kept secret for a little longer" Jane admitted. "I have been in some discomfort these past weeks and there was always a chance it might come to this. The King will be furious." As Anne put her arm around her shoulders, Jane finally began to weep.

Jane did not know who told the King what had

happened, but someone evidently did because he presented himself at her bedside bright and early. The fear in her face as she looked up at him was real, fuelled by the fact that she could not read his thoughts because his face was totally expressionless.

"You were right to delay the announcement" she said at last, when he did not immediately speak.

"I am well experienced in such circumstances" he replied. "Are you recovering?"

"I am, thank you."

"Then I will leave you to rest. I have cancelled all upcoming events for the next week or so, to give you time to regain your strength. Your physician tells me that you have suffered no lasting damage and that we may begin trying again almost immediately. Perhaps next time we will be successful."

"Your Grace!" Jane called urgently to him as he was leaving the chamber. Pausing, he looked back at her. "Did Doctor Butts say if it was a male or female child? I was so distressed last evening that I forgot to ask."

Averting his eyes, he opened the door. "Male" he replied shortly, before slamming the door none too gently behind him.

Cromwell was waiting in the King's ante chamber. "What is it?" the King barked, as he strode past without even bothering to glance across.

"Your Grace." Cromwell followed his obviously angry monarch into the watching chamber, sincerely wishing himself anywhere rather than there. "I have been informed that the Imperial ambassador has written to the Lady Mary, urging her to submit to your demands."

"Then he is aware that I do not jest in this matter?"

"He has told her that her life will be in danger if she continues to defy you."

"Good." The King sat down heavily in his great chair, which creaked loudly in protest. "Whilst we are about that matter, alert the judges that in the event of the Lady Mary ignoring all good advice, they will be required to proceed against her for treason."

"Your Grace, that would mean certain death should they find her guilty."

"If she wants to die for her convictions, then that is her affair. I would hope that a daughter of mine would have more sense but the situation is in her hands. Perhaps Chapuys's words will sway her."

Jane was up and about the following week. Although her ordeal had been traumatic, she was anxious to put it behind her and show the King that she had both strength and fortitude. She had conceived easily enough the first time and she would do so again. Making her way to the King's chamber, she paused outside his door when she heard voices within.

"How is the Queen?" Cromwell asked.

"She does well enough" the King replied. "It is a shame about the child but she is still young and with any luck will quickly conceive again."

"I must say that Your Grace is remarkably magnanimous in the face of such disappointment."

"There is little point in being otherwise. What is done is done, and it is not as if there were not warnings that all may not be well."

"Did the physician have any insight as to why she was so beset with problems?"

The King sighed so heavily, Jane clearly heard the exhalation. "He wonders if she is meant for breeding; he fears she may struggle in childbirth built as she is. I am beset with doubts as to my wisdom in pursuing this."

Jane had heard enough. Pushing viciously at the door, her presence was announced as it slammed loudly against the wall. Both men turned quickly at the commotion.

"Your Grace." Cromwell bowed low.

Ignoring him, she stalked up to her husband and poked him in the chest with her forefinger. "So you believe you have chosen badly, did I hear right? One early miscarriage and that is me earmarked for the Tower?"

"I did not say that" he protested. "I only wonder if the getting of an heir might put you in danger, that is all."

Jane glared at him. "I appreciate your concern for my safety, but I would not have married you if I did not think that I could give you children. My mother is even slighter than I, yet she brought ten children into the world with very little trouble. There is no reason why I cannot do the same."

"I would be most grateful were you to provide me with ten children!" The King did his best to defuse her anger by throwing in a lighthearted quip.

"Then there is no time like the present." As the King's mouth dropped open in surprise, Jane turned towards Cromwell and jerked her head in the direction of the door. Cromwell did not need second bidding. Anxious to distance himself from a domestic situation fuelled by the woman he had

mistakenly thought to be meek and obedient, he

exited with astonishing speed for one who generally moved at a more sedate pace.

Turning back to the King, Jane surveyed him boldly. "Surely it is too early to try again?" He was not sure he liked this new dominant Jane, he preferred her to let him take the lead in such things.

She shrugged. "Who is to say? You need an heir, I am here to do my best to provide one. Why delay?"

Chapter Thirty-Five

"Your Grace, is there news of the Lady Mary?" Jane spoke gently and timidly, not wanting to anger him.

"None" he replied. "She will have had Chapuys's letter some days ago and I had hoped for a response before now. It seems as though she is determined upon her course."

"Is there nothing more that can be done, short of proceeding against her for treason?"

"I am out of patience!" he struck the arm of the chair as he spoke. "I have given her every opportunity to reconsider, yet still she proves as stubborn as her mother."

"The Lady Mary is indeed stubborn" Jane agreed. "But if she came to court, all could be forgotten and I could be a friend as well as a step-mother to her."

"How many more times?" his exasperation was clear. "She is more than welcome to come to court once she submits to my demands and proves herself a dutiful daughter." The little eyes narrowed with suspicion as he turned to look at her. "Why are you so anxious for her welfare?"

Jane paused to think, she would have to tread carefully not only for Mary's sake, but also for her own. "Because to have her with you here, and behaving as you expect, would give Your Grace such peace of mind and would also please the people greatly. Should this matter proceed to charges of treason and eventual execution, the people would be horrified and it could cause the ruination of the country should the Emperor decide to take action."

He looked at her sharply. "You are well informed."

"I place Your Grace's welfare and happiness above all things." Jane bent her head in apparent reverence as she spoke, which pleased him.

"Very well Jane, for your sake, I will try one more time. I will have Cromwell write to her. He is a master with words and will be able to leave her in no doubt of the consequences if she does not comply. I believe she has a certain respect for him and added to what would have been said in Chapuys's letter, and knowing her friends are also in danger, she must surely see that she must submit to me in this."

"I thank Your Grace." Jane said quietly. "I am sure she will do her duty to you as her father and her sovereign. I would be so happy to have her here for since you have elevated me, I have no equals at court only inferiors. The Lady Mary would be more than an equal and as we are close in age I am sure that we will be united in both a sisterly bond and in our love for Your Grace."

Cromwell acted swiftly, composing a letter which reminded Mary that she had previously told him of her humble wish to obey the King in all things and professing astonishment at her continued contrariness. He reminded her that with her mother dead and her friends not only incarcerated but in peril for their lives, she was alone and that the King was her only close family. He enclosed another copy of the articles for her to sign along with a suitable letter for her to copy out and send to the King confirming that she agreed entirely with the content of the articles.

The next few days were tense, but finally a messenger arrived from Hunsdon. The King eagerly tore open the small package, and inside found the signed articles and Mary's letter humbly begging his forgiveness.

Relief swept through the court like a raging tide, but whilst they celebrated, at Hunsdon Mary had fallen into a deep depression horrified at what she had done. In signing the articles she believed she had not only betrayed her mother, but her own beliefs. The Imperial ambassador wrote to her immediately he heard of her capitulation, telling her that he well understood what it had cost her to sign the articles and promised to contact the pope and request a dispensation for the action she had been forced to take in the hope that it would alleviate her conscience.

Jane was of the opinion that Mary had done entirely the right thing. It was better to be alive and complicit rather than dead and forgotten. After all, who would even remember what Mary had sacrificed her life for in a few years; by appearing to agree to the King's demands, she had saved her life. What she held in her heart need not be known by anyone.

The following day, the King wrote Mary a warm and gracious letter full of paternal blessing. Jane also wrote, expressing her joy at the reconciliation between her and her father. Both letters received prompt replies; Mary was especially warm towards Jane, telling her that she remembered her from her time in service to Queen Catherine and recalling their first meeting.

Jane was anxious for Mary to meet her father in order to rekindle their relationship, but the King decreed that a meeting could not be engineered until the celebrations for their marriage were concluded. Just one appointment remained; they were expected at the Mercer's Hall so that she could witness the ancient ceremony of setting the city watch. Surrounded by city dignitaries and observed by a large crowd, she stood in the window overlooking the Mercer's yard, the absolute centre of attention. There were more eyes on her than there were on the ceremony.

Whilst interested in the ceremony, about which she had heard much, Jane nevertheless mostly revelled in her audience and despite her reservations about those in the crowd who were rowdy and unrestrained, went out of her way to smile, wave and acknowledge them all.

After leaving the Mercer's Hall they went to York Place to spend the night. Jane was pleased to see that the royal apartments had been stripped of the former occupant's belongings and all was ready for her to take possession. She looked around with satisfaction, idly wondering what had happened to Anne Boleyn's very fine set of silver hair brushes.

The following day they were seated on a high platform outside York Place to watch a staged water battle between four ships. It was a little loud and violent for Jane's taste, but the King appeared to enjoy the entertainment very much, until one of the guns was accidentally fired at the sailors, injuring two of them quite badly. Jane averted her eyes from the ensuing chaos, noticing several men in the water who seemed to be in danger of drowning. Most were hauled to safety in the nick of time, but one man disappeared under the water never to resurface. Distressed at seeing the man drown, Jane stood up abruptly. The King had also seen enough, so together they returned to the gatehouse and took seats overlooking the jousting yard, where a tournament was held in honour of their marriage.

Early in July, Henry and Jane rode to Hunsdon for the long-awaited meeting with Mary. As Mary emerged from the house, she found herself soundly embraced by her doting father. Jane was little more reticent, but greeted her warmly, then looked on with delight as Henry loudly proclaimed his blessing whilst Mary knelt before him.

Raising her up, he embraced her once more then they all moved into the house for refreshment. Looking at his daughter with tears in his eyes, Henry told her "At last, she who did you so much harm and prevented me from seeing you for so long has paid the penalty."

The late Queen was a very convenient if not entirely

accurate excuse for Mary's treatment, but Jane was more than happy to support that and used the opportunity to raise the subject of the young Elizabeth's status. "Your Grace, I well know the vile and vindictive behavior of Queen Anne so surely it is not appropriate for her daughter to be known as Princess?"

The King looked from Jane to Mary thoughtfully. "It is certainly not appropriate that Elizabeth should take precedence over Mary. Worry not, it shall be dealt with."

After a joyful two days spent reacquainting himself with his eldest daughter, Henry and Jane prepared to take their leave. As a parting gift, Jane gave Mary a large and valuable diamond ring, whilst the King presented her with a heavy purse and promised that she would never have to worry about money ever again. She would shortly have her household reinstated and return to court. Whilst Mary was joyful at the prospect, privately she knew that she could never forgive herself for what she had to do to gain her father's forgiveness.

The issue of the lawful succession had to be dealt with, so the King summoned Cromwell to begin the process of having parliament repeal the original Act of Succession and pass an amended version. It was to make clear to all that the marriage with Anne Boleyn was refuted and that Elizabeth was therefore illegitimate and barred from the succession. Mary was also illegitimate and similarly barred. Henry's heirs were to be the children of his most dear and entirely beloved wife Queen Jane.

Having written down the gist of the new Act,

Cromwell read it carefully before laying down his quill. "Parliament can deal with this swiftly; I will have it properly drawn up and presented without delay."

The King nodded with satisfaction. "Just one more thing, I wish to include a clause so that if the Queen bears no sons, I may choose my own successor."

Cromwell added a postscript to the notes he had written. "A wise decision Your Grace, although I am sure that the Queen will bear you many sons."

"Then you are more confident than I."

Cromwell looked up sharply. "Your Grace?"

"Since our brief hope came to nothing, she has shown no sign of conceiving again."

"But Your Grace, it has only been a matter of weeks since she miscarried, I am sure that in the fullness of time…"

"I do not think I will be a father again." The King interrupted Cromwell's effort at reassurance. "I have not the energy or enthusiasm and I doubt that she has the capability to carry a child to full term."

Cromwell looked down at his notes. "Then the additional clause allowing Your Grace to name the heir would see you nominate the Duke of Richmond?"

"I would."

Cromwell rose to his feet and gathered his papers thoughtfully. "Your Grace is aware that the Duke's health has not been good these last months?"

The King waved off Cromwell's concern. "The boy is young, no doubt he just suffers a temporary illness due to the malodorous summer conditions. It cannot be more than that… or is there something you are not telling me?" Henry had observed Cromwell's averted eyes and his solemn expression.

"Your Grace, it is thought that the Duke's condition may be more serious than just a passing ailment." Cromwell knew very well what it was that afflicted the boy and had hoped that it would not fall to him to tell the King. He thought quickly, aware of Henry's stare boring into him. "He fell ill last month" he began, "around the time of the late Queen's trial."

"And?" The King's stare was unwavering.

"It was said that the late Queen cursed him before her death. As you know she always hated him as she was afraid that he might inherit the throne ahead of her daughter."

"Enough of gossip and hearsay. What ails the boy?"

"He coughs blood daily."

The King's eyes widened in disbelief. "He has been poisoned? You think that Queen Anne somehow contrived to have him murdered?"

"No, I do not believe that. What would that avail her when she had already been repudiated by Your Grace. Perhaps it should also be said that supporters of the Lady Mary would have equal concerns about him taking precedence over her."

"Conspiracies, all about me!" The King's eyes darted around the chamber as though he expected to see would-be assassins appearing from the walls.

Now the King's mind was diverted, Cromwell delivered the devastating truth about Richmond's condition. "The Duke's condition, according to his physicians, is due to a disease of the lungs. He has consumption."

"Consumption!" the King echoed, his face betraying his shock. "Then he will surely die. It seems but yesterday that I watched my father carried away by the same affliction." Looking about him for his chair, the King grasped the padded arm and sat down heavily on the cushioned seat.

Cromwell, a man not easily moved to pity, watched him with compassion. "Your Grace must keep faith with the Queen, she is your best hope for securing the succession."

Chapter Thirty-Six

The King rose to his feet, crossed to the fireplace and kicked at a protruding log, sending a shower of sparks dancing into the hearth. "I'm bored Jane" he said, leaning against the brickwork and staring down into the orange flames. "I want entertainment."
From his place at the table, where he was inspecting military and state documents ready for the King's signature, Norfolk looked up, alert.
Pushing himself away from the fireplace with a grunt, Henry stalked over to Jane's seat in the window embrasure, where she was stitching at her embroidery frame. She kept her eyes lowered, concentrating on her tiny intricate stitches. "Jane!" he bellowed.
Jane jumped and looked up at him with frightened eyes. "Your Grace?"

"Can you entertain me Jane?" he asked belligerently. "Can you write me a masque, a play, a song?"

Jane shook her head mutely.

"Well, can you sing for me, play the lute?"

She shook her head again.

With a cry of rage, the King aimed a punch at the stone alcove and wheeled away. For a moment he stood motionless, rubbing irritably at his grazed knuckles, then turned to look at her once more. "Your predecessor could" he growled. "She could do any and all of those things, just like that" he snapped his fingers as he spoke. "Oh, how she could entertain…". His voice trailed away and his eyes misted over with sentimentality as he remembered. "Eh Norfolk?" The little eyes shifted to the man working at the table. "Is it your opinion that our court was a brighter place with her in it?"

Norfolk shifted uneasily in his seat wishing he was anywhere but trapped in a chamber with an irritable King and a mute Queen. He was also wary; in agreeing with the King he could be opening himself up to treasonous accusations over favoritism towards his disgraced niece. But to disagree could equally bring down the royal ire upon his head.

"Norfolk!" The King was waiting for a response, his narrowed eyes boring into Norfolk's skull.

Norfolk cleared his throat and licked his lips nervously searching for a diplomatic reply. Suddenly it came to him. "There was certainly much entertainment to be had, Your Grace" he said in an even and solemn tone.

Jane looked up sharply. Henry continued to regard him steadily for a moment, then nodded slowly and turned his attentions back to his wife.

"What use are you Jane?" Henry demanded. "What earthly use to me is a woman like you, who has no courtly accomplishments, no interest in politics, little education and who so far has failed to perform her primary function, to deliver a prince?"

From somewhere, Jane found her voice. "God will send us a prince in time Your Grace, I am sure of it." She injected far more confidence into her statement than she felt, but it seemed to satisfy the King.

"Let us hope so Madam, let us hope so".

Crossing the chamber, he joined Norfolk at the table, seating himself at the head of it and gathering up the sheaf of papers lying there. "What is this?" he growled, thrusting a sheet into Norfolk's face.

"Plans for the Queen's coronation Your Grace, as you requested."

Henry glanced across at Jane, who had looked up in interest, then back to Norfolk. "Who gave you the authority to proceed with this?" he asked.

Norfolk was confused. "Why, you did, Your Grace."

"And are the plans advanced?"

Norfolk considered. "Progressing, Your Grace, I would say."

"Then halt their progress." Very deliberately, he caught hold of the parchment and tore it in half.

From her seat at the window, both men plainly heard Jane gasp. Norfolk glanced across at her, then back at the King. "Does Your Grace wish to postpone the event until later in the year?"

"Call it that if you wish." The King was non-committal. "Let it be known that we feel it is not appropriate for lavish celebrations at a time when my people are dying from plague and pestilence."

Shooting a murderous glance at Jane, he continued.

"I also see no reason to spend lavish amounts of money on a Queen who may well prove to be barren. We will review the situation in the spring."

Jane flushed and bent her head to her sewing. It seemed he had set a time limit for her fertility. If she had not conceived by spring, what would happen to her?

The following month, as the plague tightened its grip on the city, the court set off on a summer progress. Jane hoped that the change of scenery would lift the King's depression and reinvigorate their relationship, which of late had become sour. He had been angered by her rearrangement of both her household and other court positions. She was intent on erasing all memory of Anne Boleyn from the court, removing all relatives and friends of the former Queen and actively promoting all her own relatives and acquaintances to any positions which fell vacant. Whilst he had no problem with banishing unhappy memories, he resented her efforts to appoint whom she liked without any reference to himself. It rather put him in mind of his maternal grandmother, Elizabeth Woodville, who had embarked on a similar campaign to surround herself with family members and acquisitive friends. It was of course long before his time, but he had heard how unpopular her actions had made her.

The progress was due to be short compared to other years, mainly because when the plans had been drawn up, Henry had been mindful that Jane would have been nearing the sixth month of her pregnancy, so had been fearful of overtaxing her. Therefore arrangements had been made for stays only in the county of Kent, each one within easy riding distance of the next.

The object of the progress was to visit Dover, to see the newly begun pier. It was a costly venture, but one which Henry felt was justified, given the importance of the port. The first stop was at Rochester, where they spent a few nights at the ancient castle, whose keep dominated the bank of the river Medway. More than a century earlier, it had been owned by Henry V's widow, Catherine of Valois, and it was the same royal apartments used by her to which Jane was shown on her arrival. She looked around herself disdainfully and then ran her finger across some of the wooden surfaces. She wasn't at all surprised to find that they were covered in dust; the place looked as though no soul had even crossed the threshold since the old Queen had died. Looking at the great carved bed, she wondered idly if the Queen had actually breathed her last in it.

"Henry." She turned as the King came through the door.

"Look at this" he looked about himself in interest. "Nothing much seems to have changed in here over the last century."

"I hope the bedlinen has been." Jane was speaking more to herself than him, but he was quick to reassure her. "My great-grandmother only sometimes came here, the castle was gifted her to aid her financially after the King died, before she married my great-grandfather Owen Tudor."

Jane was relieved. "So she didn't die here?"

"Oh no. It was in London I think." He looked at her in amusement. "Are you fearful of ghosts?"

"Not at all. I just like to know who has been here

before me that's all."

"Quite right. I must confess that I have neglected to order this castle the improvements it so badly needs. We shall refurbish it, and you may choose exactly how you would like these apartments to be. Then when we visit next year, all will be as you want it."

Jane looked around her with new eyes. She knew exactly how she would like it to be. "Your Grace is most generous" she murmured.

"I can be" he said. "I can be very generous to those who please me."

Jane stifled a sigh. There it was again. The inference that all would only be well if she produced a prince to order.

After a few days at Rochester, they moved on to Sittingbourne, and from there to Canterbury. They visited the cathedral, praying for some time before the shrine to Thomas Becket and leaving offerings to the murdered saint.

They were still in Canterbury when they were informed of the death of Henry's illegitimate son, the Duke of Richmond. Henry was distraught; he had been fond of the boy and had taken an active interest in him as he grew up. Now, unless Jane gave him a son, there was no-one upon whom he could settle the succession. Of course he had other illegitimate sons but their mothers had not kept themselves exclusively for him, and he was therefore unconvinced that they were truly his offspring. Even though Richmond had been given a royal upbringing and had a royal title, it may still have been difficult for the people to accept him as the next King. The other boys had been brought up by their mothers away from the court and the public eye and would be even less likely to be acceptable to the populace. In general, the people remained loyal to Catherine's daughter Mary, and Henry feared for the country if he were not able to leave a legitimate son to succeed him.

On the last leg of their ride to Dover, the public, who had been scant up until then, turned out in great numbers to cheer them as they passed by. Jane thought that the people of Kent were a great improvement on the Londoners she had so far encountered. The Kentish might be equally poor, but they were less ragged and appeared cleaner than their London counterparts. She waved, smiled and nodded at them and won a fair few hearts. The King was gently amused as he watched her; if only she would smile a little more often in London, he was sure that the people there would be equally won over. In repose, Jane's face had a naturally disdainful expression which did not endear her to the masses.

On the homeward journey, they stopped briefly at Leeds Castle, for which the King had a particular affection, before taking the road to Greenwich. They intended to finish the progress with an extended hunting trip. Jane was keen to take part, and the King was pleased that she wanted to keep company with him. All in all, their time away from London had been a great success. Jane had endeared herself to the people, and more importantly, they had repaired their relationship and both had renewed hopes that it would not be long before they were blessed with a child.

They had not long been back at Greenwich before the

needs of another of Henry's children were brought to the fore. Lady Bryan, governess to the young Elizabeth had complained to Cromwell that the child had no clothes that fitted her, she was growing so fast. Without her mother's care and intervention, her needs were being neglected. In the hope of melting the King's heart, Lady Bryan had written of Elizabeth's intelligence and Tudor temper. At not even three years of age and obviously in ignorance of the amended Act of Succession, the child had asked Lady Bryan why it was that yesterday she was addressed as my Lady Princess, yet today only as Lady Elizabeth.

The Lady Mary also added her pleas for Elizabeth's care. Now Elizabeth had been removed from the succession and was no longer a threat to her, she found herself sympathizing with the little girl, only too aware of what it was like to be ousted from royal favour.

It was the only thing upon which Jane and Mary really disagreed. Jane did not like the child, she found her far too clever and precocious for her young age. Although the red hair and imperial manner clearly marked her as Henry's daughter, she had her mother's eyes, and for that reason Jane preferred to avoid her.

Rather than consulting and quite possibly angering the King, Cromwell dealt with Lady Bryan's complaints himself, quietly authorizing new clothes and linens for the child. The King had become notoriously touchy at the mention of Elizabeth's name, and it was better for all if she was not mentioned in his presence.

Chapter Thirty-Seven

At the end of the summer, the Lady Mary arrived at the palace with great ceremony. She was richly dressed and followed by her new household, all equally well attired. On being informed that the King and Queen were in the King's presence chamber with his ministers, she left her household on the ground floor and processed regally up the wide staircase.
As she was announced, the King stepped forward and embraced her with great affection, then stood back whilst Jane did the same. All the while, the courtiers applauded politely. Some of them were pleased to see Mary back in favour, others less so.
With tears in his eyes, Henry took Mary by the hand and presented her to his ministers. "There are those of you" he told them, "who would have had me put this jewel to death." At the stunned silence which followed, and as the ministers looked at each other in

shock, Jane tried to intervene and diffuse the situation.

"Your Grace, it would surely have been a great pity for you to lose your chiefest jewel in England."

The King then turned to her and pulled her forward, placing his hand on her stomach. "No" he said. "The chiefest jewel in England is Edward. My Edward."

Mary looked from one to the other, then began to sway slightly as all colour drained from her face. Her last thoughts as she lost consciousness and crumpled to the floor was that even on her triumphant return to court, her father had to make it clear that her importance to him paled in comparison to the potential birth of a son.

Horrified to see Mary insensible on the floor before them, both Jane and Henry hurriedly stooped to revive her, Jane calling for wine then gently raising Mary's head and encouraging her to drink.

"Come, daughter". When she was seemingly recovered, Henry held out his hand and pulled Mary gently to her feet, holding her steady as she swayed once more. "Jane, perhaps you and Mary could take a turn about the room until she is fully restored."

Hesitantly Mary began to move, leaning on Jane, as together they began to circle the large chamber. The colour quickly returned to Mary's cheeks and she mumbled her thanks to Jane for her assistance.

"I had not realised you were with child" she whispered. "Many congratulations."

"But I am not" Jane protested. "I have no idea why the King decided to indicate to all that I was."

"I do" Mary replied grimly. "It was a less than subtle reminder to me to know my place and not to expect to take precedence over any child you may have."

"It troubles me greatly that the second Act of Succession still disinherits you" Jane confided. "As his eldest child, you are his natural successor."

"He means to maintain his stance that I am illegitimate" Mary replied. "Even though he knows that his marriage to my mother was perfectly legal thanks to his holiness providing a dispensation. I may have signed his articles agreeing to his repudiation of his first marriage, but that has no bearing on what I hold in my heart."

"You did what you had to do, and thus saved your life."

"But it is not easy to live with" Mary admitted.

"I find it all grossly unfair!" Jane exclaimed. "You have done all he asked and you are still barred from the succession. Just because you are a woman, it does not mean that you cannot rule well and wisely. I warrant illegitimacy would not be an issue were you male."

"My father has a horror of leaving his country without a male heir. He looks back in history and recounts what happened to the country when last a woman inherited."

"But these are different times" Jane urged. "I see no reason why a woman could not manage this country."

"Do not let my father hear you say that" Mary whispered, as they drew near to where the King stood, watching them quizzically.

"You two whisper incessantly" he observed. "About what do you talk so earnestly?"

"We are just getting to know each other again, Your Grace" Jane replied. "I will so enjoy having the Lady Mary here with us."

"I know you women like to whisper confidences together" he said jovially. "I can see that you and my daughter are going to be great friends."

"That is my most fervent wish" Mary declared, smiling first at Jane, then at the King.

Jane was wearing her newest gown, a sumptuous thick piled velvet the colour of autumnal beech leaves. Matched with Henry's recent gift of sable sleeves, she felt every inch a Queen and was on her way to his chambers to show him her finery.

As she turned into the privy passage and passed the men at arms who smartly saluted her, she saw a woman exit the privy chamber. It was only as the woman turned and came towards her that she recognised Lady Lee, the former Margaret Wyatt, friend of Anne Boleyn in life and her relentless champion in death. She was annoyed to see that Lady Lee's clothes were almost as fine as her own.

"Lady Lee" Jane stopped in front of her and bestowed a haughty half smile. "How nice to see you at court, what business do you have with the King?"

"Jane." Lady Lee acknowledged her greeting with the slightest inclination of her head which immediately had Jane bristling at the lack of respect shown. "This is but a fleeting visit; I was seeking permission from the King to visit the Lady Elizabeth, to honour the promise I made her mother. The King was pleased to grant my request".

Jane absorbed that information, then tried again. "Come Lady Lee, we are old friends you and I but you should remember that I am now your Queen and as such demand due deference. I understand that your loyalties very much lay with the late Queen, but I am mistress here now."

Margaret Lee's simmering anger with the sly, smug creature before her finally boiled over. "I am very much aware that you are Queen, but I think you should not have too much pride in how you achieved such lofty status. And as for us ever being friends, I think your memory may be at fault."

Jane's naturally pale complexion appeared to whiten even further as she fixed Margaret with a cold gimlet stare and took a step closer. "I will have you know that I am leading the King back to the true church."

"I am not concerned with what you do, but how you attained the position from which to attempt it. You made Anne's last few months a misery, flaunting your association with the King at every opportunity and relishing in her misfortune."

Jane tossed her head, folded her hands across her stomacher and looked at Margaret from half closed eyes. "She was a witch and a heretic and she deserved all she got. She shamelessly enticed the King away from the true Queen and delighted in her exile."

Margaret grimaced and shook her head. "She did no more to Queen Catherine than you did to her. The difference being that at least Catherine died in her own bed when her time came. Anne was butchered. How do you think that felt Jane, to be young, full of health and vigour and to know that your life was about to be taken from you in the most brutal way?"

"Then she should not have sought to make the King a cuckold, should she?"

"You, as well as the rest of the world know that those charges were false, trumped up by Cromwell at the

King's behest. Her only crime, if it may even be called a crime, was to not provide the King with a male heir." Margaret brought her face close to Jane's and continued. "Because that is what the King demands of his wife, a male heir. How goes that for you Jane?" With a flourish, Margaret swept her skirts aside, sidestepped Jane and continued on her way. Jane turned to watch her go, her lips pursed speculatively, then calculatingly rubbed at her cheek energetically to make it redden and ran the rest of the way to the King's chamber, bursting in dramatically.

The King was slumped in his great chair and not in a good mood. He had one of his frequent headaches and was feeling maudlin. At Jane's sudden appearance he turned and scowled.

With no heed for his feelings or temper, Jane launched straight into a tearful tirade. "I have just met Lady Lee in the passageway. I went out of my way to be pleasant to her but she insulted me. When I tried to talk further with her, she slapped me and stormed off." She stroked her reddened cheek and looked at her husband expectantly, anticipating rage against Margaret and a call to have her arrested. Instead, other than the briefest of glances at her, he remained silent and unmoved.

"Did you hear me?" she moved closer, speaking imperiously. "Lady Lee has both disrespected my position and used violence against me."

Angered by her insistence, he heaved himself up from his chair and stalked irritably towards the window before turning to face her. "I find it hard to believe that Lady Lee would strike even the lowest household servant, never mind a Queen. There was never a more even-tempered, considerate woman than she. Furthermore, I hear she is an exemplary wife to Sir Anthony and a devoted mother to his sons". As his face darkened to a purplish hue, Jane realised her mistake. "I see little devotion in you Jane, now you have attained your ambition to be Queen. Lady Lee immediately saw my discomfort and fetched me wine and a cold cloth to soothe my brow. Where is your concern and compassion? All you seek is to bring trouble to the door of a good woman because she was a loyal friend of your predecessor and therefore will have no truck with you."

Crossing the chamber in rapid strides, he took Jane's chin in his hands and tilted her reddened cheek towards the light. Not seeing any finger marks on her skin to indicate a blow, merely a slight flush, he stepped away from her, pulled the door open and motioned to the guard to come near. "Was there an altercation between Lady Lee and the Queen out here just now?"

The guard shook his head energetically. "Not that I saw, Your Grace. The two ladies stopped and talked briefly, that is all".

"And one did not move to strike the other?"

"Indeed not."

The King dismissed the guard, then opened the door wider, indicating that Jane should pass through it. Mildly affronted at being caught out, although not in the least ashamed, she stepped into the corridor. The King stood in the doorway looking down at her, his expression blank and unreadable. "Remember that here Jane, the walls have ears and liars always get their comeuppance. Perhaps you should give some thought to the fates of others who have sought to mislead me."

As the echo of the slamming door echoed through the stone passageway, Jane flounced off in the direction of her own chambers, pausing only to throw a venomous glance in the direction of the guard whom she considered had betrayed her.

Chapter Thirty-Eight

It had been four months since the miscarriage, and with the King almost continually exasperated with her, Jane was feeling more vulnerable with each day that passed.

Waking one morning and taken with sudden nausea, she dared to hope that at last she might be able to give the King the news he craved. Much as she wanted to share the possibility of a child with him, she considered patience would be the best course of action. It was far better to say nothing until she was sure; to give him good news only to later admit she had made a mistake could further damage their relationship.

It had lately become her habit to take a seat in the corner of the King's chamber whilst he was about the daily business of ruling the country. She always kept quiet and never expressed any opinions, even when asked, which was not often. She was doing her best to recapture the docile, obedient reputation with which she had come into the marriage.

So quiet was she, bent over her embroidery frame, that he often completely forgot that she was even in the room and spoke freely to his ministers and advisors about matters both at home and abroad. Whilst not appearing to pay any attention, Jane in fact absorbed everything which was said. She had an excellent memory and was fast building up an impressive knowledge of current affairs.

On that particular morning, Cromwell was briefing the King about the progress of the dissolution of the monasteries. It seemed that the royal commissioners had now moved on to the county of Lincolnshire and had split into three separate units. One was engaged with dissolving the smaller monasteries, another was assessing and collecting the taxes levied by the crown and the third was examining the clergy for their fitness to fulfill their calling, concentrating on their morals and their politics.

The King was aware that the commissioners were unpopular and very much resented and was concerned at the reports of a growing grievance against him as the instigator of the business. Cromwell, who was in charge of the commissioners, was openly accused of encouraging the King to line his own pockets by having his men invent scurrilous charges against innocent clergy. Wild rumours regarding the King's religious policies began to circulate attracting even more men to the cause. It was said the all possessors of gold coins would be fined and that gold and jewels belonging to parish churches would be confiscated. Furthermore, fines would be payable to the King if poor men ate white bread and other delicacies and high fees would be charged for wedding, christening and funeral ceremonies.

Once the commissioners moved on to the town of Louth, the situation escalated. The vicar denounced the commissioners from his pulpit prompting the townsmen to gather the following day and take the keys of the church from the churchwarden in order that the silver and jewels contained within their church could be protected. Led by Nicholas Melton, a cobbler in the town who dubbed himself Captain Cobbler, the townspeople entered the church and rang the bells to sound the alarm across the district before assembling behind the church's three large silver crosses to walk in procession to mark the first Sunday after Michaelmas. Melton declared to all that if was as well to follow the crosses that day because if they were taken by the commissioners then they could follow them no more on holy days.

Later, forty of the townspeople set out for the nearby nunnery of Legbourne to offer their protection. There, they came across two of Cromwell's men whom they captured, took back to Louth and imprisoned.

As Cromwell recounted the events, the King grew increasingly angry that his royal commissioners had been so hampered and interfered with whilst carrying out their work.

Jane, sitting quietly in her corner, struggled to take in the huge volume of information. Occasionally she risked a glance at the King, or Cromwell, but dare not let them catch her eyes on them or give them any indication that she was paying attention to anything which was said.

In the days which followed, more alarming information reached the court. The rebellion had spread to nearby Caistor. The people there rose as one and declared to the commissioners that they would forfeit no more of their gold, silver and jewels in taxes. The commissioners were informed that 20,000 local men were advancing so immediately tried to make their escape. Some were captured, and the few who did get away immediately returned to court to inform the King of the rebellion.

Within a very short time, almost the entire county had risen to the cause and it was said that more than 40,000 men had assembled and planned to march on London. To give themselves credence, they had bound a number of local noblemen to their cause; some joined willingly, others had to be coerced by threats. Lord Hussey was forced to join when a contingent of rebels visited his house and swore to burn it to the ground unless he agreed allegiance to them.

The King's first instinct on hearing the latest news was to muster his own army and ride out to meet the rebels long before they approached the capital. As he made this assertion, Jane cried out in horror and hurriedly got to her feet, her embroidery frame hitting the stone floor with a loud crash. "Your Grace! How will we fare without your presence and strong guiding hand?"

"Be at peace Jane and do not worry. This menace must be dealt with at first hand for I cannot allow an army of that size to come near."

"I will ride with Your Grace."

The last thing the King wanted was a wife at his side, getting in the way of his campaign and potentially getting herself captured and ransomed.

"No Jane" he reasoned. "I need you here, to act as regent in my stead."

Highly delighted although she was, and quite sure that she could do an excellent job, she pretended humbleness and trepidation. "Your Grace, how can I possibly rule in your stead?"

"You will have supporters" he told her. "I will leave my most trusted nobles and clergy to protect and advise you in my absence."

"I much appreciate your confidence in me" she told him. "Your kingdom will be in safe hands."

"I know it" he told her kindly, before turning away to begin finalizing his plans.

As it turned out, Jane's joy and excitement in her approaching regency was premature. As more reports reached court about the ever-increasing size of the army, the King had second thoughts and decided that it would be better if he stayed in his capital.

Jane hid her disappointment as best she could, although she admitted to herself that it was also tinged with relief. It would have been no easy task and she would not have been free to rule exactly as she wished because Henry's advisors would police her every move.

In early October the rebels reached the outskirts of London and made camp, sending a delegation to the King to negotiate their terms. Henry, dressed in his finest and most imposing attire and flanked by his ministers, met them with barely concealed resentment.

"Set out your demands" he barked.

One man stepped forwards, snatching his cap from his head and twisting it anxiously in his hands.

"You are the leader?" the King asked, noting the man's uneasiness and privately thinking that he had rarely seen a man less suited for leadership.

"No, Your Grace" he began. "We are as one and have elected no leaders. I have been asked to be spokesperson."

"Then begin."

Clearing his throat, the man began to speak. "We demand that the dissolution and suppression of the monasteries be stopped and that the church be allowed to continue to enjoy its ancient liberties." Pausing, he glanced anxiously at the King, who encouraged him to continue with a wave of his hand. Clearing his throat again, he continued. "We demand that there be no more taxes except in times of war, that England be purged of heresy and that the heretical bishops be deposed and exiled. Finally we ask that Your Grace only take noblemen as your councillors. All those not of noble birth such as my lord Cromwell should be removed and punished."

As he finished, he bowed and stepped back to his compatriots. The King surveyed them all in silence for a moment, then began to speak in an icy monotone, his anger clear but carefully controlled.

"Starting with the question of the monasteries, you should be aware that what I do, I do by an Act of Parliament and this was therefore not begun by any councillor or councillors as you would try to persuade all to believe. No house where God was well served has been suppressed, only those where vice, mischief and abomination of living was prevalent. Those houses performed no service to the poor or sick but spent their wealth in the pursuit of vice and profligacy." He paused and glared at the small band of men, some of whom took a step back. "Furthermore, I have never heard that a prince's councillors and prelates should be appointed by rude and ignorant common people or indeed that they are suitable persons to decide councillors fit for a prince. How presumptuous are you, the occupants of but one shire, and that the most beastly in the kingdom, to find fault with your King for the electing of his advisors and to take upon yourselves contrary to God's law and man's law to seek to rule your prince to whom you are bound by all laws to obey and serve with your lives, lands and goods. You have behaved like traitors and rebels and not the true subjects you like to call yourselves."

The little group had been edging further and further backwards as he spoke. When he had finished, they executed hasty bows and all but fled from his presence. Once back with the remainder of the army, the decision was taken to disperse as quickly and quietly as possible in the hope that the King would not seek retribution against them.

Cromwell was soon able to bring the welcome news back to the King that the rebels had abandoned their cause and appeared to be returning to their homes.

"That was a fine speech Your Grace and I am pleased to report that the danger has been averted, only a few stragglers remain and will soon be gone."

"I am pleased to hear it." The King was not only pleased but relieved that the episode appeared to be over.

"Will Your Grace send men into Lincolnshire to reinforce your message?"

"It remains an option" the King replied. "However, if all remains quiet then I do not feel it will be necessary. These were just a number of disgruntled peasants with no organization or even weapons to speak of. I well understand how a few discontented voices can suddenly swell into an alarming number, but I think they were sensible enough to realise that I will not be told how to rule my kingdom."

"And the commissioners will continue with their work?"

"I see no reason why not. They should be encouraged to be even more zealous in rooting out vice amongst the clergy."

Suddenly the King remembered Jane, who had quietly witnessed everything from her seat in the shadows. Turning in her direction he held out his hand. "Jane?"

Hesitantly she came forward, eyes downcast. "You see why I could never die leaving my kingdom in the hands of a woman? It takes a King to put down a rebellion and it takes a King to keep it down. Do you understand now why it is vital for us to have a prince?"

"Yes, Your Grace" she replied meekly. From what she had heard, she thought that many of their demands were perfectly reasonable, but she knew the King well enough to understand that he would never agree to any demand which was forced upon him by a rabble. Much as she wished for the suppression of the religious houses to stop, it was not a matter she could raise without prior and careful preparation.

Chapter Thirty-Nine

As relieved as Henry was that the Lincolnshire rebellion had been put down so easily, it was not long before yet another uprising was reported, this time in Yorkshire.

It had been started by a lawyer named Robert Aske, who had been travelling through Lincolnshire when their rebellion had broken out. On his return to Yorkshire, he spread the news and it was not long before the town of Beverley took up the cause. Encouraged, Aske rode there and spoke so eloquently to them that they immediately accepted him as their leader and spokesperson. Having seen the Lincolnshire rebellion fail for the lack of leaders and organization, he urged the people to ready themselves and meet on Skypworth Moor the following day to elect their captains.

Once organized into military units with a captain in charge of each, the men progressed through the county gathering supporters and holding aloft banners depicting the crucifix, the five wounds and the chalice. At the head of the army marched priests holding large crosses which caused their ever-increasing throng to be dubbed the Pilgrimage of Grace.

At Windsor the King had been informed of this new uprising and had immediately gathered his ministers about him. Whereas the Lincolnshire army had been a ragged and disorganized band of peasants, their sheer numbers had been a concern. From reports coming out of the north, it seemed that this new army had every chance of posing even more of a threat. Although the numbers were presently nowhere near the might of the Lincolnshire army, by all accounts it seemed that the Yorkshiremen were well organized and had strong leadership. It was expected that the numbers would swell once they moved towards London and the King felt that this was a threat to the safety of himself and his family.

Wasting no time, he ordered the Tower of London to be fortified, with the intention of using it as a refuge for the court and his family should the city come under siege. Mary and Elizabeth, at separate households away from the capital were ordered to join him at the comparative safety of Windsor. Then should they eventually need to take refuge at the Tower, they could all travel together under heavy armed guard.

Mary arrived first, followed several hours later by Lady Bryan and the young Elizabeth. Jane greeted Mary with much enthusiasm, pleased that she would at least have someone with whom to discuss the events. She was less pleased to see Elizabeth, who stared at her with frank interest from Anne Boleyn's eyes and asked her how she liked wearing her mother's crown.

Jane, outflanked by the fiercely intelligent three-year-old, smiled stiffly and had one of her ladies direct Lady Bryan and her charge to the rooms which had been allocated to them. Watching the child, who was already possessed of some of her mother's grace, exit with Lady Bryan, Jane resolved to have as little to do with her as possible; this view was reinforced when the child looked back at her just before she turned the corner, a piercing stare making Jane feel as though Elizabeth had already assessed her and found her wanting.

Later, she and Mary discussed both the rebels and their demands, and Elizabeth.

"What think you of my young half-sister?" Mary enquired.

"I find her unsettling" Jane admitted. "She stares at me from her mother's eyes and seems to see into my very soul. I well remember finding the late Queen's gaze similarly disconcerting."

"She is certainly astonishingly perceptive and intelligent for one so young" Mary replied. "She is fortunate in Lady Bryan, who cares for her as though she were her own daughter. I well know how hard life can be once a mother's love and protection are lost."

"Even a mother like Anne Boleyn?"

"It has to be said that she was a good mother." Mary could hardly believe that she was defending the woman who had caused untold suffering to her own mother. "She tried very hard to persuade my father to let Elizabeth grow up at court, but of course the child of a sovereign, even if only a lowly girl, must have her own abode and household. Given the distance involved to Hatfield, she managed to visit frequently."

Jane nodded in reluctant agreement.

"However, as a step-mother, I admit found her lacking." Mary mouth twisted in a grimace as she recalled the angry letters, words and threats.

Jane looked about her, then lowered her voice even further. "And what think you of the rebels demands?"

"Mostly unfeasible" Mary replied. "At least those of the Lincolnshire mob. The dissolution has gone too far now for it to be brought to a satisfactory halt, much as I would wish it. We can only hope that the larger monasteries and abbeys are spared. I am horrified by the unnecessary force which I hear has been brought to bear on those smaller establishments."

"I would wish it halted" Jane shuddered. "What began as a simple survey into the usefulness of these places has become nothing more than an excuse to seize as much gold and valuables as possible. I am sure the King was led into this folly, surely it cannot have been all his own doing?"

"I fear it was." Mary replied. "When it first began, it was put about that it was all the doing of the former Queen, but in truth it was down to my father in collusion with Cromwell. The monasteries and wealthy abbeys were seen as remaining loyal to the pope, so as he ushered in the new religion, he began sweeping out what he called popery and felt it only right and proper that all the riches and lands formerly held by the monks should revert to him. By putting it about that many of the richest establishments were hotbeds of vice assisted the process, and the Act of Parliament made it legal"

"And you think that was just vicious rumour?"

"No" Mary admitted. "I believe that some were as evil as has been put about, but there is no doubt that others were implicated simply because they had assets my father coveted."

"Is there nothing we can do to change his mind?"

Mary looked at Jane pityingly. "Do you really think that the entreaties of a couple of women like ourselves would have any effect? Not only would he be angry because we tried to interfere, he would be suspicious of our motives. No, I have only just been accepted back at court, it would be folly to anger him yet again."

"Then it is down to me." Jane spoke with conviction and determination. "Perhaps if I beg him publicly; maybe when the entire court is present, it might move him?"

Mary shook her head warningly. "Have you not learned anything from your time with him? He will feel humiliated if you do something like that in front of others, and from that humiliation will come anger like you have never before encountered. You are playing a dangerous game which could end very badly for you."

"I do not care!" Jane leapt to her feet with the light of religious conviction in her eyes.

"He needs to understand that his only salvation is within the catholic church, his new religion will avail him nothing. He is already excommunicated and pretends not to care when in fact the knowledge chills him to the bone. He must return to the true church, then he will stop this senseless persecution of those he feels are loyal to the pope."

Mary got to her feet and laid her hand on Jane's arm. "If you confront him in public, you could be writing your own death warrant. I have seen him condemn men to death for less."

Jane put her hand over Mary's. "Worry not. I will choose my moment. He will listen to me, I am sure of it."

More determined than ever to get her point across, Jane watched and waited for her chance. If she had but heeded Mary's warning and paused to consider the King's state of mind, her entreaty might at least have been heard. Jane was devout in her beliefs and like other committed catholics at court, only paid lip service to the new religion, believing that God would know what was in her heart no matter what heretical ceremony she was forced to accept. With the King anxious and concerned about the latest uprising, it was ill-advised for her to call his religious policies into question.

In front of a court assembled to discuss the threat from Yorkshire, Jane took her stand. "Your Grace, do you not consider that this latest uprising and the one before may be God's retribution for your treatment of the monasteries?"

Henry had been discussing the situation with Cromwell and only half heard what she said.

Turning around slowly, he fixed her with a stern gaze. "I would be obliged if you would say that again, for I cannot believe my ears."

"I said, does Your Grace not consider that this rebellion has been allowed by God because of your treatment of the monasteries?"

As he absorbed the implication of her words and became aware that most of the court had also heard and were awaiting his response with bated breath, his eyes narrowed and he took a menacing step towards her.

Jane stood her ground, her head held high, her gaze challenging.

"Who are you to tell me that God is punishing me for my actions? From what lofty eminence do you presume to judge me?"

Jane felt her courage begin to ebb away and glanced fearfully towards Mary, who had her eyes averted from the scene.

"Well, Madam?" the King roared. "Answer me!"

Throwing herself to her knees, Jane put her hands together as if in prayer and looked up at Henry beseechingly. "Forgive me Your Grace, but it seems to me that all this trouble could be averted if you would but lead your people back to the true church. These rebels but do God's work; surely He looks down in disapproval upon His servants being ousted from their communities whilst their treasures and lands are confiscated. I beg you, return to the true church then the rebels will have no cause to promote."

For answer, the King, now visibly trembling with rage, turned his back on her, stalked slowly across the chamber assembling his thoughts, then turned to face her. The thunderous expression he wore had turned stronger characters than she into quivering wrecks, and although inside she was terrified at what she had done, outwardly she maintained a serene dignity.

"Get up" he spat. "It is demeaning for you to beg thus."

Mutely she got to her feet, mentally bracing herself for what was to come.

"How dare you presume to speak on behalf of God and seek to call down His judgement upon my head for crimes you imagine I have committed. You of all people, who as my wife and my Queen should be my most loyal supporter in everything I do. I have told you before not to meddle in my affairs yet you persist in defying me. I strongly advise you to remember what happened to your predecessor and if you wish to avoid a like fate, I suggest you keep your opinions to yourself in future and never again try to berate me in front of my court. Am I understood?"

Jane raised her chin fractionally and stared coldly at him determined to avoid showing the terrible fear she felt. "Yes, Your Grace" she said at last. "You are understood."

Chapter Forty

By mid-October almost the whole of Yorkshire was up in arms. Upon joining the army, the rebels swore an oath to maintain God's faith and to restore the true church by purging the country of heretics. They also vowed to preserve the King's person, and like their Lincolnshire compatriots, aimed to have only the nobility serving in high office. All low born councillors were to be removed and punished for their evil influence on the King.

When faced with foot soldiers numbering more than 20,000 and a company of more than 4,000 horseman, the city of York yielded. At the head of his army, Aske rode up to the gates of York Minster and posted an order on the railings, telling monks and nuns from suppressed houses to re-enter their monasteries
and nunneries as they had the full support and

protection of the Pilgrimage of Grace.

The city of Hull surrendered to the might of the army on October 20th and the following day Pontefract Castle followed suit. Aske had observed the advisability of recruiting noblemen as captains when in Lincolnshire, and followed the same concept, using threats when persuasion failed.

The King sent the royal army northwards under the command of the Duke of Norfolk and the Earl of Shrewsbury, with instructions to observe but not to draw close enough to invite confrontation. The King's army numbered but 15,000 and highly trained although his soldiers were, it would be folly for them to engage with Aske's army which by now was said to number over 40,000 troops.

Representatives were sent between the two camps in an effort to find a compromise, but Aske would not negotiate with Norfolk unless any agreement was fully supported by the King. After a further delay, it was agreed that Aske and Norfolk would meet at Doncaster and then Norfolk would consult with the King before any decision was reached.

The meeting was short and to the point. The demands Aske outlined were the same as the Lincolnshire men had put forward, the only difference being that Aske spoke with eloquence and reasoned thought and had a huge and organized army at his back, rather than the leaderless rabble which had scattered in the face of the King's anger only weeks earlier.

Rather than send a messenger, Norfolk rode south himself, meeting the King at Leeds Castle, near Maidstone. Jane had accompanied him and was also present in the privy chamber when Norfolk strode in. With very little preamble he began barking out the rebel's demands. He was tired, he was angry and at sixty-three years of age was beginning to feel that he was a little too long in the tooth to be galloping about the country on what he termed a fool's errand.

The King listened attentively and without interruption until Norfolk finished his tirade. "Much the same as before then" he commented.

"Indeed Your Grace."

"And the rebel leader, Aske, what sort of man is he?"

"Well educated and intelligent. He is a natural leader and his men are well trained and more than ready to act on his every order."

Henry rubbed at his beard thoughtfully. "The most dangerous type then. How is the mood in the north? Is it ripe for conflict or will reasoned negotiation win the day?"

"We are sorely outnumbered, Your Grace" Norfolk admitted. "The people of Yorkshire and neighbouring counties are behind Aske and his demands; even those who do not march with the army are supporting the cause."

"Is there a danger that they will march on London?"

"I believe so, although from what Aske said, I do not believe that he really wants to use his army as a fighting force. It seems the numbers are more to indicate the support for the cause and it is obvious that they do not wish to overthrow or threaten Your Grace's person in any way; their primary aim is that you restore the monasteries and other religious houses. However, they are well drilled and armed, so force cannot be ruled out."

"We must play for time, in an effort to take the sting

and impetus from them. Tell him I wish to call a truce and will issue a general pardon to all involved for any offences so far committed as long as the army disperses peaceably. Assure them that their demands will be fully considered and that I will be open to negotiation."

Norfolk could barely believe his ears. He had expected rage, threats, menace; anything other than the King's quiet acceptance and reasoned response. "I will ride back immediately and convey your response to Aske."

"Surely you will rest and take refreshment before embarking on yet another long ride?" Jane voiced her concern sincerely. He was not a young man and his exhaustion was evident.

Norfolk glanced at her and shook his head. "This matter if left could result in civil war, so although I thank Your Grace for your concern there is no time for rest when conflict could be imminent." With hasty bows to both, he strode away.

"He has the energy of a man half his age" Henry commented, as they stood at the window watching Norfolk gallop through the park.

"Your Grace is indeed fortunate in such a general" Jane agreed. "Hopefully once he acquaints the rebels of your generous concessions, the danger will be averted."

The King did not reply and seemed distracted by his thoughts. "We should return to London without delay in case the situation should worsen."

"Very well." Jane turned to face him and was taken aback by his savage expression. "What ails Your Grace? I thought with your generous pardon and promise to consider their demands, you would be of the opinion that the situation is under control."

"The situation will not be under control until Aske and his captains suffer the fate of all traitors!"

Jane was shocked at his vehemence. "But Your Grace, you spoke of pardons and negotiation!"

"And you thought I meant it?" He all but laughed in her face. "Rebellions are not put down with kind words and promises, they are put down with violent retribution. Men such as Aske will always conjure up new demands and once I am seen to show weakness, there will be no end to it. I may bide my time, but they will come to rue the day they belittled my kingship. They will bend to my rule, not I to theirs."

Once Norfolk acquainted Aske with the King's request for a truce and gave him a promise that their demands would considered and negotiated, he stood his troops down. Satisfied with the King's word, Aske told his men to go home to their families.

Within a week of arriving back in London, Jane discovered that the pregnancy she thought had started six weeks earlier was in fact another false dawn. Whilst very glad that she had not told the King and raised his hopes, she found the disappointment very hard to bear on her own.

The winter of 1536 was the coldest for many years and by mid-December, the Thames was frozen so hard that it was possible for merchants to drive their horses and carts across it from one bank to the other without mishap.

In early December the King was alerted to more rumblings of discontent in the north, so to avert the chance of the army reforming, extended an invitation to Robert Aske to come to court and spend the Christmas season with him. Aske was delighted to accept and arrived a little over a week later.

A few days before Christmas, Jane's brother Edward requested an audience which she was pleased to grant. As he approached her, she imperiously held out her hand for him to kiss, leaving him in no doubt that she expected all the reverence due to her as his Queen and not any familiarity as his sister.

"This is an unexpected pleasure" she began. "Have you been keeping well?"

He brushed her polite enquiries aside in his usual brusque manner and got straight to the point. "News from Wolf Hall. It seems our father has died unexpectedly."

Jane was taken aback. "I have not seen him for many months" she mused. "Had he been ill, do you know?"

"I do not know" he replied flippantly. "I have not seen him for some time either."

"And our mother, what of her?"

"Relieved to be rid of him if she has any sense, but she will no doubt put on a good show of grieving for the old rogue."

"I will write to her" Jane decided. "As Queen, it would not be appropriate for me to attend his burial, but I will let her know that I am thinking of her. You will attend the burial I assume?"

"Not if I can help it" he replied cheerfully. "I am sure I can conjure up estate business at some far-flung property on whatever day he is interred. Our mother will have our other siblings for support and they will no doubt display the proper grief for the death of a father. I on the other hand do not mourn him."

"I thought you had forgiven him for whatever occurred with Catherine?"

"Forgiven him? No. Learned to accept it, yes."

"Oh Edward, your bitterness will be your undoing."

"If I am bitter, then it is what he made me. He has been all but dead to me since it happened. I may have spoken to him civilly in these later years, but any love I held for him died the moment the affair came to light. I do not mourn his death and it would be dishonest to pretend otherwise."

The court was to spend Christmas at Greenwich, although the frozen river meant the journey had to be made on horseback from Hampton Court rather than by barge.

Once ensconced in the warm and seasonally decorated chambers of the palace, Jane spared a fleeting thought for the sullen Londoners who had turned out to watch them on their journey. Some of them were so sparsely and raggedly clothed she had wondered how they had not frozen to death. Gone were the happy cheers and waves, instead they just stared dully at the sumptuously furred court as it had passed them by. Jane supposed they were probably used to harsh conditions, and then promptly forgot about them.

With mounting unease, she watched Henry laugh and talk with Robert Aske. So jovial were the pair, one would assume that they were lifelong friends. Jane knew that Henry detested the man and all he stood for and was astounded at the ease with which he put on the show of friendship. Jane likened it to a cat taunting a mouse before the kill.

Aske, clever man though he was, was totally won

over by the King's show of friendship and understanding. They spoke briefly of the rebellion and the changes it hoped to effect and Henry promised he would hold a parliament in the north to properly enact the rebel's demands and even vowed that when Jane was crowned, the coronation would be held at York.

When Aske returned north in January, he met with many of his rebel captains and soldiers, praising the King for his hospitality and understanding. However, some were wary of the King's promises, seeing them as just diplomacy to lure them into false security. It had been nearly two months since the army disbanded, yet still there was no proof of the King's good intentions and nothing had changed. No monastic lands had been returned and there was no move towards ridding the court of the likes of Cromwell and the heretic archbishop Cranmer.

Despite Aske urging peace and patience, fighting broke out amongst various factions of the army and local townspeople. When reports of the unrest reached the King, he dispatched Norfolk to deal with the problem, which was fast escalating and had spread almost to the Scottish borders. Norfolk was provided with a large enough army to suppress any pockets of dissent and had the King's order to execute rebels in every town and village which supported their cause.

In Cumberland, he had to suppress a peasant mob numbering close on 6,000 as they advanced on Carlisle. Although they scattered when the King's army approached, some seventy-four were captured and hung, some on trees in their own gardens and villages. Others were hung in village squares, town greens and in churchyards. Many of those captured were rebellious monks or clergy but the King's order was that all rebels captured should be executed without pity or consideration of their circumstances.

The King was kept abreast of the developments in the north and Jane was alarmed at the pleasure he took in destroying all who tried to defy him. He strutted about the court like a peacock, relishing in the fates of those who could not stand up for themselves. With this new bravado came the inevitable wandering eye; Jane often surprised him in close conversation with one court beauty or another, which made her all the more anxious at her continuing childlessness. The King had also been making wild statements to all who would listen; he again avowed that he would have no children by Jane and that he was getting too old to bear the continuous disappointments. He airily announced that most people in England thought that Mary was the most suitable heir to the throne anyway and saddled as he was with a barren wife, what could he do about it?

For Jane, history seemed to be repeating itself. She had seen Henry's two previous wives suffer repeated miscarriages and still births. She had heard him openly blame them for their failures which then led to him using any means he could to rid himself of them. She could clearly see where it was all going to lead and took the only steps she could to protect herself. She retreated into her shell, becoming quiet, obedient and shunning limelight. Once she had behaved in that manner to contrast herself to Anne Boleyn, now it was no longer an act, it was a way of preserving her life.

Chapter Forty-One

The unrest in the north continued during the early months of 1537, culminating in an attempt to retake the city of Hull, led by Sir Francis Bigod. With much of the army dispersed, Bigod only had a modest following and his efforts were easily crushed by Norfolk and the royal troops.
Meanwhile, back in London, Jane again dared to hope that she might carry the royal heir. She had maintained her new docile and meek persona for almost three months and not only had it kept her from angering the King, it had lured him back to her bed. She was aware that he continued in his dalliances with other ladies of the court but had

resolutely ignored the provocation, reasoning that her only chance of maintaining her position was to keep her opinions to herself, avoid confrontation and quietly go about the business of getting herself with child.

As before, she decided to keep the information to herself until there was no doubt. Also, whilst his mind was so occupied with the rebels in Yorkshire he was paying her little attention by day, so would not notice the extra efforts she took to attempt to maintain her fledgling pregnancy. She avoided exercise as much as possible and spent long periods just sitting quietly with her embroidery. She was optimistic that she was correct in her calculations and planned to give him the happy news at the beginning of March, after she had consulted her physician.

Never had the weeks dragged by so slowly and when at last she felt the time was right, rather than summon Doctor Butts to her chamber and alert her ever watchful ladies of a potential pregnancy, she chose to visit him secretly in his rooms. After a very perfunctory examination and discussion of her symptoms and recent health, he was pleased to confirm her suspicions; there was no doubt in his mind that a child was on the way and the happy event was to be expected in mid-October.

Anxious to share her news, Jane went straight to the privy chamber where she found the King in consultation with Cromwell. One look at his face told her that it was not wise to interrupt, so she quietly withdrew and returned to her own rooms.

After the merest glance at his Queen, and relieved that she had sensibly quit the chamber, the King returned to the matter in hand. "This has gone too far!" he roared, striking the table in his customary fashion. "After all Aske's promises he has failed to quell these outbreaks of violence and now the time has come for me to take action. I revoke the pardons I so generously bestowed on this rabble and I want them all rounded up; every rebel leader who took part in either the Lincolnshire or Yorkshire uprisings is to be arrested and sent for trial."

"Even Aske, Your Grace? He has done his best to prevent the rebels rising again."

"He may have tried, but he has failed, and now he must pay the price for that failure. Send riders to the Duke of Norfolk immediately, I want this matter dealt with once and for all."

It was late in the afternoon before Jane dared to approach the King. Hesitantly she knocked on his door before opening it a crack and peering round. Seeing him slumped in his chair gulping wine from a goblet, she opened the door wider and entered the room, making sure to close it behind her.

"Why do you persist in creeping about like a mouse" he snapped irritably, upon seeing her.

"I do not wish to disturb your important business" she replied meekly. "I saw you were deep in discussion with Cromwell when I came by earlier and needed to make sure that you were at last alone."

"Oh yes?" Draining the last dregs with relish and placing the goblet on the table, he rose to his feet and moved towards her. "Why do you wish to see me alone?"

Jane lowered her head and smiled to herself, before raising her gaze to his. "Can you not guess?" she whispered coquettishly. "At last I can give Your Grace the tidings you sorely wish to hear."

He looked suspicious. "There is much news I would wish to hear" he began, then as Jane continued to smile happily at him, his eyebrows raised in surprise. "You mean you are with child?"

"I am" she replied smugly. Furthermore, I have consulted good Doctor Butts and he tells me that we can expect our child in October."

"That is indeed welcome news" he began cautiously, "however, you should not place too much store on it until you are past the danger of early miscarriage."

Jane was puzzled. "I had thought Your Grace would have been overjoyed."

"I am Jane, I am. But with so many disappointments over the years, I have learned to accept such news with caution."

"All will be well this time, I know it" she told him earnestly.

Catching hold of her face, he kissed her forehead gently. "Let us hope so. Keep me informed, and if all is well in another month, I will notify the council."

Piqued, Jane pulled free and scowled up at him. "I had expected more enthusiasm from you. This is your prince!"

"It may be my prince" he reminded her. "As I said, give it another month and I might begin to believe, but until then, I would be grateful if you would keep this matter to yourself."

"Very well" she replied coldly. "I will take my leave then and allow you to get back to your important business." She glanced meaningfully towards his goblet as she spoke.

He followed her gaze, then glared at her. "It is not your place to tell me what I should and should not do" he told her crossly. "I have many state matters to consider and since I am the one who has to make the decisions, I shall arrive at my conclusions by any means I choose. I suggest you leave me to my business and go about your own."

Norfolk wasted no time in implementing the King's new instructions. The first twelve prisoners were apprehended in Lincolnshire and sent south for questioning and trial. At the end of the month, all twelve were executed. The news of the executions sent shock waves through the entire country, especially the north. All those who had been involved in the uprisings went to ground and hoped that the King would let things lie.

Once March had passed by and Jane continued in good health, the King began to let himself hope for a happy outcome. He sent word of the pregnancy to Norfolk and announced that he would not travel more than sixty miles from Jane in case she experienced any irrational fears for his safety. Now he was beginning to believe, he did not want her emotionally disturbed in case it endangered the infant.

The King informed the council in early April and the matter was discussed at length. The decision was made not to make a formal announcement until such time as the child quickened.

Jane was feeling extraordinarily well, and although her ladies had not been told of her condition, some of them guessed. However they were wise enough to take their cue from Jane and not discuss it openly. She continued with her quiet living and by early May, there was no hiding her condition as her skirts would no longer fit her and she had to advise her ladies to not lace her bodice too tightly.

Her whole household soon got to know and there was subdued celebration in and around the royal quarters. Jane allowed them a little exuberance, then called them together and spoke sternly. "You are all now aware of my happy condition" she began, pausing as a ripple of applause broke out around her, "however, I have to advise you that it must be kept to yourselves. On no account do you share this news with anyone outside these chambers, is that understood?"

Whilst her maids scowled, the older ladies exchanged knowing glances.

"Your Grace," As the Countess of Rutland stepped forward, all eyes turned to her. "Without wishing to pry, might I ask if all is going as it should?"

"It is" Jane confirmed. "Why do you ask such a question?"

"It is just that in the past, tidings of an expected royal infant were spread abroad readily, and I think we are puzzled as to why you wish it not to be so."

Jane pursed her lips and sighed loudly. "I see no reason why I should be expected to explain myself to you" she began "but if you must know, I prefer that the rabble are kept in ignorance of my condition. It is no-one's business but mine and the King's and I prefer to keep it thus for as long as possible."

Eleanor Manners frowned. "When you say 'the rabble' I assume you refer to the King's subjects?"

"Thank you, Eleanor" Jane snapped. "I know very well that they are the King's subjects, but they are also loud, grimy busybodies and I like them not."

"But it might be good for the Londoners" Eleanor persisted, despite Jane's forbidding stare. "They have been much upset by the talk of rebellions in the north, might it not be a timely distraction for them to hear some glad tidings for a change?"

"It is none of their affair" Jane replied, after a moment's pause. "The King has decreed that the information should be kept close until such time as the child quickens, after that, I suppose I shall needs must endure the populace fawning over me. But until then…" She left the sentence unfinished and treated them all to another of her baleful stares.

"Your Grace." Eleanor Manners bowed her head and curtsied respectfully before moving back into the ranks.

As a cold and breezy April gave way to a more temperate May, there were signs that at last the north was settling into a lasting peace. At the beginning of the month the last of the rebel captains were captured and brought to trial, amongst them the unfortunate Sir Francis Bigod, Lord Darcy and Lord Hussey. Aske too was finally apprehended and sent for trial along with the rebel nobles.

Jane was relieved that the conflict appeared to be over even though it had not much affected her since the King became aware of her condition. Up until then, she had been present at most of his strategic meetings and had gained a broad understanding of just how ruthless he could be to those who crossed him. She saw at first-hand how he would break promises without compunction and twist all situations around to suit himself, manipulating events or people until he had achieved his ends.

Since her pregnancy had become known to him, she had been firmly excluded from such councils of war, as he believed that rough talk and details of the violent skirmishes might upset her and the infant. Such exclusion did not suit Jane, she preferred to be fully informed on all matters which might affect the King's mood, so that she would know when to tread carefully with him.

In the event, she did not need to worry about the King's tempers, which could blow up over the merest upset. He was solicitous towards her in the extreme; anything she wanted she could have, and should she wish to speak with him at any time, he would dismiss any minister or noble in order that her wish be granted.

However Jane had one last involvement with the Pilgrimage of Grace when she received a letter from Sir Marmaduke Constable, whose father Sir Robert was one of those rebel captains imprisoned and awaiting trial. He begged her to intercede with the King for his father's life citing a blood link between her and the Constable family through a shared Wentworth ancestor.

Jane agonized over the letter for several days; she sympathized with the rebels and privately supported many of their demands but dare not speak up for Sir Robert, mindful of what had happened when she last challenged the King. So paranoid was he about his absolute power over all that she could not be confident that even her pregnancy would protect her against his possible ire. She did not reply to Sir Marmaduke or mention the contents of the letter to anyone, just quietly threw it on to the fire at the earliest opportunity. If it came to a choice between her safety and that of Sir Robert, there could only be one outcome.

When she next encountered the King she made sure to watch and listen carefully to everything he said and did, just in case he had heard of the arrival of Sir Marmaduke's letter. She knew only too well how information regarding even the most significant word or action inevitably found its way back to Henry. In this instance it seemed that he was unaware, making her doubly glad that she had been sensible enough to burn the evidence.

Chapter Forty-Two

On 27th May, Jane felt her child move for the first time. Henry was overjoyed when she told him the good news and wasted no time in informing the council of the joyous occasion.

When the Duke of Norfolk, who was still in Yorkshire keeping the peace, was informed he ordered Te Deums to be sung in churches throughout the county and bonfires to be lit in celebration. The people of Yorkshire and beyond had been unaware of the coming child and were ready to celebrate. To capitalise on their elevated mood and to demonstrate the bounty of both the King and the nobility Norfolk sent four hogsheads of wine from his own cellar to be distributed amongst the people of York.

Similar celebrations took place in London and beyond. There was a public service of thanksgiving in St Paul's attended by the lord chancellor, lord privy seal, lords and bishops. Also in attendance were the mayor, aldermen and representatives of various city guilds resplendent in their liveries. Huge bonfires were lit and widespread prayers offered for the safe delivery of the child.

To commemorate the occasion, the King presented Jane with a golden casket filled with beautiful jewels and gold trinkets. Jane's eyes widened as she assessed the richness of her gift, picking up handfuls of jewels and allowing them to run through her fingers in wonder. "Your Grace is too generous" she told him. "These are wondrous things."

Henry puffed out his chest in pride and beamed down at her beneficently. "It is my pleasure. My treasury is happily full to overflowing with such richness and beauty and it is only fair that you as the mother of my son, should share in this bounty."

The smile faded from Jane's face as she quickly dropped the jewels back into the casket as though they burned her fingers and took a step back. "Where did these come from?" she asked suspiciously.

"Why, my treasury, as I just said" he replied jovially.

"No, I mean before they were in your treasury?"

He looked puzzled and scratched at his beard absently. "I do not know for sure" he admitted, "they were part of the haul brought back by my commissioners, forfeited from low and disreputable religious houses."

"Then they are stolen!" Jane exclaimed with distaste, backing away even further.

"Nay, sweetheart" he protested. "They are the rightful property of the crown now; they were no doubt inveigled from some unsuspecting merchant in return for a false relic of some saint or other."

"Really?" Jane looked from the casket to the King, her doubt clear.

"Certainly!" he exclaimed. "Far better that they should adorn your royal person than be salted away in some greedy abbot's coffers."

Jane looked again at the casket and could not help agreeing with him. The jewels were far too beautiful to be locked away out of sight. She may not agree with the suppression of the monasteries, but these were the King's property now and who was she to throw such a gift back in his face.

Her mind made up, she beamed at him. "I thank Your Grace, I will treasure them and long remember the happy occasion on which I received them."

The King stepped forward, took her hand and raised it to his lips. "I hope that there will be many more such occasions in the years to come."

Jane blushed prettily and smiled up at him. "I do hope so Your Grace, if God so permits."

In early July, the last rebel captains paid the ultimate price for their foolishness in defying their King, Sir Robert Constable amongst them. Only Aske remained and the King planned to make a particular example of him. On a market day in mid July, he was taken to York and chained to a scaffold. There was to be no merciful quick death for him, he was left there to die from exposure and starvation, with armed guards ensuring that no person went near to offer him food, water or comfort.

Meanwhile the suppression of the monasteries was continued with renewed zeal by the King's commissioners. It seemed that the worst had been routed out and now the commissioners were coming across more and more smaller establishments where no fault could be found. A list of these was sent to the King for his consideration. Although he had originally specified that those found to be serving the community and without sin would be allowed to continue, he was ordering more and more of them closed anyway because of the large amounts of valuable land they possessed.

Now the distasteful business of the Pilgrimage of Grace had been concluded, Jane was once more allowed to sit in on the King's meetings with Cromwell and other ministers. On one particular morning in late July, the matter of the nunnery at Catesby in Northamptonshire was raised. The commissioners recommended that it be kept open as it was discovered to be in perfect order with all the nuns found to be pious and devout in their religious observations. There was no question of any sin or immoral behavior. Due to its situation, Catesby priory was a lifeline to the poor and sick in the local area so Cromwell recommended to the King that the findings of the commissioners be upheld and the nunnery be allowed to continue as it had over the past one hundred and sixty years.

The King read the commissioners' report carefully, noting their praise for the prioress whom they found to be a wise, discreet and very religious woman in charge of nine nuns, all of whom were devout and obedient. He was inclined to follow the recommendations until Cromwell volunteered the fact that the prioress, in fear of suppression, was prepared to buy the priory from the King for 2,000 marks. The King looked up sharply. "What? What did you say?"

"The prioress offers to purchase the priory from Your Grace for the sum of 2,000 marks" Cromwell repeated helpfully.

"Does she now. And where, pray, would a simple prioress acquire such a sum?"

Cromwell shrugged eloquently. "I presume there have been a number of offerings over the years which even given the cost of the priory's good works, amount to a substantial surplus."

The King's little eyes fairly gleamed with greed. "If she is withholding monies which should be spent on the poor and sick I fail to see how such a glowing report has been submitted." The King tapped the report to emphasise his point. "I suspect bribery here."

"Surely Your Grace's commissioners are above bribery?" Cromwell was shocked at the suggestion.

"My dear Thomas, no-one is immune to bribery, be he king or commoner."

Cromwell shifted uneasily from one foot to the other, mindful of the fact that the prioress had offered him the sum of 100 crowns should he succeed in persuading the King to complete the purchase.

"No, there is certainly skullduggery afoot." The King had made up his mind. "I want the priory duly suppressed and the resulting monies sent to the treasury."

"Your Grace!" Jane stepped forward, her face full of concern. "Perhaps you would permit me to buy the priory from you? Then I can ensure that it is properly run and continues to serve the community."

The King rounded on her crossly. "All I require of you Madam is to bring my son safely into this world. I will not tolerate you trying to meddle in my affairs, as I have told you before. There is no place in the politics of this kingdom for a woman's opinion or interference and I would thank you to return to your embroidery."

Meekly Jane did as she was bid. Turning to Cromwell, Henry tossed the report in his direction. "Deal with it" he ordered.

Jane had learned her lesson. Over the following weeks, the fates of dozens of other establishments were discussed and no matter how appalled she was at the outcomes for some of them, she kept her mouth shut. It was not that she did not possess a forceful enough personality to get her views across for she had great strength of character and could construct logical arguments. Her biggest downfall was that she let her emotions carry her away which immediately led to her opinions being dismissed. The King was a great believer in a strong and ruthless regime to discourage insurgence and he had no room for sentiment. The injustices Jane witnessed caused her great distress and she was aware that when her predecessor had found a cause to stand for, she had done it without fear of consequence. Jane had a stronger sense of self-preservation and a natural fear of angering the man who held her very life in his hands.

As her pregnancy progressed, further honours were bestowed on her family. Her elder brother Edward had become Viscount Beauchamp in the weeks following her wedding and now it was the turn of her brother Thomas. He was given the valuable stewardship of Chirk castle and other Welsh border castles, and then gifted the manor of Holt in Cheshire.

Although Jane kept her religious views to herself, the King allowed her to observe certain catholic holy days and feast days. He knew she took no comfort in the new religion and resolved not to stop her doing anything which made her happy; he even consented to the court keeping to the tradition of eating fish on Fridays.

It was not long before Cranmer became uneasy at what he saw as the relaxing of the rules which shaped the reformed faith. Already it was an uphill struggle to persuade the people to let go of the long held holy days and by allowing the court to observe even a few of them, the King was doing the faith no favours at all. Unsure of his reception should he presume to lecture the King over his laxity, he approached Cromwell with his concerns.

Cromwell did not like Archbishop Cranmer, but he had a healthy respect both for his intellect and for his achievements in the establishment of the reformed faith. Therefore he listened gravely to his concerns and found himself agreeing to much of what was said.

"I do not presume to dictate to the King as to how he negotiates this treacherous path to further establishing the Church of England" Cranmer began, "but I cannot condone the open celebration of former feast and holy days at court."

Cromwell sat back in his chair and steepled his fingers together as he formulated his response. "I share your concerns Archbishop, but as you are only too well aware, the King will stop at nothing to appease the Queen in her current condition. He is of the opinion that the more content she is, the better the chance of a safe and successful delivery. I do not believe that it is any secret that the Queen remains as devout a catholic as she ever was and that she will do anything in her power to persuade the King to abandon this new faith and return to Rome."

Cranmer's expression accurately represented his horror. "Do you believe there is a possibility that she may succeed?"

Cromwell shrugged. "I have no idea, I only know that she is more influential now than she has ever been. Should she deliver the longed-for prince, there will be no holding her and we will all be in peril. Over the past months the pope has made several approaches to the King, offering to welcome him back into the fold if he chooses to renounce the new religion. So far, he has rejected all pleas from Rome, but that is not to say that another request in the future may not be considered."

"Is there anything which can be done?"

"I do not believe so." Cromwell pushed himself to his feet, to signify the interview was concluded. "One thing though is for sure; the King thoroughly enjoys his new title as Supreme Head of the Church of England and will not easily give it up. Should the Queen not produce the required prince, he may repudiate her in the near future. Removing her, a stubborn catholic, will not be a problem so long as the reformed faith still holds sway."

Chapter Forty-Three

In June, the new Imperial ambassador arrived at court. It seemed that the brother of the King of Portugal was actively seeking a bride and the ambassador had been sent to approach the King with regard to a match with his daughter Mary.
Loath though she would be to lose Mary, Jane was thrilled at the possibility of a good marriage for her and was pleased when the King allowed her to sit in on the negotiations. The Emperor supported the proposed marriage and sent letters assuring the King and Queen that the young man was highly regarded in Imperial circles and would be a good husband for Mary.
Jane was very much swayed by the possibility and as someone who had become Mary's very good friend,

could see how advantageous such a match would be for her. She promised the ambassador that she would do her very best to encourage Mary to consider the proposal carefully.

In the same month, the question of the monasteries entered a new phase. The King, impatient at the time it was taking to enter and assess all the religious houses, decided that the quickest method would be to bring an end to all of them. The smaller ones could be dispatched without too much difficulty, it was the larger and wealthier establishments which may prove troublesome. On Henry's authority, Cromwell sent letters to all, encouraging them to submit voluntarily, offering suitable incentives to all who complied. Jane watched on sadly as the King continued in his efforts to sweep the last vestiges of the catholic faith aside. She believed it would all end in misery and bloodshed and was appalled at his lack of empathy for those clerics who had served their communities diligently for decades.

As she moved into the sixth month of her pregnancy Jane began to develop cravings for sweetmeats, in particular marzipan and sugared almonds. This was followed by an insatiable desire for quail, peas and cherries. She required nothing else on her table and dined morning noon and night on roasted quail and peas, followed by cherries and sweetmeats. The King joked that he feared the child would be born with wings and a beak.

When it became clear that her desire for quail was not abating, there was a concern that there would not be enough birds in the kingdom to satisfy her.

Pleased that she had such a huge and healthy appetite, the King did not want her upset by the lack of birds so sent messages to the governor of Calais, Lord Lisle, asking him to acquire as many good fat birds as he could and send them across the channel without delay, and if he could find cherries and peas, to do the same.

Lord Lisle mentioned his new and onerous task to his wife, who saw an opportunity to press again for an appointment in Jane's household for their daughter Anne Bassett. Personally delivering a large batch of birds for Jane, Lady Lisle begged an interview, ostensibly to acquaint the Queen of the numbers she had brought.

Delighted with the delivery, for she had been running short and had needed to limit her intake, Jane invited Lady Lisle to take supper with her, which she accepted with gratitude, planning to raise the subject of both of her daughters during the meal. In the event, Lady Lisle did not have to do a thing as Jane had remembered their earlier conversations regarding an appointment.

"Are your daughters both settled now?" Jane enquired, tearing her quail meat from the bone with obvious enjoyment.

Lady Lisle was delighted that the Queen had remembered and relieved that she did not have to engineer the conversation.

"I regret not" she replied. "Both of them are currently in want of employment."

"And are they at court?" Jane's mouth was so full, that Lady Lisle had to strain to make out her words.

"Why yes" she replied after a pause. "They accompanied me in the bringing of the birds and both sit yonder." She gestured to a table further down the great hall, where the two girls sat with their aunt.

Jane followed Lady Lisle's pointing finger and saw two young girls, both dressed in the French fashion, sitting demurely with an older woman. "Which is Anne?" she asked.

"Anne sits on the left, her sister Catherine beside her."

Jane nodded enthusiastically. "Anne is the prettier of the two, you may bring her to meet me tomorrow and if I find her satisfactory, I will take her into my household."

Lady Lisle was overjoyed. "I thank Your Grace from the bottom of my heart" she exclaimed. "I will bring Anne to meet you in the morning."

"Make that the afternoon" Jane told her. "I often lie late in bed."

"But of course." Lady Lisle risked a discreet glance at Jane's stomach and thought she was a very goodly size considering she still had nearly three months to go.

"You are aware of the requirements for my maids?" Jane spoke sharply, not appreciating Lady Lisle's scrutiny.

"I am not. I assumed we would be told on the morrow?"

"I can tell you some of the conditions now so that you are prepared for the expenses. She will need at least two changes of clothes, one damask and one silk. Also double gowns and kirtles of silk, matching headdresses and suitable jewellery. She will need her own servant to wait upon her, for which she will have to pay, and also supply her own bedding."

Lady Lisle nodded gravely. "I see."

Jane wiped her greasy fingers on a napkin, then

turned to glare at Lady Lisle. "I was not finished" she reproved. "I observe that both of your daughters are dressed in the French fashion. This is not acceptable at my court, I require my maids and my ladies to dress in the more modest English style complete with gable hoods."

"Yes, Your Grace." Lady Lisle was chastened by Jane's sudden show of petulance but not surprised. She had been warned by others that the Queen's moods were variable and that she thoroughly enjoyed wielding what limited power she had. "Whilst Anne's new gowns are being made, will it be acceptable for her to continue wearing what she already has?"

Jane pursed her lips and looked hard at Anne Bassett. The girl was pretty, petite, brunette and looked very fetching in her French hood. It was all rather too reminiscent of that other Frenchified brunette. She turned her most unforgiving stare on Lady Lisle. "Assuming I accept her, I will allow her to wear what she has until suitable replacements have been acquired. But I warn you, it will not be for long if she wishes to keep her employment with me."

Cromwell did not usually dirty his hands with petitions from the needy, but he had made an exception in this case. Running his eyes over the neat script in front of him, he read the sad tale of a young woman, widowed early and the mother of two young children who upon the death of her husband no longer had a house of her own and was forced to live on very reduced means and rely on the hospitality of others. Many a young woman could tell a similar story, but this was not just any young woman, this was Elizabeth Ughtred, sister of the Queen.

Elizabeth had thought of a way out of her destitution; she begged the grant of one of the dissolved abbeys as by selling the goods, she could at least keep a roof over her children's heads until such time as she found another husband.

Cromwell could not help but be gratified that she had appealed directly to him, rather than approach her sister the Queen. He wondered if she was astute enough to realise that Queen though she may be, Jane had very little power or influence at court and would be forced to beg the favour from the King. At least she would if she actually wished to help her sister and Cromwell was not so sure that she would. He knew how piqued Jane had been when her younger sister had found a husband so easily whilst she herself had been overlooked, for it was his business to know all things about all people. Particularly those people close to the King.

If Elizabeth Ughtred needed a husband to support her, he knew the ideal candidate. His own son Gregory was in want of a wife and the sister of the Queen would be a most advantageous match for him.

Elizabeth accepted Gregory gratefully and the marriage went ahead within a matter of weeks. Jane was not directly informed of her sister's remarriage but came to know about it through court gossip.

Although she had never been close to Elizabeth, she was nonetheless annoyed that her sister had not sought her help or approval.

Anne Bassett was interviewed, scrutinized and

accepted as a maid of honour by the Queen.

Although Jane had kept her word to allow Anne to begin her duties still attired in her French fashions, it quickly became clear that a young pretty girl in such fetching and often revealing attire attracted much male attention. After the King had stared at her continuously throughout the duration of two consecutive meals, Jane decided she had to act. It was not difficult to know exactly what was running through his mind, and Jane was not prepared to suffer any competition, especially with a girl who had more charms than Jane could ever hope to acquire in a lifetime.

Before retiring that night, she called Anne to her and told her in no uncertain terms that on reflection, she felt that Anne's attire lowered the tone of the court and that she had leave to return home until such time as her new wardrobe was complete.

Very much downcast though she was, Anne had no choice but to follow the Queen's orders. Within a week, the minimum dress requirements were received from the seamstresses so Anne carefully dressed in the modest style required by the Queen and presented herself for approval. Jane ran a satisfied eye over the girl's apparel; dark coloured silk which covered her to her neck, the Queen's cypher prominently displayed on her bodice, and well above the required minimum of pearls

decorating her girdle and the gable hood. Jane nodded slowly, bestowed a brief cold smile and then jerked her head to the side to indicate that Anne

should rejoin the other maids. The girl had been transformed from teenaged temptress to dowdy insignificance most satisfactorily and Jane was sure that the King would not look her way again.

As the weeks dragged by agonizingly slowly, the weather suddenly became much hotter. Jane could not settle and wandered from room to room complaining of the heat, pursued by a flurry of ladies and maids carrying fans to cool her whenever she dropped into a chair. As the court was at Greenwich, the Queen also liked to walk in the gardens if the sun was not too hot; the privy garden abutted the river bank and she liked to catch what breeze she could from the river.

On one such day she was walking slowly along the path by the river when she heard a commotion from the opposite river bank. Ever curious, she stopped beside the clipped yew hedge and craned her neck to see over the top of the thick foliage. Her ladies, taking their cue from the Queen, did the same.

Jane had risen up on tiptoe, but still could barely see over the top of the hedge. Looking around in frustration, she spied the Countess of Sussex, easily the tallest of her ladies, watching events on the opposite bank with interest.

"Mary, what is going on?" Jane asked crossly. "Is it some sort of celebration, or has there been an accident?"

"I cannot say for sure, Your Grace" Mary shook her head and frowned. "There is a gathering of townspeople just outside the gates of Archbishop Cranmer's house and they appear to be trying to lift up someone who has fallen."

"Fallen, how?" Jane craned again, trying to see.

"Your Grace" Eleanor Manners had stepped forward. "It is not advisable for Your Grace to stretch too much, it may disturb the infant's comfort."

"Very well." Jane immediately relaxed and placed both hands over the mound of the child. "Thank you Eleanor, I had not thought of that."

Mary was still looking over the hedge at the group of people; there was movement amongst those closest to the person on the ground, then suddenly as one they all seemed to draw back in horror. "Oh." Mary's soft exhalation immediately captured everyone's attention.

"What is it?" Jane demanded. "Another drunkard I suppose."

"I suspect it is a little more serious than that" Mary began, "from trying to help the person, everyone has drawn back holding their mouths and pointing." She continued to watch and strained to listen to the cries coming from the onlookers. Gradually the voices became louder as more and more people were drawn towards the group through natural curiosity, and Mary finally grasped what was being said. Shocked and distressed, she raised her hands to her face and turned towards the Queen, her eyes downcast.

"Mary?" Jane reached out to her in concern. "What is it? What did you hear?"

Mary raised agonized eyes to Jane's face. "Plague" she whispered. "It is the plague."

Chapter Forty-Four

Jane was terrified. Pestilence was bad enough at any time, but with her child only two months away from birth, she knew only too well that it was imperative that she keep herself healthy. Should she contract the sickness and cause harm to the child, the King's disappointment and rage would be immense. She did not believe that he would be overly concerned if she suffered, but should the child be affected there was no question that she would be held to blame.
In an effort to protect herself, she ordered the windows overlooking the river to be sealed and let it be known that she would not be accepting any visitors whilst the disease was rife in the city. She even turned away Archbishop Cranmer, since she had first-hand knowledge that someone had died at his very gates.

It was not good for the child, she knew, but she could not stop herself pacing about her apartments and worrying that sooner or later someone would bring the disease into the palace. It was no consolation that she felt very well in herself because the onset of the disease was always sudden and it seemed to target generally fit and healthy people. The King, hearing of her mounting distress, was concerned enough to dismiss his ministers and come to her chambers. He was alarmed at the sight of her; she was sweating, pale and seemed on the point of collapse.

"Jane, this will not do." Gently he steered her into a chair and signalled for wine. "Here, drink this and calm yourself."

"I cannot" she waved the goblet away and looked up at him in desperation. "I am so afraid" she confided. "Once the plague reaches the palace all will be lost, I know it."

"There is no need to be so alarmed" he soothed. "As yet, it is not widespread and I have ordered that no-one must leave the palace to visit the city."

"But kitchen supplies come in every day, who is to say that the pestilence will not be carried in with the flour or the grain?"

"That will not happen. The merchants leave the sacks in the granaries, they do not have direct contact with the kitchen hands. Be of good cheer; it is unfortunate that people are dying but so far the numbers are small in comparison to previous plague summers."

"I do not feel safe." Jane looked around fearfully, gripping the King's hands with surprising strength. "I want to go far from here. Please, can we leave for the country?"

"I would not wish to go too far with you in this

condition" he began, "would you feel better if we went to Hampton Court?"

Jane shook her head determinedly. "No, it is right on the river and the pestilence always comes off the river."

The King begged to differ, but he did not want to agitate her further by disagreeing with her. "Windsor then" he offered. "The infection will not have travelled that far and all reported plague cases are so far within the city walls."

"Yes, Windsor." She brought his hands to her face and kissed them gratefully. "Can we go now? I do not want to spend another night here."

"Of course" he told her. "I will make the arrangements immediately and we can ride within the hour, if you feel strong enough?"

"I have to be strong enough because if I stay here I will surely die and the child with me."

Henry was used to neurotic pregnant women, but something about Jane's panic bred a similar fear in him. "Order your women to pack what you need and rest quietly. I will send for you as soon as all is ready for the off."

Because of the suddenness of the departure, the household numbers at Windsor would be much reduced, but Jane was not concerned about that. If anything, she felt that the less people around her the better. Henry was true to his word and by suppertime they were safely within Windsor's ancient walls.

"You will be content to remain here until it is time to withdraw to the lying-in chamber?" the King asked her after they had eaten.

"I think so" Jane replied. "Although the river is close I do not fear the approach of the pestilence as much here and I do in the city."

"And you are still happy for the child to be born at Hampton Court?"

"Oh yes" Jane smiled happily. "It is my favourite of Your Grace's royal residences and there is nowhere I would rather be when my time comes."

"That is good" the King nodded with satisfaction. "If you are feeling strong enough to walk a little way, I have a gift I would like to show you."

Jane perked up immediately. "A gift? For me?"

"For you both." Henry nodded towards Jane's swollen body as he spoke. "It is a happy coincidence that we are here because this gift was made by local craftsmen in the town."

Jane smiled vacantly; she had no idea what he was talking about but rose to her feet with as much energy as she could muster. "I am ready" she announced. "Pray lead the way."

From the King's privy chamber, they moved slowly down the long corridor to the watching chamber and from there into an adjoining large room which Jane had not seen before. There, in the middle of the chamber was a very large bed. Jane looked at it for a moment then turned to the King questioningly. "It is for you, for your lying-in" he gestured grandly towards the huge piece of furniture. "Do you like it? I think it very fine and I want my son born in the best that English craftmanship can produce."

Jane looked at it in silence. She did not like it all and thought it worse than monstrous. It reminded her uncomfortably of Anne Boleyn's great bed at Greenwich, the bed she had hated on sight because of its enormity and vulgar gilding. This bed was remarkably similar and quite possibly even larger. The head and footboards bore her badges and the royal coat of arms whilst the posts were elaborately carved with birds and foliage. The whole thing was heavily gilded and hung with royal blue velvet curtains embroidered with phoenixes and hers and Henry's initials.

"Well?" The King was waiting anxiously for her reaction.

"It is very large" she observed.

"You don't like it!" Henry's face fell in disappointment.

"I do!" she lied. "It is as you say, very fine."

"Then why do you look so unimpressed?"

Jane looked at him, wondering if she should just tell him the truth and get it over with. It would not make any difference, she would still have to accept the bed and give birth in it, although it was so wide that she felt sure that the physicians and midwives would have to climb on it in order to assist with the birth.

She took a deep breath. "You remember the bed in the Queen's chamber at Greenwich, the one I wanted you to remove?"

He looked at her suspiciously, little eyes so narrowed they all but disappeared into the folds around his eye sockets. "You mean the French gilded bed? Of course I remember, it is the most expensive item of furniture I have ever commissioned."

"This reminds me of it, it is so similar."

Baffled he looked from her to the bed, then back to her. "There is no comparison!" he roared. "This bed is altogether bigger and finer, and furthermore it is English, lovingly crafted by English craftsmen, for you."

"And I appreciate it" she told him earnestly. "I appreciate both their skilled work and your thoughtfulness in commissioning it for me."

Henry's lower lip protruded making him look like a petulant child. "I do not think you do. I go to great lengths to surprise you and you all but throw it back in my face."

Jane sighed and looked at the floor. She had said her piece, now she had to find a way to accept the wretched thing and soothe his hurt pride. "I think it perhaps because I do not consider myself worthy of something so grand." She hung her head, hardly daring to breathe as she waited for his reaction.

"Why sweetheart!" She could tell from his changed tone that she had somehow managed to come up with the exact words to rescue the situation. He put one heavy hand on her shoulder and tilted her face up to his with the other. "Do not underestimate yourself so. You are my Queen and I consider this bed worthy both for you and my son."

Relieved beyond measure, she smiled up at him. "Then I am most honoured to accept your gift."

"Good. That is good!" Pleased, he hugged her briefly, taking care not to squeeze her too tightly. "I will arrange to have it dismantled and taken to Hampton Court."

By early September the worst of the plague was over and although many had died, fewer and fewer new cases were being reported. Heartened by that news, Jane and her household prepared to move to Hampton Court. In a fortnight it would be time for her to go into seclusion to await the birth and she wanted to be sure that all was ready. Although the King accompanied her to Hampton Court, once she was settled he announced that he would not be staying there with her.

"But why?" Jane was perplexed. "I had expected that you would be close by me during these final weeks."

"And I shall" he told her. "I will stay at Esher with my household. It is but three miles as the crow flies and I feel that it would be better for you to have less people around you at this time. There is always a chance of infection where there are large numbers of people. You are confident in your household and you know they have kept themselves away from pestilence. It is for your own peace of mind that I do this."

It was on the tip of Jane's tongue to ask why he suddenly feared infection, especially now the plague was dying down. She suspected he had made certain plans now she was close to her time and did not wish to be at the beck and call of a peevish pregnant wife. There was no point in arguing with him, his mind was obviously made up. She did not wish to part on bad terms, especially since she would be going into seclusion within the fortnight. "I thank you for your consideration" she told him. "I am sure I will be very well looked after here and safe from harm."

He looked mightily relieved, she thought, as he grinned widely and kissed her hand courteously. "Remember," he told her, "I am only a short ride away. If you need me, send for me and I will come."

"I will" she confirmed. "Will I see you before I retire to the lying-in chamber?"

He frowned. "When will that be?"

"It is fixed for September 16th."

"Oh yes, that is two weeks hence, I will make sure I see you before then so that I can wish you well in your labours."

As she watched him ride away, Jane was suddenly taken with a profound sense of unease. Despite his protestations of averting possible infection by keeping his household at a distance, she still wanted him near as she approached this most crucial time of her life. Although everything seemed to be going well as she approached the birth, what if something went wrong?

With a sigh, she turned away from the window and placed her hands over the child. As if sensing her concern, it moved restlessly under her hands, kicking out sharply. Jane smiled and silently admonished herself over what she believed were but the irrational fears of a pregnant woman.

Chapter Forty-Five

Despite his promise to visit, the King generally kept his distance, only spending a few days with her before she took to the lying-in chamber. On her final day of court life, he accompanied her as she walked slowly around her garden at Hampton Court and admired the beautiful white roses she had bade her gardener plant against the south facing wall. They were still in full bloom and their perfume was intoxicating as they moved gently in the soft September breeze.

"Let us sit here awhile." Gallantly the King handed Jane to the stone bench, then sat down heavily beside her. Looking about himself with pleasure at the arrangement of scented flowering plants within their neatly clipped box hedges, he told Jane that she had crafted the most delightful garden he had seen in many a year.

"Thank you, Your Grace" Jane replied gravely. "I designed a similar scheme at Wolf Hall, but this is finer I think since Your Grace's gardeners are far more skilled than the local men we employed in Wiltshire."

The King screwed up his face as he tried to recall the gardener she most favoured; he had often seen her deep in conversation with him, pointing out the beds she wished him to make and explaining how she wished them planted.

Suddenly his brow cleared as he remembered. "Chapman. That is your preferred gardener's name, is it not?" He turned to her for confirmation.

"Indeed" she smiled. "He is most knowledgeable and has been a constant inspiration to my efforts."

The King nodded, his eye drawn again to the profusion of white roses. "The white rose of York" he murmured, more to himself than Jane. "I well remember my mother's chambers were always perfumed by them. The blooms in the warm weather and the oils and dried petals in winter." His eyes misted over as he thought of his beloved mother, taken from him far too soon.

Jane glanced at him sharply, noting his nostalgic, sentimental expression. She did not want him brooding over the past, she wanted him thinking of her and the infant they were about to welcome into the world.

"We will bring him here soon, and he will sit with us and learn about the joys of nature" she enthused.

"Not in the depths of winter" the King observed dryly. "We will all be taken by the ague if we perch on stone benches."

The warm September sun which they had been so enjoying, suddenly disappeared behind a bank of dark forbidding clouds. Squinting up at the sky, the King rose to his feet and held out his hand to assist Jane to stand. "Time to go in, I think" he told her. "We have had the best of the day."

Getting to her feet, Jane stood for a moment looking around her garden. Even under brooding clouds it still gave her pleasure. As they moved slowly back towards the palace, she glanced back once more over her shoulder, imprinting the image of her nodding roses on her memory. From nowhere, she had a premonition that she would never see them again.

The following day Jane attended a special mass and then joined favoured members of her inner household in the withdrawing chamber for the final time. Together they talked of mundane matters and took light refreshments. Jane tried to pretend to herself that this was just another social gathering and that soon she would not have to withdraw into the birth chamber from which all natural light was excluded. Now the time had finally come, she was afraid. Afraid of the pain which she knew awaited her, afraid of disappointing the King and producing a dead or female child, but most of all, afraid of never seeing the light of day again. The premonition she had experienced in the garden had unsettled her and was tarnishing the approach of what should be a joyous event.

Finally she could delay her departure no longer and with the good wishes of all, moved slowly over the threshold into the birthing chamber, gasping as the heat from the roaring fire took her breath way. With trepidation she looked about her; at the tented ceiling, the sealed windows and the expectant faces of her chosen waiting women. The great gilded bed dominated the room, looking even larger now it had been fitted with its high over stuffed mattress and bedlinen. At the foot of the bed, and looking tiny by comparison, was a long, low day bed. It was there that Jane chose to seat herself, watching as the great oak doors were slowly closed, shutting out the world she knew and sealing her inside this strange womb-like environment.

There were books should she wish to read, there could be soft lute music if she wanted it, she could sew and fashion garments for the infant should she wish, but Jane refused all such diversions. All she wanted to do was pray earnestly for a healthy son, and such prayer dominated every waking hour in the birth chamber. With her ladies ranged about her, she spent hour upon hour on her knees in front of the small oratory, her eyes either firmly closed or fixed on the small statue of the blessed virgin. She prayed until she near dropped from exhaustion, only pausing in her entreaties to eat and sleep.

The onset of labour three weeks later, was so subtle she scarcely recognized it for what it was. She had an ache in her back and a tightness in her chest and began pacing about the chamber agitatedly.

"Your Grace should try to rest." Eleanor Manners attempted to steer Jane to a seat but was shaken off angrily.

"Leave me be Eleanor" she snapped. "I will rest when I see fit and not before."

"Shall I call your physician?"

"No, it is not time. I just feel uncomfortable, that is all, it will pass."

Eleanor withdrew tactfully but watched her mistress with troubled eyes. A mother herself, she knew that if Jane was not already in labour, then she very soon would be.

It was a little over an hour later that Jane felt the first painful twinge. Surprised, she rested her hand on the window ledge and bent over slightly, flapping crossly at her women as they immediately surrounded her. "Do not fuss" she ordered, "it is nothing." As the pain passed, she continued her pacing, only to be stopped in her tracks a few minutes later as more pain gripped her. As the contraction passed she became aware of a trickle of warm fluid running down her legs and swept her skirts aside with an exclamation of disgust at the sight of the pooled liquid on the floor. Looking up, she met the steady gaze of Eleanor Manners.

"I will call your physician" Eleanor said firmly, ignoring the glare which Jane directed at her.

He was there within minutes. Doctor William Butts had been a royal physician for more than a decade and was a kindly elderly man whom Jane trusted implicitly. "It is time for Your Grace to take to your bed" he told her, after a perfunctory examination during which Jane refused to lie down. "Your ladies need to dress you for the ordeal to come, to facilitate easy examination and delivery."

Jane said nothing, just stared fearfully at the great bed which squatted before her, imagining it was awaiting the time when it could swallow her up. "I do not want to" she replied, struggling futilely again the hands which held her.

"Your Grace" the physician said patiently. "I cannot care for you adequately and see your child safe into the world if you will not obey my instructions."

Wild-eyed, she glanced about her at her women, seeing the mixture of emotions on their faces. It was only when she met the calm, patient expression of Eleanor Manners that she became still and meekly allowed her ladies to take her behind the screen and replace her gown with one of the many long loose white robes set aside for the purpose.

Suitably clad at last, she climbed reluctantly on to the bed and sat up, supported by huge feather pillows.

"Your Grace should lie down" Doctor Butts directed.

"I do not want to" she retorted. "I feel perfectly well thank you, I do not believe the birth is imminent."

The physician bowed and stepped back. "As Your Grace wishes. I will wait a while and see how your pains progress."

Seeing Jane lean back and close her eyes, Eleanor approached the physician. "I am sorry that the Queen is so disobliging" she began. "She has been difficult with us these last few weeks and I suspect it is because she fears the upcoming ordeal."

"Every pregnant woman approaches the birth differently" Doctor Butts observed. "It seems the Queen's way is to fight against inevitability, but that will soon pass once her body gets on with the business of expelling the infant. She will not fight against that, nor will she feel the need to."

"Will all go well?" Eleanor glanced towards the bed.

"My dear Lady Manners, you know as well as anybody that these things cannot be predicted. In her favour, she is fit, well-nourished and relatively young. She has had a straightforward and easy pregnancy, and there is every possibility that the birth will be equally uncomplicated."

Five hours later, the pains were strong and regular and Jane was beginning to struggle with their intensity. "How much longer?" she moaned as Mary Countess of Sussex gently mopped her forehead with a damp cloth.

"It will be soon, I am sure" Mary told her, although in truth having never laboured herself, she had no idea.

"Lady Manners." Doctor Butts gestured that she should approach him. Eleanor, still outwardly maintaining her cool and unruffled air, although inside she was deeply anxious, joined him where he stood. "Lady Manners, as the senior lady present, I must inform you that I am concerned at the lack of progress" he began. "The Queen has been labouring now for many hours yet the child remains high in the womb and the birth canal firmly closed."

"Then what is to be done?" she whispered.

"There is time yet" he soothed. "The Queen will continue to suffer greatly, but I believe some fluid still remains around the child and it seems relatively undisturbed thus far."

Trying to conceal her worry, Eleanor approached the bed and smiled reassuringly down at Jane. "What is it? What did he say?" Jane asked fretfully.

"All is progressing, Your Grace, just a little more slowly than anticipated. "Rest as much as you can between pains, you will need your strength when the time comes to expel the child."

"Nobody warned me it would take this long!" she exclaimed. "I find I have renewed respect for my own mother for the hours she must have laboured to bring her large family into the world."

"It is different for every woman" Eleanor soothed. "Some can birth their children quickly and easily, others take longer. You are doing very well and coping with the pain magnificently."

"In truth, the pains have abated a little" Jane told her. "I will try to rest a little now, as you advise."

"As Your Grace wishes." Eleanor curtseyed and backed away. "If you need me, I will be just here, seated close beside you."

"Thank you, Eleanor, you are a great comfort." Jane groped for Eleanor's hand and clasped it loosely. "I confess I am afraid but your serenity gives me courage."

Chapter Forty-Six

Twenty-four hours later the situation was getting desperate. Jane was in terrible agony and screaming shrilly with every pain which tore through her body. Again and again she submitted to the physician's examination and every time he came away, his face was more grave than before.

"Is there still no progress?" Eleanor asked desperately.

"Very little" he replied. "The child's head has descended a little, but the birth canal has opened but an inch. There is no exit for the child and neither will there be unless her contractions increase in intensity."

"But she is so much pain, surely her body is doing its utmost?"

He shook his head sadly. "Because the child was so

high in the womb at the onset of her labours, her body is becoming exhausted at the effort to move the child down into her pelvic cavity whilst simultaneously stimulating the birth canal to enlarge. Furthermore, the fluids have drained from around the child, making it imperative that delivery takes place as soon as possible. It is evident from the colour of the fluids that the infant is becoming distressed. The time is coming when a decision will need to be made as to whether the King wishes the Queen to be saved, or the child. I am not confident I can save both."

Eleanor's eyes filled with tears as again the Queen's screams filled the chamber her agony causing her to twist convulsively on the great bed. "I will do it" she decided. "I will go to the King and acquaint him of your opinion."

It was with some relief that Eleanor slipped through the oak doors. As she shut them firmly, the Queen's screams were very slightly muffled, and she found her ears were ringing in the comparative silence of the watching chamber. Members of Jane's household were ranged about the room and all looked up hopefully as Eleanor appeared. Not trusting herself to speak, she shook her head and moved swiftly towards the King's privy chamber.

She was admitted at once. The King was sitting at his work table his head in his hands. As she appeared he looked up, the hope in his eyes dying as he read her solemn expression. "Lady Manners! What news?"

Eleanor opened her mouth to speak but no words came. She had volunteered to appraise the King of the situation yet had not paused to think how she would do it.

"The Queen suffers greatly and there is no end in sight" she began. "The physician is beginning to fear for the child because the Queen's body does not propel him sufficiently."

"Then what is to be done?" The King rose to his feet wearily and came towards her.

"I believe he can perform some intervention to conclude the matter, but he fears that the lives of either the mother or child may be lost during the procedure."

The King said nothing, just regarded her steadily, although he had an idea of what was to come.

"Your Grace" Eleanor said, "Doctor Butts needs guidance from you as to what he does next. He begs you inform him that if it comes down to a choice, which of the two he should save; the mother or the child."

Henry pursed his mouth, pretending to consider, when in truth he had instantly decided. "My dear Lady Manners" he began. "There can only be one option. If it comes down to a choice between the two then he must save the child. It would be regrettable should the Queen not survive her ordeal but wives are easily come by; sons, less so."

Eleanor could not hide her horror. "But Your Grace, the Queen!"

The King regarded her coolly. "Your loyalty to the Queen is admirable Lady Manners, but it seems to me that even should she survive the ordeal at the cost of the child's life, she will never have more children. Harsh though it seems, it is the child which must be preserved. Kindly direct Doctor Butts accordingly."

Dumbfounded, Eleanor curtsied and backed away. As she stood in the open doorway, an eerie howling echoed through the corridors, a sound so terrible that the King felt the small hairs on the back of his neck prickle in response.

"What is that?" he demanded.

Eleanor looked back at him not troubling to hide her scorn. "That, Your Grace, is the Queen."

The birthing chamber was ominously quiet as Eleanor slipped back through the doors. Glancing across at the bed, she saw that Jane was lying still and quiet, a deathly pallor about her face, her white gown wet with a mixture of sweat and blood.

As the physician hastened towards her, Eleanor asked fearfully "What has occurred?"

"The Queen's pains lessen as the hours progress" he told her. "I fear for both their lives unless matters conclude soon. I have mixed a potion which should stimulate her womb to do its work, and I would be grateful if you would assist me in its administration."

"How quickly will it take effect?"

"We will see a change before the hour is out. I will need you to raise the Queen up a little to avoid too much spillage."

Together they approached the bed. Jane was not asleep and turned her head as they drew near. "I cannot do it" she whispered, her voice hoarse from the long hours of screaming.

"Your Grace, we have a potion which will help you" Eleanor replied, slipping her arm under Jane's pillow and raising her a little. "Try to drink this."

"Is it poison?" Jane murmured. "I would welcome it

for I feel I am already in hell and fast losing my hold on life."

"It is a soothing elixir and it will speed Your Grace's labours" Doctor Butts told her as he tipped the liquid slowly through her barely open mouth.

Jane screwed up her face and moved her head aside, coughing and spluttering. "There is nothing soothing about that!" she exclaimed. "It tastes evil."

The physician did not answer, just expertly caught hold of her chin and tipped the remaining potion down her throat before she had the chance to protest further.

Carefully Eleanor lowered the pillow and pulled the bloodied sheet up to the Queen's shoulders. "Take your chance to have a few moments rest" she urged. "It will all be over soon."

The potion took effect within fifteen minutes and once again the chamber was filled with Jane's piercing screams as she writhed futilely on the bed, gripping and twisting the sheets as she desperately sought to relieve her torment. As the hours stretched on, there was no respite for her as her body renewed its efforts to expel the child.

Jane was no longer lucid, any attempt to speak with her was met by a glassy stare before she once again plunged into the depths of more agony than any woman should be expected to bear.

Holding the Queen down as once again her body contorted in an uncontrollable spasm, Eleanor found herself fighting to hold back tears. This was not how it was supposed to be; every woman experienced

pain during labour, but the torment the Queen was enduring was unimaginable, even for those women about her who knew what it was like to give birth. Mary, Countess of Sussex had fainted at the sight of the blood which the Queen's body was randomly expelling and had been carried from the chamber, prompting the physician to dismiss any other of the women who had not themselves given birth, believing the trauma they were witnessing to be damaging. As a rule, maids were not allowed anywhere near a birthing chamber, but Jane had asked for her particular favourites to be present, little knowing what horrors awaited.

Examining the Queen with difficulty, Doctor Butts glanced across at Eleanor. "I did not ask you the result of your visit with the King, although knowing his mind as I do, I suspect I already know his wishes. All efforts are to be directed towards the child are they not?"

Eleanor nodded wordlessly, her helpless gaze travelling from his face, to the Queen and then to the sealed and covered windows. She had no idea whether it was day or night and could not even begin to comprehend how long the Queen's ordeal had so far lasted. She herself was exhausted beyond measure and that had to pale into insignificance before the obvious depths of Jane's fatigue.

Although she seemed insensible to onlookers, Jane in fact did have some understanding of what was going on around her, particularly in the brief interludes between the pains. She had heard the exchange between Eleanor and the physician and now knew that the King valued her life as nothing next to that of the child. She wondered if it was even worth fighting to stay alive anymore, because at the moment that was all she was doing. The birthing process seemed to have left her behind and she no longer felt the pain as a physical expression, although her body and her voice still reacted to the spasms in noisy unison. She felt as though she were being tossed on a stormy ocean towards shore, one moment being drawn towards a peaceful haven, the next being snatched back into the depths in the coils of a sea monster. The rhythm was strangely soothing but with each spasm she felt as though she were being drawn deeper into the timeless depths and the blessed pulse towards shore was no more than the duration of a blink of the eye.

Gasping involuntarily as another spasm hit her, she suddenly felt many hands on her, pulling at her, pushing at her, prising her body apart. She wished she could open her eyes and tell them to stop; she just wanted to be left alone to drift in her ocean. They were hurting her, she felt as though she was being torn apart by wild animals. Suddenly finding her voice, she dug her head hard back into the pillow and summoned up a final, agonized scream.

As the sound lessened to nothing more than a whimper, a new sound was heard in the unnaturally hushed chamber; the thin, weedy wail of a newborn infant.

Jane was unaware that they had pulled the scrawny scrap from her body, but she heard the wail and managed a small smile of satisfaction before she lapsed into unconsciousness. She had done it; she had borne a live child.

Chapter Forty-Seven

There was so much blood. Eleanor struggled to believe that a body could spew so much yet still somehow manage to sustain life. For the Queen was still alive, but only barely.
As the child had been pulled from Jane's body, an unbelievable bloody torrent had followed which had been hardly stemmed by the time her body expelled the afterbirth. This precipitated another haemorrhage which refused to abate, pooling around Jane's body until it dribbled in rivulets down the sheets to the floor.
The midwives were clustered around the child, rubbing the puny grey body until it took on a strong pink glow and encouraging it to scream lustily and clear its lungs. In all the chaos and confusion, no-one

had thought to question the infant's sex, and it wasn't until the child was wrapped warmly and placed in a crib did one of the midwives say "God be praised, a prince of Wales."

Meanwhile, all Doctor Butt's attention was directed towards the Queen. Somehow, he had contrived to pull a live child from the Queen's body and his professional pride would not allow him to watch her bleed to death. She had endured unbelievable agony over the two days and three nights she had laboured and he vowed that he would do his utmost to save her.

Gradually the blood flow lessened until it was but a trickle. He could not estimate how much the Queen had lost but he believed that should she stay free from infection and be encouraged to rest and take nourishment, she may survive.

It was as Jane was being lifted into a clean dry bed, dressed in a pristine robe, that she began to regain consciousness. It came about slowly; she felt as though she were fighting her way through dark veils of gossamer guided by light and noise. It seemed to take an eternity, but suddenly she was thrust into a blinding light and surrounded by a hubbub of excited voices. Blinking in confusion, she lay still, too exhausted to even move her head and quite certain that should she open her mouth, no sound would come forth.

The first face to loom over her was Eleanor's, pale and concerned. It was hard, but somehow Jane managed to force her mouth into a semblance of a smile, which prompted Eleanor to beam widely.

"Your Grace, you are back with us at last!" she exclaimed.

Jane nodded. It took a huge effort to speak, but she managed it. "What of the child?" she whispered hoarsely. "Does it live? Is it a boy?"

Eleanor caught hold of Jane's hand and kissed it fervently. "You have birthed a healthy prince of Wales, Your Grace."

The Queen's sigh of relief was heard by everyone. "Thank God" she breathed. "I have never known such suffering but the knowledge that I have done my duty is balm to my wounded body."

"Here he is." As one of the midwives handed the baby to Eleanor, she brought him close to Jane's face then laid him beside her.

Jane blinked in an effort to focus on her child. He was a rosy red colour, his face screwed up so tight she could barely discern his features whilst his little hands waved aimlessly above his lose swaddling.

"Would Your Grace like to hold him?" one of the midwives asked.

Jane shook her head wearily. "Perhaps later" she whispered. "I feel so very fatigued."

Carefully the child was removed and the Queen raised a little so that she could slake her thirst. "Thank you" she said as she was settled back into the bed. "Tell me, has the King been informed?"

"A messenger has this minute been sent to tell him that the child is born" Doctor Butts informed her. "I thought it better to delay the news until we had attended to Your Grace."

"I should sit up and make myself presentable then." Jane tried futilely to raise herself but found she had no strength.

"Your Grace need not worry" Eleanor intervened. "The King is not presently in the palace and it will take some time for him to get here. There is time for rest and he will not expect you to be sitting up or holding court, not after your ordeal."

As the gist of the conversation between the physician and Eleanor came back to her, Jane pulled a rueful face. "He will probably be surprised that I am even alive, given that he was ready to sacrifice my life for that of his child!"

Eleanor winced, she had not realised that the Queen was aware of her conversation. "He will be delighted that you are both well" she offered.

Jane sniffed disdainfully then closed her eyes. It was too much of an effort to think, let alone talk.

It seemed to her than she had no sooner drifted off into a restless sleep than she was rudely awoken. She became aware of the sound of heavy, hurried footsteps, doors banging and raised voices. It was almost impossible to fight her way up through the sleepy depths, but she persevered and had barely opened her eyes when she felt herself almost pulled from the bed and soundly embraced. "Jane. Sweetheart!" the King's voice was intolerably loud in her ear. "We have our prince!"

Jane groaned at his rough handling and was promptly replaced in her bed, rather too robustly for comfort. She was well aware they had a prince and didn't need telling but stifled the retort which rose to her lips and instead smiled patiently at him.

But he was no longer looking at her, he had turned around his eyes eagerly sweeping the chamber. "Where is he? Where is my boy?"

"Your Grace." Curtseying awkwardly with the bundle in her arms, the senior midwife handed him the child.

"Ha!" His father's jubilation was all too much for the infant, who screwed up his face and began to wail loudly.

"Listen to that Jane" the King glanced towards the bed but did not look at her, not wishing to tear his eyes from his son. "Listen to those healthy lungs! I warrant he will not be cowed by emperors, clerics or kings. What a King he will make!"

"Nearly as great as Your Grace" Jane said sarcastically from her bed, causing him to look at her searchingly.

"Indeed." he agreed, deciding not to chide her following her ordeal.

Jane averted her eyes from father and son and attempted to lift her arm from where it lay upon the fur coverlet. No matter how hard she tried, it continued to lay there like it no longer belonged to her. Then she tried to move a leg; again, nothing happened. There was a strange jangling in her head and she began to wonder what was happening to her as her heart started to beat harder in a peculiar jagged rhythm.

Doctor Butts, who had scarcely taken his eyes from her since she had delivered, stepped forward and placed a hand on her brow. She was cold and clammy and her eyes had an unnatural, distant look to them.

"Her Grace needs to rest urgently" he told the King. "The chamber should be cleared of all but Her Grace's attendants."

Henry, unused to being told to quit rooms in his own palace, narrowed his eyes in annoyance. Then he caught the aura of concern which permeated the chamber and took a step towards Jane. Her eyes were closed and her breathing was fast and irregular. After a last lingering look at his son, he placed him carefully in the waiting arms of the midwife.

"I understand" he said, meeting the gentle but firm gaze of the physician. "You need to attend to the Queen. I will take my leave as you advise." With a nod to his gentlemen to indicate they should follow him, he turned on his heel and marched from the room. The glance he cast over his shoulder was not towards his Queen, but towards his son.

Noting Jane's waxy pallor, Doctor Butts carefully drew back her coverings and was alarmed at the sight of the large spreading bloodstain underneath her hips. Alerting the midwives, he worked with them to try and stem the bleeding and revive the Queen.

When Jane did open her eyes once more, it was with extreme annoyance. Despite the heavily draped and sealed windows, there was no escaping the sound of a dreary succession of cannon fire backed up by the pealing of every church bell within proximity.

"He failed to kill me when his son all but tore me apart, so now he seeks to send me mad with this endless cacophony" she complained.

"It is the King's way of celebrating the birth of your son and making sure all know of it" Eleanor replied. "I heard him shouting for heralds to be dispatched as he was leaving, so no doubt every church bell in England will be pealing shortly."

"I suppose." Jane moved her limbs cautiously; they seemed to be obeying her now. "Bring me a scribe" she ordered. "I must officially inform the council of the birth of the heir."

From her bed, Jane dictated a triumphantly worded letter and then took the quill and scratched her signature weakly. That done, she allowed herself to sink back on her pillows and bask in her success. For the first time since her marriage she felt safe. She was the mother of the King's son and as long as the child thrived he would never seek to displace her. Nothing could touch her now.

She spent an uncomfortable and restless night. Desperate as she was for deep and dreamless sleep she was troubled by strange dreams and racking pains throughout her body. The next day she felt no better. Her complexion, although usually pale, had taken on a distinctly yellowish hue and if anything she felt even more exhausted than she had in the hours following the birth.

Throughout the day she was frequently disturbed by all manner of well-wishers as well as multiple visits from the King, who insisted on referring to the child as Edward, even though she had not been consulted. It seemed that now she had given birth to him, he was exclusively the King's property and little to do with her. Not that she minded, and even if she had, she did not have the strength to object. Edward, as well as being created Prince of Wales, also bore the title of Duke of Cornwall, which seemed to Jane rather excessive for a child not yet two days old. He even had his own stall in the Garter Chapel at Windsor as well as a host of minor titles.

Jane's reward from the King for her labours was an enormous gold cup, which was so heavy, she could barely lift it. He placed it on her stomach so that she could admire it and see her own motto prominently engraved on the front and back. All she could feel was the excessive weight on her body so she pushed it away irritably but tried to cover up her action with a bright smile.

She did not feel well and would have preferred to be left to her own devices, but there was no rest to be had as the visitors kept coming. She was hungry but waved away all the food which was brought to her. With every hour that passed she grew more lightheaded, more nauseous and found it harder and harder to keep her thoughts anchored to the present.

Chapter Forty-Eight

On the third day following the birth, Jane began to feel a little better. She still refused the nourishing food recommended by her physician, instead demanding sweet wine and copious amounts of sugary sweetmeats. Any attempt to offer her a meat dish was met with a forbidding stare and even the quail she had so craved in the months leading up to the birth was pushed aside.

The baptism was to take place that night in the palace chapel. The King had been excitedly making arrangements for it all weekend and although she had hoped she would be spared attendance, he was determined that she should be present.

At around 11 o-clock that evening, Jane's fragile and bruised body was carefully washed before she was dressed in a simple but ornate high-necked gold robe. Next, she was wrapped in a crimson velvet mantle which was lined and lavishly trimmed with ermine before being seated before the fire to await the arrival of her ceremonial pallet. It pleased the King to have her carried regally to the chapel and even had she been capable of walking, he would not have allowed it. As she stared miserably into the flames which shot high up the great chimney, all she desired was to be left alone to sleep in the dark and quiet. Perhaps once she had submitted to this ceremony she would get her wish.

The lightheadedness was returning, so she rested her head against the back of the high chair and closed her eyes. She could hear the distant blaring of many trumpets and knew that her pallet would shortly be arriving after which she would have to take her place in the procession.

The pallet was luxurious and richly embellished. As it arrived, Jane wondered vaguely how it had been crafted in such a short amount of time. It was upholstered in crimson velvet and had the crown and arms of England embroidered across the back in gold thread. There were four matching cushions lavishly embroidered with her badge, two fashioned as squares and two as bolsters. As it was set down in front of her Jane wished it was any colour but crimson. It was the colour of blood and she had seen too much blood over the past days. She silently decided that never again would she wear anything crimson or allow it to have a place in her apartments.

Carefully she rose from her chair with the assistance of two of her ladies and gingerly reclined on the pallet with one bolster at her back, a square cushion behind her shoulders, another cushion underneath her feet and the largest bolster wedged between her body and the raised side of the pallet. Once she was comfortably settled, a large fine lawn sheet was tucked about her then topped with a counterpane of ermine lined scarlet cloth. Jane imagined she must look very fine and wished that she could see herself as the onlookers could.

Fine though her pallet and coverings were, all who observed the Queen could not but be horrified by the way she looked. Her skin was so pale as to be almost translucent and her blue eyes were sunken and dull. It was clear that she was fighting to stay awake and to be the focal point of a late night, long torchlit procession through the corridors of a large and draughty palace was the last thing she needed.

Slowly the procession formed about Jane and then her pallet was lifted high and they were on their way, accompanied by loud blaring trumpets. Jane cringed at the incessant noise and tried to squirm deeper into her covers. Despite their weight and warmth, she felt icy cold whilst the greasy smoke from the profusion of torches curled around her face and made her feel nauseous.

Fighting against the unconsciousness which threatened to overwhelm her, she concentrated on the other participants in the stately procession. She could see the Lady Mary, who kept casting concerned glances at her, walking just ahead of the Duke of Norfolk and Cranmer. Her brother Edward, newly created as Earl of Hertford was close by, and further along was her brother Thomas, carrying the young Lady Elizabeth, whose little face reflected the same tiredness which Jane herself felt. Looking around, her eye was caught by the stooped, greying Thomas Boleyn, present as a peer of the realm. Jane wondered idly what thoughts might be running through his mind as he walked behind the woman who had succeeded where his daughter had failed.

Eventually the huge doors of the chapel came into view and Jane was borne triumphantly down the aisle and into a small ante room. She saw the King looking down proudly from his gallery and summoned the strength to incline her head graciously as she passed him. Whilst the rest of the procession gathered around the baby at the font with his godparents, Jane was set carefully down on the tiled floor beside a low table of refreshments. She could not see the baptism ceremony, but she could hear it. A pile of gifts was brought to her and try as she might to open the wrappings and express her pleasure, her hands were too cold and her fingers would not work. Eleanor stepped forward to assist, exclaiming in delight as each gift was revealed whilst Jane smiled weakly and tried to keep her thoughts from wandering.

She sipped at the wine, which was very cold and caused her to start shivering, whilst refusing anything to eat. All she craved was sleep, yet in the main chapel the cleric's voice droned on and on whilst the child whimpered intermittently as each of his many titles was announced to the accompaniment of the appropriate trumpet fanfare.

Just when she thought she could bear the noise no longer, it stopped, and suddenly the child appeared before her, duly baptized and requiring his mother's blessing. Tremulously she stretched out her hand, touched the soft downy scalp and did her best to smile and graciously accept the congratulations and good wishes as she was surrounded by the nobility.

The room seemed to be spinning around her causing such dizziness that she was afraid she might vomit. She tried to concentrate on one face at a time, but it proved impossible so she gave up, and capitulated to the overwhelming need to close her eyes. She was vaguely aware of being lifted and carried through many chambers and corridors, but the next lucid moment she had was when she was lowered at last into her own bed in her own chamber, hot wrapped stones at her feet and a warm coverlet pulled high over her shoulders. The chamber was gloomy and quiet, the only light coming from the small fire in the hearth. Thankful to be away from the tented horror of the birthing chamber Jane sighed contentedly and gratefully succumbed to sleep.

She was hungry when she awoke the next day but could think of nothing she wanted to eat; the more she thought of food, the sicker she felt until the rising nausea became so insistent she had no choice but to lean over the side of the bed and vomit on to the floor.

"I am so sorry" she whispered, as Mary Norris cleared up the mess. "The impulse was so sudden I had no time to call for a bowl."

"All is well Your Grace." Having efficiently dealt with the problem, Mary stood up and draped a cloth over the bowl and its stinking contents. "I will have a clean bowl brought, just in case Your Grace requires it."

And Jane did require it; time and time again she retched painfully until there was precious little left in her stomach to bring up. The tireless Doctor Butts was summoned by her concerned ladies, who felt

that her sickness was caused by excessive sweet food on an empty stomach. "You must try to take some meat, Your Grace" he advised. "You need proper nourishment and should not give way to fanciful cravings."

"I cannot!" Jane snapped. "I have neither the appetite or energy."

"I will concoct a ginger tea for Your Grace, it will settle your stomach which in turn may stimulate your appetite." The physician bowed his way from her presence, ignoring her grimace.

"I hate the taste of ginger" she announced, to no-one in particular, as she relaxed back amongst her pillows. But she desperately wanted to recover her strength and to revel in her elevated status as mother of the prince of Wales and she knew that for that to

happen she had to abide by her physician's instructions, no matter how distasteful she found the remedies. She drank the tea and had to admit that it

made her feel a little better and so was taken unawares when her bowels started churning uncontrollably resulting in a most unpleasant bout of bloody diarrhoea.

She wished for the ground to open up and swallow her; she had never felt so embarrassed as her attendants dutifully cleansed her body and then the bedlinen, only to have to perform the same function many times over as the day wore on. The resulting malodorous stench in the chamber made her dizzy and sickly and she felt that all natural human dignity had been stripped from her, rendering her no better than the lowest farm animal with her inability to control her own bodily functions.

Her natural impatience with being handled and pulled about lessened as a fever gradually took hold; she lapsed in and out of consciousness, only becoming aware of her attendants when she felt a cool cloth mopping her brow.

The physician watched her with the utmost concern. "If she does not improve over the course of the next few hours, then it is my opinion that she is in the grip of a puerperal fever."

Eleanor nodded sadly in agreement. She had seen her sister die of the same condition and was well familiar with both the symptoms and the outcome.

"If she had but been able to take adequate nourishment, her body may have been in a position to fight through it, but she is so weak now and what little food and drink she has taken since the birth has surely been expelled by her body."

Eleanor wiped a tear from her cheek and shook her head sadly. "Arrangements were to be finalised today for her churching in three days time."

"Then you must inform the courtiers responsible that the Queen is in no condition to undergo the ceremony. Where is the King? Has he been to see her today?"

Eleanor shook her head. "He did send a page to enquire about her condition, but as you well know, he has a horror of sickness and will not come near her until he hears that she is recovering."

Doctor Butts puffed out his cheeks and looked across at the recumbent Queen. "We will know more in the morning" he advised, "but unless she shows a significant improvement..." He left the sentence unfinished and shook his head sorrowfully.

Jane passed a restless night and showed no improvement the following day. She was however conscious and complained that the light was too bright and gave her a headache. On examination, her womb was found to be enlarged and even the slightest pressure across her stomach caused her pain. Without relaying his findings to the Queen the physician stepped away from the bed and called all her attendants to him. "I regret to inform you that there is now no doubt that the Queen suffers from a puerperal fever. You must pay great attention to her and try every means to reduce the fever." He paused and looked around the circle of women, their faces betraying their horror and shock.

"Will the Queen live?" Mary Norris voiced the question all were thinking.

"I do not know" came the honest reply. "However, I believe that it would be advisable if the Queen's confessor was summoned that he may give her the sacrament of unction. It may calm her and help her to rally what little strength she has left to fight her ills."

"It shall be done." Eleanor touched Mary on the shoulder and inclined her head towards the door. As Mary scuttled off on her quest, Eleanor took a bowl of cool water over to the bed and began gently sponging the Queen's face.

Chapter Forty-Nine

Following her confessor's visit, the Queen did indeed begin to rally as her physician had hoped. It was only a small improvement in that her nausea eased, her headache lessened, and she felt able to sit up a little in bed rather than recline. Her ladies moved about the chamber attending to her needs with renewed hopes for a full recovery, although Doctor Butts warned against letting their hopes get too high.
"There is still a very long way for her to go" he warned. "It is common for the very sick to appear to be making a miraculous recovery only for them then to rapidly decline. Whilst I would bid you all to maintain a cautious optimism, you should be aware that she is still a very sick woman."

The King, informed that she was a little better, risked a very quick visit to the sick-room. "How are you Jane?" he asked solicitously.

"I feel a little better" she replied, noting that he kept his distance from her bed and did not offer a husbandly embrace.

"That is good, very good." He fell silent, unsure what to say next, then noting a certain rosiness about her complexion, turned to the physician who hovered nearby. "She is a good colour" he commented. "I trust you are pleased by her continuing progress?"

"Your Grace." With a glance towards the Queen who was listening to their exchange, he motioned the King towards the corner of the chamber, well away from the bed.

"You should be aware that the Queen's rosy appearance is not in fact a sign of good health" he began. "She has a very high fever, which is the cause of her colour."

"But she is improving?"

"A little but not significantly."

"Oh, but I thought…." the King turned half towards the bed, then back to Doctor Butts. "I thought she was through the worst?"

"Your Grace, until the fever breaks there is no knowing for sure. I am cautiously optimistic for the Queen's life, but should a decline set in, her condition will rapidly deteriorate."

"I see" the King nodded his understanding, then approached the bed warily. "I will take my leave now sweetheart and allow you to rest."

Jane turned her head and raised her eyebrows questioningly. "You have no embrace for the mother of your son?"

Henry held up his hands apologetically. "I would not wish to cause you discomfort whilst you are still unwell. I will see you again soon."

As he made a hasty exit, Jane sighed disinterestedly and turned her head towards the window, through which she could see the leafless trees whipping from side to side in a savage October gale.

"Your Grace, would you like the prince brought to you?" Jane did not recognise the voice and did not deign to turn her head.

"No" she replied dully, her eyes still on the window. "Maybe tomorrow."

On the following day, whilst not actually showing an improvement, her physician was heartened to find that she was at least no worse. Her womb was still swollen but abating a little and it did not pain the Queen quite so much as it had to undergo examination.

Baby Edward was brought to see his mother but she regarded him with a certain amount of suspicion and felt no maternal love for him. As he was laid in her arms, she recoiled a little and stiffened; he was not a heavy baby but the feel of his small body against her own caused her pain. Sensing her discomfort, the baby began to cry. Lifting him up, she thrust him at the nurse. "Take him away please" she ordered. "I will see him again when I am feeling better."

As the nurse hurried away, soothing the fractious baby with little cooing noises, Jane looked sadly across at Eleanor. "I feel nothing for him" she admitted. "Every time I see him he just reminds me of pain and blood."

"That is to be expected" Eleanor replied. "You have not seen enough of him to know him or he you. Once you are a little better and can spend more time with him, you will forget all the pain."

Jane shuddered. "I will never forget" she declared. "It is beyond my understanding how women can bring themselves to birth more than one child."

Over the next few days, the Queen did improve. Her ladies had finally persuaded her to take some very thinly sliced beef and bread which the Queen's body did not immediately seek to eject. Heartened by this, Doctor Butts, after consultation with the King's physician Doctor Wendy, directed that she should try and eat a few mouthfuls every hour, just to stimulate her digestion which in turn would allow her body to return to its normal rhythm.

The King, his mood buoyed by her apparent recovery, visited more often and was pleased to bestow embraces and kisses upon her. She still had a low fever and suffered from bouts of sickness and lightheadedness, but overall seemed to be making significant progress at last.

"I want to visit my garden" she announced, as Doctor Butts replaced her bedcovers following his latest examination.

"Your Grace that would not be wise" he replied. "The wind outside is very cold and even were you well wrapped up against it, the chill could still affect you badly and cause a setback in your recovery."

"Sister, heed his advice. You are making such excellent progress and it would be such a shame for that to be reversed through a foolish whim."

Jane turned her head slowly towards her sister-in-law Anne Stanhope Seymour and gave her the benefit of her iciest glare. She did not appreciate the familiarity of her tone and refused to be admonished by someone whom she regarded as her inferior.

"I think you will find that I am still the Queen, even confined as I am to this sickbed and I would appreciate it if you would remember that fact and address me accordingly."

Anne blinked at her in amazement, her eyes darting from the Queen to the embarrassed physician and then back to Jane. "I apologise for my lack of respect Your Grace" she said at last, curtsying deeply as she hurriedly backed away.

With a final venomous glance in her direction, Jane turned back to Doctor Butts who still stood at her bedside. "And if I should disregard your advice?" she demanded.

"Then I would have no alternative but to notify the King that you seek to put yourself at risk" he replied.

With a frown and a sigh, Jane brought her fist down hard on the furred coverlet. "Then what am I supposed to do?" she demanded crossly. "Just lay here and wait to live or die?"

"I sympathise with Your Grace, but there really is no advisable alternative. It is not safe for you to go outside; were it a different season, then it may have been possible, even beneficial, but not in late October."

"Then perhaps I may get out of bed and walk about the chamber a little?"

He shook his head. "Again, I would not advise it. You are still very weak and the slightest exercise may stimulate the bleeding to return. However I am heartened that you believe yourself well enough to leave your bed, so maybe we can review the situation in a day or so."

Jane rubbed the side of her face wearily. "I suppose you are right" she conceded, "I just wanted one more look at my white roses before they are gone."

"Your Grace, I would imagine that if any roses remain, then they have long been stripped of their petals for the wind is strong and unforgiving." Eleanor had overheard the conversation and wished to add her voice to the physician's opinion that the Queen should stay within her chamber.

"The garden is sheltered by high walls" Jane countered. "There is every chance that some remain. Eleanor…" Jane reached for Eleanor's hand and drew her closer. "Would you go down for me and bring back any which remain?"

"Of course, Your Grace" Eleanor patted Jane's hand awkwardly with her spare hand before withdrawing both. The Queen's skin burned like a furnace and was dry and unpleasant to touch. "I will go down directly."

Finding her warmest cloak, Eleanor moved quickly down the privy staircase to the garden entrance and hesitated at the door. The wind was even stronger than she had expected, battering the small evergreens and swirling the fallen leaves of the ornamental fruit trees ranged along the eastern wall into restless falling spirals. Putting up her hood, Eleanor clutched her cloak close about her and walked briskly along the gravel path towards the curved brick archway which marked the beginning of the Queen's domain. She paused under the archway, grateful for the shelter, then lowered her head and hurried through the knot garden before turning into the Queen's walled garden. There, against the south wall were the white roses, very much windswept and straggly, but with some blooms still gleaming softly behind the shelter afforded by the foliage.

Once she was closer she could see that the blooms were not perfect but intact enough that they would please the Queen with their form and their perfume. Sliding a small pair of sprung scissors from her cuff, she quickly selected the best half dozen buds and blooms then tucked them under her cloak for protection, wincing as the thorns bit into her skin.

She returned to the palace with as much haste as her dignity would allow. On reaching the ante chamber she called for a knife and set about removing the thorns from the stems before removing excess foliage and clipping the stems to a uniform length. That done, she filled a small pitcher with water and carefully arranged the blooms for maximum effect before carrying them carefully into the bedchamber, a bright smile on her face.

She had only been gone for a matter of minutes, yet it seemed that the situation in the chamber had changed dramatically for the worse. The attending ladies were gathered fearfully by the hearth, glancing nervously towards the curtained bed.

"What is it? What has happened?" Eleanor asked, placing the pitcher carefully on a side table.

"The Queen suddenly began calling out and writhing with pain" Mary replied, her face white with shock.

"It seems she has begun haemorrhaging again and even now her physician fights to stem the flow."

Wordlessly Eleanor approached the bed and slipped inside the curtains half expecting what she might see but woefully unprepared for the reality. The Queen was lying flat and unresponsive on the bed with her covers pushed aside and dragging on the floor. The lower half of her white nightgown was soaked with dark red blood, the stain creeping higher with every second. Doctor Butts and two midwives were frantically packing thick linens around the Queen's lower body, only for them to become quickly soaked and instantly replaced. Horrified, Eleanor brought her hands up to her face as the tears began to roll down her cheeks, unable to check her sobs. Doctor Butts looked up at her briefly before returning his attention to Jane. He did not utter a word and he did not need to, his expression told her everything.

Chapter Fifty

It seemed that Jane was much stronger than anyone gave her credit for. Despite the latest devastating haemorrhage, once it had been largely stemmed by the constant ministrations of physician and midwives, she regained consciousness although seemed to be vague and confused.
"What day is it?" she asked, looking around the worried faces of her ladies.
"It is Tuesday Your Grace" Eleanor offered, "The twenty-third day of the month."
"Is the child born?"
Doing her best to keep her voice steady and reassuring, Eleanor approached the bed. "Yes, Your Grace, you gave birth to a healthy prince eleven days

ago."

"Eleven?" Jane moved her head restlessly on the pillow. "I do not remember." Suddenly she started violently and tried vainly to push herself upright.

"Where am I?" she asked fretfully. "Why am I here?" Doctor Butts stepped forward and gently eased her back down on to her pillows. "You are at Hampton Court, Your Grace, in your bedchamber, recovering from the birth of your son."

Although Jane's eyes fastened on his face as he was speaking, she gave no indication that she understood what he said. After laying his hand on her forehead he bowed and withdrew.

"The fever escalates out of control once more and she is delirious" he told Eleanor. "I will have to bleed her and see if it restores her senses."

"Surely not?" Eleanor burst out. "She has done nothing over the past days but lose blood, how will it help her to lose more?"

"It is a proven method of breaking delirium" he retorted. "And in my experience, it is the only thing that can."

Eleanor shook her head and looked mutinous. "In my humble opinion, it will more likely kill her."

"Then it is well that you are not a royal physician." As Eleanor recoiled at his bluntness, he turned away and began gathering the necessary instruments.

Despite Eleanor's misgivings, the procedure did seem to bring Jane to her senses for a short while. Taking advantage of her lucidity, Eleanor fetched the pitcher of roses and placed it close to the bed. As Jane turned her head and saw them, her eyes lit up. "What beautiful roses, are they from my garden?"

"Yes, Your Grace, I fetched them at your behest earlier today."

Jane smiled sadly. "They put me in mind of long, perfect summer days. Can you bring them closer so that I may catch their perfume?"

Nodding to Mary to raise the Queen a little, Eleanor brought the pitcher close to her face. With evident delight, Jane inhaled deeply. "Beautiful, so beautiful" she murmured weakly.

Even as her fever once again soared and her delirium returned, her eyes turned again and again to the little pitcher of roses by her bed. She succumbed meekly to repeated bleedings as Doctor Butts sought desperately to bring her some respite. As the evening approached she complained of racking pains throughout her body and repeatedly threw aside her coverings in an effort to assuage her body's raging heat.

The King was kept informed of her condition, although he did not venture near; he hoped to escape to Esher for some hunting if she did not worsen significantly.

As night approached, her physician gravely informed the Queen's ladies that almost all hope for her recovery had gone. He advised that her confessor be summoned in order to administer extreme unction; he feared that should they delay, she might not be sufficiently lucid to participate in the rite.

Shortly before midnight, her ladies stood around her bed with heads bowed and hands folded in prayer as the age-old rites of the catholic church were intoned over the barely conscious Queen.

Once concluded, Jane slept peacefully for a while in the dimly lit chamber although within hours she was once again moaning in pain and moving restlessly in her bed as the fever and delirium strengthened its hold.

As night moved into day, she was bled three times more but this time nothing seemed to bring her any relief. She drifted in and out of consciousness, sometimes seeming to recognise the faces about her, other times looking at them in confusion and fear.

"It is a miracle she still survives" Doctor Butts confided. "Her body barely functions and the fever does not abate. The King should be made aware that the situation is desperate; if Her Grace survives the coming night then I believe that she may recover, it all depends if she can rally her remaining strength and break through the fever's grip."

Jane's hair was wet with perspiration, her body felt as though it was on fire and her sight was dimming. "I taunted Queen Anne" she muttered. One of her ladies bent closer the better to hear as Jane's voice was weak "Your Grace?"

Jane moved her head on the pillow to see who had spoken. It was the Countess of Rutland whose face swam into view. "Eleanor, I am so full of disquiet" she whispered. "When the former Queen lay in agony after miscarrying her heir, I taunted her and said that it would have been better had she died in childbed."

Eleanor, who had borne no love towards Anne Boleyn, was shocked nonetheless.

"There." Jane licked her dry lips and moved her head restlessly. "You share my opinion do you not, that this is her revenge. From her grave she seeks to pull me down to her personal hell to suffer endless torment for my cruelty."

"Queen Anne was many things," Eleanor soothed, "and whilst she was undoubtedly powerful in life, I do not for one moment believe that in death she holds sway in either hell or heaven. It is your fever manipulating your thoughts. Pay no heed."

"No, not my thoughts, my guilt. I rejoiced in her downfall just as I accused her of rejoicing in that of Queen Catherine. Lady Lee told me I was no better than her, and she was right."

"Hush now." Eleanor laid her cool hand on the raging heat of Jane's forehead. "Save your strength for your recovery. You are the mother of the prince of Wales and he will expect his mother in his nursery before long."

Jane shook her head as a single tear snaked down her cheek. "It is over for me; the fate I wished on Anne Boleyn has been laid at my door. I will not live beyond this night."

"While there is life, there is hope" Eleanor urged. "For twelve long days and nights you have fought for life and even when your situation became desperate, somehow you pulled yourself back from the brink. Do not give up, not now. Try to rest and perhaps later you might try to eat a little?"

Jane closed her eyes. "Perhaps," she murmured.

"She seems to feel no pain now" Eleanor whispered to the other ladies. "Surely that is grounds for hope?" Seeing Doctor Butts on the outer edge of their little circle, Eleanor encouraged him closer and asked him the same question.

"The reason the Queen feels no pain is because her body is slowly shutting down" he advised. "With every hour which passes, she draws inexorably closer to death. Only God can save her now."

Whether Jane slept or was unconscious, no-one was sure. The physician was of the opinion that if it were unconsciousness, then the best outcome would be for death to claim her quietly whilst she was unaware. He forbade her ladies from attempting to rouse her and sent a page to advise the King that the end was near.

Quietly her ladies took up their positions around the bed, praying earnestly for either a miracle recovery or a peaceful end. Eleanor's eyes kept travelling towards the door, where the Queen's brothers stood silently; surely the King would come to bid a fond farewell to the woman who had given him his heart's desire?

As the minutes turned into hours, and day turned into night, there was no sound of any approaching footsteps, no indication that the King's thoughts were with his dying Queen. The only sound in the chamber was the delicate tick from Jane's enamelled clock which stood on the shelf above the hearth. All in the chamber stood still and silent, waiting for the Queen to release her tenuous hold on life.

Shortly after the little clock had chimed the half hour, and against all expectations, Jane opened her eyes and appeared surprised to see all the figures ranged about her bed.

"I cannot see you clearly, come closer" she whispered.

One by one, her ladies approached her and leaned closer so that she could clearly see their features before kissing her hand and stepping back, stifling their sobs. Finally, her brothers stepped forward, causing her eyes to widen in surprise. "I did not expect you here" she whispered.

"Dearest sister, we could not let you depart from this world without wishing you God speed."
"I am dying then?" Jane's eyes, moist with tears sought the shadowy figure of her physician who inclined his head regretfully, not trusting himself to speak.
Jane tried to swallow her rising panic, again looking around at all who surrounded her. "I am not ready" she whispered. "I do not want to die."
"Here, Your Grace." Carefully Eleanor extracted the largest and most fragrant bloom from the pitcher and laid it on the pillow next to Jane's head.
"Thank you." Jane's breathing had become very shallow and she struggled for each breath, but somehow she managed to turn her head and inhale the fragrance. She looked at the perfect, creamy petals and wished she had the strength to touch them one last time, then looked towards the window, hoping to see the sky, but all was black outside.
"What is the time?" she asked.
"Just a few minutes before midnight, Your Grace" Eleanor replied.
Jane managed the slightest of nods in acknowledgement and took another breath, the deepest she could manage and became aware of a loud rushing in her ears followed by a sensation of falling. Her eyes momentarily widened in surprise as the dimly lighted room receded until it became just a pinprick of light before her eyes. Suddenly the s of roses was all around her, lifting her, enfolding her, immersing her in softness and fragrance. Miraculously, she could feel her fear ebbing away and those watching her crossed themselves in awe as the pain and worry was erased from her face and

replaced by a peaceful and joyful expression. With a half-smile on her lips, she forced a final exhalation and closed her eyes for the last time.

Jane the Queen was dead.

THE END

Historical Notes

Jane most likely died from a condition now known as puerperal sepsis which is an infection following childbirth. This could have been caused by the unsterile conditions or by the retention of a small piece of the afterbirth in the uterus.

Her body was embalmed soon after her death, dressed in a gold and jewelled robe then removed to her presence chamber, where she lay in state for a week, surrounded by lighted tapers. Her ladies watched over the body, clad in black gowns and white headdresses.

On 1st November, All Saints Day, she was carried through the black draped galleries of Hampton Court and laid on a hearse in the chapel for the service of Mass. The hearse was decorated with banner rolls showing her ancestral descent along with that of the King and the infant prince.

Jane remained in the chapel at Hampton Court for a further twelve days whilst the final preparations for her burial were carried out. The King wished for her to lie at Windsor and decreed that when his own time came, he would be laid beside her.

On 12th November Jane was taken from the chapel and laid on a chariot drawn by six horses for the journey to Windsor. The Lady Mary was the chief mourner and rode behind the chariot on a horse draped with black velvet. Behind her were chariots containing Jane's waiting women and noblewomen, a long procession of noblemen, 200 poor men wearing Jane's badge, minstrels and trumpet players, foreign ambassadors and clergy. Alms were distributed along the way and when the cortege reached Windsor, the 200 poor men left the procession and stood either side of the street, holding lit torches.

Jane was taken through the castle precincts to St George's chapel where a short service was held before she was left to lie in state overnight with a vigil kept around her. The following morning, nearly three weeks after her death, she was interred in a vault beneath the chapel.

Mary continued to act as chief mourner throughout as the King pronounced himself too distressed to attend. However, Henry did not mourn for long. By the end of November he was said to be not only 'merry' and accepting invitations to dine out with his friends but actively discussing potential brides with Thomas Cromwell.

Author's Note

I have never subscribed to the idea that Jane Seymour was a mousey, obliging little nonentity. Yes, there is no doubt that the King needed the solace of an easier, gentler companion to offset the demanding and often acidic Anne Boleyn, but would he really have chosen the woman that history depicts?

She was a woman who attracted no serious suitors before the King and who was believed by her own family to be destined for lonely spinsterhood. Even after she became Queen, no-one at court had much to say of her. Chapuys, the Emperor's ambassador dismissed her as 'Of middle stature and no great beauty, so fair that one would call her rather pale than otherwise. She is over 25 years old, not a woman of great wit but she may have good understanding.' He also reported her to be obedient and quoted another's observation that she was said to be rather proud and haughty.

The evidence of Jane's obvious intelligence can be seen in Holbein's portrait. The slightly narrowed gaze projected from cold, thoughtful eyes portrays a shrewd and calculating woman who was not disposed to be anyone's doormat and was prepared to do whatever it took to achieve her ambitions. The pursed mouth indicates great determination and, I think, a certain amount of artfulness. She was certainly a force to be reckoned with; something which the unfortunate Anne Boleyn did not recognize until it was too late.

So despite many historians dismissing Jane as quiet, meek and insignificant, it is clear that she was sufficiently astute to know exactly the type of wife the King would need after Anne and was adept at portraying herself as the ideal candidate.

It is common knowledge that Anne Boleyn and Henry's eventual fifth wife Catherine Howard were closely related but perhaps less known that Jane Seymour was a half second cousin to them both. All three women shared the same great-grandmother, Elizabeth Cheney.

Elizabeth Cheney was married twice. Her first husband was Frederick Tilney and their only child was a daughter they called Elizabeth. This Elizabeth also married twice, her second husband being Thomas Howard, Earl of Surrey. There were nine children from the marriage, including Thomas Howard 3rd Duke of Norfolk, Elizabeth Howard (mother of Anne Boleyn) and Edmund Howard (father of Catherine Howard).

Elizabeth Cheney's second marriage was to John Say and one of their several children together was Anne Say. Anne Say married Sir Henry Wentworth and they were the parents of six children, amongst them Margery Wentworth (mother of Jane Seymour).

Nothing is known of Jane Seymour's early life prior to her employment in the household of Catherine of Aragon. Once she came to the King's notice –
although the date of that event in itself is open to dispute – we see more of her in the records.

I have adjusted some documented events in her life to assist the flow of the story, although only by a matter of days or weeks in all cases.

Because so little is known of her, her personality and interactions with members of her family and royal household are open to interpretation. Based on my research, I came to the conclusion that it is quite possible that in life she was not dissimilar to the way she is portrayed in these pages.

Was she his favourite wife? She was certainly the only one who gave him the son he desired, but if he was truly bereft at her loss, he would have mourned her for longer than two weeks. He was an enormously sentimental man when it suited him and it certainly seems as though he had no qualms about exchanging a living wife for a living son. I certainly believe he would have remarried far sooner had a suitable bride been available. He was a man with a gift for forgetting the uncomfortable past and moving on with alacrity, so quite possibly his 'favourite' was the one he was either currently romancing or had recently married. With the exception of Anne of Cleves. Although he was initially satisfied with her looks based on Holbein's portrait and influenced by the various reports of her brought back to him, the flesh and blood woman he found himself contracted to marry was not to his taste.

Many historians point to his decision to share Jane's burial vault as an indicator of his partiality. I think he thought it only right that as the parents of the next King they should share a tomb, as had his forebears.

The vault at Windsor was supposed to be temporary, whilst a magnificent marble tomb, much gilded and complete with effigies of them both was constructed. For various reasons, this tomb was never completed so both bodies remained where they had been originally interred.

The location of the vault became forgotten and was only discovered by chance in 1813 when excavations for a new royal vault revealed the coffins of not only Jane and Henry, but also that of the executed Charles I and an infant child of Queen Anne. In 1837 a marble slab was placed over the vault to mark their resting place.

Bibliography

INSIDE THE TUDOR COURT - Lauren Mackay

JANE SEYMOUR – David Loades

THE LIFE OF JANE DORMER, DUCHESS OF FERIA – Henry Clifford

THE ROYAL PALACES OF TUDOR ENGLAND – Simon Thurley

THE SEYMOURS OF WOLF HALL – David Loades

JANE SEYMOUR – Elizabeth Norton

THE SEYMOUR FAMILY HISTORY AND ROMANCE – Amy Audrey Locke

ANNALS OF THE SEYMOURS – Richard Harold St. Maur

HENRY VIII – Francis Hackett

LIFE OF WOLSEY – George Cavendish

PRIVATE LIVES OF TUDOR MONARCHS – Christopher Falkus

TUDOR COSTUME AND FASHION – Herbert Norris

WIVES OF HENRY VIII & THE PARTS THEY PLAYED IN HISTORY – Martin Hume

Acknowledgments

Thanks to my family for the patience they showed when their evening meals were either late or on occasion forgotten. For the times I wandered around the supermarket, largely forgetting what I went in for and for the vacant stare which answered any attempts to engage my attention as I sat before the computer. With my head stuck very firmly in the sixteenth century, it was sometimes hard to remember that I had obligations to those waiting for me in the twenty-first century!

Huge thanks to Stephanie Hardwick and Melody Fisher for their support, endless encouragement and superhuman publicity skills and distribution. And to my son Nick Warwick for his advice, marketing expertise and the cover art.

Printed in Great Britain
by Amazon